BLACK OUT

"PART 3 OF THE LIGHTS SERIES"

GEORGE SHERMAN HUDSON

"THE LIGHTS SERIES"
CITY LIGHTS
LIGHTS OUT
BLACK OUT

STREET CHRONICLES

Published by:

G Street Chronicles
P.O. Box 1822
Jonesboro, GA 30237-1822
www.gstreetchronicles.com
fans@gstreetchronicles.com

Cover design:
Hot Book Covers, www.hotbookcovers.com

ISBN 13: 978-1-9384424-6-9
ISBN 10: 1938442466
LCCN: 2013931240

Join us on our social networks

Facebook
G Street Chronicles Fan Page
G Street Chronicles CEO Exclusive Readers Group

Follow us on Twitter
@GStreetChronicl

Acknowledgements

I want to thank God for giving me the strength, courage, wisdom and talent to go after my dreams and for making all of this possible.

Thanks Mom and Pop for always being the best parents even when it was rough.

Thanks Grandma for always telling me like it is!

To my kids Jazmine and Sherman...I love y'all and that little one on the way!

To my first lady, Shawna A., it goes without saying...thank you! I knew we could make this happen and we're not done yet!

To the G Street fam...we got a helluva team! Real talk!

To our production team—designer, editors, proofreaders, promoters—we couldn't do it without your help. Thank you.

I want to acknowledge all my social networking family... Angels & Goon Squad and all my Twitter, Instagram and Facebook fam. Also those who promote our books, Kisha Green, EDC Creations, Urban Reviews, OOSA Bookclub and more!

Thanks to ALL the fans who make this all possible. I truly appreciate your continued support.

~ G

Dedicated to my First Lady,

Shawna A.

Much Love

Get to know Silk.
It all began in The Gangsta Girl Short Story Mini Series

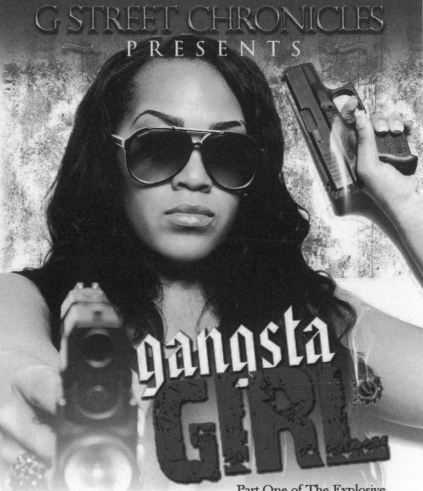

G STREET CHRONICLES

~ PRESENTS ~

gangsta GIRL

Part One of The Explosive
E-Book Series

George Sherman Hudson
Author of Drama & Executive Mistress

Chapter 1

"Walk nigga!" I screamed, as I nudged the barrel of the pistol grip pump into the back of Markel, one of Atlanta's biggest dealers and known trick.

"Damn baby girl, you ain't got to do it like this, let's…"

"Clunk!"

I tried to knock this fat Biggie Smalls looking ass nigga head off with the barrel of the gun for trying me like I'm stupid.

"Ahh! Aight!" he screamed, as a small trickle of blood eased down the back of his freshly shaved baldhead.

Sticking up niggas was way more profitable than shaking my ass for chump change at the club. I just loved how easy it was to get info out of a nigga then take him for his whole stash. I made it my business to fuck a nigga like one of his favorite porn stars, then pillow talk him and find out where the nigga held his stash. This was my second lick and I can say this shit was sweet as cotton candy. Niggas would never think I, Cassandra Jenkins also known as Silk, would be the one to take their whole stash and life in the blink of an eye.

My first lick had my adrenaline pumping like crazy. I just kept repeating my locked up nigga's words in my mind— he gave me the game on this robbing shit. I had to build up the nerve to pull it off. Watching Baby Face, a big baller from the Westside of Atlanta sleep, I slid out his bed and grabbed my nine out my purse. After making him empty his stash spot, which held $130,000, I pumped bullet after bullet in him until he stopped twitching.

Standing 5'11, black as night with wide hips and a big ass, I was a true stallion. Niggas was constantly trying to get the pussy and that was the trap. Once they push up and look into my green eyes that I inherited from my grandmother, they lose all train of thought. That's when I do my inspection on them and if shit adds up…I'm game. I used to just let rich niggas hit for a couple stacks but why get a stack or two when you can get the whole stash!

* * * * *

At one time in my life I was oh so happy. That all changed one day when I came home from high school and saw police cars and an ambulance in front of my house. As I tried to get through the crowd that was standing in front of the house, I was stopped by a big white policeman.

"You can't pass through here ma'am," he said with authority.

"I stay here. Where's my mama?" I asked with an attitude, trying to look around him.

Police were rushing in and out the house, scribbling on notepads and questioning people. Just as the officer was about to respond, I saw two black men dressed in all white push a gurney out the door with someone covered from head to toe. Seconds later another one followed with another person, also covered. I knew it had to be my mom and dad. My heart skipped a beat at the sight of the bodies—I started to scream. A female officer rushed to my side and consoled me as she explained how my mom had shot my dad and then killed herself. That was the day my life changed.

* * * * *

"Nigga open the safe!" I screamed, as Markel stood motionless in the middle of the room.

"Baby girl, you making a big mistake. Let's just act like this shit ain't even happen and go back upstairs," he said, as he slowly turned to face me.

"Nigga you got five seconds to open the safe...one...two..." I spat, as I leveled the pistol grip pump to his chest.

He looked into my eyes, turned and walked over to the safe. Seconds later the door to the safe swung open, exposing the stacks of money neatly placed inside.

"Here you go, get what you need but I promise you baby girl, you will regret this shit," Markel sneered.

This nigga must didn't know the rules of the game! When a muthafucker robbing you barefaced, nine times out of ten yo ass dead!

I loaded all the safe contents into a black garbage bag, then stepped around Markel's lifeless body. The shotgun slug blew his chest wide open.

Chapter 2

"Girl where you been? I've been calling your ass all day?" Brandi asked, as I entered the two bedroom loft we shared in downtown Atlanta.

"Out and about," I answered with a slight attitude, letting her know to mind her business.

I had met Brandi two years ago when we were both rookies at the Body Suit, a popular strip club out in Decatur. We both had big dreams to catch a baller and get out the business but up till this day, it still hasn't happened. We were cool—more like associates than friends. I had quit dancing six months ago to take up my new profession that my locked-up man Sherm, schooled me to on our weekly visits.

"Excuse me then, I was just worried about yo black ass!" she fumed, as she walked over and grabbed a pint of ice cream out the freezer.

"Ah girl, quit being so sensitive. I was out with Justice. He took me to lunch," I lied.

The whole time I was talking to Brandi I was thinking about the nice stash I had down in my car. Then the sight of Markel's body falling to the floor invaded my mind. Shit! It was well worth the hundred thousand plus some and a nice diamond necklace that had to be worth a quarter mill. The M that hung from the chunk of platinum had diamonds all through it. This lick should set me straight for a minute. I was zoned out thinking about everything when Brandi tapped me on the arm.

"Silk! Silk!" Brandi said over and over, trying to get my attention.

"Oh my bad girl. My mind was out there for a minute. I dazed way out there, shit."

"You good? That nigga got you gone like that? I know he all fine and shit but damn!" Brandi said playfully.

"Bitch please…aight the dick is the bomb!" I replied laughing but the whole time planning my next move.

Justice was the first guy I actually went out on a date with when I first started working at the club. He tried everything in his power to get me to stop dancing but his money wasn't long enough to take care of a high maintenance bitch like myself. The dick was the bomb but his pockets were slacking like hell. We had been on and off—well just keeping it real, we were just fuck friends.

"Girl me and Zay going out to the poetry Cafe tonight. You want to come?" Brandi asked, wedging the spoon into the butter pecan ice cream.

The mention of Zay sent chills down my spine. Zay was the leader of the NWM clique—they're filthy rich and treacherous. Zay was worth well over a million dollars. Like all these other rich niggas in the street, he was a pussy hound. He kept trying to push up on me behind Brandi's back but soon saw that I wasn't the type of bitch to fuck a friend's man nor for free. I never told her—I just kept turning him down but just keeping it real, I did think about fucking the nigga, then robbing him for everything he had. I quickly dismissed the thought—NWM was not a clique to be fucking around with.

"I'm good. I got some business to take care of but I appreciate the invitation."

"Girl you're going to miss a good show," Brandi exclaimed, as she placed the half eaten pint back into the freezer and headed upstairs.

Brandi was the type of broad that every man would love to fuck. She was short and thick with some fat juicy tits that jiggled every time she moved. She was black and Chinese with some pretty "suck me" lips and slanted eyes. She had all types of men trying to lock her down but only one was successful at it and that was Zay.

Chapter 3

The next day I deposited the money which totaled $112,000 in my bank account and then treated myself to a five star lunch and a bottle of wine. I was so excited to be moving into my new house in a few days. Life is finally looking up again. Just as I headed out the restaurant door my cell phone rang.

"Yeah," I answered, as I climbed into the seat of my four year old Lexus GS400.

"Girl where you at?" Brandi asked frantically.

"Just got finished eating and now headed to the furniture store. Why? What's up?"

"Girl, Zay found his cousin dead at his house today!"

"What? What happened?" I asked shocked at the news.

"Somebody shot him and then robbed him. They say it was some niggas from the Westside he was dealing with," Brandi explained.

"Do I know his cousin? What's his name?" I asked, as I thought about the lick I had pulled off yesterday.

"Mark...Markel Lane."

The mention of his name caught me off guard.

"Zay cousin...his cousin got killed?" I asked, trying my best to hide the uneasiness in my voice.

"Yeah, they out right now trying to find out who was responsible. I know they 'bout to tear the city up until they find their man."

"Damn, that's fucked up. I hope they find out who did it but they can't be too mad because that type of shit comes with the game," I told her as I navigated my Lexus down 285 in route to IKEA.

"Yeah, that's a fucked up game to be in."

"Yeah it is. I'll see you later," I said in a sad voice, yet smiling because I had pulled off another lick undetected.

Chapter 4

Zay had made a couple of calls and word on the street was that Bones, a nigga from the westside, was responsible for Markel's death. Zay called one of NWM enforcers and headed out to holla at Bones in the worst way. I had no idea that Markel was affiliated with NWM or that he was Zay's cousin. Oh well, it is what it is—bitch gotta eat too.

Zay and Dino sat outside of Bones' house and went over their plan once again.

"The nigga won't be back for a minute. He still at his poolroom but his baby mama is in there with his lil' boy. I will get her to open the door. When she does, we'll bum rush her, then set up camp til' this nigga shows up," Zay explained as Dino listened in carefully.

"Shit lets do it! Nigga should have known not to fuck with NWM," Dino said, as he tucked his .357 in his waist.

"Lets go," Zay said, looking around making sure the coast was clear.

They stepped out into the cold night air and made their way up to Bones' front porch.

"Knock! Knock!"

"Who knock!" Kia, Bones' baby mama screamed from the back of the house.

"This Zay. I got a package for Bones," Zay yelled, then looked over at Dino to make sure he was ready.

"He ain't here. Just leave it on the porch," Kia said, not moving from her spot on the couch.

Kia didn't know Zay personally…she only knew his name. Her baby daddy, Bones, dealt with his cousin Markel on a regular. Bones introduced her to Zay and Markel not long ago, at Zay's annual birthday bash he had for himself at Velvet Room every year.

"Shawty, I can't just leave this out here like this," Zay replied trying not to draw any attention in the quiet neighborhood.

"Aight, hold up!" Kia screamed mad that Zay was interrupting Basketball Wives.

She made Zay wait until a commercial came on. Slamming the remote down, she got up and rushed to the door.

"Man what's up?" she said in an irritated tone, as she pulled the door open.

Before she could say anything else, the door was pushed into her, knocking her to the floor. Zay rushed in, as Dino wrestled with Kia who kicked and scratched until Dino's closed fist connected with her jaw.

Chapter 5

I arrived home later with my furniture delivery slip and a couple of new outfits. Brandi was in the kitchen on the phone when I walked in.

"What's up girl?" I asked, as she flipped the burger in the pan.

"Shit. Just tripping on niggas in this so called game," she said disgustedly.

"What's up now?" I questioned, as I took a seat at the kitchen table.

"Girl don't tell nobody…Zay found out who killed his cousin," Brandi whispered, as if someone was in the other room.

"Oh yeah…who?" I asked, liking the news.

"Some dude from Miami that moved here a couple of years ago, named Bones. Zay knew him through Markel—they did a lot of business together. They said he had just bought some dope from Markel that same day. Zay and his friends are looking for him now," Brandi explained, as she pulled the burger from the skillet and placed it on a napkin covered plate.

"Damn for real? Can't trust nobody these days," I said, happy to know that I wasn't suspected in no kind of way.

"Yeah, shit fucked up."

"I'm tired as hell. Guess I'll go ahead and turn it in," I told Brandi, feeling good about getting away with murder.

"I'm going to watch the rest of Single Ladies, then turn it in myself."

"See you in the morning," I said, as I headed back to my room.

I stepped in my room and closed the door behind me. I thought about Sherm and the game he gave me on this robbing shit. Damn I miss my nigga. I pulled out my laptop and did a little research on Markel's murder. The police have no clues and are looking for anyone with any information to call some bullshit snitch hotline. I was home free once again.

I counted up the money in my head, knowing I had a nice stash to hold me over for a while. I walked over to my nightstand, pulled out my digital camera pouch and emptied the contents in my hand. The diamond necklace sparkled like glass, as I held it up and checked it out. While admiring the diamonds my door suddenly opened.

"Girl I forgot to tell…" Brandi started and stopped as she set her sights on the big diamond necklace I was holding.

I snapped, "Brandi why the fuck you busting all up in my shit! That's why I got to get my own shit ASAP! What you want!" I screamed, as I tried to conceal the necklace in both hands.

"First of all, I did knock and second you be busting up in my shit all the time. Who's necklace?" Brandi asked changing the subject.

"A present for Justice. Now what you want?" I asked in an irritated tone, as I stuffed the necklace back in the bag.

"Oh, some lady about a house called. She said everything is finalized and to call her when you can."

"That's what's up," I replied excitedly, knowing I was about to be living the American dream.

After Brandi left my room, I placed the camera pouch with the necklace in my nightstand drawer.

Chapter 6

" W hat the fuck! Stop!" Kia screamed, as Dino grabbed her up and slammed her down on the couch.

Seconds later Bones' ten year old son ran in the room with his pj's on.

"Leave my mama alone," he screamed, as he rushed Dino.

Before he reached the sofa, Zay snatched him up and slammed him hard to the floor. He busted out crying as Zay continued to manhandle him.

"Lil nigga, sit down and don't fuckin' move," Zay spat, as he held the lil' boy by the back of his neck.

"Please don't hurt my son!" Kia screamed, as Dino pinned her face-down on the sofa.

"Look here lady…your man killed someone very special to me, so right now I don't want to hear shit you got to say, so shut the fuck up," Zay said through clenched teeth, as he continued to hold her son by the neck.

"Please! Please don't hurt us!" Kia sobbed, as Dino pulled the roll of duct tape from his pocket and taped her hands behind her back.

"Look just be easy and shit will be cool," Zay said, knowing in his mind shit wasn't going to be cool at all.

"Nooo! Please!" Kia screamed, as she watched Dino tape her son's hands behind his back.

Just as Dino finished taping Bones' son's hands behind his back, Zay heard a car outside.

"Say bro, somebody pulling up," Zay said, peeping out of the blinds and recognizing Bones' customized Cadillac EXT truck.

"It's Bones. Put some tape on both of their mouths," Zay said, as he positioned himself on the doors' blindside.

Dino knew Bones was going to pitch a fit when he saw his lady and son tied up on the couch, so he made sure they were in plain view as a distraction.

"He at the door," Zay whispered, with his gun in his hand.

Bones stuck his key in and unlocked the door. His heart dropped when he saw his lady and little boy tied up. He rushed over to them, unaware that the people that did this were still in the house. Just as Bones reached them, he heard someone behind him.

"What the hell going on bro?" Bones asked, as he turned and faced Zay, not aware of Dino coming up behind him.

"Like the good book says, an eye for an eye," Zay said, as he tightened his grip on his gun.

"What you mean an eye for…"

Smack!

That was as far as Bones got before the butt of Dino's gun came crashing down on the back of his head. He crumbled to the floor.

When Bones came to, he was duct taped and laying face down on the floor between Kia and his son whose mouth was still covered with tape.

"Man what's going on! The money in the bathroom! Ain't no need to hurt nobody!" Bones pleaded, trying his best to look up from his awkward position.

"Come on now Bones, I see you don't remember me because if you did you would know this ain't about no money…shit…I'm already rich," Zay said, as he walked and stood over Bones' son who laid motionless with his eyes darting around the room.

"Man what's this 'bout? My face clean in these streets bro," Bones said in a pleading tone, as sweat started to form on his forehead.

"I'm just going to tell you like this…you killed someone that meant a lot to me, so I think it's only fair I do the same to you," Zay said calmly, in a sinister tone.

"What the hell you talking 'bout bro. I ain't did shit to nobody…I swear!"

"Look here nigga, I already know what's up so miss me with your bullshit!" Zay screamed, then snatched Bones lil' boy up and propped him up against the bed.

"Man, please don't hurt my son—man come on now! I ain't killed your people bro!"

"Yeah, yeah whatever," Zay said, as he pulled a hunting knife from his pocket.

"Bro man I swear…please man don't hurt my boy…he ain't got shit to do wit none of this," Bones pleaded.

"You right my nigga," Zay said, as he placed the knife back in his pocket, then reached around and pulled a glock from the small of his back and pointed at the scared lil' boy who looked at his dad for help.

"Man no please! If you gonna kill somebody…kill me!" Bones screamed, as he wiggled around frantically on the floor trying to free himself.

"In due time playa," Zay said, leveling the gun at the lil' boy's chest.

Kia's cries were muted by the tape on her mouth, as she watched helplessly as her lil' boy stared down the barrel of Zay's gun.

"Bitch nigga! This is what happens when you fuck with NWM.!" Zay screamed, as he squeezed the trigger.

The single shot hit the small boy in the middle of his chest slumping him over.

"Um! Ummm! Ummm!" Kia cried out, helplessly, as her son's blood trickled down her face.

"Aww noo! Man I didn't…" Bones started but was cut off when Dino stretched a strip of duct tape across his mouth.

"Nigga shut yo bitch ass up!" Dino spat.

"Aight now…what do we have here?" Zay said, stepping around Bones and over to Kia who was laying flat on her stomach with her head in the carpet, crying uncontrollably.

"Ummm! Ummm!" was all you heard from Bones as he watched Zay walk over and stand over Kia.

"Turn that bitch nigga around so he can get a good view," Zay told Dino, as he snatched at Kia's nightgown.

Bones watched as Zay stripped his girl naked. She wiggled around like a fish out of water trying to get away from Zay.

"This lil' bitch got a lil' buck in her with her fat pussy self," Zay said, as he rubbed his hand in between her butt cheeks and over her clean-shaved pussy.

"Ummm! Ummmmm! Ummmmm!" Bones screamed, as he watched Zay play in between his woman's legs.

"Say my nigga, you want some of this pussy?" Zay asked Dino and smiled at Bones.

"Shittt! Might as well!" Dino said excitedly, as he started to unbuckle his pants.

"Be my guest," Zay told him, as he walked over to Bones who watched with fire in his eyes.

"Yeah shawty…thank yo man for this here," Dino said as he stood over Kia, pulling his pants down.

"Pull the tape off her mouth so her nigga can hear his bitch scream," Zay ordered, as he kneeled down next to Bones and pulled the tape off of his mouth too.

"Man why yall doing this! You killed my son man! Man I swear, man I didn't kill your people! Please man don't hurt my girl!"

"Nigga, you should've thought about that when you fucked with NWM.!" Dino yelled, as he lowered himself onto Kia.

"God please stop! Nooooo! Ahh!" Kia screamed, as Dino jammed his dick into her from behind.

"Come on man nooooo! This some fuck shit my nigga! Y'all some coward, bitch ass niggas! Fuck y'all!" Bones screamed at the top of his lungs, while Dino pushed himself roughly in and then back out of his woman.

"Nigga shut up and watch my playa dick your bitch down," Zay smiled, as he walked over, grabbed Bones' lifeless son and moved him closer to Bones.

"This ain't right! No man…" Bones burst out in tears as he looked over at his son, then back over to Kia who was screaming and crying while being fucked hard and rough by Dino.

"Ahhhhhh! Shit!" Dino screamed out as he filled Kia with his juices.

"God please help me! God please!" Kia screamed and cried, as Dino lifted himself up off of her.

"You good my nigga?" Zay asked Dino, as he pointed at Kia and gave Dino a signal to finish her off.

"Bitch got some good good! Sorry it got to go to waste," Dino said, as he placed the barrel of the gun to the back of her head.

"Man please! Man let her live bro please! Don't do this maannn!" Bones screamed.

"God please forgive me for my sins I ask…" Kia instantly started praying, as the barrel of the gun rested on the back of her head.

Dino looked over at Zay to get the go ahead. Zay smiled and ran his finger across his neck and seconds later brain matter was all over the floor. The blast echoed around the room. Bones was in shock after watching his son and lady get killed.

"Damn my nigga why you so quiet?" Zay asked Bones, laughing. "Shit real ain't it! You see it don't you fuck boy!" Zay screamed.

"Shit ain't no fun now huh?" Dino added, laughing also.

Bones was through begging. He had accepted his fate.

"Man, grab the covers off the bed," Zay told Dino, as he pulled the gun up and zeroed in on Dino.

"You need all of 'em or just…" Dino stopped mid-sentence as he turned and saw Zay's gun pointed at him.

"Nigga quit bullshitting. We got to get up out this mutherfucker!" Dino said uneasily, with the bed sheets wrapped in his arms.

"My nigga…no witnesses, no case. Can't take that chance," Zay said calmly, as he put four shots in Dino's chest.

Bones looked on, stunned as Zay killed his partner in crime. Just as Zay was turning his attention back to Bones, he heard a car pulling up out front.

"Shit!" Zay said, as he ran over and peeped out the bedroom window.

Two men were getting out of a van and heading up to the house. Zay knew he had to make a move and make it fast. Grabbing a pillow off the bed, he placed it over Bones' head and fired two rushed shots—one grazed his ear and the second knocked a chunk out of his head. After firing the shots, Zay jumped out of the bedroom window.

Lendo and Cricket knew Bones was going to be trippin' because they were late dropping off the money for their last package. While walking up to the door they were sure they had heard gun shots. Cricket and Lendo retreated back to their van and grabbed their guns. Creeping back up to the house, they heard a crash around back.

"What the fuck going on in this bitch?" Lendo slurred, still feeling the effects of the lean and cush.

"Something ain't right," Cricket added, as they crept up on the house and looked in the window.

"The sofa all turned over and shit. Yeah something happening up in here,"

Lendo said to Cricket, who stood behind him trying to look over his shoulder to see.

"I'm calling this nigga phone," Cricket said, as he pulled out his old model flip phone.

After a few rings and no answer, they made their way to the back of the house. They stopped and turned around as they heard a car starting up out front.

"Somebody's leaving," Cricket said gripping his gun tight and running back toward the front of the house with Lendo right behind him.

"Fuck!" Cricket yelled. "What the fuck is goin' on here?"

He turned to see Lendo motioning for him to follow him to the back of the house.

"Yo, they came out of that window," Lendo whispered, as he stooped low and eased up on the open window.

Gripping the window ledge, Lendo pulled himself up and looked in. The carnage in the room made him throw up.

"Uggg!"

"Man…damn! You almost threw up on me. Stop drinking that shit if you can't handle it!" Cricket yelled, disturbing the peace as he moved Lendo out the way to look in.

When Cricket looked in, he almost gagged too. The stench of death, sex, sweat, and blood hit him in the face instantly.

"Let's get the fuck up out of here!" Cricket screamed, as Lendo was regaining his composure.

"For real…let's go!" Lendo said, as he took off running back to the front of the house with Cricket not far behind. As they pulled out the driveway they dialed 911.

* * * * *

Zay lit a blunt and turned up Young Jeezy as he headed back to his spot. He had fucked the nigga up that was responsible for killing his cousin, now it was time to get back on the grind. The one thing Zay didn't know was that the two shots to Bones' head, were only flesh wounds.

Chapter 7

The next day I put on my fuck me outfit and hit the highway in route to MSP where Sherm was locked up and serving a life sentence for murder. Sherm was my everything and till this day, I planned to stay down until he comes home. I pulled up in front of the prison at exactly nine o'clock. Damn, I couldn't wait to see my boo. After passing all the security check points, I was escorted to the main visitation room where I was given a small chit that had a number on it and I was to sit at the corresponding table. I had been through this on several occasions and hated it but fuck it…my baby was more than worth it.

* * * * *

I still remember the day we met…

"Damn Miss Lady, how you doing?" Sherm asked, as I bobbed my head to the T.I. song that was blasting from the clubs' sound system.

"I'm good. You know me?" I replied with a fake attitude.

"Naw, I don't know you but I'm trying to get to know you," Sherm told me, as his jewels sparkled in the clubs dimmed lights.

As bad as I tried to play hard, I couldn't— this nigga was too fine. He had the sexiest lips that partially concealed his mouth full of platinum and diamonds. Every time this nigga spoke all you could see was money.

"What you want to know?" I asked, as I picked up my drink and took a sip.

"I want to know if it's ok for me to change your life?" he asked, as he motioned for the bartender.

"Why you think I want to change my life? My life may be just fine as is," I said, with a little snap in my tone.

"What woman doesn't want the finer things in life, then on top of that, a man that gives you his undivided attention at all times."

"Shit sound good but I'm not impressed," I said, as I leaned over and whispered in his ear. "I'm the type of bitch that got to be wined, dined, pampered, then fucked real good on a regular basis—if you can handle that then give me your number…if not, move to the next bitch."

He smiled, displaying thousands of dollars worth of dental work.

"I think I may be just the man for the job," he replied, as the bartender walked up.

"What can I get for you?" the female bartender, who may have been mistaken for a man on many occasions, asked.

"Give me a bottle of your best champagne and a pen."

* * * * *

We had been inseparable after that night—right up until the night he pulled a lick and left a nigga living, who later on pointed him out in a crowded courtroom. That's why now he always stresses to me…leave no witnesses.

I almost fell out the chair when I saw my baby walk in the visitation room, still fine as hell. No matter when I come to visit, I'm always head over heels for my nigga.

"Hey sexy!" he said, as he wrapped his arms around me.

"Hey boo!" I replied excitedly, as I rested my head on his chest.

My nigga was still looking good. Just picture a bowlegged Tyrese with a mouth full of platinum and diamonds.

"Baby I got some good news," Sherm said, as he sat in the chair that was positioned directly in front of me, on the other side of a small round table.

"What's the news baby?" I asked curiously.

"This is what's up. I spoke with a lawyer and he advised me that he could get me out but…" Sherm said, as he reared back in the small plastic visitation chair.

"But what?" I asked, excitedly.

"He's going to need $250,000 and the deal is only on the table for another month," Sherm explained, with a stern look on his face.

"A month! How are we going to get that kind of money in a month?" I asked, thinking about the money I had just spent on the house and also the money I had left from my last lick which was only $145,000.

"What? You laying down on me now? You ain't going hard for your man now?" he asked, with a hint of anger in his tone.

"Baby, you know I will always go hard for you. It's just that…" I started as he cut me off.

"It's just that what? So you telling me with the game I gave you on this taking shit, you can't make it happen?" he asked, now clearly angry.

"It's not even like that. It's just that I got to get close to a nigga that's holding like that. These niggas ain't getting it like they use to and the ones that are ain't keeping that kind of money laying around," I explained.

"Change your playing field, plain and simple. You want me home?" he asked, leaning in close to me.

"You know I do. I got you," I replied softly, as I brushed my hair out of my face and thought about a good place to find a big lick.

"That's my baby," he replied, as he reached over and grabbed my hand.

Me and Sherm had been through so much and when he was home I never wanted for anything. I knew I had to do whatever it was going to take to get him home. We sat around and talked about the past and the future, until they announced visitation was over.

"You good boo?" he asked as we stood and embraced.

"I'm good baby. I got you," I whispered, as I buried my head in his chest.

"No doubt. I know my baby got me," he replied, then tilted my chin up and placed his tongue in my mouth.

This was the highlight of all my visits. I couldn't wait for the end to kiss him. His kissing and grinding never failed to get my pussy wet.

As I exited the visitation room, I looked back and saw my soldier, my best friend, my happiness, just sitting there helpless. I knew what I had to do and didn't care how many niggas had to die to get it done. I turned, blew him a kiss and mouthed—I love you. When I got in the car, I pulled my glock 40 from under the seat and placed it on my lap. Wasn't nobody in the world going to stop me from getting the money to get my man out.

Chapter 8

One Week Later…

" *M*an you're lucky to be breathing," Lendo told Bones as they sat in room 205 at South Fulton Hospital, where the doctors had just cleared Bones to leave.

"Bro that's real talk," Bones replied. He gathered his stuff to leave and thought about the man responsible for all of this.

Ever since the day of the murders, Bones was hush about the situation. The police had questioned him on several occasions and he always gave them the same story, excluding any information on the man he planned to punish…Zay.

Zay was back on his grind since the day of the murders. There was a lot of talk on the streets about the killings, even about the lone survivor. When Zay found out that Bones was still alive, he got off the scene and moved in with Brandi.

"You still ain't got no idea who did this shit bro? Word on the street is that Moonie had something to do with this shit," Lendo told Bones, as they exited the hospital

"Man the niggas was masked up but I ain't stopping until I get the nigga behind the mask. I need to go by the house, then go by my mother-n-law's and give her something on the funeral," Bones said, still playing out the scene from last week in his head.

"Aight, damn shit is crazy as fuck bro. It's fucked up how they did Kia and lil' B. I'm with you on whatever, my nigga," Lendo said sincerely, as they got in his black on black Denali.

"Yeah fam, it's fucked up…real fucked up," Bones replied with an eerie calm tone, lost in thought looking out of the truck window, as they headed to the same house that his loved ones died in.

Pulling up outside of the house brought back memories that Bones would have to live with forever. He told Lendo to wait in the truck while he went in. Yellow crime scene tape was everywhere. Tears of anger welled up in Bones' eyes as he entered the house. As he walked in, he smelled death in the air. The house was left just as it was the night of the murders, except for the obvious signs of police presence. As Bones entered the bedroom, his heart felt as if it was going to jump out of his chest. His son's blood was still visible on the bed and the big patch of red carpet next to the bed was where his babygirl and soon to be wife, Kia was raped and then shot point blank range in the back of the head.

Bones hurried across the room and pulled the nightstand away from the wall. Pulling the carpet back, he snatched the loosely fitted piece of wood out and retrieved the stacks of money he had hid in the floor. After emptying the spot, he grabbed his canvas gym bag and filled it with clothes and the money.

Walking through the house, all Bones could think about was Zay and Dino and the pain they put his family through. Dino was dead, so now all Bones wanted to think about was Zay and the way he would make his family pay.

Passing through the kitchen, Bones ducked off into the carport and grabbed a gas can. Heading back into the house he poured gas from the front room and throughout the entire house. As he stepped out the front door, he lit a match and tossed it onto the gas soaked carpet. The house was up in flames before they turned the corner.

"I feel ya bro…I feel ya," Lendo said softly, as he pushed the Denali out into traffic.

Chapter 9

I stood in the long line at Club Visions, scoping out niggas and their rides. Tonight was Ladies Night and the spot was packed. I really wasn't up to this shit tonight but I had to beat the clock if I was going to get my baby home. I made sure I remembered every face that valet parked and the car they drove. I was going to find the right lick tonight, no matter what.

Thirty minutes later I was walking into the smoke-filled, dimly lit club. I scoped out all the so-called ballers and the niggas that was gettin their cake up for real. The so-called ballers were always the ones trying to be seen, flashing money and checking their fake diamond-filled watches. The niggas with the real money always played it cool, laying low in the background. As I walked through the club I noticed all the stares and pointing. Tonight I wore a short red, tight mini-skirt that hugged my hips with some three-inch heels that jacked my ass up just enough to make my skirt rise so you could see a lil' of my ass cheeks. I didn't want to get to raunchy tonight but I had to command attention.

"Say Beautiful, how you doing. Oh, don't answer that…fine I see."

"Excuse me?" I said with emphasis, trying my best to make this clown get out my way.

"Aint no thang Beautiful. I was just trying to see what it's going to take to get to know you," he slurred, obviously drunk.

"I'm here waiting on a friend, my boyfriend sorry," I told him, as I positioned myself at the end of the bar so I could scope out the whole club.

"Y'all bitches be killing me with all that fake ass shit!" he screamed, all up in my face.

I already had shit on my mind and now this nigga was all up on me.

"Look nigga…get your broke, bitch ass out my face before I get you up out my face!" I stood face to face with him.

"Ohhh, ok bitch, you think you tough huh," he said, as he put his finger in my face.

"Smack!"

I smacked that nigga with all my might and before I could draw my hand back, he had grabbed a hand full of my hair and snatched me to the ground.

"Bitch, you put yo hands on the wrong…"

Before he could finish, a fist to his jaw sent him crashing to the floor.

"So we beating on the ladies I see."

As the stranger manhandled the man, I regained my footing and played the damsel in distress role. I watched as the at least six foot, two hundred fifty pound man slapped the wannabe baller around.

Minutes later the bouncers arrived.

"Are you cool?" they asked the big man, as he tossed the drunken wannabe their way.

"Yeah, all good. Just get him up out of here," the man said, as he came over to me.

"You ok? " he asked, displaying a mouth full of perfect teeth that had to have been the work of a skilled dentist.

"Yes, I'm alright. Just a little shook up," I replied, as I took in the scent of what was undoubtedly, an expensive fragrance.

"I'm Sly, the club manager and co-owner," he said, as he extended his hand that had on it one of the biggest diamonds I have ever seen.

"I'm Kimmie. Thanks for helping me," I told him, as I adjusted my shirt and fixed my hair.

The whole time we got acquainted, I checked out his Gucci ensemble that was head to toe. Looking at him, I know he had money but he also looked like one of them niggas that kept his money in the bank.

"You alone?" he asked, as he looked around.

"Yes, I'm afraid so. My girlfriend that was suppose to meet me here had a change of plans, so here I am…solo," I said, watching his eyes scan my body.

"I see you didn't let her stop your show. Are you going to be here for a minute?" he asked, looking at me like he wanted to eat a bitch up.

"Depends on if I need to be," I said in a sexy tone, while looking him up and down.

One thing I know, is that a pretty smile and a fat ass will have all types of men eating out of your hands.

"Yeah, you need to be. Just pull up at any one of those empty tables in the VIP area. I'll send a bottle of Ciroc over while you wait."

"That's what's up," I said, as I walked away twisting my ass hard enough to make sure he couldn't take his eyes off me.

Thirty minutes later I had the nigga all wrapped up like a Christmas present on Christmas Eve.

"How about we have a night cap at my place and talk more about your artistic side," he suggested, as he downed his third glass of Ciroc.

"Ok, that sounds good to me," I agreed, as I reached over and rubbed the inside of his thigh, slightly making contact with his hard on.

I knew for a fact that this nigga had money but where the hell did he keep it. As we walked out the club I heard someone call my name. When I turned I was eye to eye with Alfred, one of Atlanta's most known con men. Niggas from all over knew how Alfred rolled but they respected him to the fullest because he was known to use his strap.

"Hey Alfred," I spoke, as we headed to our respective cars.

"Hey girl. What the biz is?" he asked, as he looked in Sly's direction.

"What up Sly. I see you still keeping it playa," he said, as he walked over and gave Sly some dap.

I was totally caught off guard at their recognition of one another. It is never good to be the last one seen with a dead man.

"Same oh same oh—trying to get to the house," I said, trying my best to make it seem as if I wasn't with Sly.

"Good to see you again, oh my man here good people now," he said smiling, as he walked off.

Damn! I thought to myself, as I got to my car and told Sly that I would follow him.

Sly lived out on the outskirts of Atlanta in Fayetteville, a spot that's known for it's mini mansions and upscale living. As I rode behind him, I loaded my glock 40 and put an extra clip in my clutch. I changed out of my heels at the light and put on my Nike running shoes. After fifteen minutes of driving, we pulled up into a nice palatial home that had a man-made lake flanking it. The house was beautiful and obviously very expensive. This one lick alone should be the one to get my nigga out. I got my nerves together, grabbed my clutch and got out the car.

"Oh yes baby, fuck mama good! Ahh yeah! Oh shittttt! Damn I love you! Yeaaah!" Brandi screamed, as Zay fucked her in every hole in her body.

That's what Brandi loved so much about Zay. He was a true freak in the sheets and knew just how to hit her G-spot.

"Yeah boo! Give daddy his pussy! Fuccccccck daddy baby! Give it to me! I'm 'bout to cum boo!"

Even though Zay put the monster dick down on Brandi, his mind was still on Bones and trying to make sure his own whereabouts stayed a secret.

Zay had devised a plan to finish his business with Bones. He knew he would have to get to Bones before Bones got to him. Finding Bones was going to be a problem now that his spot was closed. He rode by Bones' house yesterday and saw that it was burned to the ground. Zay thought long and hard and it hit him… he was going to finish this nigga Bones off at his son's and baby mama's funeral that was scheduled for tomorrow. After fucking Brandi like it was their last time, Zay checked his cell phone and saw that Hester, one of his biggest spending customers, had called. Even though he needed to stay off the scene, he still had to eat so he got up, took a hoe bath and headed out to meet Hester with his usual order of two bricks.

As Zay headed down Old National Highway, he didn't notice the old model gray Chevy Cavalier trailing him. Making drops this time of day was really out the question but since he knew Hester well, he went ahead but what he didn't know was that he was being followed and the person in the car behind him wanted the dope he was set to drop in a few minutes.

"Move on that nigga at the next light!" the man barked, as he stayed close behind Zay.

"Man, wait till the nigga hit Flat Shoals—that way we can dip off in the old hood," the second occupant in the car said, as he pulled his .357 snub nose out from under the seat.

"Aight, we'll rush him at the first light that we get caught at. Call Hester and let him know we on him now."

Making a left at the light on Flat Shoals, Zay counted the money in his head that he was about to make off the drop off. As he rode down Flat Shoals, he noticed a car with two dudes behind him. He was sure they had been following him now for over five minutes, making every turn behind him. Just to make sure his assumptions were correct, he made a turn just to see if they would follow.

"We on him now but he must be making another stop before he get to you," the man told Hester, who had set the lick up because he was broke due to gambling a habit that he couldn't break.

"Ok just stay on him. I know for a fact that he got two bricks with him—we need both of 'em. Call me when you straight," Hester said, then ended the call.

The next light was just over the hill. The two robbers were ready to jump out on Zay if the light caught them. Just as they neared the light, it turned yellow then red. Zay, knowing now that the men were on his tail, pulled his strap out and got ready for whatever. Zay wondered how in the world Bones had found out about his whereabouts. He never suspected Hester—all he kept trying to figure out was where he slipped. Pulling up and stopping at the light, Zay watched through the rearview mirror as the two men jumped out the car and rushed his way. Instead of hitting the gas, he wanted to send a message. As the men neared, he jumped out the car and just started shooting. The two robbers were caught totally off guard. Zay hit one of them in the knee, causing him to buckle and eat the concrete. The second man was hit with two shots in the stomach, doubling him over.

"Ahhh!" the men yelled, as the bullets pierced their bodies.

"Y'all bitches thought I was slipping! Nah, Zay don't do no muthafuckin slipping! Now see what Bones got you!" Zay screamed, as he walked over to the robber who was doubled over and shot him point blank range in the face. As soon as the other man saw his friend's face disappear, he started screaming while trying his best to limp away.

"Naw...fuck nigga...where you think you going!" Zay yelled, catching up to the man.

"Man, please don't kill me man. Hester wanted us to hit you bro...ain't no beef bro, please man," the man pleaded, as Zay stood over him with his gun smoking in the cool night air.

The mention of Hester's name shocked Zay. Him and Hester had been doing business for a while and were always straight up with each other.

"Bitch, you should've thought about that earlier," Zay said calmly, as he unloaded on the man, sending bullets to his face and chest.

Hurrying back to his car, Zay put the car in drive and sped off to meet Hester. As he neared Hester's spot, he called him.

"Yo bro. I'm almost at you. Had to make another stop first. Be at you in a minute," Zay said, as if nothing just happened while mapping out a plan to end this nigga's life.

Hester didn't waste time picking up the phone and calling his two goons. He slammed his phone closed when the voice mail came on.

"What the fuck these niggas doing!" Hester screamed out loud, as he paced nervously back and forth in the front room of his apartment.

He knew when Zay got to him with the work and he didn't have money, it was going to be a problem. He walked to the back of the apartment and grabbed his sawed-off shot gun...he was going to handle Zay himself.

" **M**ake yourself at home beautiful," Sly said, as we walked in the expensively furnished three story house that had to be worth a cool million or more.

"I'll do that. How about a drink?" I suggested, trying to get this nigga sloppy drunk.

"That'll work…the bar is over there help yourself," he slurred, as he headed to the back.

I poured him up a glass of Absolute and me a glass of water. I didn't want to waste any time pulling this off, so I fast forwarded this shit.

"Damn baby!" he yelled excitedly, as he walked back in the room where I stood in the middle of the floor holding the two drinks with only my thong on.

"Oh, I did something wrong?" I asked him, as I walked over and handed him his drink.

"Oh naw, you right on point. How 'bout we go upstairs?" he asked, as he turned his glass up.

"What we waiting on?" I questioned, as I turned my water up, grabbed my clutch and followed him upstairs.

I can say this nigga's bedroom was the bomb. He had a round king sized bed that sat across the room from a custom designed hot tub, with a 52inch flat screen hanging on the wall in front of it. This was going to be the lick to set my nigga free.

"Nice room…like the set up," I commented, as I sat my glass down and climbed up on the bed.

"Glad you like it," he said, slightly staggering as he stripped down to his birthday suit and climbed in the bed next to me.

The nigga was hung like a horse and a bitch really needed a good fucking right now but I dismissed the thought and got down to business. He reached over and started kissing and rubbing on my ass. Knowing I had put myself on the clock, I grabbed his dick and caressed it one good time before I excused myself.

"Hold up boo, I got to go to the lil' girls room," I told him, as I rolled off the bed and grabbed my clutch.

"Hurry up and bring daddy back that pretty ass," he slurred in the worst way.

I went in the bathroom and locked the door behind me. Pulling the gun from my clutch I made sure it was off safety and ready to shoot. I got my nerves together as I gripped the glock and exited the bathroom. Little did I know, his on-site security guard watched me the whole time I was in the bathroom and was now rushing up to the room.

"Nigga don't move!" I screamed, as I exited the bathroom with the gun pointed at him laying on the bed.

"What the he'll you doing! What the fuck is your problem?" Sly yelled, as he sat up on the bed looking at me confused.

"Nigga make another move and I will blow your fuckin' head off. Just do what I say and I will be up out this bitch," I told him in a angry irritated tone.

"What you want?" he yelled, looking over at his bedroom door.

"Nigga, where the safe at? I know you got one. Just let me get what's in the safe and I'm out," I said calmly, hoping there was a safe.

I really was mad at myself for not doing research on this lick before pulling it off because if it wasn't a safe, this killing would be for nothing. Just looking around, I realized if there wasn't a safe, he had enough valuables to sell to get the money I needed.

"Baby, I ain't got no safe. I keep my money in the bank," he laughed crazily.

"Nigga, I know it's a safe. Well, just put it like this…your good friend that knows about your safe got me standing in your bedroom naked about to kill yo ass if you don't open the safe!" I yelled angrily.

The expression on his face gave him away—he had a safe.

"Get up slow and easy," I said in a firm tone, as I kept the gun pointed at him.

He rolled out the bed and walked slowly over to the flat screen TV hanging on the wall. He hit a button on the side and it unlatched itself and was now hanging on hinges. He swung it out and bingo…the safe was in full view.

"There you go," he said, laughing again.

"Open it!" I demanded.

This time he laughed uncontrollably, as his on-site security guard eased up behind me with his gun in hand.

Chapter 12

Zay pulled up in front of Hester's spot a few minutes later. Taking the bricks out the bag and replacing them with old clothes, he slung the bag over his shoulder and headed up to the door.

Hester peeped out of the front room window when he heard a car pull up outside. Seeing that it was Zay, he grabbed the sawed-off and made his way to the door.

Knock! Knock!

"Hold up!" Hester yelled, as he reached the door with the shot gun in hand.

Hester wondered what the hell happened to his two goons as he unlatched the door to let Zay in. Just as the door cracked, Zay kicked out and rushed Hester who had stumbled backwards with the shotgun in his hands.

"Put it down nigga!" Zay screamed, as he pointed the gun down at Hester who was frantically trying to get a grip on the sawed-off.

"Hold up man!" Hester said, holding both hands in the air.

"No sir my friend, it wasn't no hold up when you sent your lil' fuck boys at me," Zay said, as he stood over Hester who knew if he didn't make a move now he was going to be killed.

Out of nowhere Hester reached over and grabbed the shotgun and pulled the trigger, not even coming close to Zay. Zay laughed at his efforts and pulled the trigger, hitting Hester in the arm.

"Ahh! Shit! Fuck!" Hester yelled, as he held his arm.

"Damn it's fucked up shit played out like this but it is what it is," Zay said softly, as he pulled the trigger, hitting Hester one time in the chest and one time in the face.

"Fuck!" Zay screamed, thinking about all the bodies that were adding up.

Grabbing his bag of clothes, he stepped out of the door and as soon as he cleared the doorstep, police cars swarmed the parking lot. Zay didn't know that Hester was under investigation for all his illegal activities and today was the day the Feds decided to bring him down.

Chapter 13

Bones got Lendo to circle back around later that night so he could get his truck. Pulling out his cell phone, he made call after call until he got the information he was looking for.

"The nigga stay with his girl Brandi on the southside. Matter of fact the bitch dance out at Nikki's," the female voice on the other end told Bones, as he sat out in front of his burned down house.

"Oh yeah? Ok I appreciate you—I got you boo," Bones told her, as he ended the call.

It didn't take Bones long to come up with a plan for Zay and his bitch.

At eleven o'clock, Bones was climbing into his truck with nothing but murder on his mind as he headed out to club Nikki's to meet Brandi. He was going to first find out who she was and then he was going to wait till she got off, then follow her back to her spot. He planned to do the same thing to her that Zay did to his lady and more.

* * * * *

Silk doesn't know a gun is pointed at her.

Zay is surrounded by the police right outside the house he just killed someone in.

Bones is on his way to Nikki's to settle the score with Zay.

STREET CHRONICLES

~ PRESENTS ~

gangsta GIRL 2

"The Lick"

George Sherman Hudson

Author of *City Lights* **and** *Executive Mistress*

Chapter 1

As I stood with my glock .40 pointed at Sly, I noticed a figure in the back wall mirror creeping up behind me real slow, with a gun in his hand. Now I see why this nigga laughing like he all crazy and shit! I braced myself and gave the approaching person one more step before I swiftly turned and let go on his ass.

"Pop! Pop! Pop!"

The glock shook and jumped everytime I pulled the trigger. The bullets connected with him easily, hitting him in the neck and chest.

"Yeah nigga…you crept up on the wrong bitch this time!" I yelled, as I ran over to the man who was barely breathing.

I looked into his eyes and smiled, as I took him out of his misery with one shot to the face. This killing shit was getting easier by the minute.

Sly stood back in shock when the bullet from the glock pierced his longtime worker's skull. Snapping out of it, Sly tried to make a run for it but didn't get far before I let a couple of rounds go, hitting him in the leg and thigh.

"Ah! Shit!" he screamed out in pain, as he crumbled to the floor holding his leg.

"Nigga get over here and open this muthafuckin safe!" I yelled, as I rushed over to him and put the glock in his face.

"Ok! Please! Just hold o…on!" he screeched out in pain.

"Now! Open the safe!" I screamed, as I tightened my grip on the gun.

"Ok! Just please don't shoot," he pleaded, as he pulled himself over to the safe, obviously no longer feeling the effects of the alcohol from minutes ago.

"Hurry the fuck up!" I yelled, realizing that I had been in this nigga spot way to long.

A few seconds later the door to the safe swung open. Sly leaned on the wall next to the safe sweating and bleeding badly.

"Take it all— just let a nigga live, please," he pleaded, as he started to cry like a lil' bitch.

I looked over in the safe and saw four big money stacks held together with rubber bands. I instantly got excited knowing that my man was about to be free.

"I appreciate ya," I told him, as I smiled and lifted the gun and pointed it at him.

"No! Please nooo!" he started screaming just as I pulled the trigger, sending two hollow points to his chest.

I stepped around his lifeless body and cleaned out the safe. After putting all the money in a pillow case, I rushed downstairs, got dressed, then did away with the glass and bottle I had touched. After looking around making sure that I left nothing to tie me to the scene, I grabbed my clutch and headed out the door. I smiled as I tried my best not to exceed the speed limit on the way home.

Chapter 2

"Freeze!" the undercover FBI agents yelled with their guns pointed at Zay, as he stood stunned like a deer caught in the bright glow of headlights.

"Fuck!" Zay cursed under his breath, as he took off running in the opposite direction.

"He's fleeing!" the tall lanky agent yelled, as he gave chase.

Zay knew if they caught him, he would never see daylight free again. He cursed himself over and over again as he ran. He knew better than to be doing his own dirty work. He knew there was way more than enough flunkies in the crew who could be handling all this hands-on shit.

The federal agent was closing in fast, as Zay jumped the back fence of the apartment complex. Thinking he was in the clear, he looked back again…the federal agent cleared the fence with ease and continued his pursuit.

"Fuck!" Zay cursed out loud as he ran recklessly through the brush that was parallel to a side street.

Making his way through the brush, Zay ran out into the street. An approaching vehicle, with an old white man behind the wheel barely missed him. As the car came to a screeching halt, Zay ran up to the driver's door. Zay didn't give the old man a chance to say anything before he hit him twice in the face, pulled the door open and snatched him out, throwing him onto the hard concrete. Just as he was climbing behind the wheel, he looked back and saw the agent coming out of the brush.

"Zero, nine, two, fiver. The suspect is now fleeing west bound in a brown four door, late model Cadillac with Fulton County plates," the agent barked into his radio out of breath, as he watched Zay bend the corner in the old man's car.

Zay pushed the Cadillac as fast as it would go, maneuvering down back streets in route to Brandi's place. Ten minutes later, he was ditching the car in an abandoned lot and cutting through an old freight yard around the corner from Brandi's.

"Knock! Knock! Knock!"

"Open the door!" Zay yelled, as he stood outside of the front door sweating and looking around for any signs of the police.

He then remembered that Brandi went down to the club early tonight.

"Shit!" he cursed, as he looked around to make sure the coast was clear.

"Crack!"

The front apartment window shattered when the large rock connected with it. Looking around and seeing everything was still quiet, he climbed through the window.

Chapter 3

"Next up is sexy fine ass butter!" the club emcee shouted, introducing Brandi to the stage.

Brandi emerged from behind the curtain with a skimpy, all red, two-piece that didn't conceal much and a pair of red, four inch stilettos. Stepping out on stage, she dropped down to the floor and shook her ass wildly while licking her tongue out at the club's patrons. Niggas and bitches in the club went wild. Bones stood off in the back, admiring Brandi and thinking about what he had planned for her tonight.

Bones took a seat at the bar and watched Brandi as she moved her body to the rhythm, not missing a beat. Right before her set on stage ended, Bones walked up to the stage and pulled out a wad of money. Brandi, noticing the man in front of the stage with the stack of money, wasted no time making her way over to him. Bones made it rain on Brandi with all the bills, while Brandi gave her best performance.

Brandi was out to get every dollar Bones held. She turned around in front of him and dropped down on all fours, bringing her ass inches away from his face. Bones smiled and showered her with the bills, as she made her ass cheeks take turns jumping.

After dropping five hundred dollars on stage, Bones motioned for Brandi to holla at him when her set was over. Brandi, recognizing the gesture, smiled and nodded her head ok as she collected all the money that was scattered out on the stage.

"Damn bitch, you gonna leave some money out there for us?" Diamond asked playfully, as Brandi entered the dressing room with an arm full of crumpled up bills.

"I'm trying my best not to leave a dime out this bitch," Brandi replied laughing, excited about her big spender out front waiting for her.

"Get it bitch! I feel ya!" Diamond said, as she oiled up and slipped on a pair of six inch heels that matched her custom made, black and silver two piece that covered nothing at all.

Minutes later, Brandi was sitting at a corner table with Bones.

"Damn, what kind of man would let a woman as beautiful as you work in a place like this?" Bones asked, as he motioned for the waitress.

"You know a woman got to pay her own way these days. Shit as soon as a nigga start doing for you, he thinks he owns you," Brandi said, as the waitress approached with a pen and pad in hand.

"Can I get a bottle of Ace of Spades?" Bones asked the young, thick, half black-half Chinese girl, as he pulled a wad of bills out of his pocket.

"Anything else?" the girl asked.

"Nah, that will be all unless this beautiful lady here wants something extra," Bones stated, as he looked intently at Brandi, who was ready to get back on her hustle before it got too late.

"I'm good Angel," Brandi told the girl, as she started to get up from the table.

"By the way, I'm Dee...and you are?" Bones asked, already knowing everything about the woman who stood before him.

"I'm Butter," Brandi said, as she started to walk off.

"Hold up Butter. Where you rushing too? The bottle is for me and you," Bones told her, trying his best to hide the agitation in his voice.

"I got to get back on my grind, Dee. I can't feed me and mines sitting around drinking Ace of Spades," Brandi told Bones, knowing that he would fall right in.

"I feel you on that so here is $300 for thirty songs...now sit down and holla at a nigga."

The waiter was back a few minutes later with the bottle and two glasses. Bones gave her three one hundred dollar bills and told her to keep the change.

Thirty minutes later, half the bottle was gone and Bones was ready to put his plan into action.

"How about we spend a lil' time together? I'm willing to pay the price," Bones told her, feeling the effects of the alcohol.

"Sorry baby, I don't do the trick thang," Brandi told Bones and smiled.

Bones knew then he had no choice but to go to plan B and that was to follow her home. Bones also made a quick tally in his head. He planned to get every penny back he spent on the bitch.

Hours later Brandi entered her car and pulled out the lot and didn't notice the man in the truck following her.

Chapter 4

$\mathcal{A}$s I pulled up in front of my lavish new spot, I couldn't help but smile from ear to ear. I was happy as hell now that I had my dream home, a nice ride and on top of all that, I had just pulled off the lick to free my man. I grabbed the pillow case that contained the money and headed off into the house.

Rushing into the kitchen, I dumped the money out of the pillow case and onto the table. Sitting down in a chair, I made myself comfortable and took the bands from around the money. As I peeled back the bills from each stack, my heart dropped. Most of the bills were tens and twenties. After doing a count, I saw that I had no more than $15,000 in front of me.

"Fuck!" I cursed out loud, pissed off.

Time was running out. I had to get the $250,000 at whatever cost. I refused to let my nigga down. I knew I didn't have time enough to go out and scope another lick, so I came to a conclusion and picked up the phone.

"Hello," Brandi answered

"Hey girl, just checking on you," I said calmly, trying my best not to sound suspicious.

"Oh, thanks girl. I'm good, just tired as hell; on my way back from the club. You good?"

"Everything is nice but I do miss my girl and her old school fried chicken," I said jokingly, as I thought my plan through once again.

"Ah girl, go ahead on with that," Brandi laughed.

"For real…matter of fact, how 'bout we have dinner and you cook the chicken and I do the sides," I suggested, hoping that she would agree.

"That sounds good to me," she agreed.

"Well, you know Justice is going to be here, so bring Zay. It'll be a double date," I lied, as I thought about the trap I had for Zay.

"That's a date. When and what time?" Brandi asked, as the truck with Bones behind the wheel continued to follow her closely.

"How about tomorrow night at eight? Will that work for you?" I smiled, happy that the first part of my quickly devised plan had worked.

"Ok, but I'm going to have to be gone by 11:00. It's drink free night at the club, one of my busiest nights. Shit girl, you ain't forgot how drink free night is, have you?" Brandi asked, not noticing the truck behind her making every turn that she made.

"Yeah, I remember. That's cool, ain't no problem. That's more than enough time for us to eat," I assured her.

"I'll be there. Goodnight girl, I'm almost home."

"Goodnight," I smiled and ended the call.

After making sure my plan was air tight, I went upstairs and took a hot shower.

I really didn't want to hit this nigga Zay but right now he was my only option. I know for sure that he had money stashed at Brandi's spot somewhere, as much as he was in and out handling business. I also knew that hitting him would bring a lot of drama being that he is a highly respected member of NWM. Oh well, he was my only option.

I had finally decided to give this nigga what he's been after since day one but it was going to cost him…his life.

Chapter 5

Bones followed Brandi into her parking garage, then sat back and waited to see which door she went in. He noticed her looking strange at the front window of what had to be her place. He looked closed at what seemed to be a broken window. Just as Brandi was turned and started walking away from the door, pulling out her cell phone to call the police, the front door opened and Zay stepped out waving her in. A look of relief came upon her face as she hurried back up to the door.

"What happened to the window baby?" Brandi asked, as she entered and headed straight back to the bathroom to take a shower.

"It was broken when I got here. It looks like them bad ass kids next door threw a rock through it. Now that I think about it, they were out front earlier," Zay lied. Even though he knew Brandi was a ride or die chic, he really didn't need her being all paranoid and nervous right now.

"Damn lil' bad ass kids! What's up with you baby? Where your truck at?" Brandi asked, as she stepped into the bathroom and turned on the shower.

"Lil' Ceebo got it, trying to see what's wrong with my system," Zay yelled so Brandi could hear him over the running shower, as he climbed up in the bed and turned the TV to ESPN.

Bones sat out in the parking lot for hours going over his plans to get into the place without anyone being alerted. He slipped on some black gloves and a black hoodie, then exited the car and made his way up to the door. By the time he reached the door, he had his .38 snub nose in his grip, ready to let loose. He thought about trying to pick the lock and slide in but changed his mind and proceeded to climb through the broken window.

Zay was restless and couldn't sleep. He flipped the TV to the late night news to see if there were any reports about today's earlier events as Brandi lightly snored next to him. As he flipped from channel to channel, he heard a faint noise coming from the front room. After all the bullshit from earlier, Zay was past paranoid, so the noise he heard instantly sent his antennas up. Pulling his 9mm from the night stand drawer, he slid out of bed and crept out to see what was going on. Peeping around the corner, he saw a figure climbing through the broken window.

Bones had banked on everyone in the spot to be sleep when he made his move. Slipping through the window was a little more complicated than he thought. He hurried to his feet and made a quick scan of the room. Relieved that everything was still quiet, he pulled his hoodie over his head and started on his mission.

Bones crept like a cat, making his way through the pitch dark residence, trying his best not to make any noise or knock anything over. His heart raced a thousand beats a minute, as he cleared the front room and headed to the back where he thought his intended victims were sound asleep. He thought back on how Zay did his son and lady and the intensity of his anger grew stronger. He planned on doing Zay and his lady a thousand times worse. Bones gripped the .38 tight, as he turned the corner to enter the hallway that lead to the back bedroom.

Zay watched the figure come in his direction with what was obviously a gun in his hand. Zay knew he had to get a jump on the intruder, so he planned to take the nigga out as soon as he reached the hall closet. Zay made sure his 9mm was ready to fire, as Bones took his next step toward the closet door.

"Shit!" Bones screamed out, as the dark figure appeared out of nowhere and fired two shots.

All Bones could see was the fire that blazed from the muzzle of the person's gun. The first bullet struck him in his shoulder and the second one pierced his face, just below his right eye. The impact of the hollow point blew a hole in his face. Bones was dead on contact. This time he wasn't so lucky.

"Die bitch!" Zay cursed under his breath, as he walked over and flipped the light switch to the on position.

"Ahhhhh!" Brandi screamed, as she entered the room and saw the bloody figure laying out in the floor.

"Shhh!" Zay hissed, as he reached over and grabbed her.

"Wha…What happened?" she asked, breathing hard and looking back and forth bug eyed from Zay and then back to the dead man.

"Look, just calm the fuck down," Zay said firmly, as he moved the man with his foot to get a better look at his face.

"It's the nigga from the club," Brandi said nervously, as she placed her hand over her mouth.

"The club? This the nigga Bones that…that was out to get NWM," Zay hesitated, not wanting to let Brandi know the full details.

"He was at the club tonight trying to get me to trick with him," Brandi said, as she looked back over to the dead body laid out.

"Yeah he was trying to knock us off. Let's get him up out of here," Zay said, walking to the kitchen to get some gloves.

"Why don't we just call the police and say he was breaking in and you shot him."

"Last thing we need is the police in here investigating and questioning us. Don't you know the heat that will bring? We going to handle this ourselves," Zay insisted, as he came out the kitchen and threw Brandi a pair of latex gloves.

"I don't want to touch no dead…" Brandi started.

"Look, fuck all the bullshit…help me roll him up in this carpet and drag him to the truck."

"Zay…plea…"

"Put the gloves on and after we do this, you carry on with your day as if nothing happened. Ok?" Zay said forcefully, as she pulled on the gloves.

"Ok," Brandi said, as she helped Zay roll the dead man up in the carpet.

After getting Bones body in his own truck, Zay climbed behind the wheel while Brandi followed in her car. Zay drove the truck out to an abandoned ball park. He grabbed the gas can from Brandi's car, doused the truck with gas and set it on fire. They were well on their way out of the area by the time the fire trucks were dispatched to the scene.

As they rode home, Zay made sure that Brandi was well versed on the plan and he made it clear to her that if anything came out, she would go down for murder also. Brandi nodded in agreement not to tell a soul and to act as if nothing happened. Later that night, it was hard for Brandi to sleep with the smell of bleach and blood wavering through the place.

Chapter 7

The next day while I was preparing for the dinner, my phone rang and it was Brandi.

"Hey girl, what's up?" I asked, as I pulled the chicken from the freezer for tonight.

"Girl, we got to put the date off to another time. Something has come up with Zay and they need me down at the club tonight to help Sashay with her party. I am so sorry girl," Brandi told her, after she decided to go down to the club and get loose to clear her mind.

"Ah man, it's cool. We can do dinner another time. You alright ain't you?" I asked, trying my best to hide my frustration.

I was now going to have to change up my whole plan. I was going to hit Zay up one way or the other and it was happening tonight.

"I'm fine…just hate I couldn't kick it with my girl," she said sadly, as I went to my bedroom closet, pulled out my old purse and fished out the spare key I had to Brandi's place from when I stayed there.

"It's alright. We'll reschedule. Just call me if you need me girl, I'll be here," I replied.

"Ok, thanks. I'll be in touch girl," she said as we ended the call.

I knew time was running out and I was determined to get the money for Sherm's lawyer by any means necessary. I grabbed my chrome plated .380, loaded it and stuck it in my purse, next to Markel's chain that I tucked away out the movers' sight, when they moved me into my house.

I waited for nightfall before I made my move. Later in the night, I hopped in my car and made my way out to Brandi's spot. I prayed Brandi wasn't there because if she was she would have to be dealt with too…no witnesses. I felt out of place on my mission. One thing Sherm always stressed to me was to plan and never pull a lick without preparation. Right now, I hadn't planned and wasn't prepared at all but I would have to make an exception because time was running out.

I pulled up into the loft parking lot thirty minutes later. To my surprise when I was parking, I spotted Zay sitting out front smoking a blunt, talking on his cell phone. I started to retreat but it was too late—he had seen me. I killed the engine and grabbed my purse.

"Hey stranger," I spoke as I walked over to him, as he ended his phone call.

"What up sexy? What brings you out this time of the night?" Zay asked, as he took a hard pull on the blunt and held in the smoke.

"I was in the area and decided to stop by and check on my girl. She sounded like something was bothering her earlier when she called and cancelled dinner," I explained, as I stood over him with my crotch in his face.

"She's straight, everything is cool. She took off not to long ago for work." Zay said, as he pulled the blunt again and then stubbed it out.

"Ok tell her…" I started before he cut me off.

"Come in for a sec," Zay blurted out, then started smiling, obviously high off the weed.

"It may be trouble in there and I ain't trying to get in no trouble," I told him in a seductive tone, glad that Brandi wasn't home.

I held my purse close so close that I felt the bulge of the .380. I faked hesitation as I followed him in.

"Ma, you in good hands. Just follow my lead," he said, as he lead me in and over to the sofa.

"Ok, I'm following your lead. Just make sure you lead me in the right direction," I replied, as I sat my purse on the sofa next to me.

"Damn Silk, you know a nigga been trying to get at you for a minute, what up with you?" he asked, as he stood in front of me with bloodshot eyes.

"Man Zay, you know Brandi…"

He cut in, "You ain't even go to go there. Let's just keep our business our business, feel me?" he asked, as he sat next to me on the sofa.

"I'm with that, long as you with it," I said, knowing this lick was going to be real easy.

"That's a bet…come here," he said, as he leaned over and kissed me on my neck.

A few minutes later, he was pulling me up off the sofa and leading me to the back room.

"You go on back, I got to lock the door," he told me, as he nudged me toward the room.

After locking the door, Zay saw my purse sitting on the sofa and went to grab it to bring it to the back for me. When he grabbed my strap, my purse tilted and the contents hit the floor. Zay frowned as he picked up his cousin Markel's custom made diamond necklace and looked at it closely.

"Bitch," he cursed softly, as he stuffed the necklace in his pocket.

Chapter 8

"Oh fuck this pussy! Oh shit yes!" I screamed, as Zay pounded me from behind like it was his last fuck.

I really hadn't planned on fucking this nigga but I needed to get him all laid back and off guard for my next move. Shit, all in all I really did need a good fucking to relieve this stress all built up in me.

"Oh damn! Umm yeah! Throw it to me bitch!" Zay screamed, out of breath as he handled me roughly.

"Ouch! Shit stop!" I screamed, as he pulled me back way too hard by my hair.

"Slap!"

I was caught totally off guard when Zay's hand connected with the side of my face.

"Bitch take this dick!" he snapped, as he held me down and started fucking me real hard.

"Nigga what the hell is wrong with you! Let me up!" I screamed, as our good fucking turned into rape.

"Nah bitch, lay down!" Zay screamed, as he speeded up the pace and all of a sudden started shaking and releasing himself inside of me.

"Nigga get the fuck off of me! Let me up Zay," I screamed, as I started swinging back at him wildly feeling helpless.

A lucky swing connected with his right eye. I took advantage of his loosened grip and wiggled free. I ran into the front room to get my .380 out of my purse. I had nothing on my mind but to kill this nigga for violating me. I still didn't know what the fuck had gotten into this nigga, up until I grabbed my purse and my gun was gone. I turned and looked back...Zay was standing in the middle of the floor with my own gun pointed at me, while holding Markel's necklace in his other hand. I knew then that I was most likely a dead bitch.

Chapter 9

" ooking for this?" Zay asked, as he waved the gun in my face.

"Wha…Man Zay, it ain't what you think," I stammered, as I started to explain.

"Bitch, you had my cousin set up—ain't no other way in hell you going to end up with his piece!" Zay screamed, not knowing the complete truth.

"No I didn't Zay but I…"

I stopped mid sentence when I heard a noise outside of the door. Listening closely, I heard some keys. Seconds later the front door was opening and there stood Brandi looking at me and Zay naked in her spot.

"What the fuck going on in here Zay! Silk!" Brandi screamed, as she stood in the middle of the floor looking from me to Zay.

"This bitch had my cousin set up and now I'm going to show this bitch what happens when you fuck with mines!" Zay spat, as he started towards me, clearly high off the weed.

I put on my best act, hoping that Brandi would see shit my way.

"I came over here to check on you and your nigga raped me! I swear, I ain't set nobody up! I ain't did shit to nobody, he raped me!" I screamed and made myself cry.

"Zay, hold up! Is this true? Why are you naked then?" Brandi asked, completely confused.

"This lil' lying bitch had this!" Zay screamed, as he held the diamond necklace up for Brandi to see.

Brandi eyes got big as golf ball as she stared at the necklace that I told her was a gift for Justice.

"Silk that's the necklace that you said…"

Before Brandi could get the words out of her mouth, I took off barreling over her, butt-naked, trying to get out of the door. Just as I got passed her, I heard the gun blast. I didn't bother to look back, I just prayed that I would get away. I cleared the doorway and ran out into the parking lot screaming, hoping Zay wasn't behind me.

As I ran my heart out through the parking lot, I knew things was about to get real serious in the streets. I knew I would have to move out my spot and hide out until I could relocate because Zay was going to put all the NWM niggas on my ass. I couldn't believe I got so sloppy handling my business. Sherm always told me to have a plan and now I see what not having a plan meant. I had to find me some clothes and get out to my place. As I walked through the adjacent complex, I saw a car pulling in. I ran over and put on my best act.

"Hey, could you please help me. My boyfriend just beat me up and put me out naked," I cried to the young thug that was behind the wheel of the customized Hummer.

"That's fucked up Miss Lady. Climb in, I got you," he replied without hesitation, as he opened the door and let me in.

"Thank you," I said, as I slid in.

"No problem. Where you need to go," he asked, as he gave me a jacket to cover up with.

"Out to Pine Crest, please," I said, as I thought about what was about to come.

I had to get away and the more the young thug talked, the more I factored him in my get away but what I didn't know was that the man behind the wheel was the infamous Trudy, one of the most feared members of the NWM clique.

Chapter 10

"Zay what the in hell going on? It's just too much happening!" Brandi yelled, as tears rolled down her face.

"Your friend had something to do with my cousin's murder. The bitch came over here throwing pussy at a nigga, that's what she did," Zay said, unconvincingly as he pulled on his Polo jeans.

"That's a fuckin' lie Zay and you know it! Tell me the fuckin truth! Just fuck it! I don't care...I see what you all about. I know y'all was fuckin' all up in my shit! I want you to get your shit and get out!" Brandi screamed, as she started pulling Zay's clothes from the dresser and throwing them out into the floor.

"Hold up. So you telling me you don't believe me? Oh ok, fuck it then but just remember we in this shit together. Feel me?" Zay said, as he looked at Brandi with hatred, making sure she remembered her involvement in the murder last night.

"Fuck all this shit! I don't care if they lock me up—I refuse to let you hold that shit over my head. I ain't shot nobody! Fuck you Zay!" Brandi cried, as she continued throwing Zay clothes out into the floor.

Zay had seen many of his friends and associates take a fall because of a bitch. Zay refused to be sitting around in a prison cell for the rest of his life because of a scorned bitch.

So what are you saying Brandi? So you flipping on a nigga now?" Zay asked calmly , as he reached around and pulled the .380 from his back pocket.

"Zay go to hell!" Brandi screamed, as she stood with her back to him pulling his stuff out of the closet.

"Check that!" Zay spat, as he lifted the .380 and pulled the trigger.

Brandi squealed out in pain as the impact of the bullet pushed her into the closet. Walking over to Brandi, he saw she was barely breathing. Zay aimed and shot her in the back of the head.

Zay looked down at the lifeless Brandi, kicked her legs inside and then closed the closet door. He felt guilty about killing his lady but he also knew that he would have been a walking statistic if he didn't.

Chapter 11

"Nice crib Silk, you did say Silk right?" Trudy asked, as he pulled up into my driveway.

"Yeah it's Silk, Trudy. See how I remembered your name," I said with a hint of sarcasm, as he pulled the truck to a halt.

"You going to be ok?" he asked, displaying a mouth full of platinum teeth.

"Yeah, thanks so much for helping me," I said while thinking of a way to use this nigga to help me get away and hideout.

"Stay away from them crazy niggas now," Trudy said, smiling.

"Yeah, most definitely got to do that. Come on in so you can get your coat. Can't let the neighbors see me naked out here," I told him as I opened the trucks door.

Without hesitation, he killed the engine and followed me in. As we walked up to the door, I peeped him watching me closely. I raised the coat a little to give him a shot of my ass as I walked ahead of him. I wasn't feeling fucking two niggas in the same night but then I really needed this nigga's help and not to mention, my shit is sore from Zay roughing me the fuck up.

"Trudy? I've heard your name before but I just can't remember where. What side of town are you from?" I asked.

"Decatur, off Glenwood."

"Damn I done heard your name before," I said, as we made a detour to the side door when I remembered I didn't have my key.

"You sure you stay here?" he asked playfully, as I lead him around to the back door that I rarely locked.

"I think I do," I replied and smiled, as I turned the knob on the back door and pushed it open.

"Just chill in here for a minute while I get freshened up, unless you're in a rush," I said, as I flicked on the wide screen in the den and handed him the remote and his coat.

"Naw, I'm cool. Handle your business boo," he replied, as he flipped the channel and acted as if he wasn't taken in by my nakedness.

"You want something to sip on?" I asked, as I made my way to the stairs so I could go up and put some clothes on.

"Im straight appreciate it," he replied, still not acknowledging me being naked as I exited the room.

I knew I was going to have to pull out all the stops to get this nigga on my team. I also knew by tomorrow niggas was going to be gunning for me from every side of town. I had to move and move fast. As I stepped in the shower, I made a mental note to find out who this nigga Trudy was because I know I heard that name on more than one occasion. As I dried off I thought of a good place to relocate and I most definitely needed Trudy's help. The ringing of my house phone brought me out of my deep thought.

"Hello?"

"You have a collect call from an inmate at a Georgia state prison…" the automated operator said on the other end.

My palms got sweaty and my heart rate increased as I pressed 5 to accept the call.

"Baby girl, how you doing? What the move is?" Sherm asked.

"Shit's crazy out here baby. I went on a lick the other night and didn't come close to what we needed. The nigga wasn't getting it like he made out to be. Then I got problems in the street that got me having…"

"So you ain't got the money for the lawyer is what you are telling me!" Sherm snapped, cutting me off.

"I'm trying to get it. Shit ain't like it used to be out here now…" I started but got cut off again.

"Why you in the house now when you could be out making shit happen! You always coming with fucking excuses!" he screamed into the receiver.

"What the fuck was I suppose to do! I just get what these muthafuckers got! I'm doing the best I fuckin' can!" I screamed, as my bedroom door flew open.

"Whats up! You cool up in here!" Trudy screamed, as he held his desert eagle out by his side looking geeked up and ready for action.

"Yeah, I'm straight," I whispered, knowing what was coming next.

"Who dat?" Sherm asked, as Trudy turned and walked out.

"A friend that brought me to the house af…" I started, then got cut off again for the third time.

"Bitch see, that's why you ain't got the fuckin' money! You fuckin' entertaining niggas and shit! Bitch, fuck your fuck ass and I promise that you will be sorry for playing fuckin' games with my freedom," he screamed.

"Sherm it ain't even like that if you let me ex…"

"Fuck you hoe!"

"Click!"

I knew that was coming next when he heard a nigga in the background but I got more important shit to worry about like staying alive. The more and more I thought about the situation, I came to the conclusion of…fuck Sherm! I'm out here risking my life to get his ass out and he handling me all fucked. From now on it's all about me. Sherm is now officially on his own since it's like that. I got myself together and headed back downstairs where Trudy was laid back on the couch, watching Gangland.

"You up there screaming and shit like a nigga on yo ass. You good?" Trudy asked, as he sat up on the couch.

"I got to get away from here, ASAP. I know in the morning that nigga going to be banging my door down."

"What you got going on lady?" he asked, as I took a seat next to him on the couch.

I let my robe fall open just enough to see my oiled up thighs and a lil' cleavage. I could tell he was enjoying the fresh scent of my body wash.

"This nigga is heavy affiliated and crazy as hell. I know when he wake up, he coming out here and going to call himself putting me out. This is both of our house, so before I go through all the bullshit, I'm just going to pack some of my shit and be out. He can have this shit," I said, hoping to get the response I was looking for.

"Where are you going to go? You need some help?" he asked, as I purposely let my robe fall open exposing my clean, freshly shaved pussy.

"Just being honest, I really don't know right now but whatever I decide, I got to decide tonight. I know I got to get up out of here though," I told him, as he cut his eyes at the opening in my robe.

"I can put you up at my condo out in Union City, if you need a place to duck off for a minute. I use it occasionally for business. Its way out in the middle of the country," he said, falling right into my hands.

"I would hate to be a burden on you," I said, as I looked into his eyes seductively.

"It ain't no thang; its all good," he replied, gazing back into my eyes.

A few minutes later I was unbuckling his pants, getting ready to fuck this nigga like my life depended on it—which it really did.

Chapter 12

" *H*ello," Nut answered groggily and angrily, as his the ringing of his cell phone woke him up.

"Say Nut boy, I need you to meet me at the IHOP downtown in thirty minutes," Zay stressed, as he pushed Brandi's ride through the downtown streets of Atlanta.

"Man what time is it? What the hell going on?" he asked, in an urgent tone.

"I found out who was behind Mark's murder and we need to make her regret she ever was born, feel me?" he snapped, as he exited the expressway.

"She! So you telling me a bitch killed bro?" Nut asked, as he sat up in his bed, now fully woke and alert.

"If she ain't do it herself, she had a hand in it," Zay replied.

"How you know?" Nut asked, as he slid out of bed to go to the bathroom.

"I'll explain it all when you get down here," Zay replied as he pulled into the IHOP parking lot.

"Man I'm on my way," Nut said and ended the call.

Nut was the go to man of NWM. He was the go to man when someone needed to disappear. He was known around the crew for the jobs he had pulled off undetected. Zay planned to put every killer in the clique on the job...Silk is a dead woman.

Soon as Zay finished off his plate of pancakes, Nut was pulling up outside in his Dodge Ram that was a gift from all the money go-getters of the crew. The keys to the truck were given to him at the annual cookout by the man that he looked up to in the crew, Trudy.

"Man fill me in," Nut demanded, as he took a seat in front of Zay who was looking tired and disheveled.

"Look man, this is what's going on…" Zay started and explained the situation to Nut.

"What kind of info you got on this bitch?" Nut asked, as he pulled out his mental notepad.

"I know where the broad lay her head. She just bought a new house out on the southside," Zay said, as he picked up his glass of orange juice and took a sip.

"You ain't got to say no more. I got it from here on out. Bro, you look all tired and shit. You good?" Nut asked, as the waitress approached their table.

"I'm good, just been going non-stop these last couple days but I refuse to rest now for real, until that bitch is taken care of," Zay spat.

"Hi, would you be ordering sir," the petite, young black girl asked as Zay and Nut eyed her.

"Naw, I'm straight, but I do need to borrow your pen for a sec," Nut said, as he reached over for a napkin.

Nut wrote down all the info Zay had to give and then folded the napkin up and stuffed it into his back pocket.

"Thanks lil' lady," Nut told the young girl, as he handed her the pen back.

A few minutes later Zay and Nut were exiting the restaurant with one thing on their mind...Silk.

On the way back to his spot, Nut made a couple of calls to a few NWM members that may be familiar with the woman named Silk. He had plans to hit the strip clubs around the city since Zay had informed him that not long ago, she used to be a dancer. Nut knew if he could find this bitch and make her pay, he would be rewarded by two of the most respected niggas of the clique...Zay and his idol, Trudy, being that they were real close to Markel.

As he dialed number after number, not getting an answer, he tossed his cell into the passenger seat and thought about the best place to start looking for his prize catch.

Zay was in a daze as he drove, headed nowhere in particular. So much had gone on these last few days and he really didn't know what to do. He cursed as he thought about the main thing that kicked all this shit off and then slapped the steering wheel as he exceeded the speed limit riding down 285 South in the night's darkness.

Brandi was dead, Bones was dead and Hester was dead and on top of that the police were hot on his tail. Right now Zay was losing it mentally; his sanity was hanging on by a thread. After riding around for thirty minutes, Zay decided on a hotel room out of town for a couple days and then he would come back and set up shop again.

Chapter 13

I was jarred out of my sleep by the ringing of Trudy's cell phone. I looked over and he was knocked out cold, lightly snoring. Last night we had started our hardcore sex session downstairs on the sofa but before it was over with, he had me upstairs in the buck in my bed. I saw that whoever called had left a message and a text. I slid out of bed and jumped in the shower while Trudy still slept.

I knew my time was limited in the city and I knew Zay would find out where I lived from Brandi, sooner than later. After taking a quick shower, I packed up my important stuff and sat it by the door, as Trudy started to stir.

"Damn lady, what time is it?" he asked, as he sat up n the bed.

"It's 7:30 boo, you sleep good?" I asked, as I walked over, leaned in and kissed him softly on the lips.

I knew after last night, he was all mine for the taking. I planned on relocating to another city but for now I was going to take Trudy up on his offer of staying in his condo.

"Real good, thanks to you," he replied, as he reached over and rubbed my ass as I stood next the bed.

I can truly say the nigga was attractive as hell and had an air of arrogance to him that made him just my kind of man. Thoughts of Sherm invaded my mind, as I looked at Trudy in a way that was against the rules of the game. I really wanted to reach out to Sherm but I knew after tonight it was going to be nothing but cussing and screaming. I felt kind of bad that I couldn't get the money he needed to get out right away but I can say that I really tried. I had no other choice now but to fall back and get off the scene. I had made plans to write him, as soon as I got settled in my new location.

"Glad I could help. I've packed all my important stuff up and sat it by the door. We really need to be getting up out of here before this crazy ass nigga shows up," I told him, as I walked over to the blinds and peeked out.

"Fuck that nigga, he gone get in some shit he really don't want," Trudy said, as he got up and headed to the shower. "Can I get a towel?"

"I left it on the sink. I hear what you're sayin' but I just want to get as far away as possible. I'll come back and get the rest of my stuff next month, after I get situated," I said, as he closed the bathroom door.

While he was showering, I looked around to make sure I had what I needed most. I hated leaving my things but right now, getting out of here and getting somewhere safe was more important. I was startled by the ringing of Trudy's phone again. I thought about taking it to him but whoever it was, can wait.

A few minutes later, Trudy walked back in the room. "You can stay out my spo…"

"Ring!!!!!!"

The ringing of his cell phone cut him off.

"Yeah speak," he answered.

He frowned at whoever was talking on the other end of the line.

"Who is the bitch and what's her name? Your phone breaking up bro. Get somewhere with a better signal and hit me back."

"Everything cool?"

"My man trying to give me some information but I couldn't hear him."

I was anxious to get out of here but I must admit, watching him lotion down made me want to undress and go another round. I'd really broken all the rules.

Just as he pulled his jeans up, his phone rang again.

"Go 'head bro," he ordered.

"Aight, I can hear you now, so what's going on now?" he asked the person on the other end, as I stared at him.

He had a puzzled look. Where is Zay at?" he asked, as he placed his pistol in the small of his back.

My heart sank at the mention of Zay's name and now here I am again, in a tight spot. I knew it had to be about me and before long Trudy would be told what happened and he would put two and two together. Trudy! Now I knew where I heard the name at…Sherm's eastside gun connect. Trudy Waters was one of the founders of NWM and an associate of Sherm. Was the sex good enough last night for him to keep me safe from his own people, or was I going to have to kill this nigga and go for what I know.

"Baby let's get out of here," I said in an urgent tone, trying to interrupt his call.

He held his hand up as I turned to leave the room to get my pistol that I kept in the kitchen. As I turned walked down the hallway, I heard him call my name. I knew then it was about to go down.

I picked up the pace as I heard Trudy scream something, then he started calling me again. I fished the small .22 from the bottom cabinet and just as I stood back up Trudy was standing in the doorway.

With tears in my eyes, I turned and pointed my pistol at him.

G STREET CHRONICLES

PRESENTS

Part Three of The Explosive
Short Story Series

gangsta GIRL 3

"The PayBack"

George Sherman Hudson

Author of *City Lights* and *Executive Mistress*

Chapter 1

"Trudy, please just listen to me," I cried as we stood there eye-to-eye pointing our guns at each other.

Shit had gotten out of hand and the only way that I was going to stay alive was to convince this nigga to let me live.

"So you the bitch my people looking for...the one and only Silk," he spat with disgust and hatred in his voice.

"Trudy shit ain't what it look like. I promise you that it didn't go down like Zay think it did, I swear," I said in the saddest voice I could muster.

"Tell me what happened and if I detect any kind of bullshit in your story, I'm going to body you right here," he said shakily.

"Trudy I swear that it wasn't like Zay said. I was fucking with Markel—he was my nigga, that's how I got his necklace. Zay thinks I had something to do with his murder which is crazy when he always gave me whatever the hell I wanted. Just being totally honest with you, I even knew about his other bitches on the side but I didn't care because I was well taken care of. The day before he was killed, he gave me his necklace so I could get the stones reset and cleaned. That's how I got his necklace. Zay just went crazy when he saw the necklace. He didn't even give me a chance to say nothing; he just pulled his gun and came at me. I swear Trudy, I ain't have nothing to do with none of this shit," I lied as my eyes watered trying to detect the slightest sign of sympathy in this nigga.

"So you was fucking Mark huh?" he asked, lowering his gun.

When I saw him lower his gun I knew I had him, so I poured it on real thick.

Following his lead, I lower my gun too. "Trudy, he didn't even give me time to say nothing. I tried but he wasn't hearing nothing, he just pulled his gun and started shooting at me. I was so scared I didn't know what to do. That's what was going on the night I met you when I was out in the street naked. Zay was the one chasing me, not a crazy boyfriend. I don't have a boyfriend," I added in my sad and needy voice.

"Damn. Man shit! Silk you know you got me in a tight spot right now. I'm just gonna call Zay and let him know what's up and straighten this shit out," Trudy said, as he walked over, pulling his cell phone from his front pocket.

"No, wait Trudy! Please baby, don't call him because I know he ain't going to believe me. Just help me lay low for a couple of days and we'll set up a day to meet with him," I pleaded.

"What if they catch up with you before then?" he asked as he put the phone back in his pocket.

"That's why I need you to hide me until we get everything together. They will never look for me at your condo that you told me about."

There was a long pause as he stared at me. A minute later, after thinking, he answered, "Ok, but just for a couple of days." He walked over to me.

"Thanks," I said as I wrapped my arms around him and kissed him softly.

"I got you," he moaned, looking into my eyes.

I smile to myself thinking how stupid and naive niggas get after a piece of pussy. I made a mental note to kill this tender fuck ass nigga when all this shit is over with.

Chapter 2

"Look Silk don't leave here without calling me first so that I can make sure you're safe. Drive my Charger if you need to go anywhere," Trudy told me as I sat in his expensively furnished condo that was located on the outskirts of Atlanta.

"Ok, I really do appreciate you helping me out," I said as I looked over at the gun that rested on the kitchen table.

"Nobody will ever know you're here. They would never suspect that you would be at one of my spots. After everything calms down, we'll set up a meeting with Zay and kill this shit," he explained as I thought otherwise.

"Alright, I just need to get my head together. Things are just moving to fast right now. As soon as I collect myself, I'll be ready to talk to Zay," I told him sadly, while plotting my next move.

I had been plotting and planning the whole day. I now had transportation which was needed to pull off my plan. As soon as I got settled in, I'm going to find that nigga Zay and off his ass with all the rest of them NWM niggas. After getting rid of each and every one of them, I'm going to finish this nigga Trudy off and take everything he has stashed. I looked over at the .380 on the table and knew to take down the whole clique, I would need more fire power.

"You just hit me if you need anything or have any problems. Look…like I said, don't leave this condo without calling me first. I got to make some runs so just hit me later," he told me as he turned and exited the condo.

I got up and unpacked the rest of my things, dug my cell phone out of my bag and made a few calls. Before I hung up the phone I had a glock .40, a Tec 9 and a .45 automatic lined up, all equipped with silencers. My underground connect Malcolm was going to meet me tonight at 9:00 down at the Dugans on Old National Hwy.

As I hung up the phone with Malcolm, I heard a noise out front. Springing up I ran over to the table and grabbed the .380. Looking out of the blinds I saw a newspaper on the doorstep that wasn't there earlier. The newspaper man was now rounding the corner, throwing papers from the window of his old beat up Blazer. I took a couple of deep breaths and retreated back over to the sofa. I was beyond paranoid.

Chapter 3

"Man ain't no sign of this bitch nowhere," P-Nut told Zay as he pulled up outside of the third strip club of the night.

P-Nut had hit all of the strip clubs to see if anyone had seen or heard from Silk but no one could help so far.

"Man just keep looking, the bitch can't be too far without no car. Hit a couple more spots and then call it a night. I'm going to hit Trudy back in a minute to see if he has heard anything. I'm pretty sure his club connect done heard something," Zay said as his Blackberry power bar turned red, signaling that the battery needed charging.

"That's what's up. I'll hit Blue Flame last since it's on the way to the house," P-Nut replied as he got out of the car and ended the call.

P-Nut admired all the customized expensive cars as he walled through the parking lot. Entering the club, he handed the thick chocolate sister at the door a twenty dollar bill and breezed through disregarding the change.

The Gentleman's Club was one of the hottest clubs in the city that catered to professional atheletes, CEOs, rappers, and rich street hustlers. P-Nut was nowhere near as wealthy as the men in attendance tonight but you would never know because he was adorned in jewelry and sported nice pieces just the same as the rich niggas that flaunted their wealth every chance they got.

"Hey, what you drinking?" A slim, high yellow sister with a fat ass asked as he found him a spot close to the stage.

"Remy and sprite with light ice please ma'am," P-Nut replied as he scanned the club trying to see if anyone resembled the picture in his phone.

It wasn't two minutes later that a brown skin bow-legged sister with wide hips pulled up to the table.

"Hey there sexy, can I get some time?" the girl asked as she put her goods on display for P-Nut.

"Time is money, so what you doing now is asking me for money right?" P-Nut said as he looked the dime piece from head to toe.

"Just look at it like this...it will be money well spent. I will make sure that it's worth your while," the girl said assuringly as the waitress sat P-Nut's drink on the table and collected her money.

"How about we just talk for a minute because really I'm out here trying to find my lil' sister," P-Nut lied as he pulled a chair up for the girl to sit down.

"Like you said, time is money and you know I get $10 a song," the girl stressed as she smiled and took a seat next to him.

"That's all good, I'm P-Nut. What's your name?" P-Nut asked as he took in the sweet scent of the girls body spray.

"I'm Stallion," she replied as she wiggled around in the small chair trying to get comfortable.

"Here you go," P-Nut said as he handed Stallion a $50 bill.

She tucked the money in her top and leaned in, placing her elbows on the table.

"Thanks, now what you want to talk about?" she asked, batting her eyes.

"My sister. I just got out from doing a five-year bid and while doing time my mother passed and my sister was left to fend for herself. I hear that she used to dance here," P-Nut lied as he picked up his drink and took a sip.

"What's her name?"

"Silk."

"You talking about Silk from the southside that hang out with Brandi?" Stallion asked.

P-Nut wasn't familiar with her friends or where she was from.

"I really don't know but hold up," he said as he dug into his pocket, pulled his cell phone out and pulled the picture of Silk up that Zay had forwarded to him earlier.

"Yeah, that's Silk. She don't work in the clubs no more. Sherm retired her a while back but right afterward, he got locked up on some big time shit and was given hella time. Ain't nobody seen or heard from her since.

P-Nut's heart skipped a beat at the mention of Sherm's name. He was very familiar with Sherm and the treacherous robbing crew he ran with. They had held Beeno, one of NWM's own and his baby Momma at gunpoint. They took him for everything he had in his stash spot which was well over $500,000. P-Nut was paid to take Sherm out but before he could get to him, the police had him in the county on murder and armed robbery charges. Last he heard was that Sherm was down south doing time.

"So she just disappeared? Do you know where her friend Brandi lives?" P-Nut inquired, knowing Silk would most likely still be in touch with her friend.

"No, but she works down at Shak'em."

"Thanks," P-Nut said as he picked up his glass and downed the rest of the drink.

P-Nut's next stop was Shak'em to find Brandi.

Chapter 4

Everybody arrived at the northside stash house for a meeting at noon the next day. Zay had contacted all the members of NWM and told them it was mandatory that they attend. The meeting's agenda was Silk and her involvement with one of their most respected member's murder. The room in the modestly furnished split level home reeked of weed. The members didn't smoke in the house that dubbed as a duck off but it was obvious that a lot of them indulged on the way to the meeting.

Zay stood in the front of the room, pulled out a pad and started calling out names and making checks by the names of the men he saw in attendance.

"Ray Ray, Bo Ski, Man MAN, Taterhead, Buck, Rio, P-Nut, Tre, Trudy, Dee, Turk, JAY, Beeno, and Money."

Looking back over the names, he saw that all the members of NWM were in the room.

Signaling to P-Nut, Zay called him up to the front and told him to fill everyone in on his findings of the night before.

"Aight y'all this is what's up. I hit all the strip clubs that the bitch use to dance at but no one has seen or heard from her. Her homegirl Brandi hasn't been seen either, so right now we got no leads. I do know her nigga is Sherm, one of the people on our list to get rid of for the robbing our brother Beeno. The nigga is doing time now down south, so right now we ain't got shit on this bitch but the picture in our phones. We need to use all of our resources and find this bitch," P-Nut said as he paced back and forth.

Zay cringed at the mention of Brandi knowing that she was still lifeless in her bedroom closet. None of the members knew about him and her and he felt no need to fill them in. Across the room Beeno frowned when Sherm's name was mentioned. He wanted Sherm more than anything in this world for the way he had made him bitch out in front of his baby moma. Sherm had really made him look like a real live bitch and then kicked him in the ass on the way out the door, after robbing him blind. To the left of Beeno sat Trudy who looked at the picture of Silk that was sent to his phone. He knew he was in total violation and he also knew he was putting his life on the line for Silk. His palms sweated every time they mentioned her whereabouts but all-in-all, he knew they would never suspect him or find her out at his condo. He looked around the room at all the men he had sworn his loyalty to and now he sat here betraying them for a woman that he really didn't know.

After P-Nut finished speaking, Zay took the floor.

"Everybody be on the lookout for this broad, she is to be bodied on site no questions asked. She has violated everyone sitting in this room, so it's a must that we set an example. If any of you track her down, hit me up and I'll alert the rest of the crew. We got to turn the city upside down until we find this bitch. That's all for now, I'll be in touch," Zay said with emphasis as he ended the meeting.

"What up fam?" Trudy said as he turned nervously and faced Zay.

"Bro, push your connects hard, if anybody can find this broad I know you can with all your underground connects. If it's going to cost, just let me know the tag so everybody can come together for the cause. Feel me?" Zay said to a nervous Trudy.

"That's what's up. I'll connect with everybody that may be able to help," Trudy replied, thinking that right now Silk was probably still sleep in his condo.

Chapter 5

Trudy arrived back out at the condo around 2:00 p.m. When he walked in, he was surprised to see me sitting at the kitchen table half naked, counting money with a loaded glock on the table beside me.

"Am I interrupting something?" Trudy asked as he looked at all the stacks of money on the table.

"Oh hey baby! Nah you ain't interrupting. I'm just trying to see what I'm working with here," I said as he got an eye full of my bare breast and red thong.

"Oh, ok but I got a few things I want to run by you. As you know you are being hunted by the whole NWM crew and they are dead serious about taking you out. Zay stressed that if you are seen to kill you on site, no questions asked. Every one of the members got your picture in their cell phone so right now you got 13 niggas, excluding me, out looking to kill you," he said with an urgent tone.

I had planned for this shit because I knew shit was going to get crazy. One thing that I got to get Trudy to tell me is all the members names and locations which I know wasn't happening. My plan is to take all of them out, one by one, all the way up to this weak, pussy-whipped ass nigga standing before me. With his help I can take down the whole NWM crew and get paid in the process. A lil' pillow talk and some good fucking is going to get me all the info I need, guaranteed.

Ten minutes later we was fucking out of control, I needed to at least get one or two of these niggas tonight.

"Damn baby, shit," I moaned as I laid my head on his chest.

"For real boo," Trudy whispered as he ran his fingers through my hair.

"I'll be glad when all of this is over with. Baby, who are these niggas gunning for me?" I slid the question in hoping he would open up about NWM.

"Baby, you ain't got to worry, like we planned…we will meet with Zay when all of this calms down," he replied not giving me what I wanted.

"I feel that boo but it would be nice to know who to look out for just in case," I said, trying again to get him to open up.

"Won't nobody find you, you all good. Just be easy and I promise, everything is going to work out," he replied still not giving me any info.

I tried another approach.

"Who I got to meet with? Is Zay y'all leader?" I asked, playing on his ego.

"He'll naw. Zay is a respected nigga like me, Beeno and Buck. We all founded NWM, not saying everyone else is not respected, it's just that we are the OG's of NWM.

Bingo, I have names…Beeno and Buck and of course Zay. My mission tonight is to find these niggas and start eliminating them. I have names now so all I have to do now is track them down which is going to be easy since I swiped Trudy's cell phone from his car console. I'm going to send each nigga a text, set up a meeting and when they arrive, knock em off. Shit is going to be simple and to the point.

"Oh, ok so I got to meet with all of y'all?" I asked, really not caring about the meeting because by the time it's time to meet, it won't be no members left.

"Yeah, you going to be straight though. I got to make some runs today and go out to my place and take care of some unfinished business. You going to be ok out here? I gave you the keys to the car, so use it if you have to but make sure you stay out of sight," he stressed in his most irritating pussy whipped voice.

When I first met Trudy I kind of felt him because I just knew that he was an official nigga, a real stand-up dude. Over these couple of days I've seen a different side—a side that a real bitch like myself ain't feeling, so when it's his time to go, I won't have any regrets. I'll be doing all of my stand up bitches a favor by ridding them of this artificial ass stand up guy. I smiled to myself as Trudy got up and got dressed then exited the condo. As he pulled out of the driveway I pulled out his cell phone and scrolled down his contact list. I found the names I was looking for and more than likely a lot of the other names probably were members too. I laid back in the bed and went through his pictures too. This nigga must have a thang for red bitches because his phone was full of different ones. Not far down the list was my picture. I pulled up the picture info and to my surprise there was a forward list with each number that my picture had been sent. I quickly jumped up and jotted down the numbers. I couldn't wait to meet every nigga on this list up close and personal.

Chapter 6

"Man I owe you my life Bro, I really appreciate your help," Sherm told Diego as they pulled out of Macon State Prison parking lot in a black on black Phantom.

After Silk failed to come up with the money to get Sherm out, he reached back to the streets and caught up with his young protege from the hood who was now a seven figure nigga up North. Sherm was like a big brother to Diego when he ran the streets of Atlanta, trying to get rich. Sherm gave Diego the game on every level but as Diego got older he put his own twist on the game which had some strong niggas in the streets looking for him. While all of this was going on, Sherm had caught his case and was sitting on Rice Street, waiting to go to trial. Diego came down and filled Sherm in about the lick he had pulled on some dreads and how they had been beatin' the streets down looking for him. Sherm was quite familiar with the dreads and their treacherous ways, so he advised Diego to leave the city and lay low, which he did that same night. He packed and headed up North to Jersey where he had family ties. After arriving in Jersey and scoping the scene, Diego took his show on the road. In less than a year he was making millions off of heroin, guns and cocaine. Diego became the man up North in no time.

"Boy, I see you doing it big now. I'm glad mama Sandra still had her same number," Sherm said as he smiled at his young patna that was now a made man in the game.

"Bro, you know I was tryna to get at you but every time I found your ass, you was in the hole on pending transfer. Nigga you stay trying to take over them folks chain gang." Diego laughed as he pushed the Phantom beyond the speed limit down 285 in route to his Atlanta home.

"Man that shit was crazy but it's all over with, so now it's back to the basics," Sherm calls out as he reached down and turned up Jay Z that was already blasting from the Phantom's customized stereo system.

"Bro, you can stay in my Atlanta spot as long as you need. I got you thirty thousand sat to the side for clothes and shit. I want you to retire that pistol bro and rock with me on this shit I got popping. Shit so sweet bro, the only thing I do is collect and count money…feel me?" Diego said excitedly, hoping Sherm would take him up on his offer.

"You know my pistol is my bread and butter bro, but if it's that sweet on your side, I'm game. How long you going to be in town before you head back up North?" Sherm asked as he reached down and turned the system back down.

"I got to head back out tonight, so if you want to come it's cool," Diego said as he exited off the highway at the McDonough exit.

"I got a lot of unfinished business in the city to take care of but as soon as it's taken care of, I'm on my way. Like I said before lil' bro, I appreciate ya and every penny you put out will be returned. My nigga, you just saved my life, real talk," Sherm said appreciatively as he thought about how Silk left him hanging.

"Bro it's all good. You the one that gave me the game and without the game I wouldn't be the nigga that I am today. It ain't no thang, I'm just glad to see my nigga home!" Diego bellowed and smiled, displaying a perfect set of ivory capped teeth with diamond chips sprinkled through them.

As Diego turned into the gated community, Sherm took in all of the expensive mansions that sat on acres of sprawling land. Sherm was speechless as they pulled up at two big iron gates with a security booth out front.

"Hi Mr.Black, you had a guest by the name of Carmen Jenkins come by. She seemed real disappointed that you weren't available," the old, black security guard informed Diego as we sat at the gate waiting for it to open.

"Thanks Harold, oh and this is my fam Sherm. He gets all access to everything. He's going to be staying here while I'm gone," Diego told Harold as Sherm looked at the dream house and all the amenities that flanked it.

"What up Harold," Sherm said, bringing his attention back to the conversation.

"Hi sir, you ever need me just hit any of the intercom buttons that's marked with a red X. You will also see monitors throughout the premises, so if you spot anything fishy going on inside, just hit the button and holla," Harold explained and smiled showing off his one gold front tooth.

Sherm held his laugh, thinking how in the hell was this old man going to save somebody.

"Alright then Harold," Diego saluted then pulled on through the open gates, then seconds later bringing the car to a stand still in front of the beautiful home.

"Ok bro, my home is your home," Diego said as they exited the Phantom and headed in.

On his way in the house Sherm thought about his unfinished business...Silk.

Chapter 7

ater that night, I was putting on my black tights and black hoodie when Trudy's phone started ringing. I pressed the ignore button and sent the caller to the voicemail. Shortly afterwards a text came through that read...*Bro meet me at the Waffle House on Old National. We need to look into a new connect.* The signature at the end of the text read *Buck The World*, which had to be the nigga Buck.

I searched the list of numbers that was connected to my picture and saw the same number on there. I didn't plan nor prepare for tonight which was totally against the rules but I had to act fast, if I planned to see 'bout these niggas. I really didn't want to have to kill in a public place but it look like I wasn't going to have a choice.

I'm meeting Malcolm at 9:00 tonight to pick up my heat. The glock .40, Tec 9, and 9mm all equipped with silencers would be more than enough to take care of the job.

Malcolm pulled up on the side of Dugan's in his old beat up Chevy pick up truck which was a good front for a nigga that had to be worth six figures. Malcolm supplied all of down south with heat that didn't come cheap. As he pulled up beside me, I exited my car and picked up the envelope that was resting on the seat, containing the $2,500 for the guns that were brand spanking new.

"Hey lady!" Malcolm happily greeted me as he stepped out of his truck and gave me a hug.

I had been dealing with Malcolm for some time now. I met him while dancing at Curves. After finding out that he was the gun man in the city, I played middleman to a lot of his deals, making good money on the side. We had a good business relationship and I respected him for that. He never let his little head interfere with his big head...the nigga was strictly about his paper.

"Pop your trunk and I'll load you up, by the way I'm digging this new ride," he told me as he grabbed the bag of guns out of the bed of his truck.

"Thanks Malcolm, you can just drop them off on the backseat," I requested as I handed him the envelope with the money.

"No problem, you just be careful. You know the silencer alone is a decade," he stressed as he opened the car door and placed the bag on the backseat.

"I'll be careful and thanks Malcolm, you never let a sista down," I said as I closed my back door.

"Always at your service. You just call me if you need me," he told me as he retreated back to his truck.

"Will do. Take it easy," I replied as I slid back behind the wheel of the Charger.

Before I pulled out, I checked the contents of the bag and chose the .9mm for the job tonight. I placed the silencer on the end of the barrel and loaded the .9mm with the hollow point bullets that Malcolm threw in with every purchase. After loading the gun, I started the car and looked at my watch…9:30, time to meet Buck to stop him from breathing. I smiled as I headed off to my mission. I think I'm beginning to enjoy this shit.

Chapter 8

Checking my watch I saw that it was close to 10:00 now. I pulled up into the Waffle House parking lot and looked around for this nigga Buck. It was only a few people inside but I would bet my last dime that the heavy dark skin brother that sported a big chain with diamonds all through it had to be Buck.

I knew I couldn't just go in and kill this nigga. I had to get him outside some kind of way. I waited to see if he recognized Trudy's Charger but then he did say that he had just bought this car. I sat and thought for a minute, then came up with a plan but first I had to find out which one of these cars in the lot was his.

Looking through the lot I picked out two cars that would most likely be his, a new black on black Denali with big chrome wheels and a pearl white Cadillac EXT. The other cars looked more like they would be the employees' cars. As I got situated I looked up and saw a heavyset, light skin female climb behind the wheel of the Denali, so the EXT had to be Bucks'.

The Denali pulled out of the lot leaving me a spot next to the EXT. I readied the .9mm with the silencer, then started the car. I pulled on the blind side of the EXT, out of the view of the customers who sat in the front windows. Checking the scene I saw that the coast was clear, not many people were out tonight. As I stepped out of the car into the cool night air, I extended the door purposely hitting the Cadillac making the alarm go off. When I looked over, I saw Buck trying to see what was going on. Seconds later he exited the Waffle House and headed my way.

"Damn girl you done fucked up a five thousand dollar paint job!" Buck spat as he looked at the damage the car door did to the side of his truck.

"Oh, I'm so sorry. I didn't mean to hit your truck sir," I said sympathetically as I reached in my hoodies two hand pocket and gripped the handle of the .9mm and positioned my finger on the trigger.

"Damn lady, sorry ain't goin' to fix my shit," he said, turning to me and pointing to the damage to his truck.

By the time he was turning I had the gun in full view. His eyes got big as golf balls as he looked in the face that he now clearly recognized from the picture in his cell phone. Before he could say anything, I put pressure on the trigger and let the .9mm spit, hitting him two times in the chest. The impact of the hollow points knocked him back onto his truck; he slid down to the ground holding his chest. I looked around and saw that everything was still quiet. I knew that I didn't need a miracle survival on my hands, so I walked over and put a single shot to his head. The smoke from the gun mixed with the cool night air, sending up a stream of grey gas. I smiled as I climbed back into the Charger and headed out on my next mission.

Chapter 9

I got this bitch bro. Meet me at the BP gas station on Old National, the text read making Beeno smile with a sense of satisfaction. Beeno and RayRay had just confirmed a 150 kilo drop that was now safe and secure at NWMs stash spot. They were headed out to the strip club to celebrate when the text came through from Trudy. Beeno didn't waste any time turning the wide body Benz around and heading southbound to Old National.

I sat admiring the piece of work I held. I've always had a crazy fascination with guns. The .9mm was nice but this glock .40 was the shit. The silencer and the gun itself was light as hell. I knew the nigga Beeno would be pulling up any minute now, so I grabbed the gun and exited the car. More than likely they would pull in over next to the phone booth, where I had the Charger parked with the engine running. I stepped out and went into the store, buying time until they arrived.

Ten minutes later a big boy, sky blue Mercedes Benz with big shiny chrome rims pulled into the lot and just like I thought, it pulled right next to the dimly lit phone booth. I stepped out of the store into the cool night air and gripped the glock that was tucked into the white plastic bag that the cashier put my bottle of juice in. I looked like a woman that was on her way home from getting a late night snack as I walked towards the Benz. I really couldn't see what was going on inside the car because of the dark tinted windows so I walked by one time and glanced back, looking through the windshield. Beeno had another nigga with him which made me change my plan. Now I was going to have to straight up blast both of these niggas because I wasn't leaving no witnesses. Besides, I don't know which nigga is Beeno anyway.

Faking like I had dropped something, looking around on the ground and checking my pockets, I turned and headed back to the store. Before I reached the car, one of the men got out and walked over to the side of the store and started pissin'.

As I reached the car, I looked through the windshield at a man talking on the phone, looking around, more than likely looking for Trudy. He glanced at me and paid me no mind as I walked by fiddling in my bag. By time I got to the back door of the Benz, I stopped and made sure that the nigga pissin' wasn't looking. I grabbed the door handle, snatched the door open and jumped in the back seat. The interior light of the car lit up the whole inside, making the man behind the wheel turn around.

Just as he turned and looked at me sitting in the back seat, I was pulling the glock from the bag. By time he had a full view, the glock was in his face. He dropped his cell phone and let out an unintelligible sound as I pulled the trigger.

The hollow point bullet entered smoothly and exploded on its exit out of the man's head, sending brain matter all over the windshield of the sleek Benz. One shot was all that was needed to rid this nigga of his existence.

As I exited the car, I saw the nigga that was pissing witnessing the whole incident. When we locked eyes he struck out running and I gave chase. Just as he hit the bottom of the hill, he stumbled and fell. I was on his ass, there was no way he was going to fuck up my plans. Just as he sprung up, I let go a round hitting him in the back, sending him back down to the ground. As he tried to crawl away on his stomach, I stood over him and put two in the back of his head.

As I turned to head back up the hill, I heard police sirens in the distance. Picking up the pace, I cleared the hill and started to my car and just my luck an old white female was standing next to my car, writing something down on a piece of paper. As I got closer I realized it was the store clerk.

"Fuck!" I spat out loud, causing her to turn around.

I didn't hesitate aiming and pulling the trigger.

The rounds ripped through her chest with ease. So much smoke came from her body you would have thought the nosey bitch was on fire. I picked up the paper she was writing on and saw that she was jotting down my tag number.

I looked up the street and saw the blue and red lights coming fast. I jumped in the Charger, started the engine and hit the gas. Just as I was bending the corner, I saw the police speeding into the gas station parking lot. I cranked up T.I. on the car's custom sound system and laid back deep in the seat as I thought out my next move.

Chapter 10

The next morning I was awakened by Trudy as he brought me breakfast in bed. I swear this nigga was losing points by the minute. Not to say a bitch don't like breakfast in bed but damn, don't let the pussy dictate your actions, that's all I'm saying.

"Hey baby, you good?" he asked as he handed me the tray of waffles, eggs, and bacon with some fresh squeezed orange juice on the side.

"Yeah I'm good, thanks baby," I replied as I grabbed the tray, sat it on my lap and started eating.

"You seen my phone around here? I can't remember where the hell I left it," he said while looking around the room.

"Haven't seen it. Call it and see if it rings," I told him as I crunched on the bacon.

"It'll show up like it always does. You sleep good last night?" he asked as he took a seat on the corner of the bed.

Before I could answer his other phone that was clipped on his belt started ringing.

"Yeah," he answered.

There was a minute pause before he spoke again.

"I'll be there tonight. Who do you think is responsible?" Trudy asked as he stood and started pacing the room.

"Ray Ray too!" he screamed as he rubbed his hand over his head.

I know Trudy would never suspect me and anyway, NWM had beef with crews all over the city.

"Man, we all need to meet at the stash house on Fulton Industrial to put our heads together. Call everybody and fill them in on the reason for this meeting. Call Larry and see about getting some more burners for the crew. It looks like somebody done declared war on the family. I'll see you tonight at 8:00. Yeah, one!" Trudy signed off, ending the call.

"What's going on baby?" I asked, already knowing the news.

"Three of our crew was killed last night on Old National, shot up real bad," he replied sharply.

"Damn baby, that's fucked up. Who did it?" I asked, faking concern.

"Shit, we don't know but after bringing everybody together tonight, we going to find out. Just to think, these niggas out chasing you and we got muthafuckers gunning for us. Fuck!" Trudy yelled as he pulled his cell phone back out and dialed a number.

As he held the phone to his ear I heard a faint sound from the nightstand where my purse sat. Reaching over and grabbing my purse I realized this nigga was calling his other phone. I fumbled around in my purse then sat it back down.

"Damn where the fuck did I leave my phone! I ain't got nobody numbers in this shit!" he spat as he tucked the phone back in its pouch.

"It will show up boo, just calm down. I guess ain't no date for us tonight since you got your meeting," I said while thinking about how the whole crew would be together in one spot.

"It depends on how long this meeting is going to last. We got to get to the bottom of this shit."

"I feel you. We can just do something tomorrow night. I guess I'll get with my girlfriend tonight and have a couple of drinks."

"Don't get careless just because all the crew will be together tonight. I don't know if they got other folks looking for you."

I could barely conceal my excitement after hearing the news that all these niggas are going to be together in one spot tonight like sitting ducks. It's going to be real easy to get rid of the whole NWM crew. I knew the Tec 9 would come in handy sooner or later.

"I won't baby," I told him as I reached up and pulled him to me.

"I love you boo," he said with goo goo eyes.

That did it! I couldn't wait to kill this pussy whipped ass nigga! How he gonna love me already?

"Love you too, now go ahead and handle your business," I told him and gave him a soft kiss on the lips.

"I'll hit you up later," he replied.

"Ok, be careful," I said, watching him leave as I thought about my plans to take out the whole crew tonight.

I couldn't wait to be able to walk the streets again and not have to look over my shoulder.

Chapter 11

Later in the night all the NWM members sat around in the lavished furnished warehouse which dubbed as a stash house. The recent shipment of the 150 kilos sat neatly stacked on the back wall, next to the high tech safe that was full of street proceeds.

Trudy paced the room as all of the members filled in. He started calling everybody's name, skipping over the three lost members. After confirming that everyone else was in attendance, he started addressing the men.

"As all y'all done heard by now, we lost three family members last night. Does anybody know about any beef with other crews? The way our people was took out was really fucked up and I'm pretty sure that the people who did it ain't finished. Do anybody in this room got any beef with a rival?" Trudy asked while scanning the room.

"It may be the westside connect crew, you know they hate we making major moves now. Word in the street is that we are disrupting their business," Money called out from the back of the room.

"I heard they talking sideways in the streets too," Turk added.

"Ok…we'll check it out. Anybody else know of any beef?" Trudy asked scanning the room again.

"What about that nigga Blu and them out on Dill Ave., you know they stay on some takeover shit. Everytime I run into that nigga he asking about shit that ain't none of his business, feel me?" Bo Ski announced as everyone listened in.

"Bro, you know the Feds raided their spot last week and locked Blu and his cousin and them up. They to busy dealing with that right now to be gunning at us," Trudy informed the room.

"Blake Miles and Tout got into it with Beeno the other week about some short money so that may be what this is all about," Rio said, seeing the surprised looks on the men's faces at the unfamiliar news.

"I forgot about that! Blake and Tout is known for their gun play too! Don't nobody know where these niggas lay their heads?" Zay asked ready to fuck something up.

"I can find out. I know a stripper bitch that Tout fucks with. She'll give the nigga up for a few dollars. After we get him he'll let us know where Blake lay," P-Nut chimed in.

"Before we jump the gun, we need to make sure that these niggas were really the ones responsible for the hit. We need to be on point because it looks like whoever is behind this shit is moving through the crew," Trudy added.

"I would bet anything that them niggas was behind it. Bitch ass niggas!" Jay screamed as he stood up out of his seat.

"Aight bro, we got to find out for sure because as you all know, when a muthafucker cross the family he got to be dealt with!" Trudy said just as his cell phone started ringing.

Looking at the screen he saw that it was Silk. He cursed at her timing but he wasn't going to put her call off. He walked over to the side of the room and answered.

"What up?" Trudy asked as Zay stood up and took the floor.

"Hey baby, I'm about to go out for a minute but I can't find the keys to the car. Do you have an extra set?" I asked, hoping that he fell into my plan.

"Yeah but I'm all the way out here on Fulton Industrial on that biz I told you about earlier," Trudy explained quietly knowing that if the men in the room ever caught on to his deceit, they would surely kill him.

"I know you're busy and it would be dangerous for me to just pop in there but my girl is waiting for me to pick her up so we can have a couple of drinks. I'm going to catch a cab out there. All you got to do is slip out for a minute and get me the key…I'll stay out of sight. Better yet, just go out now and put it on your windshield and I'll just come through and snatch it from there," I told him, hoping he'd agree.

"Baby, you don't need to be nowhere nea…"

I cut him off.

"Baby please, just do that for me I'll stay out of sight. I really need to wind down a little tonight because I'm really stressing," I begged, thinking of my next move.

"Ok I'll lay the key on my windshield. I'm out at the warehouse on Fulton Industrial next to the Pink Tail strip club. Make sure don't nobody see you. We'll be in here for a minute because we got a lot of shit to catch up on, so I'll holla at you later tonight," he told me as I smiled while thinking how easy this shit was going to be.

"Ok boo, appreciate you. I'll be in and out without nobody noticing," I said assuringly as I flipped through his phone making a mental note of how many men were in the spot.

"Aight I'll holla at you," Trudy said as he ended the call and headed back over to the men that were listening to Zay.

"The bitch hasn't been seen, so if any of you run into her, make the bitch pay. She being real quiet right now but I know it won't be long before this bitch shows her face again," Zay told the room as Trudy walked up and took the floor back.

"I ain't going to hold y'all to long but as y'all know we just had a 150 brick drop, so we need to see how we putting this shit out. Then we need to split up the last drop take in," Trudy said as he ushered everyone over to the table that sat next to the kilos and the safe.

Chapter 12

grabbed my black cat suit and black boots from my bag. I loaded all the guns, pulled my hair back and tucked it under my hat, then headed downstairs to the car. A few minutes later, I was on my way out to Fulton Industrial to take out the infamous NWM.

As I pushed the Charger down 285 in route to the warehouse I got nervous. Even with the Tec 9 and the element of surprise on my side I still knew I could easily be killed on this mission. I was going to have to be real careful and go hard without hesitation. A few minutes later I was exiting and pulling down into the parking lot of the old warehouse. There was no sign of life outside of the building, the only giveaway was all of the expensive customized cars that were wedged down the side alley next to the building.

I tucked the 9mm and glock 40 in my small tote bag and draped it over my shoulder. I positioned the strap on the Tec around the opposite shoulder, pulled my hat down and got out of the car. The building had four doors that could have been possible entrance ways, so I eased up and put my ear to them one at a time to see if I could hear anything. When I reached the third door, I heard someone talking like they was giving a lecture. This had to be the door.

I pulled on the door and the latch gave way causing the big, heavy metal door to squeak. I paused and stood real still making sure no one inside heard the squeaking. My adrenaline pumped like crazy as I eased the door open. I peeped through the door and saw a nicely furnished area with the whole NWM crew standing, listening to the bitch nigga Zay talk. My position gave me a side back view that kept me out of everyone's eyesight but Zay, I had to beat him going in.

I eased up close as I could on the group of men than I counted…12, all of the crew was in attendance. I couldn't believe that I was about to take out a crew of niggas that ran the city, niggas that was feared by many men in the streets. I grabbed the Tec and flipped the safety to ready. One…two…three…when I hit three I bolted up with the Tec held high coughing up the banana clip of hollow points. The men were stunned at my sudden appearance. They all paused, then seconds later tried to retreat but it did no good. I had their asses.

"Fuck!" Bo Ski screamed as two bullets sent him to the floor.

Man Man reached for his gun but it was to late; a stray bullet caught him in the side of the head killing him instantly. Everybody tried their best to scramble for cover but the warehouse didn't offer any.

"Shit!" Turk and Rio screamed in unison as they tried to claw by each other to get behind the sofa. The Tec cut both men down with ease.

My heart raced as I took the niggas out one by one. When I set my sights on Trudy, I hesitated and he no doubtfully picked up on it and frowned wondering why he wasn't hit up. The rest of the crew was gunned down in seconds. It was surprising that no shots were returned but then I thought about when crews came together this way, they would usually come without heat.

I got real comfortable after seeing all the men laid out, some still moving and some out cold.

Still scrambling, Trudy ran over to a far corner and got behind a flipped over table. As I scanned the men I saw one was missing...Zay! Just as I turned, I heard a cocking of a gun behind me.

"Nigga you move, you dead," Zay said menacingly as he eased up behind me.

I held my hands up, releasing the Tec that now dangled around my neck. I knew it was to good to be true. I waited for Zay to blow me away but he didn't fire, so I turned to face him.

"Silk! What the fuck!" Zay screamed, causing Trudy to come from behind the table.

"Silk?" Trudy said, walking over, now understanding the shooters hesitation when he knew he was dead.

"Yeah, but its over. Go ahead Zay shoot me, I'm ready to die," I said with umph in my voice because I knew that this nigga was going to kill me anyway.

"So you the one that's been taking the family out! Bitch, you killed my whole crew! Fuck you bitch—die!" Zay screamed as he placed the gun to my head and pulled the trigger.

"Pow!"

Just as he pulled the trigger, Trudy rushed him, sending the bullet up into the ceiling.

"Nigga what...what the fuck you doing!" Zay screamed as they wrestled for the gun.

Zay was no match for Trudy. Trudy overpowered him and took the gun.

"Man whats up?" Zay screamed, looking up at Trudy

"Bro, sorry about this but this is my lady," Trudy said as he held him down with the pistol in his chest.

"Your lady? Wha...what! Man come on now!" Zay spat as he looked over at me with a smirk on my face.

"Yeah, his lady," I repeated Trudy's words as I dug the glock out of my purse and walked over to the injured Zay.

"Yeah, my nigga...it is what it is," Trudy said shakily.

"Baby, fuck this nigga!" I screamed as I walked over, put the glock to Zays head and pulled the trigger.

"Oh shit!" Trudy screamed as he jumped back getting away from the mess that the glock made of Zay's head.

He looked at me stunned and in shock.

"Let's get out of here," he said sharply as he tucked Zay's gun in his waist.

"Hold up," I said, stopping him in his tracks.

I walked over and stood over the first moving man and placed the barrel of the glock to his head and pulled the trigger. He twitched one time and then laid still. I went around the whole room and put a bullet in each of the niggas' heads. I knew the real meaning of leaving no witnesses.

Trudy watched me move around the room in amazement. He has now seen a side of me that he would have never imagined was there. As I finished off the last victim, I noticed a safe in the corner and stacked next to it was bricks of neatly wrapped cocaine.

"What's this?" I asked, looking over at the still stunned Trudy.

"A recent shipment of cocaine," he answered as be came out of his daze.

"Let's load this shit up then. Can you get in this safe?" I asked him as I tallied up the money in my head that could be made off the dope.

"Yeah, hold up…"

After putting in the five digit code, the safe popped open displaying what had to be over a half a mill.

"That's what's up right there," I said excitedly as we started unloading the safe and grabbing the kilos.

Trudy was acting kind of strange while we took the money and dope. I took it to be that he had just witnessed his so called girl murder the niggas that was like brothers to him but I didn't give a fuck—I hit the jackpot.

"You good?" I asked him as we exited the warehouse carrying the last load to the car.

"Yeah, everything's cool. We just need to be getting out of here," he stressed as he walked out to his car.

We placed all the take in the trunk of the Charger and agreed to meet later at the condo. Just as he got behind the wheel of his car, I flagged him, signaling for him to hold up.

"Yeah?" he yelled, sticking his head out of his car window.

"Hold up, I got something for you," I said, walking up to his car.

He had a puzzled look on his face as I pulled the 9mm and started firing. I left him slumped over the steering wheel. The horn of his car blared into the silent night as blood filled the driver seat.

Rule number one…leave no witnesses.

Epilogue

One Year Later...

The man sat at the head of the huge custom made boardroom table. As he consulted with his cohorts, he waited patiently on his new Miami connect to arrive. His old connect had been killed in a cartel war down on the coast. His right hand man had put together this meeting today so that they could come together with their new supplier and discuss prices.

"Sherm, man this new connect giving us this shit at a way better tag than Eduardo was giving. Sylvester gave these people his own personal stamp of approval."

"Aight, sounds good. I respect Sylvester's word," Sherm agreed as he picked up his crystal champagne glass and took a sip.

Sylvester was an old friend who was well respected on every coast. He supplied dealers from all over; the man was worth millions. After hearing of their need of a connect, he highly recommended someone.

They sat in the conference room of the highrise owned by Sherm, one of his many real estate ventures. Sherm was now the go to man in the city. After his release he took. D-Block up on his offer and within a year he had surpassed D-Block and was now moving over a hundred bricks a week.

"Knock! Knock!"

"Yeah!" Sherm yelled at the person on the other side of his custom designed sliding wooden doors.

"Your visitor is here sir," Deondra, his well proportioned secretary, announced.

"Send them in," Sherm yelled back as he stood at the head of the table waiting for his guest to enter.

As Silk entered, she took in the immaculate setting not recognizing the man that stood before her. As she got closer her heart dropped at the sight of the man who gave her the game and the one man she really loved.

Sherm's mouth fell open at the sight of Silk, dressed in a form fitting, expensive dress with big diamonds on her wrists and fingers.

Silk instinctively grabbed at her clutch that held her .380. Not seconds later, Sherm was reaching in his jacket, clutching his signature Desert Eagle.

Sherm and Silk's people looked on at the drastic turn of events...not knowing what had just happened...not knowing what moves to make.

G STREET CHRONICLES
~ PRESENTS ~

Silk
A Novel

**BASED ON THE DRAMATIC
E-BOOK SERIES
GANGSTA GIRL 1, II & III**

George Sherman Hudson
Author of *City Lights* and *Executive Mistress*

Prologue

Pop! Pop! Pop! Pop! Click! The .38 revolver lit up the room as Tiah pulled the trigger 'til it was empty.

"Bitch, I know you didn't!" Silk screamed as she ran into the room, where Fidel laid lifeless on his favorite recliner.

"He…he was coming at me!" Tiah lied as she loosened her grip on the trigger.

"Bitch, how in the hell was he coming at you and he's all the way over there!" Silk screamed as Tiah stood speechless.

"Now how in the hell are we going to get in the safe?" Lexi asked as she and Kya entered the front room of Fidel's spacious four-bedroom home.

After doing everything in their power to get into the five-foot, digital-lock, armored safe, they gave up.

"All this shit for nothing! Don't never kill a muthafucker until the safe is opened!" Silk screamed.

"He…he was co—" Tiah started but was abruptly cut off by Silk as she moved on her like a lion on its prey.

"Look here, bitch! This is your last fuck-up! You making this shit way harder than it has to be! The next time you take shit in your own hands, I'm going to stop you from breathing. Feel me?" Silk said angrily as she clenched her teeth and waved her Glock in Tiah's face.

They rushed out of the house pissed at Tiah, climbed back into the tinted-out, smoke-gray Chevy and left with no money.

Chapter 1

*A*fter leaving Atlanta and moving to Miami, Silk fell victim to the life of the rich and famous. Before she knew it, her funds from the NWM lick had dwindled down to a mere five figures. In need of money, Silk sat back and put a plan together, realizing she would need a team to carry it out. One night not long after that, Silk was out scouting at Blazers, one of Miami's most popular strip clubs. There, she met Lexi and Kya, two dancers on a mission to get paid by any means necessary.

After feeling the girls out for a minute, Silk invited both girls up to VIP for drinks. She caught an earful while the two girls sipped on cognac and talked recklessly about their street escapades. Silk had found her first two team members. Before leaving, they exchanged numbers, and Silk had made sure the girls knew that if they got down with her program, she would make them real wealthy.

The next day the girls hit her up, anxiously wanting to hear what they had to do to get paid. Silk instructed them to meet her for lunch at the CocoCabana out by Miami Beach. The girls sat out front in Lexi's two-year-old Chrysler 300, waiting on Silk to arrive. Twenty minutes past the scheduled time, Silk pulled up in a convertible white-on-white Bentley GT with oversized white and gold Gucci shades perched on her face. The girls followed Silk's lead as she made her way into the five-star eatery.

They were seated in a back corner at Silk's request, out of earshot of the other patrons. Silk started off running down bits and pieces of her plans. She knew she had to be careful not to expose too much too fast, so she let the two girls do most of the talking. Silk was slightly amused by the girls' down and dirty ways, but during the whole conversation, they never mentioned murder or killing, nor did they make reference to leaving a nigga stankin'. The girls had pulled some mean tricks, but they had never pulled a trigger. After a little more talking and a lot more listening, Silk laid it all on the table: Murder was essential.

At the mention of murder, Lexi's eyebrows shot up, while Kya never even flinched. Silk saw then that Kya was the real heartless one. Going over the plans, Silk also noticed that after money came into play, both girls were willing to take a life. By the time lunch was over, both of them made it clear they were ready to do whatever it took to get rich.

Two weeks later, Silk put them to the test. Pat Wilkes and his wife Nancy were found dead, bound and gagged with a bullet hole in each of their heads. Pat Wilkes's murder had other dope pushers around Oakland tucking their guns in their waistbands, ready to protect their interest at all costs. The streets were really surprised at the half-million that had been taken from the safe that stood open as the two bodies were moved from the premises. Silk made sure both girls got their hands dirty before they left; now both of them had a body up under their belt. After that day, the girls were on a rampage, always looking for the next big payday, even if it meant murder.

Seeing that she had her teammates on point, Silk set out to find someone to hold her end down. The woman had to be drop-dead gorgeous, because she would have to capture the attention of the rich vic. Just as Silk was about to call it a night, she ran into Tiah, who had just exited Club Flex. Tiah and an overweight high-yellow girl were arguing. Out of nowhere, Tiah swung on her, and seconds later, the big girl was sprawled out on the street, in need of medical attention. Silk stepped in and whisked Tiah away from the scene. She was surprised to find out the big girl was Tiah's friend, roommate, and ride home. Tiah had just found out where her lost jewelry was when Desiree, one of their mutual friends, approached them, wanting to buy more of the jewelry Bev had for sale. Tiah had put two and two together and snapped.

After helping Tiah out that night, Silk invited her into the crew because she had the looks and conversation to pull any nigga into the web. Before she accepted, Silk made sure to let her know that they didn't believe in leaving witnesses behind. Tiah picked up on the hint and nodded her approval.

Silk was proud of her choices. She now had Tiah, a dime by all standards. Tiah had heart and knew what to do and say to reel a rich vic in. Silk saw a lot of herself in the girl, but Silk also knew that Tiah needed a lot of street grooming. Then there was Lexi, the hothead of the crew. Lexi was an Amazon with a bad body full of tattoos and body-piercings. Her cute, dimpled smile was misinterpreted by many, because what it really meant was that some sinister things were about to go down. Next there was Kya, the real killer. She bore a striking resemblance to the singer Fantasia but instead of the short do, she had long, flowing dreads, dyed gold at the tips. Kya was attractive in her own way, but she wasn't a bitch to be fucked with. After the first lick, Silk knew she had a real killer on the team. All three girls resided in Brook Estates, in a modestly furnished $250,000 three-bedroom house that Silk had purchased her first week in Miami. The home was Silk's first residence upon arrival in the city.

Chapter 2

"So you think your country ass just gonna come up here to my city and put down? Well, let me explain something to you, nigga. I'm Jap, and I run New York, ya hear?" Jap screamed as he and two of his goons cornered Diego in front of the mall.

"Bro, the last time I checked, this was a free country…and just to let you know, us country niggas love how that big-city money spend," Diego said calmly, sizing the three men up as they moved in closer.

"Smart lil' bitch, huh? Well, it's like this…be up out of NYC by tonight," Jap said and smiled as he and his goons made it known to Diego that they were packing heat and wouldn't hesitate to use it.

Diego had lost his grip on Jersey and had relocated to New York, but that didn't go over well in the streets when word got out that a nigga from the A was getting it in big time and had the best prices. Now Diego was having problems with the jealous NY niggas. Sherm had told him over and over again to come back home, but he steadily refused, telling Sherm that the money was too good up the way. Besides, he knew that Sherm had the whole A on smash, and he would be left scraping for the crumbs left behind if he went back.

"So you standing here telling me to leave where I lay my head and feed myself? Look here nig—"

Before he could get the words out of his mouth, a gun came crashing down against the side of his head. The big black goon grabbed him by the collar of his jacket so he wouldn't fall, then hit him again.

"Oh! Ah!" Diego screamed, trying to wrestle free of the big man's grip as Jap got directly in his face.

"Look here, country boy…be out of my city by tonight, straight up," Jap demanded and smiled as he signaled for his goon to release his grip.

Jap was the go-to man around the city until Diego set up shop. After putting his ear to the street, Jap made it his business to track Diego down and let him know his time in NY was up. Jap had been one of the craziest stick-up kids around the New York area until he got in the game of selling dope. Even though he stood six-two and weighed only 170 pounds, he was still feared throughout the city. Jap refused to let anyone get in the way of him making his money, especially a nigga from the South.

Diego stumbled forward as soon as the big man released his grip. Bracing himself on the wall, he reached up and grabbed his head, now seeping with blood. Cursing to himself, he stumbled over to his SUV, got in, and headed home.

As Diego navigated the truck through the city streets, all he could think about was murder. Before he made it home, he called Sherm; it went straight to voicemail. "Fuck niggas!" Diego screamed as he made a sharp left, hit the curb, and busted his tire. "Shit! Shit! Shit!" he screamed as he pulled over, got out, and looked at the damage. After putting in a call to AAA, he grabbed the $30,000 from the backseat and took off walking the remaining two blocks to his house, holding his bloody head the whole way.

Chapter 3

"Damn! Why the hell my prices keep going up?" Sherm asked Rocko and Taz, who had just given him the price for the 200 kilo order Macklin gave them.

"Man, every since Eduardo got killed, we been going through this shit. Sylvester sent word on a Miami connect that will be contacting us soon," Taz said as he stepped aside so Sherm could get to his office safe.

Sherm had come a long way since last year. After he was released from prison, his young partner Diego had put him on, and when it came to getting rich, there was no hesitation. He passed Diego in the game within six months. Hitting the streets running, Sherm had hooked up with connects from L.A. all the way down to Miami. Sherm now supplied men from east to west coast, but his bread and butter was Atlanta.

He frequently thought about the woman who had left him for dead in a Georgia prison cell. He couldn't believe Silk would leave him hanging after all the shit he'd done for her. If it wasn't for Diego, he would have still been sitting in that cell, wishing for hope. Sherm had made a promise to himself to make Silk pay for selling him out.

After getting rich, Sherm polished up his appearance. He removed the platinum and diamonds from his mouth and replaced them with a $50,000 veneer job. He really favored Tyrese now with his movie-star smile. Sherm had acquired real estate all around the city. Right now, he sat in his high-rise office building, located in the middle of downtown. He made good money off the office space he leased to lawyers and other professionals on the floors below. The top floor was his, and no one but the people closest to him were permitted to step off the elevator on that floor.

He sat there with Taz and Rocko, trying to decide which way to go with the next buy.

"Bro, how 'bout we just go with Macklin on this one and get the extra we spend on the back end? This is the best we can do for now until we holla at the other connect," Rocko explained as he looked out the floor-to-ceiling window at the midday traffic.

Sherm listened as he pulled a bundle of neatly wrapped bills from the safe and walked them over to his desk and set them down.

Sherm, Rocko, and Taz were the go-to men in the city. Sherm played the back, while Rocko and Taz played the front. Even though Sherm wasn't a virgin when it came to pistol play, he delegated that job to Rocko and Taz, and neither of them would hesitate when it was time to pull the trigger.

Rocko was a loyal soldier who stood five-nine, with a stocky build that he worked on religiously in his home gym. Sherm had known Rocko for some time now. They both grew up in the same apartments on the west side of Atlanta, and Sherm had always admired the young Rocko's hustle. Rocko was three years younger than Sherm, but possessed the thinking of an older, wiser man. After Sherm bumped into Rocko a year ago at Club City Lights, they agreed to keep in touch. They met up for a couple of drinks at the local sports bar and decided to team up—a decision that made both of them very wealthy. The complete opposite of both Sherm and Rocko, Taz, was short and chubby and didn't possess a lot of the qualities necessary to be a boss. He played sidekick to Sherm and Rocko, but deep down he wanted more of the action. Sherm called the shots, Rocko controlled the streets hands on and Taz filled in where needed. The different qualities the three possessed made them a force to be reckoned with.

"Do what y'all do, bro," Sherm said, gesturing toward the stacks of money he had just placed on the desk.

"Done deal. I'll holla after I take care of everything," Rocko replied as he grabbed his leather bag and loaded it with the money, about to do business with Macklin.

"I'll be out your way later, bro," Taz told Sherm as he followed Rocko out and headed to his car, pissed that Rocko didn't even consult with him on this move.

"A'ight," Sherm replied as he flipped through the property papers that Deondra had left on his desk.

Rocko and Taz went their separate ways when they got to the parking lot. As Taz entered his car, his cell phone rang; it was Sylvester.

Rocko made a left out of the parking lot bobbing his head to Rick Ross, feeling real good. What Rocko didn't know was that Pewee and Capone had been following him for some time. The two most notorious robbers in the city sat back like police on a stakeout, waiting for Rocko to exit the office building.

Chapter 4

An hour later, Silk was pulling the Chevy into the two-car garage. She killed the engine and slapped the steering wheel. "I can't believe this shit! I know for a fact that old boy was stashing some serious money in his safe. Fuck!" Silk screamed as the girls sat in silence.

After a couple of minutes, Tiah spoke. "I'm sorry, Silk. I just thought—"

Slap! Silk's hand connected with the side of Tiah's face with lightning speed.

"Ah!" Tiah screamed out as she cowered back, covering her face.

"Bitch, fuck sorry! I just spent almost a month getting this muthafucker to bite, and you fucked it all up!" Silk screamed as she forcefully pushed her door open and got out.

Lexi and Kya didn't say a word as they got out and followed Silk into her lavishly furnished three-level home that sat right next to the shore of a sandy white beach. Silk had purchased the home a year ago because she wasn't satisfied with her first home in Brook Haven. This beach home was Silk's pride and joy.

Sitting in the home office, Silk knew that if some money didn't fall her way soon, all would be lost—both her homes and her cars. She refused to let that happen. "Look, y'all, we got to put together a move, and it got to go down this week—no ifs, ands, or buts about it," Silk explained as the girls sat around in her office in their all-black gear, listening to her as she sat perched atop her custom black marble desk.

"I may have something for us. This rich cracker out in Coral Gables been trying to take me to dinner for the longest. He's been determined every since I worked at Skybox, his favorite restaurant. I can call him and see what's up," Tiah said, trying to make up for fucking up the Fidel lick as she also fumed on the inside because Silk had slapped the shit out of her.

"Do he got dough like we like?" Lexi asked, pulling off her black hoodie.

"Dough ain't the word. He owns a construction company and two high-end car lots up in Tampa. I know he's connected some kind of way," Tiah said as she started pacing the room.

"So he stacked like that?" Silk asked, rising up off the desk and walking around to her high-backed leather chair.

"Yeah, but he ain't the type to just give a bitch the bread. He on some gotta-earn-your-keep type shit," Tiah told them. She paused, looked out the window, and then started pacing the room again.

"Can you get in his spot?" Lexi asked.

"Don't see why not," Tiah replied with confidence.

"Is he a boss or a middleman?" Kya chimed in.

"Boss, but he got connections, so we got to be real careful. He holds a lot of weight with some people high up," Tiah explained as she sat back down.

"Fuck who he knows. They bleed red just like all of us," Kya spat.

"Hit him and see what's up," Silk instructed, then leaned back in her leather desk chair.

"Pass me your phone," Tiah told Lexi as she pulled her bag from the office cabinet and fished around in it until she came out with the man's business card.

Seconds later, he was answering the phone. "Hello?" the deep male country-accented voice answered.

"Hey, Richard. This is Tee. How are you doing?" Tiah asked in her best flirtatious tone.

"Tee? I don't recall a Tee," Richard replied, trying to remember.

"Skybox...porterhouse steak, rare...the most expensive wine that the house had to offer...and a slice of you," Tiah said, imitating him.

"Oh yes! Barbie doll!" Richard replied, thinking about the sexy-fine Tiah he'd been looking for during his last four visits to the restaurant.

"Barbie doll?" Tiah asked, thinking how easy it was going to be to get close to him.

"Yeah, that is my name for you, beautiful lady. Where have you been? You okay?" he asked as he pictured Tiah in his king-sized bed, naked and straddling him.

"I'm good. Sorry I took so long to get to you. Things been crazy. I know you are a very busy man and all, but—"

He cut Tiah off midsentence. "How about dinner tonight? Best restaurant, best music, and best wine the house has to offer," he suggested, not trying to hide his excitement one bit.

"You know all that sounds good, but—"

He cut in again. "We can dine on my very wealthy friend's yacht if you—"

This time, Tiah cut him off. "Richard, I'm more of a simple girl. I'd rather just have a home-cooked meal and watch a good movie. I just love that movie *Godfather*," Tiah suggested, hoping he'd fall in place.

"Oh yeah? I love *The Godfather*! I can get my chef to prepare us a nice Italian dish while we watch it. How does that sound?" he asked, willing to do anything for the young black waitress that he'd been yearning for since he'd met her.

"That sounds great, Richard. What time, and where do I need to be?" Tiah asked, smiling and giving the girls a thumbs-up.

"Don't fret. I'll get my driver to pick you up at 6:00. Just text me your address," he said, smiling from ear to ear at his good luck.

"Okay. I'll do that now. See you later," Tiah said in a fake happy tone that Silk rolled her eyes at.

"Toodle-doo! See you in a min'!" he replied as he broke out in a square dance around his five-million-dollar mansion in Coral Gables.

"It's a go, y'all," Tiah said proudly.

"Pick up address is 298 Pinellas Point, Apartment 34. Just stand out front. The driver won't know any better," Silk said as she started calculating the plan to hit the next lick. "Y'all get right. We need to be ready to follow the driver," Silk told them as she pulled out her desk drawer and retrieved a chrome .357.

"   h, I just love this house. It's beautiful!" Tiah told Richard as he escorted her from the Lincoln limo inside.

"Well, it took a lot of blood, sweat, and tears to get this place," Richard replied as he led Tiah up to the front door that was flanked by two roaring water fountains.

"I bet it did. It's a dream home," Tiah said, trying to scope out anything that might hinder their move that night.

Richard Kilgore was a very rich man who was deeply connected with one of Mexico's most dangerous drug lords, a close acquaintance of Miguel Curasco himself. Just last year, Richard had told Miguel he was ready to throw in the towel and go legit, and before his plane landed back in the States, his whole family was staring down the barrels of high-powered machine guns. Miguel told Richard right then that retiring would mean a death sentence for him and his family. Richard reluctantly agreed and accepted the next cargo of cocaine and heroin, which he distributed with ease to his faithful clientele.

"Thanks. I do enjoy it, but it get lonely at times."

Beep! Beep! They were interrupted by the ringing of his cell phone.

"Hello?" he answered, annoyed by the intrusion.

"Hi. Is this Richard?" Taz asked, looking to speak to the man Sylvester had referred him to as he left the office.

"Yes. May I help you?" Richard asked, still annoyed but now curious.

"Sylvester gave me your number. Is this a bad time?" Taz asked, wanting to make sure the new connect had given them some good prices.

"Hold on. Please excuse me," he told Tiah as he stepped over to his kitchen.

Tiah knew it was a business call, but she wanted to know more. She eased up close to the wall and listened in.

"Atlanta. I'll ship tomorrow. I'll send my partner to meet you and discuss future prices. Atlanta Square. This is a private number from you? My people will call and set up a time. I deal in cash only, so my people will be picking up $1.2 million. Okay. And when you talk to Sylvester, tell him I said hi and that he should come through sometimes." Richard ended the call, jotted down all the necessary information on a slip of paper, and placed it in his pocket for his partner West.

Tiah was surprised at the figures being thrown around.

"Sorry to keep you waiting. Come this way," he told Tiah as he stepped out of the kitchen then led her to the back terrace.

"I'd love to see this beautiful home. How about you take me on a tour?" Tiah suggested gleefully, really wanting to scope out the scene and see how many more people were in the house.

"Anything for you, Barbie. Let's start in the kitchen," Richard replied with pleasure.

After touring the whole house, Tiah saw that there were only two more people inside, the chef and the maid. "Excuse me one minute," she said. She pulled her cell phone from her purse and texted Silk the number 2 and the house address that she had been repeating over and over in her head every since she arrived.

Silk, Lexi, and Kya sat around Silk's place waiting for word from Tiah. They decided not to follow the limo; instead, they would just go after Tiah made sure the coast was clear. As soon as they saw the text come in, they sprang into action.

"Bring some extra duct tape since he got company," Silk instructed, and they geared up and loaded their guns.

"You got the address?" Lexi asked as they all filed out the door to the tinted-out Chevy for the second lick of the night.

"Yeah. It's all in the text…400 Coral Point. We good. Let's get paid," Silk said as she put the car in reverse, backed out of the driveway, and headed out to their big payday.

"Did she say anything about security?" Lexi asked as Silk pushed the Chevy through the night traffic.

"No, so it must be cool. She ain't mention nothing but the other people in the house. We ought to be good," Silk replied, hoping Tiah had her shit together this time.

"You know these rich muthafuckers living out in these million-dollar neighborhoods think they safe," Kya added as she tucked her hair under her black skullcap.

Chapter 6

As soon as Diego hit his door, he put in a call to Lucious, his NY street connect. "Say, Lucious, you know a nigga they call Jap from up this way?" Diego asked, hoping he wouldn't have to go on a witch hunt to find him.

"Jap? Jap? Jap? Um, I can't…" Lucious paused.

"Tall, skinny, long nose nigga that keep niggas with him," Diego added.

"Oh! Japrentice? Yeah, I know that crazy young'n. What's the issue?" Lucious asked, wondering what Diego wanted with the son of his dead best friend.

"I got people from Atlanta that's trying to get in touch with him. He's kin to my girl's cousin, and they told me that he stayed up this way," Diego lied, keeping his intentions on the low, just in case they were cool.

"Oh, okay. Yeah, Jap still stay out on Cookman Ave with his baby mama and their two boys. The best place to catch up with him is over at Mrs. Ruth's, his mama's house out on Trinity—40 Trinity Avenue if I remember right. Hey, make sure you tell them I said hey when you fall through. I ain't seen them folks since Drebo was killed," Lucious said, thinking back to when his best friend was gunned down by the police in front of his own house.

Diego was glad he had lied about the situation, because there was a connection between them. He thanked God for his good luck; Jap had just been handed to him on a silver platter. "I will tell them you said what up. Appreciate ya help, bro. Be easy," Diego added, knowing that he would most likely have to deal with Lucious later on for playing him. Diego also knew there was a slim chance he would never see Lucious again anyway, because after seeing about Jap, he planned to take Sherm up on his offer and move back to Atlanta.

Later that evening, Diego pulled out his AK-47 and loaded it, being careful not to touch any of the rounds. He planned to light NY up that evening and then jet off to Atlanta. Looking at his watch, he saw that it was about that time. He grabbed the keys to the maroon Dodge Ram and headed out to Trinity Ave. in search of Jap.

Thirty minutes later, Diego was pulling up on the Ave. Things were real quiet in the old well-kept neighborhood. Diego looked at the address again to confirm it. Just as he rounded the curve, he saw the address on the small brick house, and to his surprise, Jap was sitting right there on the porch with the same two men from earlier. Diego rode by discreetly while checking out the scene. He knew when he hit the AK, the police would be called immediately, so he parked close to the house and kept the truck running.

Exiting the truck, Diego concealed the AK the best he could under his jacket as he made his way up to the house. Cutting through the neighbor's yard, he eased up to the side of Jap's mom's house. He instantly paused when he heard a door open and close. After waiting for a minute, he looked again to make sure the coast was clear. Once he saw that it was, he pulled the green ski mask over his face and gripped the AK. Just as he was about to step around the corner and let loose, a car pulled up in front of the house. Again, Diego paused and waited until the car pulled off a few minutes later. Diego then figured out that Jap was using his mama's house as a trap house. Diego waited patiently for the car to leave and bend the corner so he could get his revenge. As soon as the car was out of sight he took off and rounded the house with the AK in plain sight.

Waka! Waka! Waka! Waka! The AK spat round after round, tearing down everything in its path.

"Shit!" Jap screamed as he jumped off of the opposite side of the porch.

His goons weren't as lucky though. Just as they tried to turn and run, several rounds cut them down with ease.

"What's all this noise about?" Mrs. Ruth asked as she opened the front door and stepped out onto the porch.

Before Diego could let up, a round caught Jap's eighty-year-old mother totally off guard. The bullet shattered her skull, knocking her completely off of her feet. The AK-47 round tore off the whole side of her head.

Diego's heart dropped as the old lady crumpled to the ground. "Fuck! Damn!" Diego screamed. He said a silent prayer for the old lady while running back to his truck.

After seeing the unknown shooter turn and run, Jap returned to the house. He was in shock at the sight of his mother lying lifeless, faceless. He blacked out, and when he woke, he found himself being treated at a local hospital for a fractured leg and shock.

Diego made it back to the truck and sped away, headed back home to pack so he could hit the road that night, headed to the A.

Chapter 7

"Bump the nigga at the light," Pewee told Capone as they followed Rocko down Peachtree Street en route to make the buy.

Crash!

Pewee clipped the back of Rocko's Jag at the light on Peachtree and 14th Street.

"What the hell?!" Rocko screamed, jumping out of the car, furious at the careless driver who'd just dented up his $90,000 automobile.

Just as Rocko stepped out, Capone came from around the opposite side, grabbed him from behind, slammed him to the ground, and placed the .9mm against the back of his head. Knowing the light down the hill would turn green soon and release the waiting car, Capone signaled Pewee to move fast.

"Yo, man, what's the deal?" Rocko asked, more surprised than scared.

"Nigga, don't talk or move!" Capone spat. He held the gun steady as he watched Pewee grab the bag of money from the front seat of the Jag.

"We out!" Pewee yelled as Capone stood up, releasing his grip on Rocko.

Just as Capone let him go, he jumped up and went for the gun.

"Nigga!" Pewee screamed from behind the wheel of the car as Rocko wrestled Capone for the gun.

Rocko overpowered Capone with ease. Once he had a firm grip on the .9mm, he turned it on Capone and started to squeeze the trigger, but before he could fire, shots rang out from behind him.

Blaka! Blaka! Blaka!

Pewee didn't hesitate to pull the trigger on his .45. The first bullet struck Rocko in the arm, jerking him around, while the next two pierced his face and chest.

"Man, let's ride!" Pewee screamed as Capone jumped up from the pavement and sidestepped a hurt and bleeding Rocko.

Rocko crawled to no place in particular. His eyes were pleading for help as his breathing increased. Every time his heart took a beat, blood gushed out from every hole the .45 had made. The driver of the first car on the scene hurried to call 911. An ambulance was on the scene minutes later, but it was too late; by then, Rocko had already taken his last breath.

"Damn, nigga! You let that nigga take yo' heat? Damn, nigga!" Pewee laughed at Capone as he pushed the old beat-up Buick through the back streets of the city.

"Man, that nigga got the drop on a gangsta. It's all good though. I still won, and he lost," Capone said calmly. Deep down, he didn't like that Rocko had gotten the best of him.

"Ah, man, you went out like a real duck! Nigga, you owe me, 'cause that nigga was about to light yo' ass up!" Pewee loudly joked as he reached into the ashtray and grabbed the half-smoked blunt.

"Nah, nigga, fuck that! We even, 'cause I done saved yo' ass plenty of times," Capone injected as he snatched the blunt out of Pewee's hand and lit it.

"Yeah, whateva, nigga," Pewee replied as they cruised down through the back streets of the west side of the A, en route to Fairburn Road, where they shared an apartment with two sisters who danced together at Drop It, one of Atlanta's most raunchiest strip clubs.

Chapter 8

Sherm made a couple of calls, exited his office, and headed down to his car. As he rounded 14th Street, he saw a lot of flashing lights. Getting closer, he noticed a body lying in the street, covered in a white sheet splotched with blood. "Shit's crazy!" he said aloud as the police diverted him and the other oncoming cars to a side street.

Just as he was turning on to the side street, he noticed Rocko's Jag sitting in the middle of the street with its doors open. Slamming on the brakes, he brought his Benz to a screeching halt, pulled over, and jumped out in a hurry. The police had the area blocked off, so no one could get close to the crime scene. Sherm made a slick move and slipped around the police barricades 'til he was just a couple feet from the body. His heart skipped a beat as he noticed the foot hanging out from under the sheet was wearing an expensive cream-colored gator—a shoe Sherm had just complimented Rocko on minutes earlier, when they had sat in his office.

Sherm knew there was some foul play involved, so he calmly turned around and headed back to his car to call Taz. He wanted whoever was responsible for Rocko's murder dead.

Sherm couldn't believe he had just witnessed his partner, his right-hand man, lying in the street dead. He also knew that more than likely, the money for the buy was gone. *Who knew about the buy?* he wondered. After entertaining the thought, he figured it had to come from outside the circle. Thinking about his next move, Sherm picked up his phone and called Taz who didnt sound too upset about the hit then he called the man with all the connections, Rufus. Rufus was the biggest con man in the city who always kept his ear to the street.

"What's up, bro? Speak yo piece," Rufus said as he reached over and turned down the Isley Brothers CD that was grooving from the Phantom's state-of-the-art sound system.

"Bruh, my right-hand man, Rocko, just got hit, downtown in broad daylight. Most likely niggas was at money or a drop. Man I need you to beat the street and see what you hear," Sherm stressed as he sat outside his office building in his Benz.

"No problem. I ain't heard nothing in the street about that yet, but yeah, I'll dig up some shit for you, fam," Rufus replied. He knew he'd have a whole rundown before nightfall, because nothing that went down in the A got past his network.

"Appreciate ya, bruh. Real talk."

"I'll be in touch. I'll holla," Rufus said, ending the call and then dialing his police connect.

Sherm hung up. Seconds later, his cell phone chimed. "Hello?" Sherm asked in an irritated tone.

"Sounds like a bad time, my friend," Sylvester replied, hearing the tension in Sherm's voice.

"Nah, Sylvester. My bad. Just got a lot of shit I'm dealing with. You get my message?" Sherm asked, not knowing if Taz had made contact or not.

"Yeah. I spoke with Taz a while ago," Sylvester said as he walked out on his terrace. "I'm going to give you the same info I gave him. It's good to have everyone on the same page. You got a pen?" Sylvester asked.

"Hold up…yeah, go ahead."

"Richard is the name. He's out of Florida and can get you whatever you want at the best prices. His number is (310) 768-7897. Tell him I sent you with best regards, and he will know what to do from there," Sylvester explained again, just as he'd told Taz.

"Thanks, Sylvester. Let me get with Taz right now. I'll be in touch," Sherm said, ending the call but still thinking about Rocko's murder. Sherm immediately dialed Taz's number, and Taz answered seconds later. "You spoke with the new connect yet?" Sherm asked as he kept picturing Rocko lying dead in the street.

"Yeah, I called the connect. We did good on this shipment, and he's trying to make it better on the next one," Taz said proudly as he thought about his good luck when Rocko was killed.

Chapter 9

"The address is 400, right?" Lexi asked Silk as she guided the Chevy through the neighborhood full of expensive homes that sat on acres and acres of land surrounded by water.

"Yeah, that's it," Silk replied, seeing that the mansion that sat in front of them was the spot.

"Damn! This muthafucker paid!" Kya exclaimed while eyeing the Olympic-size pool and tennis court that flanked the million-dollar home.

"Gear up, and let's get it," Silk said as she pulled the Chevy to a halt on the street in front of the house.

"Tiah hit back?" Lexi asked as she adjusted her pistol that was tucked inside of her cargo pants.

"Nah, so it's a go. We walking straight up in the front door like we live in this bitch," Kya spat as Silk pulled her black gloves on and pushed the car door open.

The three girls walked up to the front of the house nonchalantly. When they reached the door, Silk tried the knob and was surprised when the door creaked open. "Bingo," Silk whispered as they filed in while pulling out their guns.

"Which way?" Kya asked as they walked through the foyer of the expensively furnished home.

"Let's start left, then work right," Silk instructed as she pulled her black ski mask down over her face.

Lexi and Kya followed Silk's lead and pulled their ski masks down also.

Just as they were about to enter the first room, an old Mexican lady dressed in maid's attire came around the corner, singing in Spanish, her hands full of linen. "Ahh!" she screamed as she came face to face with the three figures wearing ski masks.

Before the next scream came, Kya was on her ass.

Clunk! Clunk!

The old lady couldn't stand under the pressure of the butt of the gun. Her knees buckled, and she hit the floor with a *thud*.

"Bitch, shut up," Kya said through clenched teeth as Lexi and Silk ran over to help secure the old woman.

They checked to make sure everything was still calm, then found an empty room and dragged her in.

"Who else is in here?" Silk asked the lady, while Lexi and Kya finished duct-taping her.

"*No se!* Me don't know *nada!*" she cried hysterically as Silk questioned her.

"Bitch, you lying! You got two seconds to tell us what we need to know," Kya spat as she placed her pistol to the old lady's wrinkled head.

"I think only me, Chef and Mr. Richard...with his guest! *Si!* That's all I know! *Por favor!*" the lady explained shakily in broken English.

"Okay, cool. Where are they?" Silk asked in a calm, cool tone.

"Me last see them on second floor, in the dining room," the old lady told them as she started to cry again.

"Y'all, let's go," Lexi chimed in as she cracked the room door and looked out.

"Okay. Thanks, Mrs..." Silk said as she reached over and grabbed a pillow from the bed.

"Alverez," the old lady stated, now getting comfortable.

She was surprised when Silk put the pillow over her face and then pressed her gun into the pillow. The two shots were muffled as the feathers in the pillow jumped out and floated around in the air, some of them blood soaked, silencing the pleading old lady.

"Let's get to the money," Silk said quietly as she stepped around the hired help's lifeless body.

Lexi and Kya acted as if nothing had happened as they followed behind Silk when she exited the room.

Chapter 10

Diego knew it wouldn't be long before the NYPD swarmed the scene like ants on a picnic, so he played it cool and didn't speed as he pushed the truck through the city on the way back to his spot.

On the way, he picked up his cell phone and punched in Sherm's number, but he didn't get an answer. That was when he realized he'd been calling his old number all along. The new number was jotted down on a slip of paper on his computer desk at the house. He made a mental note to add it to his contact list. As he got closer to his spot, his nervousness eased up.

On the other side of town, Jap was going crazy as he limped out of the hospital. His mother's house had been blocked off with crime scene tape everywhere. Detectives scoured the neighborhood, going house to house looking for witnesses and clues.

It didn't take long for Lucious to hear about the shooting in his old hood. As soon as he heard that Mrs. Ruth had been killed, he hit the roof. He then put two and two together and cursed himself for going out like a new jack by giving Diego all the info needed to pull off the hit. Lucious faulted himself for Mrs. Ruth's death, the woman he thought of like a second mother. He grabbed his keys and rushed over to his old neighborhood.

Ten minutes later, Lucious was pulling his Lincoln up in front of the scene of the crime. The first person he saw as he pulled up and killed the engine was Jap, just getting back from the hospital with Tootsie, his baby-mama.

"Jap!" Lucious screamed as he jumped out of his Lincoln Town Car and headed over to Tootsie's car.

"Hey, Lucious. Man, somebody done killed Ma! They killed Bolo and Nez too," Jap said, tearing up as he leaned on the car to keep his balance.

"You okay, baby?" Tootsie asked Jap as she rubbed his arm.

"Yeah, I'm good. Man…fuck! He was after me. Had to be!" Jap spat, growing angrier and angrier by the minute.

"I know who did this, and I know where he lay his head," Lucious said in a sinister tone, still pissed that Diego had played him for the info to kill his own people.

"What?" Tootsie asked, bug-eyed and surprised.

"You really know who did this shit my nigga? You know where they rest they head? Who did this shit, bro?" Jap asked forcefully.

Lucious paused and then answered, "Nigga name Diego. He stay off of McDuffie Avenue. Don't ask how I know. Just know I know," Lucious explained as he watched the crime scene people start gathering their equipment.

"Oh shit! The nigga from Atlanta? I…wait, how in the hell he know about mama's spot?" Jap asked, now getting heated.

"Don't know, but my sources say he was behind it," Lucious told him as he tried to keep down the anger that was building inside of him for slipping like he did.

"I'ma kill that bitch!" Jap yelled as he limped over and got in Tootsie's car.

"Hold up now, baby. Don't go doin' nothing stupid!" Tootsie yelled as she ran over behind him.

"She right, bro. Just slow down and let's think this thang through. Get out and ride with me. Tootsie, you go to the house. I got bro," Lucious said, opening the car door for Jap to get out.

Chapter 11

Diego rushed in the house and started packing all of his belongings. Most everything was already packed and ready to go; he just had to tie up some loose ends. As he packed his computer, he grabbed Sherm's new number off the desk and put it in his pocket. While he was packing the last of his clothes, his cell phone rang. "Yeah?" he answered.

"Bruh, what it do? Boy, I need ya help," Lucious said as he broke the speed limit trying to get to Diego's spot as Jap rode shotgun.

"What up? What you need, peeps?" Diego asked, trying to pick up on any bullshit that Lucious might be kicking his way.

"My people from L.A. up this way trying to cop, but the nigga they dealing with is knocking their head off. I know you can get me a better price. They trying to spend seventeen bundles. Can you give 'em a good deal?" Lucious lied, trying to stall him until he got to his spot.

"Hmm. I think I can help you out. How 'bout you meet me at the gas station on the corner of 5th and MLK?" Diego told him, seeing right through the bullshit he was kicking.

"You at the house? We can just swing through there," Lucious asked, knowing that if he answered "No" and didn't give his whereabouts, he was indeed at his spot.

"Nah. Just meet me on 5th and MLK in thirty minutes," Diego told him again, now confirming his suspicion: Lucious was coming after him.

"A'ight, lil' bro. I'm on my way," Lucious said as he turned on the street over from Diego's place. "Let me out right here. I going in from the back. You just bust a right on top of the hill. He stay in the beige and black house. I know when he see my ride, he going to take off," Lucious told Jap as he grabbed his twin nines, tucked them in his waist, and got out the car. He hurriedly climbed the hill that led to Diego's backdoor.

Diego knew the heat was on. He knew they were probably on their way to his spot. He figured he had at least another fifteen minutes—that was, until he saw the black-on-black Lincoln Town Car, Lucious's car, bending the curve, speeding. "Shit!" Diego yelled, dropping everything he held and turning to run back to the house.

Jap saw Diego's retreat as he barreled down the hill to the house and knew that had to be the nigga who killed his mama. Jap pulled the Lincoln up in Diego's driveway, slung his door open, and got out.

Diego didn't wait around to talk. He bolted through the house to the backdoor, exactly like Lucious knew he would do.

Lucious sat in the old rusty lawn chair in Diego's backyard waiting. A few minutes later, the back sliding glass doors slid open and Diego rushed through them, running right into Lucious' path. "What up, young blood?" Lucious said and smiled as he aimed the two .9mm at Diego, who was in shock at his presence.

"Wh-wha…" Diego stuttered like he had seen a ghost.

"Lil' fuck nigga, you played the wrong one," Lucious spat as he squeezed the triggers on both guns.

Blaka! Blaka! The nines gave little recoil as the rounds tore through Diego's chest.

Chapter 12

"This way," Silk whispered to Lexi and Kya as they climbed the winding stairway up to the second floor of the mansion.

"Hold up! Shh!" Lexi said softly, making Silk and Kya freeze in their tracks.

"Somebody is downstairs," Kya said. They all turned and looked back down the stairs.

The chef was wheeling a cart with covered platters and champagne over to what they made out to be an elevator. Pressing themselves up against the stairway wall, they stood still and waited for the man to get on the elevator that was headed up to the second floor.

"The elevator should be to the left at the top of the stairs. We need to meet him before he get off," Kya told them as they hurried up the stairs.

"I got him. Y'all go back down and get by the elevator. We don't need a loud scene blowing our cover up here. We will deal with him downstairs," Silk explained as she pulled her ski mask off and tucked her gun under her jacket in the small of her back.

Lexi and Kya followed Silk's instructions and rushed back down the stairs to take their position next to the elevator, ready to ambush the tall, lanky, middle-aged white man as soon as the doors opened.

Silk stood next to the top floor elevator, waiting for the doors to open.

Just as the bell went off and the doors started to open, a voice called out from behind her. "Hey! Who are you? What are you doing in my house?" Richard screamed just as the elevators doors slid open.

The elevator doors opened and the chef stepped out, pushing the cart of food. "Sorry, sir. I didn't know you had another guest. I will prepare another serving," the chef said as Richard started screaming as he pulled his cell phone from his pocket.

Silk was just about to pull her pistol till Tiah spoke up.

"Yes, please prepare another serving for my best friend," Tiah said as she stepped around Richard.

"Best friend? What's going on?" Richard asked, confused but not threatened by the petite, young, beautiful black girl that he would love to put his hands on.

"Dang, girl! You spoiled it! How you get in here?" Tiah called out, trying to see which way Silk was going to move in the awkward but fixable situation.

"Surprise?" Richard asked, smiling from ear to ear.

"I wanted to give you a little extra. This is who I texted earlier when I first got here. This is my best friend, and we do everything together—I mean *everything*. Two heads are always better than one," Tiah purred as she rubbed her hands across his chest.

The chef stood speechless and wide-eyed while Silk smiled, giving Richard a flirtatious look. "Didn't mean to scare you, Mr. Richard. The maid let me in and told me to come up here," Silk explained, putting on her best performance.

"I will grab another serving, sir. Just give me one minute," the chef said as he turned and pulled the cart back onto the elevator.

"Thanks," Tiah told him as she motioned for Silk to come join them.

"Dang, girl. I hate that I spoiled your surprise. Mr. Richard, I'm sorry for the intrusion. I was just trying to help my girl out," Silk said as they all walked down the extended hallway to the theatre room.

"No problem. I'm glad you could—"

Richard stopped midsentence as loud shots went off downstairs.

Chapter 13

"Boy, this is what it's all about!" Pewee screamed as he and Capone sat in their apartment counting all the money from the Rocko lick.

"Man, this just set us all the way straight. It's gotta be over $100,000 here. It's time to trade the old Capri in for one of them spaceships," Pewee barked as he separated the bills by denominations.

"Nigga, don't just go splurging. You know niggas will start getting suspicious and shit. Got to play it low, at least for a couple months," Pewee stressed as he counted out the money in $1,000 stacks.

"Nigga, I know how to play it. You act like this a G's first lick," Capone shot back as he grabbed the pack of Newports off the table and drew one out.

Just as he was about to light it, the front door flew open, catching both men by surprise. "Hey, hey, hey!" Diva, Peaches, and Mocha—the top three hood-rats from Drop It, the hole-in-the-wall strip club—busted through the door, obviously drunk and high.

Diva and Capone had been together for eight months, and Peaches and Pewee was going into their first year. Pewee and Capone had met both women at the club one night while scoping out a lick.

"Big money ballers!" Mocha screamed as she walked over and plopped down in between them in front of the table full of money.

"Girl, get away from my man and my money!" Peaches joked as she squeezed in between Mocha and Pewee.

"That goes for me, too, hoochie!" Diva slurred as she squeezed between Mocha and Capone.

"Damn! Y'all bitches ain't right! Where y'all rich friends at?" Mocha said as she stood showcasing her jiggly ass with her black tights riding up her crack.

"Man, y'all need to hold that country-ass loud talking down with y'all drunk asses," Capone barked as he lit his Newport.

"Damn! Who y'all kill for all this loot?" Peaches joked as she picked up a couple stacks off of the table.

Her statement drew stares from Pewee and Capone. "Girl, you fucked up, talking all crazy and shit. Go back there and lay down. Come on. Let's go," Pewee said forcefully as he grabbed Peaches by the wrist and pulled her to her feet.

"Oh yeah! Hump time! Whoa! Whoa!" Peaches chanted drunkenly as she rocked back and caught her balance while Pewee pulled her to the room.

"Stash that, bro. We will get finished tomorrow," Pewee said, closing his bedroom door.

"So I know y'all ain't just gonna leave a bitch out here all by herself like this," Mocha said as she paraded around the room, making her bottom jiggle uncontrollably and enticing Capone.

"Bitch, you at home. Chill out. I'm 'bout to get me some dick," Diva slurred as she stood and stumbled back to her room sloppy drunk, calling for Capone to follow.

Mocha gave Capone a look that they were both familiar with. They had been seeing each other on the low for months. She juiced him every chance she got. Capone was more than whipped by the six-one, 200-pound, bowlegged stallion. Her exotic looks had Capone going crazy. Mocha saw the control she had over him and played up on it every chance she got. "So you doing it like that, huh? So we holding back now? That's what's up? I thought we was better than that, but I guess we ain't," Mocha spat and rolled her eyes as she walked over and stood in front of him.

Capone was beyond whipped by Mocha. He always tried to compare Diva to Mocha, and there wasn't no comparison. Mocha was everything Capone wanted, and Mocha knew he would do everything she asked, just to keep her around. "Nah, baby. I had a nice play come my way," Capone replied as he put the remaining money in the bag and looked to see where Diva was. Looking straight back to the room, he saw that she was passed out on the bed.

"Oh, she fucked up on pills, weed, and gin. She out for the count," Mocha told him with a fake attitude.

"So you tripping now?" Capone asked as he stood up in front of Mocha.

"Nigga, you ain't been keeping it real, talking about a nice play. You been cuffing all along. Miss me with the bullshit!" Mocha spat faintly, then walked off.

"Nah, baby. Straight up, we hit a lick earlier for some major bread, real talk," Capone explained as he followed behind her to the bathroom.

"What lick, nigga? You lying. Fuck this shit. You ain't hit no lick that time of day. Who you take me for?" Mocha said angrily, putting on her best performance.

"I swear, baby. Come here," Capone said softly as he pulled the bathroom door closed.

"You lying. Let me up out of here. I'm out," Mocha said forcefully as she tried to push past him.

"No, wait. Hold up, boo. We pulled a lick this afternoon, and don't say shit about what I'm fixing to tell your ass. We hit the nigga Rocko from the south side. Pewee left him laid out dead in the middle of downtown. Check the news. Don't say shit," Capone said forcefully in a low tone as he pulled her to him and kissed her on the neck.

"So you wasn't lying? Sorry, baby. You going to take care of mama, right?" she said seductively as she cupped his face and kissed him, knowing she was going to get hit off real good.

"You know I am," he replied as he unbuckled his pants and pulled his dick out.

"Quickie?" she asked as she pulled down her tights and bent over for him to fuck her from behind.

As Capone pushed himself in and out of her, all she could think about was the man who still held her heart after all these years. Her ex—Rocko.

Chapter 14

"What was that?!" Richard screamed as more shots rang out from downstairs.

"Shit!" Tiah screamed as the voices from downstairs grew louder.

Richard frantically pulled out his cell phone and started to dial 911.

"Put it down!" Silk screamed as she pressed the .9mm in his back.

"Wh-what's going on? What's this all about?" Richard asked in panic as Tiah pulled her .380 out of her purse.

"Shut the fuck up and get down on your knees," Tiah ordered as Kya and Lexi appeared at the top of the stairs.

"Tape him up," Silk told Kya as Lexi and Tiah stood by, making sure he didn't try anything.

"Look here Richard, you can cooperate and make this shit real easy, or you can bullshit me and make it harder than it got to be. All in all, I ain't leaving this bitch 'til I get what I came for. You can choose to make it easy and only lose a little money, or you can make it hard and lose your life. We only want the money you got tucked away in the safe, then we out. That said, where's the safe?" Silk asked calmly with her gun resting on his forehead.

Richard looked up at her helplessly as Kya checked the tape that held his ankles and wrists together. "Look, I can help you girls make a lot of money—far more than what's in the safe. I promise you that. If you'll just—"

Clunk! Silk brought the barrel of the pistol down on the bridge of Richard's nose breaking it instantly. "I don't need you doing shit for me but telling me where the safe is at!" Silk spat heatedly as he wiggled around in pain.

"My home office! You can have it all…just…just please let me go," he pleaded as blood rolled down his cheeks from his nose.

Silk looked around, wondering where his office was in the big house.

"It's this way!" Tiah called out, noticing Silk's confusion as she remembered the sleek, expensively furnished office from her tour of the house.

"Combination!" Silk demanded as she stood over Richard.

His eyes pleaded with her, but he finally answered, "It's 37-21-38-17," as he laid his head to the side so the blood wouldn't flow back in his nose.

"Come on, Tiah. Y'all watch him," Silk instructed as she let Tiah by to lead her to the office.

They rushed down the long corridor, past all the expensively furnished rooms, until they came upon two big cherry oak sliding doors.

"Right here," Tiah said as she pushed the doors open.

Silk kept repeating the combination to herself as they entered the office and looked around for the safe: "37-21-38-17…37-21-38-17."

"Right there!" Tiah called out, pointing to the five-foot fireproof digital safe that sat alone in a far corner.

Silk raced over to the safe and punched in the code, but it didn't open. "Fuck! This shit ain't opening!" Silk screamed angrily as she stormed out of the room, back down the hall to Richard, with Tiah close on her heels.

Lexi and Kya looked up and noticed Silk and Tiah coming their way, empty-handed. "What's up, y'all?" Lexi called out, noticing the scowl on Silk's face.

"Fuck-ass cracker! What's the combination?" Silk shouted as she stood over Richard and started beating him in the face with her gun.

He tried his best to dodge the swinging gun, but he was helpless. The .9mm took chunks out of his face and head as his wiggled around like a fish out of water. "Wait! Stop! Please! Wait!" Richard pleaded as blood flowed freely from his head and down his face.

"I told you what would happen if you bullshitted me! What's the combination?" Silk screamed as she held the gun up, about to take another swing.

"Wait! Please…you have to pause…you have to put a minute pause between each number. I'm telling you the truth!" he screamed out in pain.

"If I can't get it open this time, that's yo ass," Silk said firmly as she turned and headed back to the office.

"37…21…38…17," Silk said as she entered each number with a pause in between.

After the last number, there was a soft *beep,* and the safe popped open. Silk and Tiah's mouths fell wide open as they looked at all of the perfectly stacked money that lined the safe from top to bottom.

"Jackpot!" Tiah yelled, excited about all of the money that was about to be theirs.

"Damn! Grab that plastic bag from that chair, and let's load this up," Silk told Tiah as she looked through the other contents of the safe.

Ten minutes later, they had all the money packed up and ready to go.

"Oh yeah. I forgot to tell y'all Richard was talking to somebody earlier. He was supposed to be sending somebody to meet and pick up some money—a lot of money. He wrote down the info and put it in his pocket. I could tell it's going to be their first meeting by the way he was talking. Shit, we can pick it up," Tiah suggested.

"Oh yeah? Let's see what's up wit' it," Silk replied as they made their way back up the hall to Kya and Lexi.

"We in the money, ladies! Cha-ching!" Tiah screamed out playfully as she dragged the bag of money behind her.

"That's what's up!" Kya added as she looked at the bag of money.

"Payday!" Lexi chimed in, watching the bag also.

"It ain't over just yet. Richard, I heard you talking earlier. Now you're going to call that person back and let them know you got your partner coming to get that money. You breathe wrong and I'm going to kill you on the spot. Where's his phone?" Tiah asked as she reached in his pocket and pulled out the paper with the info on it, along with his cell.

"I-I…" Richard stuttered, still dazed from the beating Silk had put on him minutes ago.

Smack!

Lexi walked over and slapped him with her gloved hand, just to let him know they were serious.

"Dial the number Tiah and give him the phone," Lexi said as she knelt down close to Richard.

After two rings, Taz answered the call, curious as to what his new connect could want after they'd just spoken earlier.

"Hey, guy. Just wanted to let you know that my partner will be there to talk future prices and pick up the money tomorrow. I will have your first shipment delivered by 5:00 tomorrow evening," Richard shakily told Taz, who agreed without hesitation.

"Okay, cool. I'll be waiting. You got the address?" Taz asked as he thought about the work that he was going to have to put in now that Rocko was gone.

"Yes, thanks," Richard mumbled dryly as he ended the call.

"Is all the information we need on the paper?" Silk asked Richard.

Lexi, who held the paper with the info on it, answered instead. "A Georgia address, Peachtree Street, Atlanta Towers," she said, reading bits and pieces of info from the paper.

"I know where it's at. How much money we picking up, Richard, and how much you charging them a brick?" Silk asked so she would know how to deal with the men tomorrow.

"Look, y'all can have it all. Just please let me loose. I swear I'll act as if this never happened," Richard pleaded.

"Richard! Richard! Richard, you must didn't fuckin' hear me!" Silk screamed and pulled the trigger, sending a bullet through his calf.

"Ah! Please! It's $9,000 a brick, and he's getting 150. I gave him a break for $1.2 million!" Richard screamed out as he wiggled around frantically with pain racing through his body.

The whole crew's eyes grew big at the amount of money that was waiting to be picked up in Atlanta. All of them knew they could retire after this lick.

The safe contained over a half a mil', and now they had a $1.2 million pickup. They all smiled at their good fortune as Silk went over the deal with Richard, getting every detail from him while he sat there in pain. Silk was well versed in the dope game, so she picked up easily on the agreement. By the time Richard finished talking, she had already come up with what to put on the table for the men.

"Richard, appreciate ya help. It's been real," Silk said motioning for Kya to finish him off as she and the other two girls turned to leave.

"Goodnight, old bastard!"

"Please! No!" Richard screamed as Kya rested her Glock 40 on his head and pulled the trigger. The bullet from the Glock left a small, neat hole in the center of his forehead.

Everybody followed Silk as she led the way out of the mansion and to the car.

"Y'all know what it is. We Atlanta bound, early in the morning," Silk called out as she pushed the Chevy through the darkened Florida streets on the way back to her spot.

Chapter 15

The next day, Mocha called Capone early, with money on her mind. "Hey, boo. Can you talk?" Mocha asked, just in case Diva was around.

"Yeah, I'm cool. Diva still knocked out. What up, baby? You up early," Capone replied as he took his seat on the sofa next to Pewee, who was dumping the money from yesterday on the table.

"You still got me, right?" Mocha demanded more than asked.

"You know I do. How much you talking?" Capone asked, trying to keep Pewee from picking up on their conversation; Pewee would surely blast Capone if he knew he was giving Mocha money.

"I'm in need for real, baby. My car note behind, and you know I'm about to move," Mocha explained as she lay in the bed next to her coked-out baby-daddy Kalil who'd pushed her up to demanding more money from Capone after she told him about the murder that took place.

"So…what you talking?" Capone asked, again amazed at the numerous $1,000 stacks that sat in front of him on the table.

"Boy, we got close to $800,000 in this bitch!" Pewee screamed, smiling from ear to ear.

Capone also smiled at the amount of money they had as Mocha sat on the phone putting in her request.

"I need $50,000, baby. That would set me right," she said, knowing it was probably a small amount compared to all the money she'd seen on the table the night before.

"Huh? Did you say $50,000!?" Capone spat, making Pewee look at him.

"Naw, nigga. We sitting on close to $800,000!" Pewee chimed in, thinking Capone was talking to him.

"Nigga, not you. Girl, you tripping. I ain't got it like that," Capone replied. He did have it, but he refused to hand over that much money to her.

"So you can't help me with a lil' $50,000 out of all that money I saw on the table?" she asked as Kalil frowned in the background.

"Nah, baby. I ain't got it like that. I can hit you with ten stacks at the most," Capone said firmly as Pewee looked at him sideways.

"Ten ain't going to help me. I need $50,000, Capone," Mocha said, raising her voice.

"Like I said, ain't nothing on that end, straight up," Capone spat, not caring if Pewee picked up on the conversation anymore.

"Oh, so it's like that? Well, Sherm, Rocko's partner, may help me out. Yeah, I knew Rocko—knew him well enough that I aborted his baby years ago when I first came to Atlanta. Don't even trip it though. I'll just call Sherm," Mocha spat, then hung up the phone angrily, exposing more than she wanted to in front of Kalil.

Capone read between the lines real well. He knew Mocha was telling him that if he didn't pay the $50,000, she would tell Sherm. It was straight-up blackmail. "Fuck!" Capone cursed out loud, getting Pewee's attention.

"Nigga, what up? You good?" Pewee asked as he split the stacks up between them.

"I'm good. Ain't shit." Capone brushed him off as he thought about the grave mistake he had made by telling Mocha about the murder. He was familiar with the nigga Sherm, who was considered dangerous in the streets of the A, and he knew that more than likely, there would be trouble. On the flipside, if the police got word, he would be facing life in prison. Capone knew that he would have to silence Mocha by paying her or killing her. He most definitely had to shut her up, one way or the other.

"Just hit the nigga Sherm up and see if he willing to kick down for info on his patna's murder," Kalil insisted as Mocha still fumed.

"I'ma see if Capone get right first. He going to come through, but if he don't, I'm going to call Sherm," Mocha said, now thinking how things could get detrimental.

"Man, fuck waiting on that nigga! Just hit Sherm up now and see what he willing to do for the info," Kalil demanded, knowing that Sherm would have Capone killed before nightfall. Kalil hated Capone from day one, when Mocha told him about how Capone was paying for company. Kalil knew there was more to it than she was telling him, but he rolled with it because the money helped pay for his coke habit. Now he had a way to really capitalize off the man he despised, so right then Kalil made up his mind to take matters in his own hands. He would tell Sherm himself, even if Mocha didn't.

"Let's just wait and see what he do," Mocha told Kalil as she rolled over and kissed him on the chest.

"All right. We will see," Kalil said as he thought about the best way to get in touch with Sherm.

Chapter 16

After not sleeping well, Sherm got up and headed down to his personal gym and did a thirty-minute workout to relieve a lil' stress before he headed to the office for the meeting Taz had set up with the new connect.

After showering and putting on a pair of jeans and a polo button-up, Sherm sat at his home office desk and counted out the $1.2 million for the buy. The Rocko lick had set him back, so now he was forced to get extra to make up for the loss.

Rocko's funeral was set for the weekend; his preacher brother had made all of the arrangements. Sherm had offered his help, but his brother shunned him, blaming him for Rocko's death. Sherm respected his brother's wishes and stayed away during the whole ordeal. Sherm made plans to go by the funeral home early and pay his respects to his partner and be out before his family showed up, while Taz declined altogether, stating his hate for wakes and funerals.

Getting himself together, Sherm grabbed the money and headed out to the office. As he passed the exact spot downtown where Rocko had died, he said a silent prayer and promised revenge. He made a mental note to get with Rufus later to see if he had heard anything.

Arriving at the office ten minutes later, Sherm grabbed the bags and tucked his Desert Eagle in his waist as he exited the car, keeping an eye out for anybody who looked suspicious. Getting on the elevator, Sherm pushed the button for the twenty-third floor and stood patiently waiting for the elevator to reach the top. Seconds later, the doors opened, he stepped off and was greeted by Deondra, his personal secretary, along with Taz. "Morning," Sherm said as Deondra greeted him with watery eyes, still feeling down over Rocko's death.

Taz was different. He smiled and grabbed the bags from Sherm's grip as they headed back to the conference room. Sherm had love for Taz, and they went back before him and Rocko. That was the main reason Taz resented Rocko, who had come in as a partner and started running the show. Now that Rocko was dead and out the way, Taz was going to prove to Sherm that he could handle Rocko's end without a problem.

Sherm pulled out a bottle of wine and poured them a glass as they waited for the pick up.

"Bro, I contacted all the workers around the city, and everybody is in line. All the weight clientele have been contacted and given my contact info. Most had already heard about Rocko. They all offered their condolences and placed their orders. Bruh, them 150 might not be enough," Taz explained to Sherm, hiding his happiness with the fact that he was now the man running the show.

"So everybody on the same page now?" Sherm asked as he poured himself a glass of the expensive red wine that he kept on the table for guests and looked out at the cloudy sky.

"Yep. Everybody been taken care of," Taz said with confidence, thinking just how nice it would be to be in Sherm's position.

Chapter 17

The T.I. CD played softly from the rented Cadillac Escalade sound system as Silk and the team headed to Atlanta.

"After this shit here, we all need to take a long vacation," Tiah suggested as she fixed the cleavage on her Versace dress.

All the girls dressed expensively and adorned their wrists, fingers, and necks with their biggest diamonds. Silk knew they needed to look like money while going to pick up $1.2 million.

Silk hadn't been back to Atlanta since she'd taken out the NWM clique because she knew people were looking for her for all the wrong reasons. She thought about her days with Sherm as he terrorized the city. She felt bad that he was still sitting in a down-south Georgia prison, which was where she assumed he would be for life. She had tried to get the money to free him but didn't succeed causing them to fall out. Silk had crossed many people in the city, so going back to the A had her tense and paranoid. As they got closer, she thought about Brandie, Zay, Trudy, Sherm, and all the blood that had been shed by her hands. She just wanted to get the money and go.

"How much longer we got?" Lexi asked as she looked down at her diamond-filled Cartier watch.

"We coming up on the city limits now," Silk responded as she went over the figures in her head that Richard had relayed to her about the deal. Silk was well versed in the game, and she knew she couldn't seem lost when talking business with the people she was about to meet. She hoped Richard had enough clout in those men's eyes for them just to accept the price and hand over the money without all the extra talking. Not about to go in ill prepared, though, Silk had a Plan B: *If they don't hand over the money, we'll just take it.* "All y'all loaded up and strapped?" Silk asked, making sure everybody had their pieces secured under their expensive designer clothing.

"Yeah. We good and ready for whatever," Lexi spoke up for everybody.

"All right. This is the deal. We're going in to pick this money up for a shipment that's supposed to be delivered by me and Richard at 5:00 this evening. I'm going to let them know that the shipment will be courier-delivered in computer boxes. I'm putting them under the impression that Richard is handling the shipment, while I'm handling the business. Remember, y'all work for me and Richard. Ladies, we going in calm and cool, but if they don't buy into our plan, we just going to let 'em have it and take what we came to get. Everything should go smoothly, but in the event that it doesn't, be prepared to draw down and get to it. Y'all wit' me?" Silk asked, making sure there was no hesitation in the truck.

"I'm ready," Tiah spoke up first.

"Let's get it!" Lexi screamed.

"Fuck easy. Let's just wet these bitches and grab the loot," Kya joked, but she was dead serious.

"Listen, y'all. This office building is going to have a lot of foot traffic, so if we have to bust and leave, make sure you are discreet. I'm going to leave the keys under the seat just in case. Everybody make sure you keep your phone on you, because ain't no telling how this shit may turn out," Silk told them as they neared downtown Atlanta. Seeing the city again brought back a crazy feeling for Silk that made her pull her backup pistol from the arm rest and lay it in her lap.

Chapter 18

$\mathcal{K}$alil hastily left the apartment after a rough episode of wild sex with Mocha that left her still sleeping. He headed out to the barbershop on Glenwood, where he knew he could find someone who knew Sherm. As he pulled up, he saw that the shop was packed. Pulling the door and stepping in, he noticed all the stares from the old-school playas that sat in each chair. Fly Cut was owned by the well-known old playa Fly Willie. His shop catered to the old-school playas from around the city, and they were all like family. This new, unfamiliar face brought on a lot of stares.

Noticing a familiar face in the crowd, Kalil made his way over to the third chair. "Hey, Benny. I need your help. I'm trying to get in contact with the nigga Sherm that bought Volt Audio from Paco. I got some real important shit to pass his way," Kalil said, knowing Benny could contact Sherm or would at least know someone who could.

"Say, young blood. You want me to interrupt my haircut and find somebody for you…for free?" Benny said in disbelief, letting Kalil know he had to pay for the info he was asking for.

"Bro, I got some very important info for him," Kalil said again.

Benny sat back without responding. "Go light around the front," Benny told his barber, like Kalil wasn't even there.

"A'ight, man. Here a C-note. Can you help me?" Kalil asked now

Benny held up two fingers.

Irritated, Kalil reached in his back pocket. "Two? Man, come on now."

After folding and placing the two $100 bills in his pocket, Benny pulled out his cell phone and made a call to his playa patna. "Yo, money man, I need a favor," Benny said as his old-school patna Rufus lounged around his spacious luxury condo with White Girl.

"Speak ya piece, bruh," Rufus said as White Girl rubbed his feet as they watched an old Pam Grier movie.

"I need to get some digits on Sherm. Lil' jit 'round here got some info for him. He seems to be upstanding," Benny added, giving Kalil his stamp of approval.

Rufus knew that nine times out of ten, the man looking to get in touch with Sherm wanted to pass info on the murder to him. Rufus wasn't about to hesitate in helping Sherm get to the bottom of the senseless act. "His direct number is (678) 628-7974. Tell him I gave you the digits so he won't be reluctant to deal," Rufus instructed while White Girl gave him some head.

"Good looking out, bruh. I'll holla," Benny said and ended the call.

Kalil stood waiting, hoping for some good news.

"Write this down or remember it, 'cause I don't give a fuck. His direct number is (678) 628-7974. Tell him Rufus gave you the digits so he'll fuck wit' ya, " Benny said as he gave his barber a flick of the hand to resume his cut.

Kalil kept repeating the number as he pulled a pen from his pocket. He wrote the number on his hand and hurried back out to his car. He pulled his cell from the charger and dialed Sherm's number.

"Hello?" Sherm answered as he sat at the large conference table sipping on his second glass of wine.

"Is this Sherm?" Kalil asked, hoping he had the right person on the line.

"Who want to know?" Sherm replied in a snappy tone.

"Bruh, my name Kalil. I got your number from Rufus," Kalil said.

"What you need, people?" Sherm asked, calming down after hearing Rufus's name.

"Man, I got some info that can help you out," Kalil said firmly as he thought of the best way to ask for a reward.

"Help me out? What you talking about, people?" Sherm asked curiously, not really sure where the conversation was going.

"What's the reward for info on your partner Rocko?" Kalil blurted out.

At the mention of Rocko's name, Sherm set his glass down and sat up in his chair. "You got info on the hit?" Sherm asked in a serious tone.

"Can we meet?" Kalil asked, noticing the seriousness in Sherm's tone.

"Yeah, meet me now at the Urban Spoon on Peachtree Street," Sherm told him sharply.

"That'll work. I'm right up the street from it," Kalil replied as he smiled, thinking about the money he was about to make.

Chapter 19

" *Y*o, Taz, hold the office down for a min'. I got to make a quick run," Sherm said, not revealing what was going on.

"I got you. Are you going to be back before the connect arrive?" Taz asked, hoping he wouldn't so he could finally feel like a true boss and broker a big-money deal.

"Yeah. I'm just stepping out for a couple of minutes. I won't be long," Sherm assured him as he picked up the crystal wine glass and downed the remaining liquid in one big gulp.

"A'ight. I got you," Taz said, his eyes fixated on the bags of money that sat under the far table.

"Make sure you keep a close eye on that bread. I ain't trying to catch no murder case, but you know I will," Sherm said with emphasis after seeing him looking greedily at the bags.

"Ain't nobody going nowhere with that loot, bruh. Over my dead body," Taz said strongly, knowing Sherm was dead serious and also dangerous. Taz always wondered what had made Sherm put the pistol down and start dealing dope. At one time, Sherm had been the talk of the city when it came to robbing and murking niggas.

"That's my nigga," Sherm said as he rushed out the door to the elevator and down to his car. Just as he sat behind the wheel of his Benz, his cell phone rang. "Yo," Sherm answered, not recognizing the out-of-state number.

"Hi. I'm Detective Lance Tarver, with the NYPD. While conducting a criminal investigation, we found your number in the victim's pocket. We are—"

Sherm cut the man short. "NYPD? Sir, I'm sorry, but I can't help you. Have a nice day," Sherm replied and hung up, wondering what the call was all about. Before he could cradle his phone it rang again. "Sir, I just told you I don't know nothing about what y'all got going on up there…" Sherm paused. As soon as Sherm made reference to "up there," he realized the call must be about Diego.

"Hello? Hello?" the detective called out, trying to see if Sherm was still on the line.

"NYPD? Did you say victim?" Sherm asked in a concerned tone, hoping Diego was all right.

"Yes. We found your number in the deceased's pocket. We have tried to contact his next of kin, but we're not having any luck," the detective explained as Sherm pushed the Benz down Peachtree Street en route to the Urban Spoon to meet Kalil.

"So you telling me my friend is dead?" Sherm said faintly.

"Was Lance Diego your friend?" the detective asked firmly.

"Yeah." Sherm was lost for words as he thought about his two partners getting killed in the same week. He felt the game closing in on him, and now he felt he had to lash out to get the streets back in perspective.

"Sir?" the detective called out, hearing nothing on the other end.

"Fuck!" Sherm screamed as he gripped the steering wheel more tightly than normal.

"Sir, do you have a point of contact with Mr. Diego's family?" the detective asked.

"Yeah. His sister's and mama's numbers are…" Sherm gave the detective Diego's sister's and mother's number and grilled him on potential suspects.

The detective promised to keep him updated and ended the call.

Arriving at the Urban Spoon, Sherm whipped the Benz into the parking lot recklessly, almost hitting a young college student who was walking to her car. Sherm had made up his mind that it was time to tame the streets once again. He made plans to head up north as soon as his business in Atlanta was taken care of.

Kalil sat in the far corner of the parking lot in his late-model Ford Focus, smoking a cigarette while he waited for Sherm to show up. As soon as the Benz pulled in the lot, Kalil smiled and stubbed out the cigarette.

Chapter 20

" *I* can't believe this bitch done tried me like this," Capone said to himself as he got dressed. The only thing on his mind was getting his hands on Mocha. Pewee and Peaches had left to go to the mall, and Diva was out pampering herself, so it was a good time to put his plan in effect. He pulled out his cell phone and dialed her number.

"Hey, boo," she answered, hoping Capone was ready to pay up.

"Come through. I'm going to give you that fifty," he told her as he went over his plans in his head once again.

"Thanks, baby. I'm on my way," Mocha replied happily, thanking Kalil for making her go hard for more money.

Capone knew she wouldn't waste time getting to his spot, so he moved fast. After tucking the .22 in his jacket pocket, he lit up a cigarette and waited for Mocha to show. At first, he'd actually thought about paying her, but he knew she would just demand more money, so the best thing to do was to silence her for good. He loved the black beautiful Mocha, but he loved himself more.

Ten minutes went by, and she still hadn't shown up. Picking up his phone to call her again, he heard a car outside and peeked out of the blinds and saw it was her pulling up. He exited the house before she could get out of the car. "Hey, baby. Run me up to Run & Shoot right quick. I can't get in the lockbox. Pewee put the key somewhere, and he ain't answering his phone," Capone said as he got in the car, not waiting for her to answer.

Mocha backed up and sped out into the street, en route to Metropolitan to Run & Shoot. "I really appreciate you looking out for me, baby," she cooed, as if she hadn't done anything wrong.

"Baby, you know I got you," Capone replied as if everything was cool.

"We hooking up tonight?" Mocha asked as she rubbed her free hand up her thick thigh, causing he skirt to rise up, exposing her smooth black leg.

Seeing her thick, smooth black thigh, Capone started having second thoughts about his whole plan. After a few seconds, he shook it off while reaching in his pocket rubbing the butt of the .22. "Diva working tonight, so it's all good on my end," Capone replied as they neared the Run & Shoot gym.

"It's a date then," Mocha purred as she looked over at Capone seductively.

Capone fought the temptations with all his might. His hard-on was obvious in the loose-fitting jogging pants he wore. "Pull up on the side," Capone told Mocha as she entered the parking lot.

Pulling the old Saab to the side of the building, Mocha looked around for Pewee.

"I'll be right back," Capone told her as he pushed the squeaky car door open

George Sherman Hudson

and got out. He walked to the front of the building and looked around to make sure the coast was clear before heading back to the car. He walked back up to the driver side of the car and motioned for Mocha to roll her window down.

"Yeah? What's up?" she asked with a hint of attitude, thinking Capone was about to come with an excuse about the money.

"Everything good. Give me that pen over there," Capone told her, eyeing the pen he had purposely dropped on the passenger side floor.

Looking over and seeing the pen, Mocha leaned over to get it.

Capone looked around quickly one more time. Seeing that the coast was clear, he pulled the .22 out of his pocket. Before Mocha could sit back up, a loud *pop* went off. The bullet pierced the back of her head, causing her to jerk forward, but to his surprise, the single shot didn't kill her instantly.

Mocha slowly turned back and looked at him with sad eyes. The blood spurted from the back of her head from the hole the .22 made.

Capone started to shoot her again, but he heard a car coming in their direction. He looked around again to make sure no one was around, then took off to catch the bus home. He knew in due time, Mocha would be dead.

Chapter 21

Sherm pulled into the Urban Spoon parking lot and looked around for the mysterious caller. Circling the lot one time, Sherm noticed a skinny, lanky nigga standing next to an old Ford Focus. Pulling up next to the man, Sherm rolled his window down. "Kalil?" Sherm asked the man as he looked him up and down.

"Yeah...Sherm?" Kalil asked in response.

"Get in," Sherm instructed as he clicked the unlock button on his doors.

Kalil hurried around the car, jumped in, and settled into the passenger seat. "I got some info on you friend Rocko's murder. I know who killed him," Kalil said with confidence.

"Oh yeah? How you know who killed my people?" Sherm asked with aggression in his voice, thinking about both of his partners that would be six feet deep soon.

"I...uh...what's the reward for the, um...info?" Kalil stammered, uneasy at the anger written all over Sherm's face.

"I got you, nigga, but right now I need to know who killed my nigga," Sherm spat as he pulled the Benz to the far corner of the lot.

"I feel you, bruh, but...but I got to at least have a lil'...well, a lil' something before I give up a name," Kalil stuttered, obviously shaken by the man he knew was very dangerous.

"What, nigga!" Sherm snapped as he snatched his Desert Eagle from his waist and put it to the side of Kalil's head.

"Wha...wait! Man, please! It was Capone and Pewee! Please, bruh!" Kalil screamed as Sherm continued to press the cold steel to the side of his head.

After processing the info that Kalil had spat, Sherm lowered the gun and thought about the two men he was familiar with from his days sticking niggas up. Pewee and Capone were from the new generation, two heartless young niggas who'd made a name for themselves real fast in the streets. "Get out," Sherm told Kalil as he tucked the gun back in his waist.

"Man..." Kalil said as he pushed the door open to get out. As he turned and headed back to his car, he heard something hit the ground next to him. He looked down and saw a wad of money, secured with a rubber band. Then he looked over at Sherm, who was now speeding out of the lot, heading back to his office.

Minutes later, Sherm was back in the office at the conference table with Taz, waiting on the connect. While they waited, Sherm picked up the phone and called Poochie. Sherm gave him specific instructions to make Capone and Pewee disappear, then told him where to pick up his $80,000.

Chapter 22

"We're here, ladies," Silk announced as they pulled the truck into the building parking deck.

"Major people we seeing, huh?" Kya asked as she looked up at the tall building that housed lawyers and other professionals' offices.

"What did you expect when you're picking up $1.2 million?" Tiah chimed in.

"Look, y'all, don't forget I'm doing about all the talking. Y'all just watch my back and follow my lead. If these niggas freeze up on the deal, we just going to take the money, so be ready to get down if it comes to it. Turn your sexy on, and let's get this money," Silk said as they all exited the truck and made their way to the building's elevator. As they got on the elevator, Silk pulled the paper out with the info on it and saw they were going to the top floor. As soon as she pressed the button for the top floor, the elevator doors closed, but it didn't move. She pushed the button again, but the elevator still wasn't going anywhere. "What the fuck's wrong with this shit?" Silk uttered as she kept tapping the button while her crew looked around the elevator for more buttons.

"May I help you?" A woman's voice boomed from the elevators intercom.

The girls jumped at the sudden intrusion of the unseen person.

"We trying t..." Tiah started but was quickly cut off by Silk.

"I'm here to see Taz on behalf of myself and Richard. We have a very important meeting," Silk explained in her best business voice.

"Hold please," Sherm's secretary Deondra replied as she picked up the desk phone and called Sherm in the conference room.

While waiting for the lady to come back on the intercom, the girls got into their role just in case they were being watched through a hidden camera. Without warning, the elevator came to life, and the button for the top floor lit up. No one spoke as the elevator crept its way to the top.

Ding!

The elevator stopped, and the doors opened to an expensively furnished office lobby with Sherm's secretary, Deondra, sitting behind an oversized, custom-made marble desk, taking calls. Seeing the girls step off of the elevator caught her totally by surprise. She didn't expect to see such attractive young black women dressed in such classy attire with diamonds everywhere; girls like that didn't usually show up for this kind of meeting. Deondra had been with Sherm for some time now, and she was very aware of what the meetings entailed, so seeing Silk and her girls caught her totally off guard.

"Hi. I'm here to see Taz," Silk told Deondra as she approached the desk with the girls following close behind.

"They waiting on you. Right this way," Deondra told Silk as she led them over to a pair of large wooden sliding doors.

Knock! Knock!

"Yeah?" Sherm yelled.

"Your visitors are here, sir," Deondra announced.

"Send them in," Sherm yelled back as he stood at the head of the table, waiting for his guest to enter.

As Silk entered, she took in the immaculate setting, not recognizing the man who stood before her. As she got closer, her heart dropped at the sight of the man who had given her the game on every level—the only man she'd ever really loved.

Sherm's mouth fell open at the sight of Silk dressed in a form-fitting, expensive designer dress with big diamonds on her hands and wrists.

Silk froze, then instinctively grabbed at her clutch that held her back-up .380.

Not seconds later, Sherm was reaching in his jacket pulling his Desert Eagle.

Taz and the girls looked on, confused at the drastic turn of events, not knowing what had just happened or what moves to make.

Chapter 23

*P*oochie stood around six feet even and weighed about 150 pounds soaking wet. His high yellow skin tone was pale and freckled. Having been a basketball star in his younger days at Banneker High in College Park, Georgia, he was very popular until his stardom faded when a tragic car accident that killed his mom killed his hoop dreams as well. He was also cursed with a slightly disfigured nose that had him wheezing with every breath he took and a hard limp that looked as if he was dragging his right leg.

After dropping out of school, Poochie moved in with his dad and got knee-deep in the streets. He had tried his hand at every hustle the streets had to offer, but couldn't succeed in any of them. After Walt Lee saw that Poochie didn't possess any hustle, he sent him out in a different direction. Walt Lee gave his son a .45 automatic and promised him $5,000 when the job was done. Tre's death was the talk of the streets; he had been shot four times in the face at point-blank range. Poochie had killed him in front of his wife and kids, then eased off like a thief in the night. Every since that day, Poochie had been killing for the right price and for only a certain few.

Poochie and Sherm had a special relationship, being that Sherm was the only reason he was still living. Back in the day when Sherm was robbing niggas blind, Poochie had been hired by Black Steve, one of the city's biggest dope dealers, to take Sherm out. Steve knew Sherm was the one who'd hit him for the $90,000, and he wanted him dead for it. Poochie set out to take care of the job, but while trying to creep, he ended up getting crept on by Sherm. Sherm held the .9mm to his head and started to pull the trigger until he recognized Ms. Freeda lil' boy Poochie from his old hood. Sherm spared Poochie's life that day, and they'd been in touch ever since. Months later, Black Steve was found floating in the Chattahoochee River with a gunshot to the face, Poochie's signature.

The streets were very aware of Sherm and Poochie's affiliation. They knew if anybody crossed Sherm, the Grim Reaper, aka Poochie, would be on their trail, seeking their soul.

Poochie sat in his Econoline van, scoping out the club. He'd found out through one of his sources that the two niggas he was hunting was fucking with two dancers at Drop It. After getting all the info on Peaches and Diva, Poochie set out to put his mission into effect. Poochie sat in the parking lot of the club, waiting for the right chance. After seeing the crowded parking lot die down, he eased out of his van and over to the cherry-red Chrysler 300 that fit the description of the car his source had told him about. Easing up next to the car, Poochie knelt down, pulled his hunting knife from his boot, and swiftly jabbed it in the tire, causing it to go flat in seconds. Satisfied with his work, he turned and eased back into the van. While he waited for the driver of the 300 to show up, he pulled out his handheld game and played *Urban Commando*.

Thirty minutes later, two women in tight-fitting clothes approached the car. Poochie rubbed his crotch in response to their revealing clothing. He laid the game down and watched them as they entered the car, obviously unaware of the flat tire. The 300 pulled off, but before they could exit the lot, they pulled over and got out to see what was wrong with the car.

"Damn! A fuckin' flat!" Diva spat as they both checked out the tire.

Seeing them stop and get out, Poochie sprang into action, but before he got to the scene, one of the girls turned and walked back to the club to get help. Just as he was about to swoop down on Diva, an old-school customized convertible full of three dreaded-out young thugs with sparkling gold grills pulled up next to her. After a brief conversation, they all got out and went to work putting her spare on the car. Poochie retreated to the van, pissed at the interference. By the time Peaches got back, the spare was on and numbers were exchanged.

"Damn, girl. Todd was going to change it," Peaches said as she lit up the blunt of Kush.

"Boy, they did a real good job. They going to be mad when they call Pizza Hut though." Diva laughed.

"No you didn't!" Peaches called out as she passed Diva the blunt.

They danced in their seats as they passed the blunt back and forth while Poochie followed close behind in his old van, a vehicle he dubbed as his *Murder Machine*.

Chapter 24

"Hold up! What the hell going on!?" Taz yelled as he fumbled around, trying to pull his gun then realizing it was in the car.

"Shit!" Kya yelled as her and all of the other girls pulled their weapons and aimed them at Sherm and Taz.

"Sherm…?" Silk said, then paused as she held her gun on the man she still loved.

"Silk! What the hell is this?" Sherm asked, knowing Silks M.O. as he kept the Desert Eagle pointed at her.

"Hey, man, can everybody just put the guns down please?" Taz pleaded as he looked from Silk to the other girls who were clearly ready to pull the triggers if Silk gave the word.

Tiah, Kya, and Lexi acted as if Taz was talking to himself. They didn't budge and kept their guns pointed at the men. Silk and Sherm also kept their stance. They knew they had to make sure everybody was on the same page before they let their guard down. The air in the room was thick as everyone stood with their guns drawn.

Silk knew sooner or later a trigger was going to be pulled if everyone stood firm, so she spoke up. "Put 'em up, girls. Everything cool," Silk said as she also lowered her gun.

Taz breathed a sigh of relief as all the women in the room lowered their weapons.

Sherm laid his Desert Eagle on the table and took a seat at the conference table, never taking his eyes off of Silk. "You my new contact, huh?" Sherm said with a hint of sarcasm.

"Only if you agree to our terms," Silk told Sherm as she walked over and sat in front of him at the table.

"Could everyone please excuse us?" Sherm asked, wanting to speak to Silk in private.

The girls didn't budge as Taz signaled for them to follow him out of the room. Seeing their reluctance, Silk nodded her head, and only then did they follow Taz out to the front lobby.

Deondra was on the phone gossiping as Taz ushered the crew over to the leather chairs, where he sat with them in silence as Sherm and Silk conducted the meeting. They were all still lost and confused by Silk's and Sherm's reactions when they saw each other, but they all knew for a fact that the two knew each other.

"Silk, Silk, Silk," Sherm murmured as he looked across the table at Silk with diamonds sparkling and looking more beautiful than he remembered.

"How you get…how long have you been out?" Silk asked softly, surprised to see Sherm.

"You meant to ask how long have I been out since you left me to rot," Sherm spat, frowning.

"Sherm, now you know it wasn't even like that. I still remember the shit like it was yesterday. I was out literally killing niggas just to get the money to get you out, but it wasn't coming fast enough. I tried to explain shit to you, but you blew, then you heard a nigga in the background and really lost it without hearing me out," Silk explained as her eyes started to water. Sherm was the only man in the world whom Silk was weak for. She had put her life on the line for him many times, but she hated that he never gave her credit for her actions.

"I remember it like it was yesterday too. You was supposed to be out checking a sucker bout some paper, but you all up in the house—*our* house—with a nigga! I made you, Silk, and you played me! I was sitting in a stanking-ass prison cell with a whole bunch of fuck niggas and wannabes, and you out fucking and sucking instead of getting the money to free me! Now give me three reasons why I shouldn't kill yo' ass right now!" Sherm said angrily as he snatched up the Desert Eagle off the table and put it directly in Silk's face.

Silk never flinched.

Chapter 25

Poochie followed behind the girls at a longer distance than he normally would, being that it was still light outside and his van was highly recognizable. His *Murder Machine* darted in and out of traffic, trying to keep up with the Chrysler 300. Poochie cursed himself for not filling up with gas as he noticed his red low fuel light blinking on and off, but he refused to stop and kept following the 300. Five minutes later, the girls pulled into The Oaks apartments off of Sullivan Road. Poochie pulled in behind them and stayed out of sight.

"Girl, grab that bottle of Hen out of the back," Diva told Peaches as they pulled the 300 to a stop in front of their apartment.

"You got the green?" Peaches asked as she grabbed the Hen and the box of blunts from the backseat.

"You know it!" Peaches sang out, holding the bag of Kush up, dancing in her seat.

The girls were tipsy, high, and ready to party with their men, unaware that Poochie was watching them from a couple cars over as he loaded his twelve-gauge, eight-shot, pistol-grip pump. Not relying solely on his gun, he tucked his hunting knife in his boot.

After grabbing everything out of the car, the girls headed in. Poochie watched them and thought about how they would become casualties as well. Grabbing his handheld game from the passenger seat, Poochie got comfortable and played *Urban Commando* while waiting for darkness to come.

The girls walked in to find Pewee and Capone playing an intense game of dominoes and smoking a blunt while Yo Gotti rapped from the apartment's shabby sound system.

"Hey! Hey! What do ya say!" Diva and Peaches sang, one with the bag of Kush and the other one with the bottle of liquor held up high as they sashayed over to the men.

"Fifteen!" Pewee spat as he slammed the domino down, ignoring the loud and rowdy Peaches and Diva as they approached and focused more on the $500 bet they had on the game.

"You ain't said nothing. Twenty nigga!" Capone screamed back as he wrote his points down on a torn strip of paper.

"Nigga, write my money down!" Pewee snapped as he looked intently at the bones connected on the table.

"Yeah, nigga, write his money down!" Peaches chimed in jokingly as her and Diva sat on their laps.

"Bitch, yo' nigga losing like hell anyway!" Diva laughed as she grabbed the torn strip of score paper and held it up.

"Yeah, nigga. Ten more points, and I'm out. That's zeehee, nigga. You still in your first house. Double money, nigga!" Capone boasted as he pulled the blunt, held the smoke, and then passed it to Pewee.

"Nigga, it ain't over 'til it's over. Twenty more!" Pewee called out, looming over at the score paper and seeing Capone write down fifteen instead of twenty.

"Nigga, you need hope and a prayer to get out of this weaver," Capone said, laughing as he pulled bones from the bone yard.

"I can beat you and the pen, nigga. You shorted me five! You probably been shorting me the whole game! It's all good, though, nigga. Pull the two three board locked, fool. Get 'em all!" Pewee called out as he slammed his last bone on the table.

Capone grabbed all of the bones from the bone yard and flipped them over. He knew he had lost when he saw all of the sixes and fives. "Fuck! Lucky-ass nigga!" Capone said as he reached in his pocket counted out $500 and slammed it on the table in front of Pewee.

Peaches didn't waste any time grabbing the money and tucking it in her shirt. She smiled, then stuck her tongue out, taunting Diva and Capone.

"Fuck you, bitch," Diva spat laughing as she raised up off of Capone's lap.

"That's what's up! Fuck me and this $500." Peaches laughed as she leaned over and kissed Pewee.

Getting up from the table, Diva, Pewee, and Capone headed into the den and lit up a blunt while Peaches went to the kitchen and poured everybody up a glass of Hen.

"Girl, where you at?" Diva called out to Peaches as the blunt went around for the third time.

"On my way!" Peaches called out as she filled the last glass.

"A'ight. This shit is almost gone," Pewee yelled back as Diva passed him the blunt for the fourth time.

"Puff, puff, pass, nigga!" Capone barked, seeing the blunt getting too short to hit.

"Don't smoke that shit up. I'm coming!" Peaches yelled as the kitchen backdoor creaked open.

Chapter 26

"You really want me dead?" Silk asked as she looked over the barrel of the gun, looking right into Sherm's eyes.

Sherm couldn't deny that he was still crazy about Silk. His love for her outweighed everything at that moment. "What you think? What if I left you to die in a six-by-nine musty cell while I was out fucking some bitch?" Sherm asked forcefully.

"Put the gun down, and let's talk, Sherm." Silk sighed, unfazed by the gun in her face.

"You crossed me in the worst way," Sherm said as he lowered the gun and placed it back on the table.

"I didn't cross you. I put my fuckin' life on the line to get that money to free you, but all I got was cussed out 'cause you heard some nigga in the background," Silk snapped as she snatched Sherm's Desert Eagle off the table and duplicated Sherm's actions by putting the gun back in his face.

"Oh, I see you learned a lot from me, huh? So you going to kill me when I just spared you?" Sherm asked, smiling and unmoved by the shift of events.

"We even now. I just spared you. Clean slate," Silk said and smiled as she laid the gun back down on the table.

"You haven't changed a bit. You a trip. So you connected now, I see," Sherm said getting back to the business at hand.

"Yeah. Me and Richard work hand in hand," Silk replied as she thought about the way Kya had ended his life.

"Oh yeah? Hand in hand?" Sherm said with a sly frown on his face.

Silk picked up on his displeasure. "We hand in hand in business, nothing personal. What you use to always tell me? Never mix business with personal or pleasure," Silk said firmly, correcting her first statement.

"I'm proud of you. You have really come a long way," Sherm said proudly.

"Thanks. Can I tell you something?" Silk asked faintly.

"Yeah," Sherm murmured.

"I never betrayed you, and the man you heard is pushing up daisies as we speak. Everything I did I did for us, but when you flipped out on me after I was almost killed trying to get money for you, I…I just couldn't take it, so I just said fuck it. I was hurt so bad, and I thought about you every day, but I just couldn't find the courage to face you. I'm sorry, baby," Silk explained as her eyes watered.

Sherm looked at her and thought back on the last day they had spoken and remembered not letting her explain or say anything. He had cut her short and hung up the phone. "It's all good," Sherm said softly as he leaned back in his chair.

"Okay. So what's up with this deal. What we talking?" Silk asked, wiping her eyes and getting back to business.

"Taz and Richard brokered this first deal, but I think in the future, we should be getting a better price on each package," Sherm explained, sitting up in his chair.

"You know you already getting a killer deal. What more you looking for?" Silk asked, then gave him a big head-cocked fake smile.

"How about you give 'em to me at eight a piece when we buy 100 or more? Anything less than 100, we stick with original price," Sherm insisted.

Silk sat back, looked up at the ceiling, then replied. "Well, since it's you, I may be able to work that, but your orders got to be consistent at that price," Silk countered, remembering Richard's words. Silk agreed and gave in to Sherm's demands, but deep down, she was feeling bad about what was about to go down.

"That's a deal. The $1.2 million for the first shipment is ready for y'all," Sherm told her, pointing to the bags that sat under the far table.

"Okay, cool. The computers will be delivered by 5:00. Richard and I spoke on my way up. Everything will be official as soon as all the money is collected. Do I need to count it?" Silk asked with a raised eyebrow.

"Do you?" Sherm asked, remembering what he had taught her years ago: *Always count your money.*

"I trust you," Silk said, looking into his eyes and feeling bad about the whole deal.

"It's all yours, counted to the penny," Sherm told her, motioning to the money.

"All right. Hold up," Silk said as she pulled her cell phone out and dialed a number. "Everything a go," Silk said into her own answering machine.

"Get at me when you get back in Miami," Sherm told her as he raised up, walked over, and grabbed the bags for her.

"I will. Your delivery will be here by 5:00," Silk said as she walked up to Sherm and kissed him softly on the lips. Silk felt bad about pulling the move on Sherm, but she was in too deep, and there was no turning back. She knew there would be consequences later, but she was ready to face them, whatever they were.

Sherm had called Taz back in the room, and the girls followed.

Silk had Tiah and Kya grab the money as she and Lexi exited behind them.

"Bruh, you gave them the money before we got the drop?" Taz asked with a confused look on his face.

"Sylvester highly recommended this dude Richard, and I trust her. Besides, she knows I will kill her if shit ain't right," Sherm said, all calm and cool, as he poured himself another drink and thought about Silk.

Chapter 27

Poochie looked at the gas hand on the van and knew he had to move fast; he had to leave the van running like he always did on a lick. He pulled the strap to the pistol-grip pump over his shoulder as he exited the van and limped up to the apartment. Not liking his position, he turned and went around to the backdoor. As he neared the backdoor, he heard noise and laughter coming from inside. He grabbed the knob; it turned, then clicked. Poochie smiled. He pushed it enough to look through the crack. He saw one of the girls from earlier pouring liquor into glasses as she danced and sang. Poochie thought to himself how easy it was going to be. He also knew that the twelve-gauge would wake up the whole apartment complex when it went off back to back, so he made sure he had a quick exit for when he let loose, but he had decided to use his hunting knife first.

Poochie cracked the door some more and eased in behind Peaches, who was dancing and singing so loudly and drunkenly that she never heard him creeping up behind her.

Capone, Pewee, and Diva were steady getting high while Poochie invaded their household.

"Man, I'm fucked up!" Capone slurred as he hit the third blunt of the night.

"Ah, man, you can't hang, baby?" Diva cooed as she leaned over and kissed him on the neck.

"There y'all go, always trying to hunch and shit! Peaches, what the hell you doing, 'cause we 'bout to kill the rest of this blunt?" Pewee yelled as he got up to go see what was taking her so long.

"She 'bout ass out," Capone said faintly, stuck off the Kush.

"Mannnnn!" Pewee called out as he slow walked to the kitchen, high and lightheaded.

"Nigga, get right!" Diva called out, laughing at Pewee as he walked back to the kitchen.

"Girlllllll fuuuuuck yoooou!" Pewee fired back weakly with a big Kool-Aid smile on his face, high off the Kush.

Poochie moved in real slow and quiet like a cat hunting its prey. Just as Peaches was within arm's reach, he struck and grabbed her around the neck and placed his hand over her mouth. "Shh!" he whispered as he tightened his grip.

Peaches struggled helplessly as Poochie handled her like a ragdoll. After getting her under control, he freed one hand, grabbed his hunting knife, brought it up, pressed and slashed it across the soft flesh of her neck.

She gurgled as blood instantly ran from the razor cut. She kicked and squirmed, but it did no good. A few minutes later, everything went dark, and she stopped breathing.

Chapter 28

Five o'clock had come and gone. Sherm and Taz sat in the office waiting for the shipment to arrive. At 8:00, Sherm picked up the phone and called Silk but didn't get an answer. A few minutes later, he called Richard. When he couldn't reach him, he immediately called Sylvester.

"Hello?" Sylvester answered in a disturbed tone.

"Hey, Sylvester. I was trying to reach your people, Richard, to finish our business up. Have you talked to him?" Sherm asked firmly as Taz paced the room, thinking the worst but hoping for the best.

"I guess you haven't heard. I should have contacted you earlier. Thing are crazy down in Florida," Sylvester said as he took a deep breath.

"Crazy? What's going on?" Sherm asked in a concerned tone.

"Richard's daughter found him, his maid, and his chef last night, all shot to death. They say the motive was robbery because Richard's safe was found open and empty," Sylvester explained.

Sherm's first thought was Silk, and then it all registered: the phone call from an obviously shaken Richard. "Robbed and killed?" Sherm asked in an angry tone as his heart dropped. Silk had crossed him.

"Robbed and killed!" Taz screamed as he looked intently at Sherm, trying to see what was going on.

Sherm looked at Taz, then turned his attention back to Sylvester.

"Yeah, got the news last night. They say it was horrible. Poor guy was duct-taped and shot in the head," Sylvester told Sherm as he thought about his old friend.

"Damn. I'll get with you later, Sylvester," Sherm told him abruptly, then ended the call.

He tried Silk's number again, but he still didn't get an answer. Sherm knew then that he'd been got.

"Man, what the hell going on?" Taz asked as he took a seat at the conference room table.

"Man, it's some bullshit in the mix. Richard is dead. He was robbed and killed last night," Sherm said forcefully, thinking about how Silk had just played him out of over a million dollars.

"Do old girl know he dead? Wait…didn't she just call? Fuck!" Taz yelled after thinking about the day's events and realizing how they had been played.

"Silk is a very dangerous woman. She is most likely the one who killed Richard, but you know what? I respect her grind," Sherm said calmly as he picked up the bottle of wine and filled his glass.

"What? Bruh, the bitch just walked out of here with over a million dollars, and we ain't got no product! Man, how the hell you just sitting there all calm and cool?" Taz asked as he stood and started pacing the room.

"I made her the bitch she is today. Really, bro, I'm kind of proud of her for pulling something like this off, but you know what? She made one mistake. She left a witness. I taught her long ago to never leave a witness, and now I'm going to show her what happens when you do. Get ready, bro. We about to take a trip down to Miami," Sherm smiled as he picked up his wine glass and gulped it all down. He had all kind of thoughts running through his head: Rocko, Diego, and all the money he had lost over the last couple of days. Silk had just pushed him back to his old ways, where murder was the common denominator.

Chapter 29

oochie gently laid Peaches on the floor as he got ready to move in. Just as he was about to exit the kitchen, he heard someone coming.

"Girl, where yo' ass at?" Pewee called out as he rounded the corner into the kitchen.

Poochie stood just inside of the doorway and waited. As soon as Pewee stepped into the kitchen, he was met with a sharp blade in the chest. He never had a chance as Poochie dug the razor-sharp hunting knife deep into his chest, puncturing his heart. Pewee grabbed frantically at the knife as Poochie looked him squarely in the eyes and smiled. Pewee doubled over, and Poochie moved out of the way as he slammed, face first, into the floor with the knife protruding from his chest; he wiggled and squirmed in pain as he died.

Diva and Capone were in their own world—high as kites—when Poochie entered the room unnoticed.

"Mmm...yeah," Capone moaned as Diva pulled his dick from his sweats and started sucking. He laid his head back with his eyes closed as Diva took him in and out of her mouth.

Poochie was slightly excited at the show of affection as he entered the room and readied the twelve-gauge shotgun. They never looked up to see him standing in the midst of their session.

"Shit, yes! Damn, girl!" Capone called out, about to cum, but he was jolted out of the moment by a loud, ear-piercing blast.

Boom!

The twelve-gauge gave little recoil as it went off. Diva's head exploded in Capone's lap as her body fell to the floor beside the sofa.

"Oh shit! What the fuck!?" Capone screamed, looking up at Poochie, frightened while wiping frantically at all of the brain matter and pieces of Diva's face in his lap. "Man, hold up, man. Please, man! Man, come on! Man, please!" Capone pleaded as he climbed up the back of the sofa.

Poochie never blinked. He pulled the trigger twice, blowing Capone's hip off, then hitting him in the chest. The whole time, Poochie only thought about the low gas in the van that was idling outside. He didn't waste any time exiting the scene. As soon as he got outside, he saw lights coming on in neighboring apartments. Jumping in the van, he sped off with his fingers crossed, headed to the nearest gas station, hoping he didn't run out of gas.

Chapter 30

"Girls, we straight!" Lexi screamed as Silk navigated the truck back down the highway to Miami.

"Straight ain't the word. It's vacation time…Jamaica!" Tiah added as her and Kya slapped five and bobbed their heads to the Jay-Z blasting from the truck's factory sound system.

The whole while, Silk was silent, lost deep in her thoughts. She thought about Sherm, their past days and the consequences of this million dollar payday. Silk knew Sherm wasn't going to lie down and take the beating lightly. She also knew she would have to be real careful now of her every move. The crazy thoughts in her head had her wanting to just take the money back, plead for forgiveness, and make love to Sherm like she used to do. As fast as those thoughts invaded her mind, Silk dismissed them.

Silk knew leaving Sherm alive was a big mistake, but she didn't have the heart to kill him in cold blood—not the man she still loved. On another note, she was and would be ready to kill him if he came for her; more than likely, when they crossed paths, it would be a life-or-death situation. Silk watched as the sun set and then disappeared as they neared Miami. She thought long and hard while she drove, and ultimately, she planned to retire and lie back, far out of sight.

"Girl, what's up? Why you been so quiet?" Lexi asked in a concerned tone as they exited the highway en route to Silk's place.

"Thinking, girl, that's all," Silk replied as she looked down at the phone they had taken from Richard; she saw that Sherm had called three times. Silk pressed the button to let the window down and tossed it out into the night traffic.

"Pep up, girl!" Tiah shouted in Silk's direction.

"Yeah, we all the way in there. Ain't no looking back now!" Kya added as she looked over at Silk. "I don't mean to pry, but what was up with you and the nigga back there?"

The other girls instantly became quiet. They had been wondering the same thing but didn't want to bring it up if Silk didn't.

"An old friend from back in the day," Silk replied as she made a left at the car dealership up the street from her place.

"Okayyy," Kya said, faintly seeing that Silk didn't want to talk about it.

Minutes later, they were pulling up in front of Silk's spot. "Look, y'all. We got to go in here and get some rest, then get up early in the morning, split all this money, and disappear 'til shit dies down," Silk instructed as they all got out of the truck and headed in.

Kya and Tiah grabbed the money bags and followed Silk and Lexi in.

* * * * *

The next day, Silk went from room to room, waking everybody up except for Kya, who was already up, talking on her cell phone. "I'll get the money from yesterday and meet y'all in the kitchen," Silk told them as they walked through Silk's lavish home. She hurried to the back and got the money from yesterday's lick, then joined the rest of the girls in the kitchen.

They all unloaded the money from both licks and started separating it into denominations.

"Damn! This is what's up!" Tiah said as she looked at all the money spread out all over the table.

"Real talk, girl. It's time for a pampering weekend and wh—" Lexi stopped midsentence when she looked up at the gun pointed at them.

"I got love for y'all, so don't make me use this! All y'all back the fuck up to the wall!"

*K*alil called Mocha's cell phone for the tenth time but still couldn't reach her. He had been up tooting powder and drinking every since getting the money from Sherm the night before. It was unusual for Mocha not to respond to his call or to call and check in, so he kept calling and texting her.

He sat in the apartment sacking up the four and a half ounces of cocaine he had copped from Bull last night. He promised himself, *This time, I'ma grind hard, flip this money, and come up.* He knew the only way to do it was to not get high off his own supply.

Kalil sat at the kitchen table and sacked up $50 and $100 sacks. He planned to hit the trap that day and then stay down until all the dope was sold. As he bagged up his last sack, there was a knock at the door. "Mocha? Where the fuck yo' ass been, and why ain't you got your key?" he mumbled to himself as he got up and walked over to the door to let her in. Something told him to peep out the peephole before he opened the door.

To his surprise, it was the police.

"Shit!" he screamed, high off of the powder. He turned and knocked over the TV stand and stereo system as he clumsily ran to the back of the apartment.

"You hear that? It's something going on in there," Detective Snow said to Officer White as he pulled his service weapon.

"Man, I thought I was just coming over here to deliver the news about a dead gal. Now I got to kick a door in," the racist detective said as he unholstered his weapon as well.

"We going in on the count of three. We don't need another homicide on our hands today," Snow said as he tried to turn the doorknob.

"One…two…three!" White and Snow said in unison as they kicked the thin wooden door in and rushed into the apartment.

Kalil ran to the back and grabbed his .38 while trying to double back for the cocaine he'd left on the table. Before he could get to it, the two officers were coming his way.

"Freeze!" Snow screamed as he turned the corner and came face to face with a high Kalil.

Kalil instantly put his hand up in the air, but he didn't think to drop the gun. *Pop! Pop! Pop!*

Snow didn't hesitate to unload his Glock as White came up from behind him, pulling the trigger on his weapon too.

Kalil's eyes grew as big as golf balls as the bullets struck him repeatedly. The cocaine had him standing tall in the hail of bullets, but after a few seconds, he gave in, crumbled to the floor, and took his last breath.

"Shit!" Snow screamed as he holstered his gun and walked over to Kalil's lifeless body.

"You okay?" White asked as he walked over and stood over Kalil.

"Yeah. I'm all right. When we call it in, we'll let them know he was aggressive and threatening with a firearm. I will doctor up the rest of the reports so we can just sweep it under the rug. Why complain when we getting rid of these ignorant black muthafuckers?" Snow spat as he turned and walked off with White following.

Chapter 32

The next day, Sherm and Taz met in the office parking lot.

"Make sure you pack up all the heat," Sherm told Taz as they geared up for the trip to Miami.

"All taken care of, but why so much firepower and bulletproof vests for a bunch of hoes?" Taz asked as he closed the trunk on the Lincoln rental car.

"Did you see how those hoes drew down on us? Those hoes—or at least that one hoe—is not a bitch to take lightly. Knowing her like I do, I'm sure her friends ain't to be underestimated either," Sherm told Taz as he got behind the wheel of the rental.

"I hear ya. If you say so." Taz shrugged as he settled into the passenger seat for the long ride.

On the way down the highway, they talked business, politics, sports, and religion right up until they reached the Miami city limits. Then, their conversation switched to kidnap and murder. Sherm was set on finding Silk and punishing her to the max for trying him.

"How we going to find them?" Taz asked, looking around at the palm trees and expensive beachfront homes.

"Already taken care of. My Miami connect is on it," Sherm assured Taz as they turned into the hotel parking lot.

Just as they were pulling the car to a halt, Sherm's phone rang. "Yeah, Boski. What you got for me?" Sherm asked, motioning for Taz to get him a piece of paper and something to write with.

"It's 3527 Juniper Court. She is living large. The beachfront house is over a half a million out her way. She was listed as…" Boski filled Sherm in on everything he needed to know about Silk. As he ran all of Silk's details down, he eyed the new female rookie who had been assigned to be his partner. He was determined to have her naked in his bed by the end of the month, even if he had to pull rank, which he had done on previous occasions.

"Good looking out. By the way, did you get your gift?" Sherm asked, referring to the $5,000 cash he'd had Deondra wire him before they left.

"Oh, yessss…much appreciated. I will keep you up to date long as you're here. Just hit me up if you need me," Boski said as he watched the young female rookie apply lip gloss to her wide, thick lips.

Sherm knew it wasn't going to be easy to find Silk, so he didn't waste any time getting in touch with his Miami PD connect. Just as Sherm suspected, Silk was still using her deceased cousin's identity. She even had her house and gym registration in her name.

"We won't be here too long because we paying this bitch Silk a visit tonight,"

Sherm said as he opened his car door and headed to the hotel lobby to get a room.

After securing a room, they strapped up and punched Silk's address into the car's navigation system.

Chapter 33

"What the fuck is this all about, Kya?" Silk spat heatedly as she cursed herself for leaving her gun upstairs in her room.

"Just business. Ain't nothing personal. Now y'all turn around!" Kya barked as Silk, Tiah, and Lexi looked at her with pure hatred.

"If you going to kill me, you going to do it facing me! This shit is fucked up, Kya. We all supposed to be a family. It ain't got to be like this!" Lexi screamed as she waited for the right time to make a move for her gun that was lying on the kitchen table.

"Come on now, Kya. Don't do this. Please!" Tiah pleaded as her eyes started to water.

Silk knew when Kya told them to turn around what it was: She didn't have the heart to kill them face to face. Silk also knew Kya planned on leaving them dead before she exited the house. "Kya, just get the money and go. We respect your decision, so just pack it all up and be on your way. Take it all," Silk said calmly, trying to buy time to think of a way out of the situation. She would have to make a move soon if she planned on living to see tomorrow.

"Turn around!" Kya screamed, ignoring all of their pleas.

"Fuck this shit!" Lexi screamed as she went for her pistol.

Pop! Pop! Pop!

The bullets from the .45 automatic punctured Lexi's flesh with ease, causing her to grab at every entrance hole like she was trying to put out a fire. Her breathing sped up, and she fell to the floor, holding her chest.

Just as the gun went off, Silk sprang into action, knowing it was now or never. Tiah followed her lead as she ran for cover, but she didn't get far before a wild shot hit her in the back of her head, sending her face first into the soft, plush, expensive carpet.

"Fuck!" Silk said as she scrambled to get away.

Kya took off behind her as she ran upstairs, trying to get to her gun.

Pop! Pop!

Kya fired recklessly, hoping she'd get a lucky shot in as she ran behind a fleeing Silk.

Silk took the steps by twos, and in seconds, she was busting through her bedroom door, trying to get to the nightstand to get her gun.

Just as Silk reached her weapon, Kya stepped in the room. "Bitch!" Kya screamed as she let off shot after shot. The .45 automatic bullets ripped clean through Silk's leg and arm.

"Ah!" Silk screamed out in pain, holding her hands out in front of her as if she could block the bullets.

Seconds later, the gun clicked empty. Kya surveyed the damage done to Silk and knew that before long, she would be dead. She hurried downstairs to pack up all of the money. As she stepped around Lexi and Tiah, who were still fighting to live, she breathed a sigh of relief knowing that she wouldn't have to be looking over her shoulder anymore. They'd all be dead soon enough. After packing up all the money, Kya scooped the rental truck keys off the table and exited the house with a broad smile on her face.

Silk lay in the floor in a growing pool of blood. Her whole life was flashing before her as the pain from the bullets grew. A single tear ran down her face as she struggled to stay conscience and alert. She tried to crawl over to the phone, but her body wouldn't let her. On the third attempt, she blacked out.

Chapter 34

herm and Taz waited for the navigational system to pick up Silk's address. To their surprise, the address in question was only seven minutes away.

"Old girl right 'round the corner," Taz announced as he put the Lincoln in drive while Sherm strapped on his vest and loaded his Glock.

"We in luck then," Sherm said as Taz used the red-light time to put his own vest on.

"Yep. Our lucky day," Taz replied as he saw that the address on the navigational system matched the one on the lavish, expensive beachfront house that sat in front of them.

"They got the front door wide open. They must be expecting us," Sherm half-joked, looking at the light from the house shining out into the darkness of night.

"I see folks out here don't believe in locking their doors. I guess that's how it is when you got millionaire neighbors," Taz said as he pulled the Lincoln to the curb that sat opposite to the house.

"Time to make a house call," Sherm called out as he pushed his door open. He was kind of excited to be back in his old element.

"Damn, nigga! Slow down," Taz replied as he killed the engine and jumped out behind Sherm.

Sherm eased up to the front door and looked in, trying to see if he saw anyone moving about inside. He was shocked when he focused on the girl in the front room, clawing at a carpet soaked with blood. Tiah had crawled out of the kitchen and into the front room as her life seeped from her body. Sherm didn't realize he had just witnessed her last breath. "Man, look here!" Sherm said, moving out of the way so Taz could see.

"That's one of them girls that came to the office," Taz said faintly as he stepped carefully into the house with Sherm in tow.

"Hold up," Sherm said forcefully, pulling Taz back by his shirttail, knowing there could be danger lurking in the shadows of the house.

Sherm and Taz pulled their guns and, seeing that the first girl was no longer moving, they dismissed her and made their way through the other parts of the house. Taz had to catch his balance as he almost fell over Lexi, who was twisted in a grotesque position up against the wall as blood soaked the carpet beneath her.

Sherm had no doubt that the killings were Silk's work. They climbed the stairs, being real careful not to touch anything. Sherm was shocked to see Silk lying on her side in a fetal position, breathing heavily. "Silk!" Sherm called out as he rushed over to her.

"That's the head girl, the one who robbed us blind without a pistol. Bitch need to die," Taz declared as he walked over and stood next to Sherm, looking down at Silk.

"Call an ambulance!" Sherm ordered as he knelt down and checked Silk's pulse.

"Man, you know the police going to be all over our asses like we killed these hoes. I don't—"

"Call now!" Sherm said, cutting him off while bending down to comfort Silk.

Chapter 35

"Hey, baby, come on out to the Embassy Suites on Palm Avenue. I'm in Room 37. Stop and get something to smoke and sip on," Kya told her girlfriend Nuki as she stashed all the bags under the bed, the ones she'd just crossed her team out for. "Money, money, money, moneyyyy, oh money…got to get my hands on some," Kya sang as she sat on the bed. She pulled a small baggie of white powder from her pocket and dipped her long, manicured pinky nail in it, then brought it to her nose. "Ahhhhhhh," she called out as she held her head back, squeezing her nose and sniffing.

By the time Nuki arrived, Kya was good and high off the potent cocaine she had picked up on her way to the hotel. "Damn, girl! You save me some?" Nuki asked as she walked in.

"You know I got my baby," Kya said as she grabbed Nuki on her arms and kissed her deeply.

"Mmmmm," Nuki moaned as she gripped Kya's ass and grinded on her.

Kya and Nuki had been on and off ever since they'd worked together at Club Rolex. Nuki was real popular in the strip club circuit. She despised the "dyke" label. She stressed "bisexual," being that she would indulge in a little dick from time to time.

Nuki was a very attractive female, standing five-six and weighing 155 pounds, nothing but hips and ass. She was known for her sassy attitude and arrogant ways, but she didn't care. Her smooth, dark, black skin complimented her big round eyes and naturally curly hair. Nuki had dykes, bisexual women and boss niggas all around the city trying to push up on her. Out of all of them, she chose Kya, the one person who catered to her every need and accepted her coming and going as she pleased.

"Hold up, boo. Let's get right," Nuki said as she pulled the bag of weed out and licked her lips at the sight of the small bag of white powder Kya produced.

They smoked and tooted until the drugs were gone. Kya took all her clothes off and climbed into the bed as Nuki used the bathroom. Returning, Nuki stripped down and jumped in the bed also.

"Turn the TV off," Kya told Nuki, who looked around for the remote.

"What the hell you got under here, girl?" Nuki asked as she leaned off the side of the bed to look under it.

"That was going to be a surprise. It's over a million dollars," Kya said, all cool like it was no big deal.

"Girl, quit lying!" Nuki replied, getting out of the bed.

"Have I ever lied to you?" Kya asked as Nuki pulled one of the bags from under the bed.

"Girl, where the hell you get this kind of money from?" Nuki asked excitedly.

"Girl, don't worry about all of that. Just know we straight. Now come on and get back in the bed," Kya said firmly as she reached over and lightly pulled Nuki under the sheets.

All of the money had Nuki lost for words. She was speechless as Kya rubbed between her legs, getting her all wet and worked up.

"You good?" Kya asked, noticing she wasn't all the way focused.

"Yeah, I'm good, baby," Nuki replied, springing her legs wide open as Kya went down on her. Her mind was only on the money as they licked, sucked, and felt each other up.

Chapter 36

olice and ambulance sirens could be heard descending quickly down the hill, en route to Silk's beach house.

"Man, let's get out of here," Taz told Sherm, knowing the police wouldn't have any understanding when it came to them being in a house full of dead women with bulletproof vests on and a car full of high-powered weapons parked across the street.

"Just stay calm and breathe," Sherm told Silk as he moved her hair from her face and wiped her brow. It was ironic that he had come to kill her, but now he willed for her to live.

"Man, come on! You think the money here?" Taz yelled as he made a quick dash through the house looking for money; he found none.

"Who did this?" Sherm asked a half-conscious Silk as he looked down into her pleading eyes. Even though he'd gone there to deal with her, he couldn't stand to see Silk hurting like that. He knew for certain that whoever had done that to her now had all the money. "Who did this, Silk? Sherm asked again as she closed her eyes, barely breathing.

"Man, let's go! They almost here!" Taz screamed, looking out the window and seeing all of the flashing lights coming over the hill.

Sherm reluctantly turned and walked away from Silk, then hurried out of the house to the car.

They drove right past the parade of police and other emergency vehicles as they left the scene. Pulling to the top of the hill, they parked the car, got out, and looked down at all of the chaos in front of the house.

"Man, I wonder who did this shit," Sherm asked Taz as he took a seat on the hood of the Lincoln.

"Shit. They saved us the hassle, 'cause we did come here to kill these bitches and get our money back, right?" Taz asked Sherm with raised eyebrows.

"Yeah, but this…" Sherm was lost for words. He wondered if he would have killed Silk on the spot in cold blood or if he'd have let her live, as long as she returned the money. Sherm knew deep down that his love for Silk was still strong as ever.

"You still crazy about that girl, " Taz stated as he lifted up off of the hood of the car, tucked his hands in his pockets, and looked down the hill at the emergency vehicles and police cars in front of Silk's place.

Sherm didn't respond to Taz's statement. He just fished his cell phone from his pocket and punched in Boski's number.

"Boy, you made a real mess out here. Damn, Sherm," Boski said as he sat in his patrol car at the scene of the crime.

"I didn't do it, but I need to know who did," Sherm replied in a firm tone as Taz came and sat back on the hood of the car.

"Well, one of the girls is still living. She's in better shape than she look. She's just lost a lot of blood. As soon as I get a chance, I'll try to question her. I'll make sure I get the detective on the scene too. Just give me a minute," Boski said while watching the rookie's ass jiggle as she surveyed the scene with a veteran officer.

"Where they taking the girl that's still living?" Sherm inquired.

"Miami General. She'll…oh, I gotta go," Boski said, abruptly cutting off the conversation as the rookie walked over and got in.

Sherm tucked his phone in his pocket and took a deep breath.

"Man, let's head back to the room and get some rest. We need to be at Miami General early in the morning," Sherm told Taz as they got back in the car. Sherm said a silent prayer for Silk as he pushed the Lincoln through the city's darkened streets, on the way back to the room.

Chapter 37

The next morning, Kya and Nuki woke up and went at it again. After pleasing each other for the second time, they got up, showered, and got dressed.

The whole time, Nuki's mind was strictly on the money. "Baby, what's your plans for all that money? 'Cause you know if you try to put it in the bank, they're going to be asking you all kinds of questions," Nuki said as she watched Kya pulling the bags from under the bed.

"Yeah, you right. That's why I'm going to grab me a spot on the outskirts and lie low for a minute until shit dies down," Kya said as she thought back on Lexi, Tiah, and Silk.

"Girl, you don't need to be getting no spot out nowhere. You can come stay with me—that's if you fucking with me like that," Nuki said sarcastically as she walked up behind Kya and wrapped her arms around her.

Kya was moved by Nuki's statement because she had been trying to move in with Nuki since they'd met, but Nuki always stressed that it would put a strain on their relationship since they both needed their space. Kya knew it was all a bunch of bullshit. She was well aware that Nuki didn't want her staying with her because she kept an occasional visitor from time to time. Kya didn't complain. She just went along with it because she was straight up head over heels for her Little Chocolate Drop. Now, hearing Nuki ask her to move in surprised her, but she knew the real reason: all that money would accompany her. Kya didn't hesitate to accept Nuki's invitation because now she could have Nuki all to herself. "Okay, I can do that. How about you come on and help me get these bags from under here so we can go?" Kya said as she reached over and pulled Nuki over to her.

"Yes, ma'am," Nuki cooed, looking deep into Kya's eyes and seeing dollar signs.

"Come here," Kya said softly as she pulled her into an embrace and started kissing her.

Their embrace ended just as quickly as it started when a loud *bang* echoed through the room.

Knock! Knock! Knock! "Room service! It's checkout time!" The foreign lady's voice boomed from outside the door.

"Shit! That bitch scared me," Nuki said playfully as she went to look out the window.

"For real! Let's get up out of here," Kya barked as she grabbed the bags with Nuki helping her out.

As they loaded all the money into the truck, Nuki laughed and smiled. She was all touchy-feely, thinking hard about a way to get all the money for herself without the hassle of being all under Kya—literally and figuratively.

Chapter 38

either Sherm nor Taz got a good night's sleep; their minds were too focused on finding the missing millions, but Sherm had twice as much to keep him awake. Silk was on his mind heavily. Both men got up, got dressed, ate free breakfast at the hotel, and were on their way out to the hospital.

"Man, whoever did this got the money, and me knowing Silk, don't just anybody know where she lay her head. It had to be somebody she trusted like no other," Sherm said as Taz navigated the Lincoln through early morning traffic.

"They may have found her through a connect like you did," Taz replied, making sure Sherm was keeping an open mind about the situation.

"No. This is something else. How many girls was found in that spot again?" Sherm asked for confirmation.

"Three," Taz replied, then thought about where Sherm was going with his assumption.

"How many girls came to the office? It was four, right?" Sherm asked trying to picture the last girl who wasn't accounted for.

"You and me done seen it plenty of times—the double-cross and then the triple-cross," Taz spat, thinking hard and trying to remember what the other girl looked like since he now knew where the money was.

"Yeah, we got to track that bitch down. Hopefully we can get some info from Silk on her," Sherm said, hoping they were on the right track.

"I hope so too. We find the missing girl, we find the money," Taz said as he followed the navigation system's directions to the hospital.

"Silk got to be able to tell us something, because even with my connect, we got to have something to start with," Sherm added as the navigation system told them to turn left and go three miles and their destination would be on the right.

A few minutes later, they were turning into the parking lot of Miami General. They made two circles around the lot before they found somewhere to park. After exiting the car, they hurried in through the big glass double-doors and looked around for the receptionist's desk. Finally locating the desk at the end of the main floor hallway, they got their story together as they approached.

"Hi, ma'am. Could you help me find Samantha Cooper?" Sherm asked, knowing the name wouldn't register.

"One minute," replied the big black girl with blonde weave. She popped her gum and rolled her eyes at the latest Facebook post as they stood there waiting. "What was her name again?" she asked as she logged off Facebook and pulled up the hospital room log.

"Samantha Cooper. She was admitted last night," Taz chimed in.

"Sorry—no Samantha Cooper," she told them as she looked once more through the hospital log.

"She was rushed in here last night with a gunshot wound, along with two other girls," Sherm said firmly.

"Oh! You talking about the Jane Doe from last night. The other girls died! That was messed up. What happened?" the girl asked, hoping to get some juicy details for the hospital gossip line.

"It's a long story. Maybe we can talk about it later. What floor is she on?" Taz stepped up and asked, flirting with the girl just in case the police had asked her not to divulge any info on the Jane Doe.

"Humph. She up on the fifth floor, Room 324. Who is she to y'all?" she asked, looking Taz and Sherm up and down.

"We're her family," Sherm said as he walked off, headed to the elevator.

"Okay, so what's up? Where you from?" the girl asked as Taz smiled at her.

"I'm from Atlanta. How about I get with you before I leave? Is that cool?" Taz asked as he turned to leave.

"That's all good," the big girl said and smiled.

"Later," Taz said as he quickly walked off to catch up with Sherm.

The girl didn't waste time picking up the phone to fill her home-girl in. "Girl, it's two fine-ass niggas coming up your way. They here to see that girl you said you know from the club you used to dance at," the girl said as she pulled Facebook back up on the job's computer.

"Oh yeah? As bad as I need some new-new from a new boo? Woo-woo!" the girl on the other line sang out.

"They straight from the ATL, shawtyyy!" the big girl said with a Southern drawl, then hung up the phone.

Sherm and Taz exited the elevator on the fifth floor and looked for Room 324.

As they made their way down the hallway to the room, a thick, light-skinned sister dressed in a bright yellow nurse's uniform pulled up on them. "Hi. May I help you guys?" the girl asked as she stepped in front of them, displaying a mouthful of gold teeth. Sherm and Taz were stunned at all the gold the thick, fine young girl had in her mouth. She was obviously once a female who played the streets, but she'd changed her life. It wasn't just the gold teeth that gave that assumption; the many tattoos that adorned her neck and arms spoke volumes about her past as well.

Taz zeroed in on the girl's big ass and thick thighs as he spoke. "We looking for our people. She was shot last night with two other girls. The lady downstairs told us she's in Room 324," Taz told her as he looked her from head to toe while Sherm veered off.

"Tell your friend it's right around the corner and half-full of police. Ain't nobody getting in that room until they say so," she said loud enough for Sherm to hear, which made him stop in his tracks.

"What they got going on?" Taz asked.

"They questioning her about what happened, but she ain't talking. The last time I went in there, they was fussing and cursing because she wasn't helping," the girl explained.

"Damn. We need to get to her," Sherm said, now focusing his attention on the girl.

"I can help you fine gentleman out. Just hold up a sec'. And by the way, y'all can call me Goldie," she said as she walked off.

"I'll make sure you are well compensated," Sherm called out.

"Don't even trip. Me and Silk go way back," Goldie said as she disappeared around the corner.

The mention of Silk's name coming from the girl made Taz and Sherm look at each other.

Chapter 39

"You sure me moving in won't come between us?" Kya asked Nuki as they pulled up into her loft's parking lot.

"Come on now, Kya. I think we know each other well enough now to make it work," Nuki replied, still trying to think of a way to separate Kya from the money.

"Yeah, I think we'll be all right," Kya said with confidence as she killed the engine.

"Come on. Let's get settled in. Wait…before we go any further, I want you to be honest with me," Nuki said, looking over at Kya as she tapped the steering wheel nervously with her long, manicured nails.

"What's up, baby?" Kya asked curiously.

"Where you get all that money, Kya?" Nuki asked firmly, noticing the nervousness in Kya.

"Can we not even go there? Let's just have a good time, enjoy the money, and be happy," Kya said as she pushed her door open to get out.

Right then and there, Nuki knew something wasn't right. She knew Kya was nervous about the situation with the money, but she wondered why. "Look, Kya, I need to know where that money came from before we get out of this truck. Or don't you trust me?" Nuki asked sadly as she ran her hand through her hair.

"Look, Nuki, let's just not—" Kya started but was cut off.

"What's up, Kya? Where'd you get the money? You don't trust me! That's exactly what it is, ain't it? You don't fuckin' trust me! Can you tell me how in the hell we going to be together when it ain't no trust? Huh? Tell me!" Nuki yelled as she turned in her seat and looked directly at Kya, who returned the gaze.

"Okay, okay!" Kya screamed as she slapped the steering wheel.

Kya thought long and hard before she filled Nuki in on the information that could put her in prison for life. She truly trusted Nuki and wanted to prove it, so she started from the top and ran the situation down to her. She justified her turning on the crew by saying they'd tried to cut her out of her take. That way, Nuki wouldn't think she'd crossed them out just for greed.

"You killed your friends? Silk, Lexi, and Tiah—them girls you hang with all the time, the ones you lived with?" Nuki asked, surprised and shocked.

"Yeah," Kya said faintly, hoping Nuki wouldn't change her mind about anything they had planned.

"Damn," Nuki said softly as she constructed her plan in her head. She now knew how she was going to separate Kya from the money without a problem.

Chapter 40

"Hey, y'all, follow me!" Goldie called out to Sherm and Taz as she led them to an empty room and pulled a linen bag from a closet.

"Are you going to be able to get us in to see Silk?" Sherm asked as she grabbed the two doctor's coats and gave each one of them one to put on.

"Good look, good look," Taz told her, admiring her cleverness but more impressed with her bulging hips and thick thighs, the physical attributes he valued so much in a woman.

"Here. Put these around y'all neck," she said, handing both of them stethoscopes.

"I've always wanted to be a doctor," Sherm joked as she handed both of them clipboards and pens.

"Well, congratulations, Doctor…Long. Yeah, I think Long will fit you perfect," Goldie said, looking down at Sherm's crotch.

Sherm didn't respond. He just gave her an approving glance while Taz stood in the background, smiling.

Taz knew when it came to women, Sherm was always serious and never showed any signs of weakness or interest—not off the top anyway. That was why Taz was shocked at the softness Sherm had for this woman Silk. It was the first time Taz had seen Sherm go soft for a woman, especially when it was one who'd crossed him. "So what's next?" Taz asked, getting back to the business at hand.

"We're all just going to walk down to the room and act like we need to see the patient for the test y'all are going to run later. I'm going to distract them while y'all go in to see Silk. Look, y'all just ignore the police out front. I got them. Shit, just act like a couple of doctors." Goldie smirked as she inspected Sherm and Taz to make sure they looked the part.

"I appreciate your help. By the way, how you know Silk?" Sherm asked as they all exited the room, looking official.

"I used to dance at a club she hung out at all the time. I turned her on to some nice people that paid off in the end, and long as I lined them up, she kept me straight. I been wondering what had happened to her. She just disappeared off the scene," Goldie told them as they made their way down the hall to Silk's room, omitting the life-and-death situation she and Silk had shared.

"Sounds like the Silk I know. Is she okay?" Sherm asked as they turned down the hallway where two uniformed policemen sat outside of a room, looking like they were guarding the person inside.

"Yeah, she's good. She lost a lot of blood, but that's it. She was lucky the bullets didn't do any major damage. She's been in there arguing with the police all morning. She's all right," Goldie replied as she picked up the pace and walked ahead of Sherm and Taz. She knew the police would be occupied watching her rather than paying attention to the two doctors.

The two police officers instantly set their sights on Goldie as she walked up and displayed her goods.

"She's conscience and alert but is having breathing problems," Goldie said, loud enough for the police to hear as Taz and Sherm walked up, looking like seasoned doctors.

"Okay. We'll run a couple of tests and see what we find. Oh, and can you change the dressing on the patient in Room 210?" Sherm told Goldie, putting on his best performance while Taz walked behind him, scribbling on his clipboard.

The officers paid them no mind as they walked in the room.

Chapter 41

*N*uki and Kya sat around all day, watching TV and making out. Nuki was so sick and tired of Kya and the constant caressing, but she knew she had to stay down and play the game if she was looking to get paid. They had made plans to hit the mall later in the evening, which made sucking her tits for the fifth time that day more tolerable for Nuki.

Kya dozed off while Nuki watched *Meet the Browns* and thought long and hard about her plans. When the 5:00 news came on, the top story was the shootout on Lexington that left two dead and one in stable condition. There was a $5,000 reward from Crime Stoppers for the arrest and conviction of the person responsible. Nuki was more focused on the million-plus that was stashed in her bedroom closet than the measly $5,000 they were offering; her real reward would be the space she needed to disappear once Kya was arrested and all the money would belong to her. She made sure Kya was still out cold before she grabbed a pen and strip of paper to jot down the reward hotline number. Then she eased to the back room and dialed it, toll-free.

"Crime Stoppers. May I help you?" the woman on the other end asked in an official tone.

"Yes. I have information on the murder that happened last night out on Lexington. I know who killed the women," Nuki whispered as she peeped out to make sure Kya was still sleep.

"Could you please give me your name and phone number? That way, if your information leads to an arrest and conviction, we can contact you about the reward money," the woman told Nuki, who walked back over to the door again peeping out to make sure Kya was still in the same position.

"I'd rather not, but I can tell you the person responsible is Kya Nelson, and she's staying with her friend at 7661 Decker Drive. She's been running around bragging about the murders," Nuki whispered.

"So, ma'am, you're telling us the killer is a female by the name of Kya Nelson and is living with a friend at 7661 Decker Drive. Is that correct?" the woman asked, confirming the info as she entered it into the computer.

"Yes, and she's there now," Nuki added, hoping they'd take her seriously.

"Okay, ma'am. Are you sure you want to remain anonymous? Do you want to give me your information for the reward, just in case you change your mind?" the lady asked again.

"No. I'm positive. It just feels good to be doing the public a favor by getting a killer off of the streets," Nuki said in a victorious tone.

"Thanks so much for the information, ma'am. I am passing it along to the proper authorities as we speak," the lady assured Nuki.

"You're quite welcome," Nuki told her as they hung up. She tiptoed back into the room and lay on the sofa with Kya, patiently waiting for the police to arrive.

Chapter 42

"Um, excuse me, Officer, but we need to speak with the patient for just a second—you know, doctor-patient confidentiality," Sherm insisted as the hard-edged female officer tried her best to pry info from Silk, who was lying back in her bed with her eyes closed ignoring her.

"No problem. I will be back, ma'am," the officer said firmly as she stepped from the room.

"Look, I'm feeling fine. Can I get my release papers now so I can get up out of here?" Silk barked with her eyes closed, thinking about what Kya had done to the girls.

"All I want to know is where my money at—that's if you want to live," Sherm said calmly as he walked over to the side of the bed and leaned over her.

Silk instantly rose up like she'd seen a ghost. "Wha...Sh-Sherm! What the hell!?" Silk called out as she frantically tried to get out of the bed.

Smack!

Sherm hit Silk with a swift backhand that instantly silenced her and sent her back down to the bed. Before she could shake it off, he had his Desert Eagle in her face. "Look...I'm the fuckin' reason you're still living. Calm the fuck down and tell me where the fuck my money at," Sherm said through clenched teeth.

Taz went over to the door to make sure the police hadn't heard anything. Peeking out, he saw all of them, including the manly female, being entertained by Goldie, who had their full attention.

Silk knew she was in a no-win situation, and seeing Sherm there with a gun in her face, dressed as a doctor, was proof enough to know shit was serious. Tired of living on the edge and reckless, Silk gave in, even though she wanted Kya for herself. Silk had planned to make her wish she had never crossed her and then collect all the money, but now she was left with no choice but to turn her over to Sherm. "Kya. She shot all of us and took the money. She was staying at my other spot, but now I don't know where she is. She turned on us and took everything. She killed Tiah and Lexi," Silk said softly as she closed her eyes.

"So this broad got all my money—the money you crossed me for? I made your ass, and this is how you repay me? By taking from me?" Sherm asked as he pressed the gun to the side of her face.

"Look, man, we got to bounce. That bitch going to be back in a minute," Taz said, peeking back out the door at Goldie and the officers.

"What's the best way to find this Kya girl?" Sherm asked as he moved the gun and tucked it back under the doctor's coat.

"She hangs out at Lucky's, and she fuck with a lil' black bitch named Nuki who's real known around town. I know she probably caked up with that bitch now," Silk spat, getting angrier as she thought about Kya's disloyalty.

"Nuki? Okay. But if you lying to me, the next time I—"

He was cut short as Silk cut in. "It's the truth, Sherm. Honestly, I didn't want to go through with the initial plan when I found out it was you, but we was too far in to turn back. I didn't want to do it, I swear. It really bothered me to do that to you, but there wasn't no turning back. I knew you would come looking for me and wouldn't stop until you found me. I thought about the shit the whole ride back home. I know it wasn't right because it didn't feel right. I'm tired of it all, Sherm. I just can't take no more of this. Please do me one favor when you find that bitch Kya. Save her for me. After that, I'm through with all this shit," Silk said, teary-eyed.

"Okay. You have my number. Call me when you're well," Sherm replied, still finding himself soft for Silk.

"Bro, here she come," Taz called out to Sherm as he rushed over to the bed and pretended to be taking notes.

"Is it okay if I ask her a few more questions?" the woman officer asked as she stuck her head through the door.

"I ain't got no talk!" Silk blurted out as she dismissed her with the wave of her hand.

"You're going to have to be easy with her. She needs some rest. You may want to hold your questions for a later day," Sherm recommended as he and Taz walked in her direction and exited the room.

"How's she doing, Doc?" Goldie asked, pulling herself away from the officers in heat.

"She's coming along real well. She's lucky. She'll be up at at 'em in no time," Taz added as they all headed down the hall to the elevator.

"Good, because she's a good person," Goldie said as she eyed Sherm.

Taz started to say something but caught himself before it came out. Sherm agreed with Goldie and gave her a sly grin.

"How about dinner on you for all my hard work?" Goldie asked Sherm, looking him up and down.

"We may be able to do that. Just hit me up," Sherm replied as he scribbled his number on the clipboard he held and handed it to her.

She wrote hers on a patient sheet and handed it to him.

"We appreciate ya help with yo' slick ass, shawty," Taz said and smiled as they took the coats and stethoscopes off and gave them to her.

"Nah. I just know how to make shit happen," Goldie replied and smiled, showing off all the shiny gold teeth in her mouth.

Taz and Sherm entered the elevator and headed down to the first floor, bypassing the receptionist desk. The big girl was still totally consumed with Facebook on their way out the door.

Chapter 43

$\mathcal{N}$uki watched the rest of the news, and just before it went off, there was a knock at the door.

Knock! Knock!

"Who is it!?" Nuki screamed, knowing it was most likely the police.

"Detective Bonner with the Miami PD. Could you please open up so I can have a word with you?" The whole time Bonner was talking outside the door, the fugitive squad was covering the loft from every angle.

"Okay," Nuki said, opening the door so he could enter, along with a uniformed officer.

"We are looking for a Ms. Kya Nelson. Is that you?" the detective asked, looking back and forth at the two women, trying to see which one was Kya.

"That's Kya over there asleep. Is there anything I can help y—"

Before Nuki could get the words out of her mouth, the detective had pulled his gun, and the officer threw the door open and waved in the fugitive squad. Before she knew it, her loft was full of men in black with guns everywhere.

"Get down! Freeze!" the detective screamed as the fugitive squad moved in on the girls.

Kya was jolted out of her sleep by all the commotion that was taking place. "Wh-what's going on?" Kya asked, scared and nervous, just as the detective alerted the other men that she was the one they were looking for.

"I don't know!" Nuki called out as she was pushed to the floor by the uniformed officer.

"Kya Nelson, you are under arrest for murder," the detective told Kya as he roughly handled her, placing handcuffs on her wrists.

"What!? I ain't murdered nobody!" Kya screamed as they snatched her up. She looked over at Nuki as they pushed her to the door.

"I got you," Nuki mouthed.

"Explain that to the judge, ma'am," the big black, burly officer told her as he led her out of the loft, past the fugitive squad members and Nuki, down to the waiting police car.

After all the chaos and commotion, Nuki looked out her window to make sure all the police were gone and the coast was clear before she went to the back to pull out all of the money. It took her over an hour to get an accurate count; $1.43 million was all hers. She had big plans for the next day: house shopping, car shopping, and clothes shopping. She was going to shop 'til she dropped. She took a shower, jumped in the bed, and forced herself to sleep like a kid the day before Christmas.

Chapter 44

Sherm and Taz headed straight down to Lucky's, the famous hip-hop spot on Miami Beach, looking for the girl name Nuki. After stopping at the corner store and getting directions, they pulled into the club's parking lot ten minutes later. As they entered the club full of women, they knew off the top that they were in a dyke club. The few men in attendance mingled about, not really getting any action from the beautiful, attractive women; however, the women who showed interest in the other women were welcomed with open arms. Picking up on the vibe of the club, Sherm and Taz headed over to the bar.

"What can I do for you gentleman?" the tall, thin, boyish-looking female asked them.

"We looking for our friend Nuki. Have you seen her tonight?" Taz asked as Sherm scanned the crowd for Kya.

"Nuki? Hmm. I don't know a Nuki." She shrugged, tapping her finger on the bar and giving Sherm and Taz a pay-me-and-I'll-remember look, which they picked up on instantly.

Sherm reached in his pocket and pulled out a $100 bill and tossed it across the bar to the girl.

"Oh! That Nuki ain't been in tonight. She is usually in around this time, but she ain't showed up yet tonight," the girl told them as she stuffed the money in her jeans pocket.

"How can I find her? It's very important," Sherm asked as she gave him the same pay-me-and-I'll-remember look as before.

Sherm laid another $100 down on the bar.

"She stay off Juniper Street in the Sun Lofts, Number 5. Was once a good friend of mines, but that's a long story," the girl said as she tucked the bill down in her pocket.

Sherm motioned for the girl to come close, as if he had a secret to tell her. As soon as she leaned in. he grabbed her by the back of her neck with a death grip. "Look here, bitch. If this info ain't correct, I'm coming back, and I promise you won't like it. Time is money, and wasting my time is wasting my money. You feel me?" Sherm spat as the girl tried to wiggle free. He didn't release her until she agreed.

"Let's ride, my nigga," Taz called out to Sherm after repeating the info to himself.

Sherm and Taz took one last stroll through the dimly lit club to see if they ran into Kya before heading out to Nuki's place.

Chapter 45

*I*t was getting late, and Sherm and Taz were getting restless. The ride out to Nuki's place was longer than expected, not to mention the two times they got lost before stopping and getting directions. By the time they exited the highway, it was dark, and the streets were deserted.

The Sun Lofts were just up over the hill a couple miles off the exit. As they reached the top of the hill, the lofts came into view. It wasn't what they expected in that rundown side of town.

"Let's find Number 5, get the money, and get the fuck out of Miami," Taz said as he pulled the Lincoln into an empty parking space.

"Yeah. Real talk, because I done lost too much money fucking with these hoes. There's 5 right there. Let's get in and get out," Sherm told Taz as he handed him the Glock while he readied his Desert Eagle.

Sherm and Taz weren't aware of the big bust that had just taken place hours before. They exited the car quickly and walked briskly toward the front door.

"How you want to do this? Kick-in or knock-out?" Taz asked, trying to see which method of entry Sherm wanted to use.

"These muthafuckers too close, then it's quiet as hell out here. A kick-in will be too loud. Let's knock out," Sherm said as he surveyed the scene, checking to see if anyone was out and about.

"Duck off, " Taz told Sherm as he knocked on Nuki's door.

Knock! Knock! Knock!

Nuki jumped up when the loud knocks echoed through the loft, scaring her up out of a deep sleep. "Who the fuck is this now?" Nuki sighed as she walked through the loft barefoot, with only a t-shirt on. "Who knockin'?" she screamed through the door, but no one responded.

Sherm and Taz stood there, ready and waiting for her to open the door.

"Man, who the fuck is knocking?" Nuki said to herself as she cracked the door open to see if anyone was out front.

Sherm and Taz watched as the door cracked. Taz, the bigger of the two, rushed around Sherm and roughly drove his shoulder into the door with Sherm following him up, pushing. The force of the door caused Nuki to stumble backward and fall. Seconds later, Sherm and Taz was standing in the middle of her dayroom.

Chapter 46

"Look, Ms. Nelson, we have all the evidence we need to put you away for life, but if you can help us, we can greatly reduce that," Detective Baylor told Kya as they sat across from each other in the interrogation room.

"I didn't kill nobody, so stop trying to get me to say I did!" Kya snapped, hitting the table.

The detective saw that Kya was going to be hard to crack, so he tried another approach.

"Look…we know you didn't work alone. Just give us the other person involved, and we'll cut you some slack," the detective offered, unbelieving that Kya was responsible for all the shooting that went on in that house that night.

"Look…for the fifth time, I don't know what you are talking about. You bust up in my spot while I'm asleep and arrest me for murder. I need to call my lawyer. I want my one phone call!" Kya yelled as she pushed away from the table and stood up.

"Oh, okay. Well, I'm through trying to help you. I tried to help your ass, but fuck it. You'll die in prison behind this shit. They may just give your ass the table," Baylor snapped, picking up all his files, angry because he couldn't get anything out of Kya that would give them probable cause to book her on murder.

"I ain't going to get shit, 'cause I ain't done shit!" Kya screamed as she started pacing the room.

"Have it your way," Baylor said as he turned and left the room.

"I want my phone call!" Kya yelled as he slammed the door closed and locked it.

As soon as Baylor left the room, he went around the corner into another room, where surveillance equipment was set up to monitor the interrogation room. He, two more detectives, and a uniformed officer watched as Kya kicked the chair and table over in anger.

"She did it," the old black female detective told Baylor as they watched Kya nut up in the room.

"I know she did. It's just fucked up that we don't have anything to tie her to it but an anonymous phone call. She wouldn't put herself there no kind of way. She's no novice to this shit," Baylor said, watching the monitor.

"I see. She's smart," the uniformed officer added.

"Look…just book her on obstruction so we can at least hold her for a couple more days or until she makes bond. I think we may be able to trip her up by then. She's going to put herself in that house by then, one way or the other. Put her up on 6 West, with no protective custody for her ass. Pass the word around that she killed her baby, and they'll eat her alive. Shit will be so crazy for her smart ass that she's going to be our best friend before it's over. She's going to do whatever she can to get up out of there," Baylor told the uniformed officer as the rest of the crooked civil servants gave their approval. "All right, y'all, I'm calling it a night. By tomorrow evening, I'm going to be looking for full cooperation from Ms. Nelson," Baylor said as he got up and exited the room.

The uniformed officer picked up the cordless phone from the table and called the booking desk. "Connie, could you please send a jailer down to interrogation and process this new intake. Do me a favor and put her on 6 West. Let your girl Buela know she's a baby killer. I'll see you tonight, as soon as we get off. I promise to have you home before your husband gets there," the officer said, smiling as his other crooked cohorts listened in.

Kya was moved upstairs to 6 West late in the night while all the girls were asleep except for Buela, who was awakened and given the word of the baby-killer who'd just been brought in.

Chapter 47

"Help! Help!" Nuki screamed, looking up at the two men standing over her.

Before she could scream again, Sherm was on her. He slapped her with the barrel of his Desert Eagle repeatedly until she shut up.

Blood trickled down her face as she begged and pleaded for her life.

"Where the fuck Kya at?" Taz asked as he walked over and looked down at her.

"Please don't kill me. Whatever Kya did to y'all, I ain't have nothing to do with it. The police came and locked her up today for killing somebody. I swear I don't know what's going on," Nuki said softly as she sobbed heavily.

Taz and Sherm looked at each other.

"Locked up? That bitch locked up? Where she locked up at?" Sherm spat as he grabbed a hand full of her hair and yanked her around.

"No, please! I swear the police came here today and locked her up. She at the city jail. They locked her up for murder, I swear," Nuki cried as she grabbed at Sherm's hands that were locked in her hair.

"Where the fuck the money at?" Taz asked as he walked through the loft.

"Ain't no money here. I don't know about no money. If she had money, it's got to be in her hotel room where she been staying," Nuki lied, hoping they believed her.

"So you telling me my money ain't here? If I find it in here, then, I'm justified in killing you, right?" Sherm said calmly as he bent down and got face to face with Nuki, releasing her hair.

Nuki's heart was broken. She had sent Kya to jail for the money, and now she had two men who might kill her because of it. She now had second thoughts about it all. The million dollars didn't look so appealing now, with her life on the line. "It's in the bedroom closet. Just please don't hurt me," Nuki pleaded.

Taz shot back to the bedroom to find the money. "It's here, bro!" Taz called out from the back as he pulled the bags from the closet.

Sherm reached over and snatched the phone cord from the wall. Nuki didn't care about him killing the house phone because she could use her cell phone to call for help. Seconds later, the phone cord was wrapped around her neck; finally, she realized what he was doing.

"Ah! Hel...Ugh!" Nuki moaned as Sherm pulled the cord tighter and tighter until her voice was cut off. She frantically kicked out and scratched at the cord that was wrapped tightly around her neck. Her eyes bulged, and her tongue stuck out as Sherm put his knee in her back and pulled the cord until his muscles gave in.

"No witnesses is my number one rule, lil' Nuki," Sherm whispered under his breath as he released the cord and let Nuki's body fall to the floor.

Minutes later, Taz stepped into the room with the bags. "Jackpot!" Taz announced as he stepped in the room.

"All good. A full circle. Let's get up out of here," Sherm replied as he helped with the bags while exiting the loft.

Chapter 48

The next day, Silk was up and moving around. She had refused to lie up in the hospital like she was on her deathbed. With no money, no car, and no clothes to put on Silk called down to the receptionist desk and asked to see a nurse.

Minutes later, an old white lady with bright red puffy hair walked through the door. "Good morning!" the lady called out as she all but skipped into the room, startling Silk.

"What the...excuse me, ma'am, but I was looking for Nurse Wells. Is she on duty today?" Silk asked, hoping Goldie was at work.

"Oh yes, Goldie. That's her nickname, and it so fits her. Did you see all of those gold teeth she's got in her mouth? It just amazes me that she—" The old lady rambled on until Silk interrupted.

"Excuse me, ma'am, but could you please go and get her for me?" Silk said firmly with a hint of irritation in her voice.

"Oh, okay, no problem. Just give me a minute to find her because people are hard to find in this place. I remember once long ago when I—"

"Ma'am, please just get Goldie for me!" Silk snapped, holding her head and scaring the old lady, who took off out of the room in search of Goldie. Silk flipped the channels on the TV while she waited for Goldie to show up.

An hour later, Goldie walked through the door with fresh bandages so she could change Silk's dressings.

"Damn, Goldie. I thought I was going to have to put out an APB on yo' ass," Silk joked, looking at the girl who'd helped set up some of her first licks when she first arrived in the city. She also thought about how close Goldie came to losing her life.

After pulling off one of her licks, Silk felt Goldie could become a problem, so she set out to get rid of her. Goldie was the only link to her and the killing of Steed, one of Miami's biggest white-collar street veterans. Silk knew if the word got out and back to Steed's brother Crack, who was also Goldie's baby-daddy that all the streets of Miami would be looking for her, and she wasn't ready to relocate so soon. Even though Goldie was the one who set the lick up, Silk still didn't want to take no chances on her talking, so she set out that night to get rid of her. Silk caught her coming out of her apartment, heading to her car, when she jumped down on her. As Goldie got in her car, she heard a *click*. Silk pulled the hammer back on the .357 and placed it behind Goldie's ear as she sat in the driver seat. Goldie didn't waste time begging and pleading for Silk to let her live. Goldie was the first and only person that Silk had set out to kill, had a clean kill, and didn't pull the trigger. Since then, Goldie had continuously thanked Silk for sparing her life. In some kind of twisted way, she also felt as though she owed Silk, and up 'til the time that Silk had disappeared from the scene, she'd been Silk's puppet. Seeing Silk come in the other night, Goldie had jumped up, ready to do whatever her savior asked.

"Girl, that old lady just told me you wanted me, and we've been talking all morning. What's up? You all right?" Goldie asked as Silk eased up out of the bed and onto her feet for the first time since she'd been shot.

"Look...I'm up out of here, but I need you to get me some clothes, and I need to borrow your cell phone and your car. I'll come back to get you when you get off," Silk told Goldie in a tone that obligated her to meet Silk's demands.

Goldie paused for a second to think. She wouldn't even let her own sister drive her new Avalanche truck, but now she was standing there with Silk demanding her keys. "Girl, I—"

"What time do I need to pick you up?" Silk asked as she walked up, invading Goldie's personal space.

Goldie knew she could easily take the petite Silk, but she also knew the consequences behind it would be severe and deadly. If it had been any other female coming to Goldie like that, she would have put her in her place off the top, but Silk was different; she had Goldie shook.

"I get off at 10:00 tonight. Just try to be here by 9:45 because I might get off early," Goldie said as she handed her keys to Silk.

"A'ight. I got you. Now I need you to get me some clothes, because I can't walk out of here in this hospital gown," Silk told her as she looked out the window at the hospital parking lot.

"I got some extra scrubs. I'll get them for you," Goldie told Silk as she turned to leave the room.

"Hey, where you parked at, and what you driving?" Silk called out, looking down at the keys, then down at the parking lot.

"Oh, damn, my bad. It's a lime-green Avalanche truck with some twenty-fours on it. Silk, please be careful wi—"

Silk cut her off. "What you waiting on? Go get the scrubs for me," Silk said, not caring to hear what Goldie was talking about.

Goldie picked up on Silk's attitude, so she cut the conversation short and hurried out to get the extra scrubs for Silk. Minutes later, she was back, but the room was empty, Silk was gone. Goldie slammed the scrubs to the floor and looked out the window to the parking lot. She cursed while watching Silk pull out into traffic in her new truck. She crossed her fingers, hoping Silk was going to be back to get her later when she got off.

herm and Taz slept later than they wanted to. After recovering the money, they'd decided to get a room and leave early in the morning, but now they had overslept, and housekeeping was making rounds, asking people to leave or pay up for another day.

"Damn! We needed to be on the road before nine, and it's raining. Shit!" Sherm said as he and Taz gathered everything to leave.

"We still should make good time if the rain slacks off," Taz added as he grabbed the money bags and followed Sherm out of the room.

The rain came down hard as they packed the Lincoln. Getting in behind the wheel, Sherm timed their arrival to the city and knew he wasn't going to be able to meet with Roscoe at 6:00, so he made a mental note to call him and cancel. Plugging his phone in and adjusting his seat, he got comfortable for the long ride home. Taz pulled out his iPhone and caught up with the news as he settled in.

Pulling out of the hotel parking lot, Sherm pulled the Lincoln to a halt at the red light.

Out of nowhere, a small compact car smashed into the back of them, crumbling the back of the rental.

"Wha…fuck!" Taz screamed as Sherm gripped the steering wheel for dear life.

"Shit!" Sherm screamed as he jumped out of the car in the pouring rain.

The young white girl stood in the middle of the street in the rain, apologizing over and over with her cell phone, the cause of the wreck, still in her hand. She pleaded with them not to call the police because she didn't have a license or insurance.

Sherm agreed, knowing the million-plus dollars in the trunk could possibly come into question. Now they were stuck in Miami without transportation. Sherm thought for a minute and then pulled out the patient slip from his jacket pocket that Goldie had scribbled her number on the day before. Climbing back into the Lincoln, he grabbed his cell phone and made two calls: one to a tow truck company and the next to Goldie.

Taz waved the young white girl on and then hurriedly unloaded the money bags and headed back to the hotel to get a room until they could line up some proper transportation.

Goldie's phone rang twice, and then a familiar voice answered. "Yeah?"

"Silk?" Sherm asked, confused and looking at his phone.

As Silk pushed Goldie's Avalanche down Main Street, she noticed her phone beeping. Just as she was about to silence it, she recognized the number starting with 404 and ending with 6655.

Chapter 50

" Why in the hell they watching me like that?" Kya said to herself as she stood in line for the morning meal. Kya didn't get any sleep the night before—just tossed and turned, trying to get comfortable in the small metal bed that was bolted to the wall. As she waited in line for cold grits and eggs, she tried to loom off all the stares that came her way from the rough-looking, hard-edged women who'd already been sentenced to long prison sentences.

The floor she was put on was specifically designated for violent offenders who had been sentenced and were waiting to be transferred to start their lengthy prison sentences. Most of the women who walked around on 6 West would most likely be old and gray before they were released back into society, and that was only if they lived that long.

As Kya grabbed the tray of cold food, she turned and walked back to her bunk. Just as she was about to reach her bunk, Buela stepped in her path, cutting her off. Kya didn't realize the tag that was put on her when she was dropped in the dorm, and she was unaware that early that morning, Buela and a couple more girls had already been plotting and scheming to teach the baby-killer a lesson.

"Excuse you!" Buela spat, frowning at Kya while bumping into her, causing her to drop her tray.

"Naw, bitch, excuse you!" Kya snapped back, ready to get down for hers.

Buela smiled at Kya's feistiness, which fueled her fire even more. "Bitch? Bitch!" Buela smiled as she walked over and stood directly in Kya's face.

Kya was raised fighting in the projects of Miami, which taught her to swing first, so she did. *Smack!* Kya open-handed the big girl, causing her to stumble backward.

Buela was caught totally off guard by Kya's aggression but welcomed the challenge. Shaking the lick off and regaining her footing, Buela rushed Kya like a raging bull. Kya balled up her fist and began administering blow after blow to Buela's dropped head, but it didn't stop Buela from picking her up and slamming her to the hard concrete floor. Before Kya knew it, three more girls jumped in; they were on her like a pack of wild dogs. They punched, kicked, and slapped her as she called out for help. The other girls in the dorm knew to stay out of the way so they wouldn't face the same fate as Kya.

The jailer looked on as they pummeled Kya 'til she was swollen and bloody. Seeing enough, the jailer and a couple more officers stormed in the dorm. "Break it up! Break it up!" the jailer yelled as they pulled the women off Kya, who was balled up in a fetal position with her arms over her head. "Take her down to medical. All y'all on lockdown!" the jailer yelled to the women who stood around watching the beating. "You come with me," the jailer told Buela as the other jailers locked all the other women in the dorm down. The jailer waited for the other guards to get on the elevator with Kya before leading Buela out to the lawyer visitation booth. "Good job, Buela. Here you go," the jailer commended Buela, then gave her a pack of cigarettes, an ounce of weed, and a cell phone.

"No problem. You know I got you," Buela responded as she went back into the dorm and split the goods up with her crew.

"All y'all need to get a phone card. This muthafucker ain't got no minutes," Buela announced and smiled as she held up their new toy in celebration.

Meanwhile, Kya was getting stitches down in medical for the damage to her face. Kya didn't want to have to go back upstairs, so she was willing to agree to anything and everything the detectives brought to her attention, just as they knew she would.

Chapter 51

"Yeah, it's me, in the flesh. I see you still love the women," Silk told Sherm as she pushed Goldie's truck down the main streets of Miami as the pain medicine wore off and the pain from the wounds started to kick in.

"You back alive, I see. Where's Goldie?" Sherm asked.

"She's busy. What you need?" Silk asked playfully as the pain started to get unbearable.

"We need some wheels. Lil' white girl smashed our rental this morning, and now we stuck out at this hotel," Sherm explained as the rain came down harder.

"What happened with the money business?" Silk asked curiously, already scheming on a plan to trick Kya out of hiding and get the money back.

"Come on, now. Ain't shit changed on this end. Money in the bank," Sherm boasted as he sat looking at the cars go around his disabled rental.

"Where the bitch Kya at?" Silk asked, knowing more than likely that Kya was dead already if she'd crossed their paths.

"Wasn't lucky enough to get her before they arrested her for murder. Her friend Nuki wasn't too glad to see us though," Sherm told her as Taz jumped in the passenger seat and gave him the room key, then jumped back out in pouring rain.

"Oh. So she locked up in the county?" Silk asked, formulating a plan in her head as a sharp pain crept through her stomach.

"Yeah. You coming to help us get back to the city or not?" Sherm asked, looking at his watch.

"Yeah. Give me a minute. I got a lil' business to handle, and then I'll be there to help y'all out," Silk told him as she tried to remember her good friend Bonnie's number.

"A'ight. Now I'm pressed for time though," Sherm told her in a firm tone that brought back memories.

"I got you. Where y'all at?" Silk asked as the rain pounded the windshield of the truck.

"Red Roof Inn on the main strip, right across from the Super Walmart, Room 305," Sherm told her, looking down at the hotel room key Taz had just gave him.

"I'll be there," Silk said as she turned down the street she lived on.

After pulling up in front of her spot, Silk got out and walked with a slight limp as she headed up to the front door. Picking the mat up, she removed the spare key and unlocked the door. Her heart skipped a beat when she saw the bloodstained carpet and all the other remnants of the shooting. Silk's blood boiled as she thought about how Kya had done the crew. Hurrying upstairs, Silk put on some sweats and a jacket, then went to her nightstand to retrieve her snub-nosed .38.

When she got back in the truck, she picked up Goldie's cell phone and called her good friend Bonnie.

"Hi. May I help you?" Bonnie asked as she looked down at her cell phone, not recognizing the number.

"Hey, girl. This Silk. I need you to do me a favor. Can you look up Kya Nelson and let me know what her status is?" Silk asked her good friend that owned Bond Out Bonding LLC as she climbed back up into the truck.

"Give me a minute," Bonnie told Silk as she pulled up the information on her computer.

"Is she there?" Silk asked anxiously.

"One minute. Yeah, I got her right here. She's got an obstruction charge with a $5,000 bond," Bonnie relayed to Silk.

"Obstruction? No murder charge?" Silk asked, surprised.

"Nope—just obstruction. I can get her for you if that's what you want," Bonnie offered as she printed the booking information off for Kya.

"That's exactly what I want. How long will it take you to get her?" Silk asked as she headed in the direction of the jail.

"I'll get with Stan, and we can have her out in less than an hour," Bonnie told Silk as she placed a big mug shot of Kya in a folder and labeled it.

"Okay, cool. Her sister needs to be on the bond. Her name is Regina Jenkins, and I'll let her know she can pick her up in an hour," Silk told Bonnie, making sure no one could put her at the jail or link her to the bond.

"Okay. No problem. Just tell them she will be out in an hour. We squared up with this one," Bonnie told Silk as she processed Kya's bond.

Silk agreed, then made a couple of stops to waste time, waiting on the hour to arrive. After getting caught in downtown traffic, Silk made her way down to the jail. The rain wasn't letting up as she turned into the beat-up parking lot of the city jail, looking for Kya.

Kya was called and told to pack it up as she sat down in medical. The detectives were licking their chops, waiting for daybreak so they could take her back to interrogation. Their plans went down the drain when they got word that Kya was bonding out.

Silk sat out front in the rain, waiting on Kya to come out.

A few minutes later, Kya emerged from the building with a big bandage on her head.

Silk pulled the truck around, waved, and blew to get Kya's attention.

Kya looked up and saw someone waving for her to come on. She knew Nuki would rescue her, so she didn't waste any time getting over to the truck so she could get out of the rain. She limped across the lot to the truck, shielding herself from the pouring rain.

Silk grabbed the snub-nosed .38 revolver off the seat, and by the time Kya reached the truck, she had it positioned to fire.

Kya grabbed the passenger side door and pulled it open. She looked up at the person behind the wheel, expecting Nuki. Her heart dropped as she focused in on Silk with the gun pointed at her. She was stuck like a deer in headlights. Her legs couldn't move fast enough before the loud *boom* echoed inside the truck. The bullet from the .38 hit her square in the face, jerking her head back. Kya fell backward and lay sprawled out on the concrete, as if she was looking up at the rain. Her blood followed the same path the rain took as it drained itself from the parking lot.

Silk reached over in pain, closed the door, and drove casually out of the lot to meet Sherm.

Chapter 52

*S*herm and Taz sat around the room making calls and catching up on business while they waited for Silk to arrive. Taz wasn't too thrilled about Silk coming to help, especially with over a million dollars lying around. He just straight up didn't trust her. A couple hours after he'd talked to her, she finally showed up.

Sherm peeked out the hotel room window when he heard a horn blow. He looked out and saw Silk sitting behind the wheel of a new, brightly colored, customized truck. He waved her in, and she waved him out, neither wanting to get out in the pouring rain. Sherm gave in, knowing she was more than likely still in pain from the shooting. He ducked his head, ran out and jumped in the truck with her.

"It's like we are meant to be," Silk joked as Sherm wiped the rain from his face.

"Yeah, really, but look here. I need some wheels ASAP," Sherm told her, admiring her on the low in her sweats.

"That shouldn't be a problem, but right now there's a tornado watch, and it's not a good time to be out. You need to just lie over one more day until all this bad weather blows over. You can stay out at my spot," Silk suggested as the sky grew darker and the rain pounded the pavement.

Sherm thought about what she said and agreed. "We need to talk anyway," Sherm said, looking disheveled and tired.

Since leaving the hospital, Silk had been feeling weak and in pain, but she was determined to push her body to the limit. Sitting there now with Sherm, she just wanted so badly to be comforted by him like old times. She wanted him to just hold her and take all the pain away just like old times. "Yeah, we do need to talk. So, come on, let's head to my place so we can do that," Silk told Sherm as she looked over at him seductively.

"That's cool, as long as you got enough room for my patna," Sherm insisted, not about to leave Taz out.

"I got more than enough room. He can take the guest room, and we can share my bed if that's okay with you," Silk cooed as Sherm looked at her, nodding his head in agreement.

"Just like old times," Sherm added.

The whole time Sherm and Silk were out in the truck, Taz was packing the money in the nightstand drawer by the bed. He just didn't trust Silk. He put the Bible, phone books, and old newspapers in the place of the money; he wasn't taking any chances with Silk. After he saw that everything was safe, he would double back with Sherm and get the money. He knew if he told Sherm, he would say that he was overreacting, so he kept it to himself.

After talking with Silk, Sherm returned to the room and told Taz to pack up because they were going to chill at Silk's spot until the next day due to the tornado warnings. Taz reluctantly agreed as he grabbed the bags and followed behind Sherm to the truck, glad he had stashed the money. As they climbed in the truck, Taz and Silk traded angry stares, and they all settled in for the ride out to Silk's. Taz put the hotel room key in his jacket pocket and patted it, glad that he was thinking ahead.

Back at the house where Kya had shot down the crew, they all exited the truck and proceeded in. They all tried their best to ignore the bloodstained carpet as they walked through the house. Silk showed Taz the guest room as they walked by to the den. Taz nodded and didn't say anything as he followed behind Silk, carrying the bags that Silk kept in her view. A half-hour later, Silk was making everyone drinks as they watched the game. Sherm declined, and Taz gladly accepted his share as the vodka took its toll.

"Man, I'm beat," Taz told Sherm, interrupting his and Silk's intimate conversation.

Silk looked at him and rolled her eyes as he stumbled back to the room.

"Damn, bro, you ain't had but two drinks," Sherm joked, but at the same time surprised that the two small glasses of vodka had Taz stumbling.

A few minutes later, Taz was laid out across the bed, breathing hard. A short time later, he started vomiting, and seconds later, he couldn't breathe at all. He felt like someone had their hand around his neck, choking him. It took approximately seven minutes for the poison to work. By then, Taz had stopped breathing and was lying face down in his vomit.

Silk and Sherm headed back to her bedroom, where they expressed love for each other and climbed in the bed.

"Damn, I missed you," Silk told Sherm as they undressed and climbed under the comforters.

"Missed you too. I'm going to be gentle. Don't worry," Sherm said as he navigated his tongue around the bandages.

"Thanks," Silk said as she cursed Taz for drinking Sherm's glass of vodka.

They made love slow and easy. Silk thought about all the old times they'd spent with each other. She knew things couldn't be the same between them anymore because she was not that Silk anymore; she really didn't know who she was anymore. Her love of money and the good life would forever come first.

Minutes later, Sherm had climaxed and was fast asleep. Silk faked an orgasm and was easing out of the bed while Sherm lightly snored. Creeping into the den, she grabbed her .9mm and looked in on Taz, who was dead to the world. Satisfied with her work, she crept back to her room, where she stood in the doorway and aimed at the bulging comforters; there was no way she could look at Sherm's face as she took his life. A single tear ran down her cheek as she pulled the trigger. She unloaded the sixteen bullets into the bed, knowing that Sherm wouldn't survive, so Silk didn't even bother pulling the comforter back.

Sherm hid in the closet, peeping out at his former lover who thought that she was killing him. He was devastated. He stayed hidden until Silk exited the house with the money bags. He badly wanted to confront her, but he knew that wasn't an option without a gun. He cursed himself for leaving his gun in the car.

Silk took her time and poured lighter fluid throughout the house and lit the curtains on fire on her way out.

Sherm scrambled to the back of the house after smelling the smoke. He rushed in to wake Taz but saw that he was dead. "Fuck!" Sherm screamed as he exited the house, disgusted at himself for believing in Silk.

Silk pushed the truck down the highway en route to her new city. Hours later, she was entering Alabama city limits, and found a hotel right off of the expressway. After paying the old man at the counter, she was given a key to her room. Silk lugged the bags up to the room and placed them on the bed. The pain she was in was now unbearable. Climbing up on the bed next to the bags, she reached over to inspect her take. Silk knew it was enough for her to finally retire. She opened the first bag and pulled out a phone book. Her heart dropped, and she frantically went to the next one and found it full of newspapers, another phone book and a Bible.

"Please, God, no!" Silk said, seeing that there was no payday or retirement.

The mental pain on top of the physical pain was too much to bear. Silk was tired and couldn't take any more. She reached over and grabbed her gun from her bag and put it to her head. The tears rolled down her face as the loud *boom* woke the people in the room next door.

Sherm cursed as he walked down the dark street with nothing but his boxers on. He swore to kill Silk the next time he saw her, without a second thought.

* * * * *

A Day Later

" *I*'m off the clock. You got the rest of the rooms on that side," the female maid told Marvin, the neighborhood crack-head.

He didn't even argue, being that he really needed the job to help pay for his crack habit. In Room 305, he stripped the bed and cleaned the bathroom. Just as he was about to leave, he checked the nightstand and had to pinch himself when he saw all the money. He wasted no time packing it in his laundry bags. He inspected it again before he threw his housekeeping attire to the floor. He whistled and smiled, showing all three teeth as he walked home with the bag full of money.

G STREET CHRONICLES
~A NEW URBAN DYNASTY~

WWW.GSTREETCHRONICLES.COM

Chapter 1

*R*eal woke up in the hospital, handcuffed to the bed.

The doctor looked down on him, took off his glasses, and placed them in his shirt pocket. "You're lucky to be alive, son. You lost a lot of blood," the doctor said as he circled the bed, checking Real's vitals.

Real lay there speechless, trying to reflect on what had gotten him to that point. All he could remember was B-Low's face and the sharp, handmade knives penetrating his body one after the other.

"How much longer will you need to keep him here, Doc?" the female prison guard asked. She couldn't take her eyes off Real. Even in his current condition, she thought he was sexy as hell.

* * * * *

Sergeant Shonnie Turner and her accompanying officer walked into the dorm with Real, who'd just been released from the hospital.

"Cell 117 is open. Put him in there," the correctional officer working the hole said.

"You know he can't have a roommate until the investigation is over, correct?" Shonnie said to the dorm officer with authority in her tone.

He glared at her with a scowl on his face. "I'm aware of that, Sergeant," he snapped. He was obviously still angry that Shonnie had been promoted to sergeant, while he'd been overlooked for the position.

Shonnie just smiled victoriously and walked off with her accompanying officer to escort Real to his cell.

"I need a mattress and a pillow," Real demanded as he limped along behind them, still in pain from the attack.

"What do you think this is, the goddamn Holiday Inn? We'll get you some supplies in a minute," the escort said as he opened the door and stood to the side for Real to enter.

"I ain't going in there till I get a mattress and a pillow," Real said firmly, even though he knew he was in no shape for physical contact.

"Look, Mr. Walker, we said we would get you a mattress and pillow. Please move inside your cell," Shonnie said, taken in by Real's good, yet rough looks. The hospital stay had knocked a few pounds off of him, but his chiseled, fit body still had her in awe. His eyes had caught her attention off the top, the same eyes that he was staring at her with now.

"Sergeant, straight up, I need a mattress. You know if you lock me in there without one, I ain't gettin' one till tomorrow, and that ain't gonna work."

"My word, I got you. Just give me thirty minutes," Shonnie said as she walked over and looked directly in Real's eyes.

Real stared her down and stood his ground.

The accompanying officer frowned at Real; he wanted nothing more than to be given permission to rough the prisoner up and nearly salivated at the thought. "Sergeant, he's holding us up. We have another transfer waiting," he said, hoping to use force to put Real in the cell.

"Don't you think I know that? I don't need you telling me my job, thank you," Shonnie snapped, keenly aware that the prejudice young white officer was just itching to bring physical harm to the young brother.

"A'ight, Sergeant. I'll take you at your word," Real said as he stepped into the room.

In a great deal of pain, Real walked slowly over to the desk and sat down on the hard, cold, metal stool. He looked around the small, musty, cramped cell, where condemned men had scribbled and carved their innermost thoughts and feelings all over the wall. *Back in prison again? I can't believe this shit,* he thought. He ran his hands over his wounds and instantly became angry. Every time he touched a bandage, he thought of B-Low and his crew, who'd almost killed him. If it hadn't been for the third-shift officer passing out call-outs for the next morning, he would have been dead. The officer had opened his room door to give him his call-out for classification and noticed the blood-soaked sheets and called the code. As Real sat there thinking about the events that had led up to the assault, his door popped open, and a mattress was slid in by the inmate who worked in the hole, accompanied by an officer.

"Appreciate you, bro," Real said as he slowly stood and limped over to the door.

"Are you Real? They said you was paralyzed," the man said, picking up the pillow and tossing it on top of the mattress.

"Do I know you, bro?" Real asked, looking the man up and down.

"Nah, but I know '*bout* you. Niggas from Atlanta been screaming your name since that shit jumped off. You a legend in the city, bro," he said, then stepped back so the officer could close the door.

"Yo, what building B-Low in?" Real asked, positioning his mouth in the crack of the door so the inmate could hear him.

"He in H-2. Bro, you need anything, just get at me. They call me Doobie," he said as he turned and started walking off.

"Say, bro!" Real screamed through the crack.

Doobie stopped in his tracks and came back to the door. "What up?" he asked.

"I need a banger ASAP," Real said in a serious tone. He'd already vowed to himself that as soon as he got out of the hole, there was going to be bloodshed.

"I got you first thang in the morning, bro," Doobie said as he turned and walked away.

Neither man knew that Bohog, one of B-Low's gang members, was next door listening to their exchange. After Doobie walked off, Bohog stood on his bed unscrewed his light and retrieved his cell phone from his stash spot. "B-Low, man, that nigga Real back from the hospital, over here in the hole next to me. The nigga Doobie who works over here is helping him tool up, so you best be on point when he gets out. My battery low, so I'll get at you when Tag get me a charged one.

Sitting in his cell, smoking weed with three of his gang members, B-Low said into the phone, "That's what's up. I'll holla." After he clicked off the call, he turned to his crew. "Yo, NoLove, you know that nigga Doobie?"

"You talking 'bout the nigga who work over in the hole?" NoLove asked, taking a pull from the blunt.

"Yeah."

"Sure I know 'im. What up?" NoLove asked, pulling on the blunt really hard once more before he passed it off to BodyBag, a notorious killer from the Yamacraw projects, one of the roughest, most dangerous projects in Savannah, Georgia.

"He need to be leaking and by last movement tonight," B-Low told him in a sinister tone.

Chapter 2

Shonnie made her last rounds in the hole before her shift ended. She was responsible for making sure all the inmates were safe and secure; her supervisor's way of making sure she did her rounds was to check her signature on every room chart.

"Sarge, that ass phat!" an inmate called out from his cell.

"Suck this dick, bitch!" another inmate chimed in, grabbing his crotch.

Shonnie was used to the unruly inmates bad-mouthing her from behind their locked doors. It all came with the territory of being a woman working in a male correctional facility. She had to have a tough skin. "Y'all fuck niggas lay down," she shot back as she continued to make her rounds.

Tap! Tap! Tap!

Real was lying in his bunk, lightly snoring, when the light tap on his door woke him. "Yeah?" he said as he rose up, squinting and trying to see who was at his door.

"You got your mattress and pillow, right?" Shonnie asked as she watched him get out of his bunk and limp over to the window.

"Yeah, and I appreciate you keeping your word," Real said, taking in the perfect features of Shonnie's face. In a lot of ways, the sergeant reminded him of his love, Constance. She had smooth, caramel skin, stood about five-two, was slightly bow-legged, and had a thick bottom with wide hips and thick thighs. She filled out her uniform nicely.

"Who was responsible for your hospital stay? What you got going on? You just got here," Shonnie asked as she sneaked a peek in at his chiseled body and the slight bulge in the front of his boxers.

"Ain't no thang. I'm good," Real said, sticking by the code of the streets and refusing to make a statement to a correctional officer, no matter how hot she was.

"I guess that mean you're not gonna tell me, but that's cool. You just be careful," Shonnie said, locking on Real's brown eyes, which were also locked on hers. With that, she smiled and walked off.

She couldn't stop thinking about Real as she made the remainder of her rounds. She tried to shake off the thoughts as she started her rounds upstairs, but before she left the dorm, she found herself back downstairs at Real's door. "Do you need any pills or anything? I can get the nurse down here if you need some meds," Shonnie said, feeling like a little girl with a schoolyard crush.

Real looked up from his mattress. "Nah, I'm good," he replied, recognizing the interest from the woman on the other side of the big steel door.

"Have a good night then," Shonnie called as she headed to the briefing room to end her shift.

Shonnie had been working for the Georgia Department of Corrections for three years. It had taken her no time to rise through the ranks at CSP, and she'd recently been promoted to the sergeant position. She was proud of that, one of the few admirable accomplishments in her life.

Shonnie had been born and raised in Glennville, right up the road from the prison. Glennville was in deep south Georgia, and it was common to encounter chickens and cows while walking the dirt roads. Shonnie had been raised by her grandmother since she was a toddler. Her mother had died in a house fire before her first birthday, and her father, an army veteran, was a drug addict who roamed around their small town, pushing his supermarket buggy full of junk that he saw as valuables. When her grandmother, Ellie, had passed a year ago from heart failure, Shonnie's world had virtually crumbled. Fortunately for her, Moe swooped in. At first, he was most definitely her knight in shining armor, but it wasn't that way anymore. Now, Shonnie dreaded that her shift was about to end, because she really didn't feel like dealing with Moe and his drinking.

She'd met Moe a little while after her mother had died, and back then, she'd seen him as the perfect man. He was a little on the heavy side when they first met, but his love and care overshadowed his physical imperfections. Now Moe was twice the size he was back then, and ever since he'd been laid off, he'd been drinking more and more. Moe had made a 360 and had changed drastically for the worse.

To make matters worse, their perfect relationship had turned into a nightmare for Shonnie. She hated all aspects of it, and the lovemaking was the worst. Their intimate moments had turned into a wrestling match between her and a fat, musty, drunk who mindlessly humped away until he got a nut, paying no attention to her needs whatsoever. Their daily life always ended in an argument, and those arguments ultimately ended up with handprints on the side of Shonnie's face. She was an officer of the law, but she could do little to stop the domestic disputes in her own place. After the beatings and verbal abuse, Moe always ended up on his knees, crying and begging for Shonnie to forgive him. She had attempted to leave on several occasions, but she always gave in to his begging and apologies. Deep down, she worried that if she tried to leave, he might actually try to kill her. Even her sergeant status at the prison couldn't save her, as her power only existed within the gates where 1,800 condemned men were housed, most for the rest of their lives.

"A'ight, Sergeant, have a good night," the old white sergeant said when he came in to take over her shift.

She grabbed her jacket and headed to the door. "You too," Shonnie replied, then exited the office and made her way home to her own personal prison.

Chapter 3

The sun had changed places with the moon, and the yard was pitch black, with the exception of the circle illuminated by the huge floodlights.

"Church call! You got five minutes to report out, or you ain't goin'! Last call for church!" Officer Knight said as she stood in the doorway signing inmates out to church.

"Nigga, come on. They building already on the walk," NoLove told BodyBag as he pulled his state-issued skullcap over his head and adjusted his shank, a homemade knife also known as a banger, in the waist of his pants.

"Nigga I couldn't get my banger. Shit stuck in the damn heater," BodyBag spat as they signed out with Officer Knight.

She was eager for the dorm to clear out so she could sneak off into the officers' bathroom with her man Raze, a two-time felon back to serve a life sentence for murder. "Closing the door! Church call is over!" Officer Knight called out as she looked around the dorm and saw that most everyone had gone up to the night's church service.

Raze stuck his head out the door and gave her the signal, and seconds later, she disappeared into the officers' bathroom. A few minutes later, Raze eased through the dorm and waited until the coast was clear so he could duck inside the bathroom. There, he saw Officer Knight waiting for him, with her pants already down to her ankles.

"That's his dorm right there," NoLove said as they rounded the walk to J-building, where Doobie was housed. "That's old man Carter working the dorm. Ain't shit to get passed him," NoLove said as they blended in with all of the other inmates headed to the multipurpose room to attend church.

Old man Carter didn't pay them any attention and just held his head down, looking intently at his clipboard, trying to sign the exiting inmates out to church. They walked right past him as if they were assigned to the dorm.

"Yo, Smurf, where Doobie room?" BodyBag asked the dorm barber.

"He up in 211," Smurf said, thinking nothing of it. After all, many inmates came looking for Doobie, who often delivered food and other contraband to their partners in the hole.

NoLove and BodyBag climbed the steps and headed to his room. They didn't bother knocking; they just slammed the door open.

"Who…what…what up?!" Rod, Doobie's roommate, screamed as he jumped up and pulled his dick out of the mouth of the dorm punk, Diva.

"Damn, my nigga! You get down like that?" BodyBag called out, surprised to see his little homeboy from Savannah engaging in homosexual activity.

"Man, ain't nothing. What y'all up to?" Rod asked, trying to hide his anger and embarrassment.

"Where Doobie?" NoLove demanded, frowning at Diva, who was standing against the back wall with white juices running out of his mouth.

"He in the shower," Rod said. He kept his head down in shame as they turned and exited the room. As soon as they walked out, Rodney walked over to Diva.

Clunk!

"Ah!" Diva screamed when Rod hit him in the eye and slammed him into the wall.

"I told you to lock the damn door!" he screamed, punching him in the face again.

Diva's eye swelled up immediately, and he held it as he wailed, "I thought I did lock it, boo! I'm sorry! Stop, Rod!" Diva screamed as he tucked himself as far as he could into the corner of the small room.

Rod halted his assault, walked over, pulled his dick out, and grabbed the back of Diva's head, forcing him to continue where he'd left off. Diva looked up at Rod with his manly features as he caressed his manhood with his mouth.

NoLove and BodyBag walked down the range, past the curious inmates who stood back watching them as they made their way to the shower. Only one shower was occupied, and they knew it had to be Doobie.

"Yo, Doobie!" BodyBag called out just to make sure.

"Yeah? Who dat?" Doobie replied, lathering up with the state-issued soap. He was facing the back wall, enjoying the sprinkling hot water, when the men entered. He felt the cool breeze flow in when they pulled the shower curtain back, but before he could turn to see who it was, it was too late.

"Fuck nigga!" BodyBag called out as they rushed him.

BodyBag swung and hit Doobie with a two-piece, dazing him, while NoLove pulled his banger from his waist. NoLove was like Jason from *Friday the 13th*, brandishing the crude, homemade blade. He jabbed Doobie with the knife mindlessly, as if he had no conscience at all, piercing Doobie's chest, head, neck, and back and spraying blood all over the tile walls and floor.

"Oh! Ah! Please! Why y'all on me?" Doobie screamed as he tried to fight his way out of the shower.

The soap and water granted the knife easier entry into Doobie's bare flesh. He scuffled and fought back for a few minutes, but soon, he'd lost too much blood and fell into shock. He slumped to the shower floor, shaking uncontrollably with blood gushing from what looked like a hundred stab wounds.

"Let's go!" BodyBag called out. He was proud of their work, and Doobie would definitely have to be taken to the free world hospital, just like B-Low ordered.

They stepped out of the shower wet, breathing hard, and bloody. The inmates in the dorm just stood back silently, watching the two make their way out of the shower, down the stairs, and out the front door, right past old man Carter, who was still staring at his clipboard, trying to get his building count right. None of the inmates said a thing, as they knew BodyBag and NoLove were B-Low's goons, and no one wanted to get mixed up in that kind of heat.

"What y'all room number?" old man Carter asked, unaware that they weren't even assigned to his dorm.

"Uh…187," NoLove said and laughed as they exited the dorm and disappeared in the darkness.

Chapter 4

A little after 9:00 p.m., Shonnie pulled up at the small, two-bedroom bricked-in trailer that she shared with her fiancé, Moe. As she parked, she noticed that all the lights were off. She was glad to see it, because that meant Moe was most likely already asleep, and she wouldn't have to deal with him. "Thank you, Jesus," she mumbled as she killed the engine, grabbed her work bag, and exited the car.

Stray dogs barked in the distance as she stuck her key in the front door. The lock clicked, and she pushed the door open, only to have it stopped by the chain lock.

"Shit!" Shonnie cursed, realizing she'd have to wake Moe in order to get into the trailer.

She thought about the back door but dismissed that idea; she'd never get past the inside bolt lock.

Knock! Knock! Knock!

Shonnie stood back and readied herself for whatever mood Moe was in. A few minutes passed, and he still hadn't come to the door.

Knock! Knock! Knock! Knock!

Shonnie was tired and getting angrier by the minute while waiting for Moe to come open the door. After thirty minutes—a whole damn half-hour—he still hadn't come to let her in. She paced around the front stoop for a moment, then decided to circle the trailer. Unfortunately, it only had three windows, and those were way out of her reach. She went around to the bedroom window and tossed a couple rocks at it, hoping to wake Moe from his drunken slumber. When that didn't work, she went back to the front door and pushed it open as far as the chain would permit, then yelled through the opening as she continued to knock, "Moe? Moe! Hey, open the door!"

Moe didn't stir. He was lying across their bed, passed out drunk, thanks to the empty gallon liquor bottle that was tipped over on the floor.

Shonnie screamed until she started crying in frustration. She walked back to the car and pulled out her cell phone, considering calling 911. She quickly killed that thought though. In their small town, her business would be the hot topic at her job and all the other town gossip spots, and she refused to listen to her co-workers talking about her tumultuous home life. She was suddenly very pissed off that they didn't have a house phone and that Moe didn't carry a cell.

"This is crazy! Oh God, please just help me!" Shonnie screamed. She hit the car horn a couple times, then tilted her seat back, pulled her jacket off to use as a cover, and cried herself to sleep.

Chapter 5

*R*eal woke up the next morning to the sound of a tray being shoved through the flap on the door.

"Chow call, buddy," the old black militant officer called. Then he flooded Real's cell with light using the switch outside the room, which only officers had access to.

"Man, turn that light off!" Real snapped, squinting and trying to block the bright light out.

"Wake-up call! House rules. Standby for the shower," the officer called out like a broken record as he closed the tray flap and proceeded to the next room.

After the inmates ate breakfast, the hole orderlies were called to the dorm to clean up and pick up trays.

"Yo, playa, where Doobie at?" Real asked the young, clean-cut brother who looked as if he'd just started doing time.

"Man, some dudes fucked him up last night. They went at him in the shower—so bad the nigga had to be taken to the free world hospital! They sent me over here in his place," the young boy said as he followed the other two orderlies' lead and started picking up the trays from the floor.

Bohog sat at his door listening to the exchange and knew B-Low had moved on his word. The thought didn't even cross Real's mind, though, that he was the reason Doobie was laid up in ICU, with a fractured rib, two internal organ punctures, and a lacerated skull. The man was barely alive.

Real laid his towel, soap, t-shirt, and boxers on the bed and did a few subtle stretches—whichever ones his small, confining quarters would allow—while he waited for the officer to arrive at his room to escort him to the shower.

A few minutes later, the officer was back at his door. "Let's ride," the officer said, motioning for Real to stick his wrists out the tray slot so he could be handcuffed and safely taken for his morning scrub-down.

After his shower, Real sat in his room and nursed his wounds. He changed his bandages and inspected himself. Most of his injuries were healing pretty well, and on the ones that seemed to be recovering more slowly, he applied the ointment the doc had prescribed. More than anything in the world, what Real wanted was B-Low, but he knew he wouldn't be let out of the hole until the investigation was over, and that would be another thirty days.

Chapter 6

Shonnie was jarred out of her sleep by Moe, pulling her car door open.

"What in the hell you doing out here, baby?" Moe asked with a slur, still reeling from his gallon of liquor.

Shonnie tried her best to keep her cool, but she was far too overcome with rage. She'd worked hard all day, only to come home to a drunk fiancé who couldn't even let her in the house for a good night's rest. "What in the hell you think I'm doing out here!? You locked me out the fuckin' house last night, then passed out with your drunk ass! I work all fuckin' day to keep our damn lights on, then come home to get off my feet and can't even get in my own damn place 'cause your fuckin' ass is drunk with the chain lock on the door!" Shonnie screamed as she rose up out of the car.

Smack! Before both of her feet were planted on the ground, a hard right backhand caught her totally off guard.

"Ah!" Shonnie cried, as she climbed on out of the car and attacked Moe. She swung wildly and caught him with a lucky strike that busted his lip, angering him beyond measure.

"You bitch!" Moe screamed. He grabbed Shonnie, whom he easily had a hundred pounds on, lifted her in the air, and slammed her to the ground.

"Argh!" Shonnie grunted as the ground knocked the breath out of her.

"Yo' stupid ass!" Moe screamed as he stood over her, slapping her repeatedly in the face.

"Stop it, Moe! Stop!" Shonnie shouted as she got up on her knees and scurried away.

Moe let up on his assault and headed back in the house, leaving Shonnie sitting in the middle of the yard, in tears. Her prison uniform was caked with red dirt, and her weave was barely hanging by its visible tracks. Shonnie was tired of her life. She so much wanted the old Moe back, that Prince Charming who'd sworn to always protect her and make her happy. She slowly got to her feet and made her way in the house, where she found Moe, who was tending to his busted lip and gawking at his hung-over self in the bathroom mirror.

"Stupid-ass bitch!" Moe spat when he caught her reflection as she walked by the bathroom.

Shonnie entered her room, stripped out of her filthy uniform, and checked her face in her bedroom mirror. She noticed swelling around her eye and on the side of her face. She searched for her reddish foundation, hoping it would come in handy to cover her injuries when she got to work later.

As she peeled off the dirty, sweaty polyester uniform, Moe entered the room, holding a wad of tissue to his lip. Instantly, a slight hard-on grew in his pants when he took notice of Shonnie's smooth, thick, flawless body while she stood there in front of the mirror in her panties and bra. He walked over and grabbed her by the waist.

"Get your fuckin' hands off me, Moe!" Shonnie demanded through clenched teeth as she rubbed her hand over her bruised face.

"Aw, come here, baby," Moe said, pulling her to him roughly.

Shonnie bit her tongue; the last thing she wanted was another beating. She knew if she put up any kind of resistance, Moe would get angry and lash out, so she played it safe.

"Look, Moe, I gotta get ready for work," she said softly, even though she was boiling inside.

"You ain't gotta be at work for hours," Moe said with a slight slur.

"I gotta go in early today, baby. We've got a…staff meeting," Shonnie lied as she tried to slowly pull away.

"I said come here," Moe said in a firm tone, nearly jerking her over to the bed.

"No, Moe. I can't. I've really got to get ready," Shonnie began to snap but quickly calmed her tone.

Moe acted as if she hadn't said a word and then pulled off his dingy cargo shorts and stained boxers.

"No, Moe. Seriously," Shonnie said as the sickening stench from his sweaty boxers invaded her nostrils.

"I said come here," he repeated.

Shonnie knew that threatening tone well, so she cooperated.

Moe climbed on top of her and clumsily searched for her wet opening with his oversized manhood. When he found her wet spot, he jammed himself into her, showing no mercy or tenderness whatsoever.

"Owww!" Shonnie cried out in pain as he tore through her insides.

Moe mistook her screams of pain for pleasure, and that only enticed him to go at her harder. Shonnie cried and sobbed as he smothered her with his smelly body, humping her like a dog in heat. Longing for escape, she pulled her mind away from the act and forced herself to imagine that she was on a white, sandy beach, walking hand in hand with her perfect man. The faster he humped, the farther she took herself away from their bedroom. Shonnie hated her life, and the worst part of it was the man Moe had become.

"Ahhhh yesss!" Moe called out, releasing inside of her with a nasty grunt.

Shonnie cringed when his sweaty, wet, unmoving body lay on top of her for what seemed like forever. Only when she nudged him did he get up off of her so she could head to the shower. With the water as hot as she could stand it, as if she hoped to somehow sterilize herself of him, she scrubbed and scrubbed away, trying to wipe all remnants of Moe off of her skin. Her tears of pain had become tears of anger.

By the time she exited the shower, Moe was knocked out in the bed, snoring and still naked. Shonnie crept across the room to the closet and pulled out the snub-nosed .38. She looked down at the gun, then back over at the still unconscious Moe. She quickly dismissed the homicidal thought, dropped the gun back in the box, and continued to ready herself for work.

Chapter 7

"Bro, the nigga was screamin' like a bitch," BodyBag bragged to B-Low in the rear of the dorm, where they sat on small trashcans, kicking it.

"Look, when the nigga Real hits the compound, we gonna have that bitch nigga airlifted out this bitch," B-Low, recalling the vicious assault he'd gone through in the gym cage a year ago, courtesy of Real, who'd ordered it from the street.

B-Low was still furious about the sexual assault, and every time he walked into the gym, he was reminded of the incident and the HIV-positive status he had as a souvenir. He wanted closure, and he felt that dealing Real the same fate would afford him that. B-Low was nothing near the man he used to be, and he really no longer cared if he lived or died. The one thing he did know for sure was that prison would be his permanent home.

"Oh yeah, he's gonna be dealt with royally," said NoLove. The six-two, yellow, tattooed, bald-headed thug smiled, revealing a mouth full of gold teeth.

"We need to torture the fuck nigga, but on the real, I don't think that nigga got the heart to come out the hole," said BodyBag, the short, ashy, bumpy-faced goon whose gummy smile made his yellow chompers look like baby teeth.

"He'll be out. I know he comin' out," B-Low said. He knew Real was no coward and would come out prepared for war.

"Fire in the hole! Twelve! Twelve!" Raze screamed from the front of the dorm.

A quartet of officers, led by Sergeant Shonnie, entered the dorm.

"Say, duck my phone in the spot," B-Low said as he quickly fished his cell phone from his pocket and passed it off to NoLove.

NoLove quickly did as he was told and ducked into his room to hide the phone and the shanks.

"Man, I want me some of that," BodyBag said, eyeing Shonnie up and down as she walked through the dorm with three male officers, making rounds and doing random shakedowns.

"The sergeant is a bad bitch. They say her nigga is the weight man down this way and that he got that country shit on lock," B-Low said, passing on the prison gossip.

Shonnie and the other officers made their way over to where B-Low and BodyBag were sitting. "Hey, y'all, what you got going on back here?" she asked with her hands on her bulging hips. She looked at them with an arched eyebrow; she could tell they were up to no good.

"We just cooling, Sergeant," B-Low said, leaning up against the wall.

"Pat them down and search these two rooms," Shonnie ordered the other officers.

After patting B-Low and BodyBag down, the officers dispersed to the rooms.

"Whoa!" one of the male officers called out when he glanced in NoLove's cell.

NoLove knew the room was dirty and that they'd throw him in the hole if they searched it and found the phone, the shanks, and other contraband, so he'd pulled one of the oldest deterrents in the book. He'd stripped down naked, greased up, got into bed, closed his eyes, and started stroking his penis.

"What? " Shonnie asked, looking at the officer.

"Uh, I say we come back to this one. Looks like he needs a little…private time," the officer said as he quickly made his way to the next room.

Shonnie couldn't help her curiosity. She looked then yelled into NoLove's cell, "Get yo' nasty ass up!" As soon as she saw his erect penis, all lubed up and hanging there, she screamed and quickly turned away.

B-Low and BodyBag laughed because they knew NoLove was up to something crazy that involved his private part. They laughed even harder when they saw Shonnie's backside wiggle loosely as she walked away.

After Shonnie did her routine search of the dorm, she dismissed the officers and headed to the hole to sign the charts. Strangely, she found herself anticipating that part of her daily duties, and she was sure that had something to do with Real.

As soon as Shonnie and the officers exited the dorm and were out of sight, Mrs. Knight and Raze ducked off into the officers' bathroom for a quickie.

"Man, that nigga time up. He gotta break bread. He needs ta make that bitch look out for the team, or he gotta go, straight up," B-Low told BodyBag as he watched Raze dip off into the bathroom behind Officer Knight.

"Just say the word, bro," BodyBag said in a serious tone, rubbing his palms together like some cartoon villain eager to pull some mischief. "Just say the word."

Chapter 8

$\mathcal{S}$honnie entered the hole dorm, walked over to the officer's desk, signed the logbook, and proceeded to make her rounds.

"Stankin'-ass ho! You ain't shit!" an inmate yelled, awakening the other inmates and starting off a chorus of insults and screams.

"Yeah, ho, suck this wood! Let a nigga put this dick in that phat-ass bitch!" another inmate called out.

The once-quiet dorm was soon filled with disrespectful catcalls.

"Y'all niggas need to lay y'all bitch asses down," Shonnie screamed. She was in no mood for confrontations; she'd already taken enough shit from Moe.

Real peeked out the crack in his door and set his sights on Shonnie, who was directly across from his room signing charts, about to make her way over to his room. He quickly got down and did a couple sets of pushups. Real had always been physically fit, but his hospital stay had taken a bit of a toll on his physique, and he refused to be seen that way by the attractive sergeant. By the time Shonnie got to his door, he was glistening from the mild sweat that came from the back-to-back sets of pushups and the dry heat of the hole.

"Hey, Walker," Shonnie called out as she looked in his room.

Her heart skipped a beat when she zeroed in on Real, standing in the middle of his room in his boxers, doing side stretches and working up a sweat. She counted more than a six-pack in his bulging stomach muscles, and she was so amazed with Real's anatomy that she was temporarily stuck in a daze. Her private parts twitched at the sight of the glistening man, looking at her with those light brown eyes that undeniably made her feel some kind of way. Even behind bars, he put Moe to shame.

"Hey, Sergeant, how you doing?" Real asked.

Shonnie glanced at the bandages on various parts of his body. "I'm good. How 'bout you? How you coming along?" Shonnie asked, still in awe.

"I'm straight. I'll be back in shape in no time," Real said, staring into her stressed eyes.

"Good," she replied flatly, still caught in his gaze.

"You lyin'."

"What?" she asked, snapping out of it a bit.

"You're not good, and you're not happy. I can hear it in your voice. What's wrong?" Real asked.

His concern caught her totally off guard, but he was right on point with his assumption. Nonetheless, she didn't want him to know that. "Why do you say that?" Shonnie asked, trying to hide whatever signs Real was picking up on.

"Like I said, I can hear it in your voice. I can see it in your eyes too," Real said as he walked up to the doors window and fixed his intent gaze upon her.

"I…uh, well…you know…" Shonnie stuttered, then paused and took a deep breath.

"You stressing about something," Real followed up.

"This is crazy. I have to…well, you have a good day now, Mr. Walker," Shonnie said, snapping out of the strong feeling that was overwhelming her. She wanted to tell him the truth. She wanted to tell him he was right. She wanted to scream, *You're right! I'm not happy. I hate my man. I hate my life…and you are so fuckin' fine!* But she knew she couldn't say any of that, so she just turned and quickly walked away from Real's room. She knew if she stood there staring into his brown, seductive eyes any longer, she'd end up spilling her guts. Not only would that be inappropriate, but it would also be way out of character for her.

"Okay, whatever," Real mumbled to himself as he watched Shonnie turn and head to the front exit without even finishing her rounds. He knew he was right about her, and he had hit the nail on the head.

As Real watched her rush out the door, he heard someone knocking on the wall. "Yeah?" Real yelled, annoyed by the noise.

"Come to the window, bro," Bohog called out from next door.

Real didn't know his neighbor and was in no mood for making small talk. "Why? What's up?" Real called out again, virtually ignoring his request.

"You got anything to read over there?" Bohog asked, trying to strike up conversation with the man his crew had hit up; he was most definitely not looking for literature.

"Naw, my nigga, I ain't got nothing," Real snapped, resuming his stretches. He was desperate to get his body and health back up to 100 percent.

"Fuck nigga," Bohog whispered under his breath as he closed his window and lay back down.

Chapter 9

One month later…

"Richard Walker, pack it up!" the dorm officer called out as he looked at his list of inmates to be released back into the prison population.

Real had healed quite nicely and was in better shape than before the assault, thanks to his daily workout regimen. He knew he had to be ready for war when he hit compound.

While dragging his property out of the room, he noticed that his next-door neighbor was also being released. Real did a double-take when he set eyes on the six-five, 300-pound gorilla who was cutting his eyes at him, but then he ignored the man's cold stares as he readied himself to go back into the population.

The ID officer rounded up all the men up and escorted them out of the hole and to their new housing assignments in the regular population. Real kept a sharp eye out for B-Low as they exited the hole and rounded the walk. He remembered Doobie telling him that B-Low was in H-building, so at least he knew which side of the prison his enemy was housed on.

Real, Bohog, and a couple more inmates were escorted to the opposite side of the compound. Real was the only one who was placed in E-building, aka The Thunder Dorm, which was also used for new arrivals. As soon as Real entered the dorm, he heard someone call out his name.

"That boy Real!" Iron Head yelled excitedly as he rushed down the stairs to greet the man whom he'd so looked up to years ago at GSCP. "Boy, what up! You ever hear from Tino or Yaki? Ever since they set it off with the Crips down here and got transferred, I ain't heard from 'em. Why the hell you back? What happened?" Iron Head asked, remembering back on the last time they'd seen each other out in the yard at GSCP with Yaki and Tino, after setting it off with some gang members.

"Man, it's a long story. Boy, look at you! You done got big as hell! What the fuck you been eatin'?" Real said, slapping the young goon five while pulling him into a half-embrace.

"Nigga been banging on the workout, bro. I heard 'bout the play with that nigga they call B-Low. Shit, bro! Whatever on yo' mind can be on that nigga's ass," Iron Head said in a serious tone.

"What you think on my mind, my nigga?" Real shot back as he held up his shirt, displaying his many wounds.

"You know my fam' is GF all out the A, shawty," Iron Head filled Real in.

"GF? Who dey?" Real asked, dumb to the fact.

"They's a clique of real niggas from the A who's setting a tone for the city behind these walls. All my li'l niggas TTG!"

"TTG?" Real asked, again unfamiliar.

Iron Head laughed. "TTG means trained to go! TTG!" Iron Head called out, bringing a crew of young thugs from Atlanta to attention.

Real looked around and noticed that all eyes were on him and Iron Head as they stood in the middle of the dorm. "Okay. Real talk," Real said as he looked around at the ready, willing, and able army of young thugs.

"See? Them soldiers ready to ride! All you gotta do is kick it off," Iron Head said as he dapped Real up again, letting the soldier boys know everything was all good.

"Let me g—"

"CERT team on the walk with the buggy coming this way! Fire in the hole!" someone screamed, cutting Real and Iron Head off.

"Shit! I'll holla at you in a min'," Iron Head said as he took off to his room to hide his cell phone that was charging at the head of his bed.

"Everybody on the wall! Stop!" the three hulking CERT team members screamed as they rushed the dorm.

"Fuck! My nigga, you straight?" Iron Head whispered to his li'l partner, Ace, as they stood with their hands on the wall.

"Hell naw! I got my shit on me," Ace replied, desperately trying to figure out a way to get his cell phone off of him.

"Damn, my nigga!"

"All y'all on the wall! If you're in your room, you've got exactly two seconds to get out here and get ya ass on the wall! Anybody who tries to stay in his room will be locked down. This is your first and last warning!" the short, stocky Bulldog screamed out. The inmates had given him that nickname with good reason, because he was always snarling at everybody, and he definitely had the build.

"Hey! Help! Help!" Iron Head screamed out as Ace flopped around on the ground, shaking and slobbering from his mouth, faking a seizure.

"Get medical down here! All y'all lock down...NOW!" Bulldog yelled, pissed that his shakedown had been sidetracked by a medical emergency, which overrode the routine search.

All the inmates filed into their rooms while the CERT team hovered over Ace, waiting for medical to arrive. Five minutes later, medics carted Ace off to the infirmary, and no one was aware that he had a cell phone stashed in his boxer briefs.

As soon as medical cleared the dorm, Bulldog went back into action. "Everybody back out now!" he barked, knowing his shakedown would now most likely be in vain.

Chapter 10

"Girl, this shit is getting way out of control! You see that nasty bitch lettin' them niggas dig all up in her onstage? I know it's hard for a bitch out here, but it ain't that serious," Fire said to Tasty as they sat in the dressing room getting ready for their next set onstage.

"See? That's the problem with bitches. They stay all up in the next bitch's business!" Black Stallion said out loud for all the dressing room to hear, directing it especially at Fire, her nemesis.

"Shit like that is why bitches is always getting their asses whooped!" Fire shot back, standing.

"Bitch, you always in the next bitch's business. The only reason I ain't gonna fuck you up right here and now is 'cause I got a quota to meet. Consider yourself lucky, ho. You get a pass tonight," Black Stallion said as she continued to fix her hair in the mirror. She knew the petite white Fire was no match for her.

"Bitch, don't give me no pass! Your ass the one lucky!" Fire screamed.

"Girl, come on," Tasty said, grabbing Fire by her wrist and pulling her out of the dressing room.

"Y'all bitches' days are numbered," Black Stallion said as she watched them exit.

Club Exposé was one of Atlanta's most popular strip joints. The establishment was owned and operated by Giovanni, a popular mobster. Giovanni was a man with many ties in politics, in the street, in religious organizations, and in many other factions of society. The mob had put him in place to run their string of high-class strip clubs. GSHS LLC was the controlling entity of Exposé, Pearlz, Star Light, and Hollywood, four of the trendiest, most upscale strip clubs in the states. The clubs generated millions, so the mob used them to launder their illegal gains. Not only did the mob trust Giovanni, but he was also the son of Dominic, the godfather.

"Hey, Giovanni," Fire flirted as he made his way through the club.

"Hello, ladies." Giovanni was definitely a ladies' man inside and outside the club, so he had no problem stopping to greet both of them before he made his way through the club, stopping to make small talk here and there with the midday lunch crowd.

"Girl, that muthafucker know he fine," Fire said, staring at the sleekly dressed, clean-shaven, gray-eyed Giovanni who displayed a mouthful of perfectly straight, white teeth when he laughed as he entertained a circle of male patrons.

"Yes, he sho is. And that only makes his money ten times finer," Tasty agreed, looking hungrily at the powerful, wealthy men.

"I really appreciate y'all coming out here. Any word on my nephew yet?"

Giovanni asked Bill Leonard, a prominent criminal attorney for the state of Georgia.

"Yeah, we're working really hard to pull everything together, but like I told you from the start, it's gonna be a lengthy process. I promise you we will get the results you've paid us for," Bill said, eyeing the bronze, blonde-haired, blue-eyed, thick and shapely Fire as she climbed onto the stage. *She has to be the baddest white girl in the whole state of Georgia,* he thought.

"Okay. I totally understand, and I know your word is like gold. Shit, our word is all we got. If a man's word isn't any good, he'd be better off dead," Giovanni said, making sure Bill picked up on the threat. Giovanni knew he understood clearly, as did his two cohorts that accompanied him.

"Giovanni, you have my word that Emilio will be home soon."

"I knew it was a good idea to hire you. If you or your men need anything, just let me know. As you can see, we employ the most captivating woman in the state of Georgia. Whatever or whoever you want, it's on me."

As Giovanni walked off, he couldn't help thinking about Emilio, his nephew who he'd raised on his own since his sister had died. The poor kid had been sitting in Georgia prison for close to six months on a murder charge.

Chapter 11

"Man, I'm fuckin' tired of this shit," the young Italian said as he picked up his property that the CERT team had thrown everywhere.

"I feel ya, man. By the way, I'm Real." He extended his hand to the young man.

"Emilio," the young Italian replied, firmly shaking Real's hand like a truly distinguished gentleman.

"How long you been down?" Real asked, unpacking his property and placing it in the locker.

"Going on seven months now," Emilio replied as he did the same. "You just getting in?"

"Yeah, but this is my second bid."

"Damn, man. What you back for?" Emilio asked curiously.

"They say murder, but you know how that go," Real replied, still sticking by his code of denying guilt, despite having been found guilty.

"Yeah, me too, but I'm not really worried about it. I'll be out soon," Emilio said with total confidence.

"I feel you," Real replied. He'd heard those same words on several occasions during his first bid from men who knew deep down they were never going to walk the streets again. "How old are you, young blood?" Real asked, realizing the youngster couldn't be too far beyond the legal limit.

"Twenty-two."

"Where you from?"

"I was born and raised in New York, Manhattan, but I moved to Atlanta with my cousin a couple years back to help out in one of my uncle's clubs," Emilio said as he put the remaining clothes in his locker.

"What club?" Real asked, pulling out his Bible and laying it on his pillow.

"Exposé, out in Buckhead. It's one of Atlanta's—"

"Most popular, upscale strip clubs. Yeah, I know the place."

"You do?"

"Yep. Been there a time or two myself," Real said.

"So you're familiar with our spot," Emilio said, not at all surprised, being that it was one of Atlanta's premiere spots for the rich and famous.

"Yeah, I owned the G-Spot," Real added, recalling all he'd heard about Exposé and its mob ties.

"G-Spot? I've heard a lot about that place too. It's the 'hood club, right?" Emilio asked, not realizing it might be taken as an insult.

"Nothing 'hood about it—just frequented by blacks, and upper-class blacks at that," Real said firmly.

"Yeah, it was a nice spot, a real classy place," Emilio stuttered, trying his best to cover for his sloppy comment.

"So who'd you kill?" Real asked.

"It was a mistake. Me and my friend were drinking and playing around with a loaded gun at his place. Next thing I knew, the gun went off, and he was bleeding like shit from his neck. By the time the ambulance arrived, he was dead. They knew it was a mistake, an accident, but his father, who just so happens to be a top-ranking city official, didn't think so. He pushed the issue, so here I am, facing a life sentence. After all his crying to the D.A. and the tough-on-crime talk, his dad was killed in a botched robbery. It's cool though. My uncle got me the best lawyer in the city," Emilio said.

Real had doubted him before, but now that he knew the kid had some powerful ties. "Well, I wish you luck. I'm gonna do the same as soon as I get my paperwork back from the courts," Real told him.

Just then, two young thugs walked by the room real slow, paused, and walked on. Having been down before, Real knew something wasn't right about that, especially when they circled back around and stepped into the small, cramped room.

Chapter 12

"Say, bro, this ain't what we asked for," B-Low told Raze as they sat in his room unwrapping the package that Officer Knight had just dropped off to Raze.

NoLove and BodyBag stood outside the door.

"My nigga, that's all she could cop from her li'l country spot," Raze said, feeling like a real chump for being extorted by B-Low and his crew.

"Nah, bro. This ain't gon' work, so this is what I'ma do. I'm going to keep this, and you're gonna get your girl to bring two more flops and another pound tomorrow," B-Low said, snatching the pound of weed and cell phone which inmates referred to as a flop in the Georgia prison system. B-Low placed the weed back in the bag, then tucked the phone under his mattress for the time being.

"Nah, bro, that ain't happening. Ain't no way in the hell she gonna be able to—"

Smack!

"Look, nigga, that *is* happening, and if it don't, you best pack your shit and get up outta here," B-Low spat as he stood over Raze, who glared up at him with daggers in his eyes.

Raze wasn't a goon, but he wasn't a chump either. It took everything in him not to jump up and attack B-Low. The only reason he didn't was Officer Knight. He'd finally worked his way in the dorm with her, which made their trysts far more convenient. He was sexing her on the regular, eating home-cooked meals, and getting contraband, drugs, and cell phone drop-offs daily, which was earning him a nice profit. Raze knew if he struck back at B-Low, all those fringe benefits would come to an end, because he'd be forcibly relocated. So, he bit his tongue and balled his fist up but never made a move. "A'ight, man. I'll see what's up," Raze said through clenched teeth. He lifted up from the bed, rubbed his hand over his head, and exited the room.

NoLove and BodyBag weren't the only ones watching him when he exited the room. Officer Knight sat behind her desk, and she had her eye on the room as well. She knew B-Low and his crew were up to some crooked business with Raze.

"Say, my nigga, what we looking like?" NoLove asked B-Low as he entered the room.

"A cool pound, and you know I full-court pressed the nigga for more tomorrow," B-Low said as he looked over at the spot under the mattress where he'd tucked the cell phone; he had no plans to mention the flop to them.

"Bet. Let's sack this shit up and hit the block," NoLove called out as he pulled the weed from the bag and spread it across the desk.

"Nigga, roll one up first so we can see what this shit hitting like," BodyBag chimed in.

B-Low looked out the door window at Raze, who was at the desk talking to Officer Knight. The officer was wearing a crazy frown on her face, staring over at B-Low's room. "Man, that nigga telling this bitch something, and now she picking up the radio. Y'all put that shit up till I see what's up with this nigga," B-Low said, watching them closely.

"Nigga, you just being paranoid. Get some fire and light this up," BodyBag called out, handing B-Low the sloppily rolled joint.

Raze had indeed gone to Officer Knight with the demands but tried to make it sound like some legit dealings.

The officer knew better though, especially since no money was being exchanged. "Raze, you act like I'm a slow bitch or something. I ain't about to let them niggas think they can muscle us just 'cause they know how we roll. I got something for they ass. I'm 'bout to get they ass shook down, and I know they got something in that room," Officer Knight said, picking up the radio to call the CERT team, who was busy harassing inmates out on the walk.

"No! Don't go doin' no crazy shit like—" Raze tried to object, but she cut him off.

"X-1, could you give me a twelve?" she said into her radio as she watched Raze storm off to his room.

A minute later, her desk phone was ringing. "What up, Meka?" her cousin Bulldog asked.

"Look, cuz, you need to come down here and do a full-ass shakedown on Room 117. They got something going on in there. When I tried to check it out, one of the inmates got in my face like he was tryin'a hit me or some shit," she lied, knowing her cousin would come running if he thought she was in danger.

"In your face? Gonna hit you? Be right there!" Bulldog yelled. Then he clicked off the line and rushed to check on his favorite little cousin.

Two minutes later, someone started yelling from the front of the dorm, "CERT team coming across the yard! They running too!"

All the prisoners who had contraband to hide scrambled around in a panic, trying their best to get their illegal property out of sight.

"I knew it! That fuck nigga!" B-Low screamed as they frantically grabbed the weed off the desk.

"Where they at!" NoLove asked as he and BodyBag tucked the weed.

"They just came in, and they coming straight this way. Shit!" B-Low yelled. He pulled the door closed, quickly grabbed his toothbrush from his locker, and jammed it in the seam of the door, making it hard to open.

"Flush this shit!" NoLove called out to BodyBag as the CERT team got to their door.

"Open this door!" Bulldog demanded, pounding on it.

Boom! Boom! Boom!

"Officer Knight, unlock all the locks."

Bulldog knew they had the door jammed, as that was nothing new to him, so he knew he'd have to kick it open. On the third kick, the door popped open. "All y'all put ya hands on the wall!" he wailed while the other three CERT officers rushed the room.

The weed smell was strong, but much to the officers' embarrassment and anger, no weed was to be found; it had all been flushed.

"Officer Knight, lock this dorm down and get over here," Bulldog instructed as he pulled his black gloves on.

"Lockdown! Everybody to your room," Officer Knight called out as she went around and locked all the inmates in.

"So, y'all threatening my officer, huh? A bunch of tough guys, right?" Bulldog mocked as he turned each man around and got in their faces.

"Man—" BodyBag said. He was ready to snap, but he knew Bulldog was just looking for an excuse to use force.

"Man what? Y'all some hoes! Jump bad now! Do it!" Bulldog spat as the other CERT officers shook down the room.

"What's up?" Officer Knight said as she entered the room.

"Which one is the tough guy?" Bulldog asked, looking at each of the men.

"Him," she replied, pointing to B-Low, aware that he was the group leader.

Before B-Low could protest, Bulldog had him locked around the neck in a submission hold.

"Ahh! Let me go!" B-Low screamed as the other officers handcuffed NoLove and BodyBag, then escorted them out of the room.

"Nah, nigga, you bad. Get in *my* face!" Bulldog spat as he applied pressure.

"Ughhh!" B-Low cried out.

The other officers walked back in and joined Officer Knight as she searched their room.

"Yeahhhh, boy, how that feel? I love this shit!" Bulldog said excitedly as he kept the pressure on the hurting B-Low.

"Lookie here!" Officer Knight called out when she found the cell phone shoved under the mattress—the phone she'd given to Raze.

"Let's go, gangsta," Bulldog said, releasing his grip and pulling out his cuffs for B-Low.

"That ain't my shit!" B-Low called out, mad as hell.

"Yes it is, but don't worry. Your boys are gonna be keepin' you company," he said, grabbing B-Low by the arm and shoving him out the door.

B-Low looked at Officer Knight, then glared up at Raze's room, making sure they both saw the revenge in his eyes.

Raze knew as soon as B-Low got out of the hole, it was going down, and he made up his mind right then to take advantage of the situation. "Fuck!" Raze screamed, punching the wall.

" Make sure the paperwork reflects those figures and fax them over to me," Giovanni told his Houston club manager. He was happy to hear that $2.7 million had been cleared through the clubs without a hitch.

"Damn, baby. Can Mama get some attention?" Black Stallion cooed as she walked over and sat in his lap.

Giovanni was aware of the rules. There was to be no cavorting with the dancers in any of the establishments, and Giovanni was a stickler for the rules, up until he met Black Stallion, his dream-come-true. She was tall, thick, and black, with smooth, flawless skin and European facial features. Her smile was his real weakness. Her plump, thick lips and pretty, perfect, white teeth just did something to him. Black Stallion was a scandalous bitch, and she had the rich Giovanni eating out of the palm of her hand.

"You get all the attention, darling," Giovanni cooed as he rubbed his hands over Black Stallion's thick, soft, smooth thighs.

"I don't feel loved," Black Stallion said in a baby voice, leaning down to kiss him on the neck.

Giovanni couldn't get enough of Black Stallion and her mind-blowing sex. "You know I love you, baby," he replied as he caressed her slim waist and plump, oversized backside.

"Love you too," she replied, feeling his erection grow inside of his pants. She jumped off his lap and knelt down in front of him and unbuckled his pants. "Now, give your baby her pacifier, Daddy," she said softly as she pulled out his hard dick and started sucking.

"Oh yeah, baby! Yes!" Giovanni moaned.

She looked up at him while swallowing more than half of his manhood, caressing his balls with her soft hand. "Mmm…" she moaned while deep-throating him.

"Suck this dick, baby! Yes!" he called out while thrusting his hips forward, fucking her in the mouth.

Black Stallion slid her mouth from around his dick and stood up. "Good, baby?" she asked as she leaned in and kissed him, purposely making him taste himself.

"Oh yeah," he said as he turned her around and bent her over his desk.

"Bad boy, Giovanni," she said as she reached back, slid her g-string o the side, and opened up her wetness for him to enter.

"Beautiful," he said as he guided his throbbing hardness into her pussy.

"Yeah…oh God…yes!" she called out as he long-stroked her slowly.

Black Stallion enjoyed the quickies with Giovanni, and she also knew she had to have his nose wide open before she made her move.

"Oh yeah, darling! This is so fucking good! This is good stuff!" he called out as he sped up his thrusts.

Black Stallion got in the groove and started throwing her ass back into him, slapping it against his thighs. She used her vaginal muscles to squeeze his dick with her walls as he pumped in and out of her. She glanced back and saw that his eyes had rolled back in his head, and he was moaning as he humped her. "Gimme that thick nut, baby!" Black Stallion called out as she reached back and spread her ass cheeks so he could go deep, then started throwing her big, jiggly ass toward him, causing his knees to weaken.

"Oh fuck! God, yes! Yeah, baby! I love you!" he screamed as his body began to tremble violently.

Black Stallion knew she had him, but she went the extra mile anyway. She lifted one leg and put it on his desk while he kept stroking. She looked back once, then squeezed his dick as hard as she could with her pussy muscles, making him cum instantly.

"Ahhhhh!" he called out, sinking his fingers into her soft, plump ass.

"Gimme all that thick, white nut baby!" she hollered seductively as he emptied himself inside of her.

"Oh shit! Damn, baby," Giovanni said plopping back in his office chair, breathing hard and sweating.

Knock! Knock!

"Yeah?" Giovanni answered, out of breath.

"Hey, boss, we got an issue out here. Could you come to the bar?" asked Fred, the head bouncer.

"A'ight. Be right there," he replied. He stood, pulled up his pants, and straightened his clothes.

"I gotta sit down for a minute," Black Stallion said, lying back on the office couch.

"Okay. I'll be right back," Giovanni said before hurrying out to the bar.

As soon as he left, Black Stallion jumped up and opened the office door. She glanced both ways down the hall to make sure he was gone. She spotted him and a couple of the bouncers having a heated conversation with the bartender. She eased the door closed again and quickly ran over to his desk. She grabbed a pen and a piece of paper and copied down everything that looked important, especially banking information. She went through every drawer and jotted down any vital information she could find. Ten minutes later, she was exiting the office, ready to call it a night.

"Bitch!" Fire called out just loud enough for Black Stallion to hear as she exited the dressing room on her way out the door.

Black Stallion stopped in her tracks, then just ignored her with a big smile on her face, knowing her stripping days were nearly over.

Chapter 14

" Say, homey, can you step out for a minute so we can holla at dude?" the first young thug asked as his partner stood off to the side with an obvious bulge under his shirt.

Real had a feeling the men were up to something, but he didn't know for sure. "Yeah cool," Real said, looking over at Emilio, who was standing there with a confused look on his face, watching him as he stepped out the room.

"You know what it is. Give us the flop and the jewelry," the first thug demanded as he closed in on a terrified Emilio.

"What's up with this? Come on, man. Y'all ain't gotta do it like—"

Smack! The open-handed slap sent Emilio to the floor.

"Look, bitch, just give up the goods…NOW!" said the second man, holding a long, sharp shank and closing in on a cowering Emilio.

Emilio shakily started unfastening his watch as the two thugs stood over him.

Real heard the yelling and peeked in the door out of curiosity. He was surprised at what was going down but ignored it; his first bid had taught him an important lesson: See and don't see. So, Real just stood outside the door checking out his new home.

"Where the phone at, crack! You lucky I ain't pulling them pants down to get at that ripe ass!" the thug with the sharp tool snapped.

"Fuck that! I'm 'bout to get some of this white ass," the second man said as he started unbuckling his belt.

Emilio's eyes grew as big as golf balls as he watched the man pull out his dick and start stroking it while walking in his direction.

Real knew it was none of his business, but he stepped in anyway. "Yo, what up, playas? What's going on?" Real asked, looking from man to man.

"Say, my nigga, stay out of our business before we put you in it," the first thug said with attitude as he turned and faced Real.

"Nigga, who the fuck you?" the second thug said, pulling his clothes back up and fastening his belt.

Emilio had taken off his watch and was now taking off his chain. He cowered in the corner, shaking like a frightened animal.

"Put ya shit back on, shawty. Ain't nobody taking your shit!" Real said to him. Then he turned to the thugs. "Yeah, nigga, I'm in your business!" he spat, ready to smash the young punks. He could sense fear from a mile away, and it was thick in the room. Even though the young thug had the banger, he lacked the heart to use it, and Real picked up on that.

Just as Real was about to air the two young thugs out, Iron Head knocked on the door and stepped in. "What up? What y'all got going on in this place?" he asked, looking at the awkward scene.

"Nothing but these niggas gettin' up outta here," Real said with emphasis, staring hard at the two intruders.

"Yolo, what the hell y'all up to? Chris, what you doin' with that tool?" Iron Head asked the two wild, thugged-out booty bandits who were trying to make a name for themselves in the joint.

"Shit cool. You got that," Chris said to Real as he turned and walked out of the room.

"It's all good, bro. We out," Yolo said with much respect to Iron Head. He looked Real up and down before he exited.

"Boy, you already got it popping 'round this bitch," Iron Head joked as he looked over at Emilio, who was placing his jewelry back on while wiping the sweat off his brow.

"You good li'l bro?" Real asked.

A visibly shaken Emilio answered, "Yeah, man. Thanks. That's some bullshit!" Emilio yelled as he dug into his mattress and pulled out his cell phone.

"They was 'bout to rape and rob li'l man," Real told Iron Head, who figured it was something on that level.

"Yeah, I figured that. What's funny about it is that neither one of them niggas built like that. They gay as fuck and TTG ain't in they blood," Iron Head said as him and Real stepped out of the room.

"I know. I picked up on it off the jump," Real replied as they walked over to the big window and looked out over the yard.

"So what's the move on B-Low?" Iron Head asked.

"Tomorrow. Get me two tools," Real said as he stared out over the yard, thinking back on how his life used to be.

"I got you," Iron Head said, and he walked off leaving Real to his thoughts.

* * * * *

"Yeah, Uncle, I understand, but I'm ready to go." Emilio said, pouting as his eyes began to water.

"Look, I just spoke with the attorneys, and they assured me that you'll be home soon, but if you have a problem like that again, let me know. Better yet, give me the name of the man who helped you out," Giovanni said, sitting on the corner of his office desk.

"His name is Real, and he said he used to own the G-Spot," Emilio said, keeping his eye on the door in case the thugs came back.

"G-Spot? I've heard about it. When you get a chance, get him on the phone so I can speak with him."

"Okay. I'll call you back then," Emilio said, ending the call. He wiped his eyes, stuffed his phone back in his mattress, and put on his best tough-guy look.

Chapter 15

$\mathscr{I}$t was almost time for Shonnie to end her shift. She looked at her watch as she did her last rounds to the buildings. She stopped in F-building, signed the book, and answered any complaints or questions the inmates had before heading over to E-building. As she entered E-building, she was approached with the same issues: stopped-up toilet, no ice in the cooler, and clothes that hadn't come back from the laundry. She handled it all the same. "Give me your name, and I'll check into it," she told the men as they approached her with problem after problem. She hurriedly signed the books so she could get away from the crybabies, but as she was on her way out the door, she heard a familiar voice calling her name.

"Sergeant, can I speak with you for a minute?" Real called out, walking in her direction.

Shonnie recognized the deep voice immediately. "Um, hi, Mr. Walker. What's your issue?" she asked, looking up into his soft brown eyes.

Her attraction to Real was unreal. She noticed that he'd put a little more weight on his chiseled frame and had also grown his hair out; it was now thick and wavy. His smooth skin looked soft to the touch, and his thick lips made her want to give in to his every demand. Shonnie found it hard to contain her true feelings in Real's presence, and that scared her. She hated that his presence had such an effect on her.

"Why haven't I seen you around? You ran out on me while I was in the hole and never came back. What's up with that? Ever since you left, you've been on my mind," Real told her, looking down into her eyes.

His gaze had her wanting him to just take her into his arms. "Uh-huh..." Shonnie mouthed, shaking her head from side to side but still listening.

"Seriously, Sergeant, I find you extremely attractive. Gettin' straight to the point, I wanna get to know you," Real said so softly that no one else could hear.

"You finished?" Shonnie asked, still attentive to his words.

"One last thing, I want to make you happy, something I can tell you haven't been in a long time. Look over my situation just for a second and let me in your life, and I promise to bring joy with me. You are so beautiful," Real told her, still gazing into her soul through her eyes.

Shonnie took a deep breath, dropped her head, then looked back up at Real. "Okayyy. Um...well, we'll talk," Shonnie said, trying her best to hide her blushing.

"I'm gonna hold you to that now," Real said, watching her turn and leave. He knew he'd gotten his point across, but for some reason, he felt guilty. He was sure Constance was looking down on him, and the things he'd just said to the sergeant made him feel like he was betraying his real love.

Shonnie ended her shift a little early, since her supervisor wasn't in. She was ready to get home for some much-needed rest. Day in and day out, she prayed to God, asking Him to bring back the Moe she'd met so many years ago. Her home life was nowhere near what she'd dreamt of and hoped for.

As she came up over the hill, she noticed a small red car in the driveway. She knew Moe didn't have many friends, so she assumed the car to belong to one of his many family members. "Shit! I don't feel like this shit tonight," Shonnie cursed out loud as she pulled in next to the car.

She grabbed her work bag and climbed out of the car. The closer she got to the house, the louder the music seemed. Shaking her head in disgust, she stepped in. As soon as she entered the house, the strong smell of sweaty, funky ass hit her. She covered her nose, dropped her bag, and headed to the back.

"Ooh yeah! Uh-huh! Fuck this pussy, Daddy!" Mabel called out as Moe pounded her from behind.

Shonnie stood at the doorway in shock, totally lost for words, watching her man pound away at his own cousin. Shonnie knew that making a scene and lashing out would be of no use. It took everything in her power to just turn and walk away, but she did. Shonnie went to the front room, turned on the TV, took her shoes off, and got some rest. She didn't care what was going on in the back of the house. She didn't care about any of it anymore. As far as she was concerned, it was over between her and Moe, and she wasn't going to give him another chance. As she sat there watching *Love and Hip Hop*, she heard someone coming from the back.

"Shonnie?" Mabel called out, startled by her presence.

"Yeah, Mabel? You finished, you nasty bitch?!" Shonnie snapped as looked over her shoulder, still holding the remote in her hand.

Mabel didn't respond. She just covered her face and ran out the door. Her 300-pound, five-four frame shook and wiggled as she raced to her car.

Seconds later, Moe came from the back. "Shonnie?" he said, equally surprised to see her.

"Get your shit and get out of my house," Shonnie said, all cool and calm.

Moe knew then that he'd been caught with his pants down—literally. "Get out? I ain't going nowhere," he said, then walked to the kitchen wearing nothing but his boxers.

"Get out of my shit now, Moe!" Shonnie screamed, finally losing her cool.

"Bitch, who you talking to?" Moe slurred, obviously drunk as usual.

"I'm calling the police. You getting up out of here," Shonnie said grabbing the phone.

Before she could press 911, a large hand was around her neck, lifting her up off the couch and choking her.

"Ca...ca...ukk!" Shonnie coughed out, trying to pry his hands from her neck.

"Bitch, I'll kill you, you understand?" Moe said as he slammed her to the floor with a *thump*.

"Ow! Get out! I hate your ass!" Shonnie screamed as she cried hysterically.

"Bitch, *you* get out," Moe demanded, walking over to stand over her.

"I hate your ass! Die, nigga!" Shonnie screamed with venom in her tone.

Moe didn't take her words lightly. He reached back and began pummeling her with his closed fist. The licks sounded off as they solidly connected. He beat her like a man while she tried her best to cover her face. When he was finished, she had a large lump on her head, a black eye, and a busted lip. He'd beaten Shonnie bloody, and he only stopped because he was out of breath.

"Ow! God, please! Ah!" Shonnie cried out as she balled herself up.

Moe didn't say another word. He just got up and walked off to the back, then lay across the bed. Two minutes later, he was snoring.

Shonnie got up on her knees, crawled across the room and grabbed her phone to dial 911.

Chapter 16

"   how call! Chow call!" the dorm officer yelled through the door, alerting the men that breakfast was being served.

Real, Iron Head, and two GF members filed out of the dorm, all strapped with shanks and ready to wreak havoc on B-Low as soon as they got the chance. As they rounded the walk, they looked out for any yard officers. Seeing that the coast was clear, they stepped through the gate and quickly headed to the other side of the compound, where B-Low was housed.

"Ain't nobody out at the gate, shit sweet this morning," Iron Head said as he led the pack, ready to put in some work.

"Yeah, shit goin' down," the young GF member said, all crunk and ready for action.

As Real walked with the men, he thought about how crazy his life had become. He'd once again been a successful club owner, a distinguished, classy, young, rich black man worth millions. Now, he was crossing a prison compound with a homemade knife, ready to kill someone. Real hated what his life had became, but he knew he had to adjust to his current living conditions. "They building just now going out," he called out just as they reached the north gate.

They walked through the open gate and rounded the walk discreetly.

Coming up on H-building, Iron Head bumped into one of his GF members. "My nigga Slack! Boy, what it do?" Iron Head called out as he gave the old chain gang vet from Atlanta some dap.

"Bruh, what's happening?" Slack said, smiling a sideways grin—a habit he'd become accustomed to every since his front tooth had been knocked out while shadowboxing.

"Boy, you still over here? You been real quiet. You know a nigga name B-Low over here?" Iron Head asked as Real and the other two members watched the passing inmates who were walking to and from chow.

"Man, them niggas got locked down yesterday. Word on the street is that Raze had his li'l bitch, Officer Knight, put the folks on them. Him, NoLove, and BodyBag got snatched up behind that shit. Niggas in they crew lurking for that nigga Raze as we speak. B-Low's right-hand man just went to look for the nigga. He been ducked off hiding and shit, but one thang they don't know is that Raze will buck back. Just being real, I don't think he'd do no shit like that. Raze ain't no snitch. Me and that nigga grew up in this shit together, and I know him better than that. They just hating on shawty 'cause of that bitch. They just better be about it when they do run up," Slack explained.

Just then, Real noticed the big man who'd left the hole with him coming through the gate. "Who that nigga?" he asked, still feeling uneasy about the big man.

Everyone looked in the man's direction.

"Oh, that's the nigga right there. That's Bohog, B-Low's right-hand man. He back over here looking for Raze," Slack said.

Real suspiciously eyed Bohog and another man easing through the gate.

"Look, y'all boys need me, just holla, 'cause I gotta go to medical," Slack said, saluting the men and stepping off.

"Say, bro, that nigga B-Low in the box. What's next?" Iron Head asked Real, who was still watching the big man.

Everyone was silent, waiting for Real to speak.

"Better now than never. Since his patna ain't available, we might as well ride on him," Real said in a sinister voice, eyeing the two men rounding the walk.

Chapter 17

"I swear, man, I didn't take it! Come on now, Giovanni! You know we go way back. I'd never steal from you, man!" Enric explained as Giovanni and his enforcer, Lurch, stood in the front room of his plush high-rise condo.

"What you're saying is that I'm stupid as fuck and can't count my own damn money! Is that what you think? Huh?" Giovanni said with force as he paced the room.

Lurch, true to his name, just stood there, silently and unmoving.

"No, man! Giovanni, come on now, man. Let's just go over the books again and make sure everything adds up. Maybe I made a mistake. The other clubs deposited their take, and the other outside business was factored in, so I don't understand where the mess-up is. Just let me go over the numbers one more time with you so we can get this all figured out," Enric pleaded as sweat matted the few thinning strands of hair that he'd combed over the bald spot on his head.

"Lurch!" Giovanni called out to his enforcer, who knew what he wanted without him even having to ask.

Enric had been working as a bookkeeper for Giovanni for over a year. He was good with numbers and was never even a penny off with his calculations, but lately, Giovanni had been questioning his loyalty. Enric had been totally loyal to Giovanni, but Giovanni felt like something was up, and he was set on Enric proving his loyalty.

"Hold up, Giovanni," Enric called out as Lurch passed Giovanni the Cobra 9mm.

"Tell me the truth then, Enric," Giovanni said. When Lurch handed him the silencer, he slowly screwed it on the end of the weapon.

"I swear, Giovanni! God knows on Mother Teresa, man, that I've been straight up! I bleed loyalty to you and the family!" Enric called out as Giovanni cocked the gun back.

"Loyalty? Okay. Well, here's the deal…" Giovanni paused for effect.

"Yeah?" Enric asked nervously.

"Show me how loyal you are. Shoot yourself." He extended the gun out to Enric, who looked up at him like he was crazy.

"Shoot myself? You mean…*kill* myself?" Enric mouthed as he shakily grabbed the gun.

"No! Just a shot in the leg or arm. Your choice. That will show me how loyal you are," Giovanni said as he stood back and smiled.

Lurch had already pulled his Desert Eagle out, just in case Enric tried something funny.

"Come on, man. Giovanni, I swear I'm loyal to you, man! This is not necessary,"

Enric cried out while looking at the gun that had just been handed to him.

"Okay. Hand me the gun, and we'll see the extent of your loyalty. You stole the family's money," Giovanni said, reaching for the gun.

Pop! Out of nowhere a shot rang out.

Lurch flinched at the sound of the gun blast.

"Ahhh!" Enric screamed. He dropped the gun and held his leg, which felt like it was on fire from the gunshot wound.

Giovanni smiled as he bent down and picked up the gun. "Good. You are a loyal man, Enric, and that is exactly why I employ you," he said as he disassembled the silencer from the gun and handed it back to Lurch.

"Ahhh! You fuckin' happy now?" Enric called out in pain as blood started to soak his pant leg.

"Get some medical attention, and I'll call you tomorrow," Giovanni said as he turned and exited, with Lurch following. Giovanni was aware that his tactics were over the top sometimes, but loyalty was very important to him, so he decided there was no such thing as going too far when it came to testing it. No money was missing, and the books were right down to the penny, but Giovanni was just in a testing mood, and Enric was the chosen one.

As they exited the condo, Giovanni's phone rang. "Hello?" he answered, climbing into the passenger seat of the black Lincoln Town Car.

"Hey, baby. Mama need some of that in me," Black Stallion said seductively into the phone, following up on her employers' demand to get Giovanni's wallet, where he kept all his account numbers and other vital information. The information from his office desk turned out to be useless.

"Sounds good to me. Just give me a little time to get there," Giovanni said, thinking about Black Stallion's mind-blowing sex.

"Meet me at the French Quarter in Cobb at 1:00, Room 207," she told him.

"You got it," Giovanni responded as they pulled up into Quick Mart for gas.

"I'll be waiting. Bye," Black Stallion said, pondering her employer's instructions. If she couldn't get Giovanni's wallet while he was alive, she'd have to kill him.

Chapter 18

Shonnie looked in the mirror and burst into tears. After the police saw her face, they didn't waste time with questions. They immediately snatched Moe up and charged him with assault. Shonnie had made up her mind that it was over. The police had urged her to go to the local hospital, but she'd flat out refused. The swelling had subsided, and the only visible sign was the black eye. That was what had her crying in the mirror. "Damn it," she said as she stripped down and got in the shower.

Minutes later, there was a knock at the door.

"Coming!" Shonnie called to the locksmith she'd hired to change all of her locks.

She hurriedly slipped on a pair of sweats and a tank top, then went to the back door to let him in. She let the Mexican in and gave him specific instructions on what she wanted. It took him a little under an hour to change the locks on the back and front door.

"Thanks so much, and here's a tip for coming right over," Shonnie said, handing him an extra $10.

"*Muchas gracias*," he said as he packed up his tools and wobbled his overweight frame down the front door stoop.

Shonnie went back and forth on her decision to go to work. Knowing she didn't have any leave time left, she went to her room and searched for some makeup to hide the black eye.

As she got ready for work, Real's words kept playing through her head. She couldn't believe she was actually thinking about him, about the things he'd said. She couldn't lie to herself any longer though: She was undeniably very interested in inmate Walker. Shonnie knew personal dealings with an inmate was grounds for immediate termination, so she had to formulate a way to get to know him without anyone knowing.

Chapter 19

*I*ron Head, Real, and the two thugs rounded the corner behind Bohog and his associate.

"Catch that nigga when he gets to the corner by the laundry," Iron Head told his two GF members as he and Real cut across the yard, trailing behind Bohog, who'd split up from his partner to look for Raze.

The two young thugs crept up on the man as he slowly walked by the building, looking in windows. Out of nowhere, they pulled their homemade knives and pounced on the unsuspecting man.

"Oh sh—" he started but couldn't get the words out before the sharp blades penetrated his skin, barely missing vital organs. "Ah! Shit!" the man screamed as they continued their assault.

"GF nigga!" the young thugs screamed as they stabbed him again and again relentlessly.

"Ow! Oh!!" the victim yelled out.

He tried to break away and run. It was no use, because the two GF members had his shirt in a tight grip and kept on sticking him like two wild animals ganging up on their prey. The other inmates on the walk stopped and watched the action, which alerted the walk officers.

"Ten-ten! Ten-ten! In front of H-building," the young white, freckle-faced female officer screamed into her radio as she watched the violent scene.

Officers came from everywhere after hearing the code.

Still, the two GF members wouldn't let up; they intended to leave their mark. They knew the assault would earn them their stripes, and it would be talked about from prison to prison. From there on out, they'd be labeled as real niggas. The two men continued to assault the third, who was lying face down in his own blood, having a seizure.

Bohog slipped in the chow hall after seeing all of the officers rush the yard. He knew something was going down, but he didn't know what it was. Real and Iron Head loved the way things were working out; Bohog was in the chow hall with no police around.

"The nigga in the back far corner," Real told Iron Head as he looked through the chow hall door window.

"Let's air this nigga out then," Iron Head said as he pulled his shank out.

Nobody paid Real or Iron Head any attention. Most of the inmates were busy getting extra trays, and others were trying to see what was going on out on the yard.

Real and Iron Head walked through the chow hall discreetly and casually crept up behind Bohog, who had his back to them, looking out the window.

"Shit," he mumbled when he saw the man laid out, face down and bloody. He had no idea it was his partner.

As soon as he decided to abort his mission, find his partner, and head back to the other side, a sharp object pierced his right shoulder, causing him to scream out in pain. He jumped up out of his seat and quickly got on his feet.

Real was still amazed by the big man's size, but that didn't deter his follow-up to Iron Head's assault. Real circled the man and plunged his shank into his stomach twice.

"Umphh!" the man cried out. He doubled over, not knowing where the next stab was coming from.

Next, Iron Head stuck him in his back and the back of his neck continuously, until he went down. Real was on one side and Iron Head on the other, stomping and kicking the big man until he was still.

"GF, bitch!" Iron Head called out as he and Real ceased their assault and rushed out of the chow hall, back to their side of the compound.

Minutes later, a gang of police rushed the chow hall after a code was called from the back kitchen officer. Both assaults called for outside medical attention. They looked for the assailants, but they were long gone.

"Word will reach the nigga B-Low soon. He gonna know shit just got real," Iron Head said as they passed through the gate and headed back to their dorm.

"Yeah, that nigga gonna see me," Real added, still thinking of what his life had become.

They entered the dorm and went to their rooms, where they cleaned up and sat back to wait for the word about the morning attacks.

"Is that blood?" Emilio asked Real, looking down at his pants and sneakers.

"Don't know what you talking about," Real said. He bent down, untied his shoes, and stepped out of them.

"Oh, okay. Whatever. My uncle wants to talk to you," Emilio blurted out as he dug in his mattress and pulled out his cell phone.

"'Bout what?" Real asked. He had no idea what a mob affiliate would want with him.

"I told him about you and what you did for me. It's probably about that," Emilio said, discreetly dialing Giovanni's number.

"Hey, nephew. How are you doing?" Giovanni asked calmly as he and Black Stallion lay in the king-sized, soft hotel bed.

"I got my roommate right here with me," Emilio said, looking over at Real.

"Put 'im on," Giovanni said.

Black Stallion lay next to him, knowing she couldn't leave the room without his wallet. If she did, her employer would chastise her to the third degree.

"Yeah?" Real said as he got on the line.

"Hey, um..."

"Real," Real said.

"Hey, Real. I really appreciate what you did for my Emilio."

"No problem. He's a cool li'l dude stuck in a bad situation. It's all good," Real told him as he listened carefully, making sure no officer was coming around.

"Yeah, politics got my little man in a bad predicament, but we're working night and day to free him. I requested to speak with you to see if you could do me a favor," Giovanni said as Black Stallion eased out of the bed to the bathroom.

"What's that?" Real asked curiously.

"I need you to make sure he stays safe until we're able to get him up out of there."

"I really don't—" Real started but was abruptly cut off.

"Name your price, and I'll pay whatever you ask. When do you get out?" Giovanni asked.

"I got life, but I'll work shit out. I'm just waiting to get a good lawyer on my case."

"Look, I employ the best criminal appeal lawyer in the state. He's already got one of Emilio's feet out the door, and he could do the same for you. If you promise to keep Emilio safe, I'll retain him for you as well."

Real didn't have to think twice about the offer. "Okay. It's a done deal. I'll make sure no harm comes to your boy."

"Thanks. The lawyer will be out to see you next week. After we hang up, text me your full name."

"Got it."

"Emilio also told me you used to own the G-Spot. Sounds like you're quite familiar with the nightclub business," Giovanni said.

"Yeah, I guess so," Real replied.

"Maybe when we get you out, you'll consider working one of our spots," Giovanni offered. He knew Bill would more than likely find Real a loophole to get him out.

"I'd like that," Real said, not believing his good luck.

"Take it easy, my friend. Please put Emilio back on."

Emilio knew from hearing Real's side of the conversation that his uncle had hired him a bodyguard. "Okay, Uncle. All right. I'll call you then. Bye," Emilio said. It was a great feeling for him to know somebody like Real had his back.

Real took the phone from Emilio, text Giovanni and handed the phone back.

The whole time Giovanni was on the phone, Black Stallion was in the bathroom, scandalously tucking his wallet away.

Chapter 20

$\mathscr{G}$iovanni and Black Stallion took advantage of another round of wild sex before it was time to check out.

"I think I'm gonna keep this room for another day. Let me give you some money to pay them on the way out," Giovanni said. He got out of bed and began to look for his pants.

"No need. I got it," Black Stallion hurriedly called out, so he wouldn't grab his pants and see that his wallet wasn't there.

"Um, okay. Why so generous all the sudden?" he asked as he lay back down and pulled the thick comforter over himself.

"'Cause you my boo," Black Stallion said, smiling as she got dressed.

"What time you coming back?" he asked, trying to hide the fact that she had him whipped.

"Who says I am?" she said playfully.

"Me," Giovanni said firmly, then smiled.

"Tonight around 10:00, as soon as I get finished at the hair and nail shop," Black Stallion lied. She knew it was their last tryst, because for the info she was about to turn over to her employer, she'd be paid enough to relocate and retire.

She exited the hotel, bypassing the front desk, and quickly got behind the wheel of her little green Nissan Altima. She headed north, past Buckhead, to meet with her employer. She turned into the Lexington Arms upscale housing development and looked for the realtor's show house. Minutes later, she found the lakefront home, with a boathouse in the back. She pulled in the driveway, next to her employer's red Benz. "Hey," Black Stallion said when she entered the expensively furnished show house, overly excited that she'd pulled the job off for her employer, the one female she'd ever considered a real boss bitch.

"Have a seat," her employer told her.

Black Stallion walked over and sat on the arm of the sofa. "Here ya go,," she said, digging Giovanni's wallet out of her purse.

Black Stallion's employer had been working with Giovanni for some time now, and she knew where he kept the vital information for all his clubs. She knew the average person wouldn't find the contents of his wallet of no use, but every number sequence and bank code made perfect sense to her, and she knew exactly how to put them to good use. "Good job. I guess he's still unaware that you have it," she said as she examined the contents of the wallet.

"Yeah, for now anyway," Black Stallion told her as she admired the sexy, classy, dangerous woman who sat before her.

"Good. Well, I know he's gonna have a fit tomorrow when he calls me for the club's nightly take. The good thing about it is that you can kiss your dancing days goodbye. When I access these accounts, I'll set you straight," she said, digging through Giovanni's designer wallet. She knew exactly what accounts all the random numbers were connected to.

"Thank you, 'cause my feet sure is tired," Black Stallion joked to the baddest bitch she knew.

Her employer stood and cracked the blinds to make sure the coast was clear.

"Um...you just want me to call you later then?" Black Stallion asked, hinting about her cut for the work she'd put in. The last thing she wanted to do was anger her employer.

"Call me tonight."

"Okay." Black Stallion stood to leave, hoping her accomplishments had put her in her employer's good graces and that she'd secured a seat in her organization. She smiled, then grabbed her purse and headed to the door.

"Hey!" her employer called out.

"Yeah?" Black Stallion said, turning back around.

"Thanks," the employer said as she pulled the trigger on the small-caliber pistol, hitting Black Stallion two times in a chest.

Black Stallion clutched her wounds and crumbled to the floor.

The shooter walked over and saw that she was still breathing. "Goodnight," her employer said. Then she placed the barrel of the pistol to the back of her head and pulled the trigger again. Killing was something she'd mastered.

Chapter 21

Shonnie arrived at work a few minutes late. As she took over the shift, she noticed a special briefing going on.

"One man is barely living, and while we were trying to get that situation under control, we received another call from the kitchen officer concerning another assault. Things are really getting out of hand around here," the shift lieutenant informed the officers. "If you see anyone out of place or on the walk without a pass, you are to call it in immediately. Officers, if your inmates are out of your building without a proper pass, you will be held accountable. Everyone also needs to be out on the sidewalk during all mass movements. Keep your eyes and ears open, people. We need to find out who was behind the stabbing in the kitchen, because it looks like we may have a murder on our hands, and you all know we're surrounded by murderers," the lieutenant said, luring a chorus of light whispers from the room. "Everyone, let's work together and get order back in our prison. Y'all have a nice day…and be careful out there." He ended the briefing, then abruptly went to his office to tend to the paperwork for the two assaults.

Shonnie stood in the back of the room listening, but all she could think about was the beating she'd just been handed by the man she'd planned to marry. After listening to the lieutenant, she placed her belongings in her locker and hit the walk.

She'd had to force herself to come to work. She felt like shit and ached all over, courtesy of Moe's bullshit. Her first stop was E-building to visit her crush, Richard Walker, aka Real. She bypassed all the other buildings, but just as she reached the E-building front door, an inmate called her.

"Hey, Sergeant! Can I speak with you for a minute?" he asked as he quickened his step in her direction.

"Yeah," she replied, not wanting to be bothered with all of the petty issues and complaints.

"Sarge, there's a two-man cell open in my building. Can you get me moved into it?" the young, clean-cut inmate asked as he cut his eyes across the yard.

"That's out of my hands. Only the unit manager can make moves," Shonnie told him.

Just as she was about to walk off, he stepped up into her personal space. "What if I give you the name of the two people who stuck that dude yesterday in the chow hall?" he whispered, looking around to make sure no one was in earshot.

Shonnie hated snitches, but yet she had a job to do. "All right. Are you tellin' me you know who did that in the kitchen?"

"Sho do."

"I'll call you up to security after my rounds," she told him, looking at her watch.

"No need. Here you go," the man said as he slid her a note containing the names of the men responsible. The note, which inmates referred to as a kite, also held his name, building, and the room he want to be moved to.

"Okay. I think I can convince the unit manager to move you. Do I have all the info I need?" she asked as she tucked the note in her pocket.

"Yeah, it's all there, but please throw that away when you're done, Sergeant. It's got my name on it, and I ain't trying to get caught up in no bullshit," he explained, still cautiously looking around.

"I got you," Shonnie said as he turned and walked away. She watched him walk off and meet up with a group of young thugs, greeting them with a crazy hand and finger movement. *How fake and phony,* she thought, shaking her head.

She knocked on the glass door of E-building to get the officer's attention. As soon as she stepped in the door, she pulled the paper out of her pocket, curious about who was responsible for the chow hall assault. As she read it, she ignored the inmates calling out about fire in the hole. When she saw the one particular name on the paper, her heart dropped. "Damn!" she said, causing the dorm officer to look up.

"You okay, Sergeant," he asked, pausing on his hourly log entry.

"Yeah, I'm cool. Um…is Richard Walker in or out?" she asked, having second thoughts about getting to know Real.

"He in. You need him?" he asked.

Shonnie nodded.

"Richard Walker!" the officer screamed across the dorm.

Shonnie lost her train of thought when Real approached, dressed down in a pair of white shorts and a wife-beater. She was absolutely mesmerized by his fit frame and handsome features.

"What up?" Real asked, looking from Shonnie to the dorm officer.

"I need to speak to you for a minute in the counselor's office," she said. She led him to the small, windowless office where inmates went to discuss personal matters with counselors and other administrators.

"What up, Sergeant?" Real asked as he entered the room behind her and pulled the door up.

"You know what's up, Richard Walker. And to think, I really was feeling you till now."

"What you talking about? What's up with you?" Real asked, confused.

"Y'all may have a murder on your hands, and don't lie like you ain't have shit to do with it, cause I got a kite right here with both of y'all's names on it," she said, pulling out the note that bore his and Iron Head's full government names.

"What? Who, me? I don't know what you talking about," Real said with a straight face, sticking to his code of denial.

"Oh, here we go again. How can I trust you if you can look at me in my face and lie so easily?" Shonnie asked, pissed.

Her words touched Real, and he knew she was sincere. Real was feeling Shonnie, so much so that he broke his own rules and told her the truth about it all.

Ten minutes later, Shonnie stood, wide-eyed and in total shock at Real's story. The incident in the kitchen stemmed from years ago, when Real was on the street and had been set up by his right-hand man Cash. She was saddened when he told her about Constance, his true love, a casualty of his lifestyle. "Look, I won't say nothing about this, and I'll do what I can to put you somewhere else at the time of the incident, but I'm going to need you to just chill out. I came to work today just to see you. I know that sounds crazy, but it's true. Since we met, I've been having thoughts about you, and that's not like me. I ain't trying to lose my job over this either, and if you're gonna be wrapped up in bullshit like this, I might as well not even go any farther with this," Shonnie said, looking up at Real who was standing over her, looking down into her pleading eyes.

"I hear you. I'm cooling, my word," Real said. He desperately wanted to take her into his arms and kiss her.

"Promise?" she asked, imagining his soft lips pressed up against hers.

"I promise," Real replied sincerely, really feeling Shonnie.

"I'm going to call you up to security later tonight when administration leaves, so be on standby," she told him. She ripped up the note with is name on it and exited the counselor's office.

"Everything okay, Sergeant," the dorm officer asked as Shonnie signaled him to pop the door to let her out.

"Yeah, everything's fine," Shonnie said as she tried her best to remember the names of the gang members and the other individuals Real had mentioned so she could drop a note to the unit manager to get them transferred.

Chapter 22

iovanni called Black Stallion repeatedly but kept getting her voicemail. "Bitch!" he screamed as he frantically searched the hotel room for his wallet. He hoped his assumptions were incorrect.

A knock on the hotel room door interrupted his search.

"Yeah?" Giovanni called out as he snatched the comforters off the bed, still searching.

"Room service, sir. It's checkout time," the young hotel worker said, looking back at his clipboard.

"You must be mistaken. I'm paid up for another day," Giovanni yelled as he looked under the bed for the third time.

"Um, I'm sorry, sir, but this room has not been purchased for another day, according to my roster. Perhaps you should call downstairs to get a verification, because I'm scheduled to clean this room at checkout time," he said, double-checking his paperwork.

"Fine. I'll be down in five minutes," Giovanni called out.

Not only had the bitch taken off with his wallet, but she'd left him high and dry and hadn't paid for another night in the room. He couldn't believe Black Stallion had crossed him. There was only $490 in his wallet, and he would have freely given that to her if she'd have asked. What he really was vexed about was all of his bank information; now he would have to look it all up again. He wasn't worried about her using it because he was sure she had no clue what information went with which banking institution. What he didn't know was that her employer was one of his own top people; had he known that, he would have quickly changed and closed all of his accounts. Black Stallion's employer was very familiar with his banking institutions, so it turned out that the missing wallet was actually worth millions.

After Giovanni got dressed, he quickly exited the room and headed to the club, on the hunt for Black Stallion. He rushed downstairs to the car, and as soon as he buckled up, his cell phone rang. "Hello?" he answered sharply.

"Hi, Giovanni. I've got good news for you."

"Good. I can use some. Shoot," Giovanni said.

"The court has finally ruled in our favor with a summary judgment. Emilio's case has been dismissed due to a legal technicality. They're preparing the papers for his release now, so you may want to get someone out there to pick him up," Bill said, excited for another victory, thanks to placing the right amount of money in the right person's hands.

"Yes! Thanks, Bill! I'll get out there immediately," Giovanni said happily, but inside he was still seething and bitter over Black Stallion. Disloyalty was something Giovanni simply would not tolerate, and she'd betrayed him big time.

"Also, I've done a little research on that Richard Walker you asked me about. You wouldn't believe what I found in the transcripts of his case."

"What?"

"Man, that trial was fucked up, misconduct all over the place. I'm 100 percent sure we can find a loophole and get him walking on at least one technicality," Bill assured him, knowing the right amount of money would ensure that Real would be a free man, and Bill's own record of wins would remain astonishing.

"Great, but my main concern is Emilio, and I'm glad you took care of that. Just keep me updated on the Walker case as it moves along. I'll talk to you later," Giovanni said. He ended the call, glad to know his nephew would be out from behind bars soon.

He pulled into the club parking lot and parked next to a customized Maybach with big, flashy rims. That car was parked in the spot that was clearly marked for him. He stepped out of his Porsche Panamera and cursed Black Stallion.

"How you doing, Mr. Giovanni?" his club security guard greeted as he held the door open.

"Nice lunch crowd," Giovanni said. As he walked through the club doors, he noticed a group of rowdy men throwing money at two dancers onstage. "What's going on over there? You need to handle that," Giovanni snapped, alerting his head bouncer to get on the job. The screaming men were making it rain, but they were also spitting liquor and making rude remarks, conduct that was way out of place for such an upscale club.

Club Exposé was an upscale, five-star establishment that catered to CEOs, lawyers, doctors, political figures, and other dignified officials.

"Yes, sir," Bruno said, then quickly approached the group of men in the VIP area. "Excuse me, gentlemen, but I'm going to have to ask you to refrain from your present conduct or leave," the big man said to the New Yorkers, in town to film a rap video for their upcoming new release.

"What? Man, miss me with that shit! These hoes ain't complainin', are they? It's all good, brotha," the tall, well-built, stocky, bald-headed man said. He was wearing plenty of bling, the custom diamond necklace could be seen from across the room and so could the platinum grill. He ignored Bruno and went right back to shouting and showering the girls with money.

"Sir, I'm gonna have to ask y'all to leave," said the bouncer, an ex-MMA fighter, eyeing the three black men, all of whom were built like football players.

"Ha-ha-ha! This guy here a fool wit' it! You hear this shit? He tryin'a put Big Lou out the spot! White boy, you must not know who you talkin' to!" Big Lou said, getting in Bruno's face.

Brent and Casey, the other security guards, heard the commotion and quickly walked up on the scene and stood behind Bruno for backup.

"I don't know who you are, and truth be told, I don't fuckin' care. I told you and your boys to get on outta here," Bruno fumed, balling up his powerful fists.

"Oh yeah?" Big Lou questioned, turning his back to club security and continuing with his rude behavior.

"Fire! Nicki!" Bruno screamed, signaling for the girls to get off the stage.

"Hold up now! What's up with that? We're payin' customers, man!" Lou said, spinning back around. When he saw the cold, hard look on Bruno's face, he said, "Okay, I see what's up!" and swung, catching big Bruno totally off guard with a blow to the chin that knocked him out cold.

"Fuck!" Casey called out as he and Brent went into action.

Even though Casey and Brent were trained in hand-to-hand combat, they still were no match for the three hulking dudes who'd grown up fighting on the mean streets of New York. In an instant, the club went crazy. Dancers were running and screaming while all the dignified professional patrons bombarded the door.

Giovanni and Lurch quickly exited the back office to see what was going on. To their surprise, their men were suffering a real beat-down by a group of baggy-clothed black men adorned in gaudy jewelry. Giovanni grabbed Lurch by the arm when he started to head toward the melee. "Handle these fools outside," he said, motioning for the DJ to cut the music and turn the lights on.

The group of men stopped their assault as soon as the lights flickered on. Giovanni watched them hurry across the floor to the club exit, then he walked over and checked on his security, while assessing the damage to the VIP area. Five minutes later, he heard gunshots ringing out in front of the club.

Lou and his friends had retreated to his Maybach, parked in Giovanni's reserved parking space. Lurch stood in front of the car, and before Lou could throw it in reverse, he had an AK-47 aimed at the front windshield.

"Oh fuck! Lou screamed. He and his passengers ducked down while he fumbled to get the car in reverse.

Lurch unloaded on the men in the car missing the driver by inches and hitting two of the passengers. People in the lot heard the shots and ran for cover while Lurch effortlessly proceeded to take the lives of the men who'd dare to disrupt his boss's establishment. The bullets ripped through the car as the driver sped out of the lot. The driver ducked low and prayed that he didn't succumb to the same fate as his friends. A fun night out of town had turned into a nightmare.

"Fuck!" Lou called out while speeding away looking for some immediate help.

Lou wiped the sweat from his brow and let out a sigh of relief when he got out of harms way. Just as he got his heartbeat to calm he heard a loud noise, an 18 wheeler's horn. Lou didn't realize that he had drove right through the intersections red light. The truck was coming too fast, way too fast to stop. The metal collided and the car went up in flames killing Lou instantly, the only living occupant of the car. The ball of fire and black smoke could be seen from miles away. Back at the club cops were swarming the parking lot, talking to Giovanni.

"No problem, Johnson. Everything is okay—just a couple groups of brawlers. They sped out of the lot, one car shooting at the other, but we're okay," Giovanni told his old police detective friend, one of many he had on the payroll.

"Good. Just checking on y'all. Have a nice day," Johnson said, winking at Giovanni knowingly.

"Thanks, y'all," Giovanni said as he and Lurch turned and headed back into the club to get ready to pick up Emilio.

milio was on top of the world. "Man, this bid is over for me!" he called out when he came back to his cell from the counseling room.

Real was sitting at the desk reading his daily scripture when Emilio burst in. He finished Psalm 91 before acknowledging his cellie. "What you mean, young blood?" Real asked as he closed his Bible and turned on his stool.

"Man, I beat the case on appeal! I just got an immediate release!" Emilio smiled from ear to ear while grabbing the few items he planned to take with him, including his photo album and some old letters.

"What a blessing, bro! Get out there and make shit happen! You know the world is waiting for ya!" Real said, excited for young Emilio, whom he'd really taken a liking to.

"Man, don't worry. I got you, Real. The lawyer will be to see this week. Bro, that man my uncle hired is the best at what he do. Oh…take this. The code to unlock it is 3974," Emilio told Real as he handed him the cell phone he no longer needed.

"Appreciate ya," Real told him as he opened the phone and checked it out.

"Man, you kept it real with me and looked out, and I appreciate you. My uncle's number is the only one saved in the contacts…oh, and a couple of them Moco Space freaks. They all yours," Emilio joked.

Real dapped him up and gave him a half-embrace. "Be easy out there, man. I'll hit you up," Real promised as the officer called his name.

"You too, bro," Emilio said before he hurried out of the room to take the long walk to freedom.

Real was happy for the young brother, but as soon as Emilio left their cell, it hit him. His heart was suddenly heavy with thoughts that he might never walk the streets again. Real's eyes watered as he thought about everything that had happened in his life. He hated the way things had turned out and sincerely wished he could reverse the hands of time. He daydreamt about walking hand in hand with Constance on a sandy beach, telling each other knock-knock jokes and just enjoying life. His smile quickly dissolved into a frown when the screams of her assault and murder replayed in his mind. Real got up, closed his room door, dropped to his knees, and recited the most heartfelt prayer he'd ever prayed.

He felt renewed as he stood and gathered his thoughts. He pulled out the cell phone but realized he didn't have anyone to call. He walked over to the window and looked out at all the razor wire. *I used to have endless contacts, and now I ain't nothin' but a number in the damn Georgia prison system,* he thought. He lifted the phone and looked at Giovanni's number, then closed the phone again, tucked it in his pocket, and lay back on the bed. He dozed off but was shortly awakened by Iron Head knocking on his door.

"They calling you to security, bro. Man, they probably done found out about the chow hall move," Iron Head said, with a hint of worry in his tone.

"Nah, I doubt that. That fine-ass sergeant broad was in here earlier looking for somebody to do ice call tonight, and when she got no volunteers, she picked me. It's all good," Real lied. He'd long ago learned to keep everyone out of his business, even his closest friends, unless they were directly involved.

"Oh. Well, I ain't even see her fine ass in here. I was probably ducked off, fussing with that crazy baby mama of mines," Iron Head said with relief in his tone.

"Yeah, you had your flap up," Real said. He got up and grabbed his toothbrush and washcloth. "Anyway, I'll holla at ya later."

"Later, bro."

* * * * *

A few hours later, Real was exiting the building and rounding the dark walk. As he rounded the curve, he spotted Shonnie standing in front of security. All of the other administration had left for the day, and Shonnie was over the shift because the lieutenant who usually supervised it had to leave early.

"What up, Sergeant?" Real asked as he approached her.

"That's Shonnie to you," she said, smiling and taking in his perfect face.

"Oh...my bad," Real said as he followed her lead into the security office.

"So, um...how does this work? I'm sorta new at this," Shonnie asked as she stared him down, feeling awkward about being alone with an inmate in such close quarters.

Real walked up to her, until they were face to face. "First, we need to hug to make sure the chemistry is here," he said, grabbing her in a tight embrace that made her tingle all over.

"Well? Is the chemistry there?" she asked, looking into Real's alluring eyes.

"Hmm. I'm not sure, but I do have another way to find out," Real said, then leaned in and kissed her softly on the lips.

Shonnie's whole body warmed up as they embraced and tangled tongues with one another. She knew from the first kiss that Real was all she needed. "What about now?" she asked, not wanting him to let her go.

"Well, the chemistry is definitely there. We soulmates," Real joked as he looked into her face. He quickly noticed the black eye that she'd tried to hide behind her makeup. "What the—"

Before Real could inquire about her eye, a call came in over her radio. "Ten-ten! Ten-ten! D-building!" the man's voice boomed over the radio, alerting all officers of an inmate altercation that required immediate assistance and backup.

"Shit!" Shonnie called out. Since she was filling in for the lead supervisor, she had to be on the scene.

"I already know, but I got a cell phone now. Give me a number," Real said, grabbing a pen and piece of paper from the desk.

Shonnie quickly jotted down her cell phone number. "I'm going straight home, call me tonight," she told him as she made a quick exit and took off running across the field to D-building.

Chapter 24

Earlier that day, after leaving the dorm, Emilio stood in the ID room of the prison, waiting for his ride to show up. Only an hour had passed, but it seemed like forever. To kill time, he made small talk with the new arrival who'd just been transferred from GSCP. The criminal acted as if his two life sentences were nothing. Emilio thanked God over and over in his head for his good fortune.

"Your ride's here," the ID officer said to Emilio when he stuck his head in the door.

Emilio walked out of the prison feeling like he'd just hit the Powerball for millions. Freedom was really that valuable. As he crossed the parking lot, he eyed the black Cadillac ESV extended edition sitting in the middle of the lot with Lurch behind the wheel. Emilio walked to the Escalade with his head held high and a big smile on his face.

Giovanni stepped out of the truck. "Young Emilio, welcome back to the real world!" he called out as he embraced his nephew, who was more like a son to him.

"Unc, man, thanks for getting me up outta here," Emilio said sincerely. He knew if it wasn't for his uncle's money and connections, he'd still be sitting in the small, musty cell.

"Come on. Let's go. This place gives me the creeps." Giovanni smiled as they climbed up into the truck.

"My man Lurch!" Emilio called out, bringing a smile to the silent man's face.

As they rode home, Giovanni had a heart-to-heart with his nephew concerning the clubs, the mob family ties, and his future. "You'll be held in the highest regard. The other families will no longer see you as little Emilio. They'll only see Emilio, the made man. They will trust you and look up to you on a whole different level. They're gonna look at you as my protégé and my predecessor, and you will run the clubs in my absence. The clubs play a vital part in our organization, and they keep a lot of us out of prison. I am going to bring you before the families during our next meeting and let them know. From now on, you need to be in the mindset of being a made man," Giovanni explained.

Emilio listened intently. He was about to be thrust, head first, into the central point of the family organization, and failure was not an option. "I understand," he said as they entered the city limits and took the downtown exit.

Lurch pushed the truck through downtown traffic, then detoured to a side street that led to the club. Just as they approached the lone stop sign, a tinted-out cargo van pulled up next to them. Two masked figures jumped out the side door, brandishing high-powered assault weapons.

Emilio noticed the masked figures first. "Lurch, go! GO!" he screamed, but not before the two masked figures pulled the triggers.

The bullets tore through the Escalade effortlessly as Lurch punched the gas, sending the truck flying forward. They were lucky, and no one was injured on the attempt.

"Shit!" Giovanni screamed as Lurch sped away, deviating from the club and heading out to Giovanni's north side home.

"What the hell was all that about?" Emilio screamed, shaken by the gunfire. "Who were those guys?"

"I have no idea, but somebody is gonna answer for it!" Giovanni spat, running his hand through his frazzled hair.

* * * * *

The green van pulled up in the driveway of a run-down house, and the three masked women climbed out. They knew their employer was going to be beyond pissed at their failed attempt. They walked into the old house, a frequent meeting place for the crew. All three of them had their heads down, like school kids about to be scolded.

Jalel, Miraj, and Amber were well trained by the employer who'd recruited them all from Clappers, the raunchiest strip club in the city.

When they walked in, they found their employer sitting at the kitchen table. A gold-plated .45 Magnum and matching gold Louis Vuitton bag were sitting in front of her. "So when's the funeral?" the employer asked.

"Well, we don't know who was hit. They, uh…sped away," Miraj said, knowing their employer was not going to be happy with the news.

"What!? Are you telling me some of them might still be breathing? Which one of you stupid bitches is to blame for this?" she said, eyeing each woman harshly.

Not one of the girls dared to speak a word.

She picked up the gold-plated .45 off the table.

"Um, we might have got him," Amber said, trying to pacify the situation.

"Right, but there's another issue. Which one of y'all thought it would be all right to tap into my resources and to be so bold to use *my* name with my underground connect?" the employer asked, setting her condemning eyes firmly on Jalel, her newest recruit.

"Uh, well, I was just…I was trying to find out about my baby-daddy, 'cause he—"

The employer cut her off. "So you use *my* resources to check up on some dick? You know what I despise? I despise a weak bitch who lets some dick control her! That is NOT what my organization is built on," the employer said, standing up. She walked around the table and stood behind the girls, who dared not move and continued facing forward.

"It wasn't like that."

"Bitch, you stepped way out of line." With that, she lifted the gun and pulled the trigger, sending Miraj's brains all over the makeshift desk.

"Ah! Oh God!" Jalel screamed, thinking the bullet was meant for her.

Amber turned with a confused look on her face, wondering why was Miraj had been killed over Jalel's wrongdoings.

"Y'all are ya sisters' keepers. This is how shit go around here. When one of you fuck up, all y'all fuck up. You need to keep the next bitch in line, or it just might be you who end up paying for her fuck-up. Besides, I wasn't digging her new highlights anyway," the employer said as she tucked the gun in her purse.

"So...umm—" Amber started.

"Clean her up, and I'll be in touch," the employer said as she exited.

Jalel and Amber followed their orders, even though it wasn't easy wrapping their good friend's body up in carpet while discussing a possible dumping ground for the it. They carried Miraj off to the van. Amber jumped behind the wheel and headed to an under-construction housing development she knew about. Jalel sat silently in the passenger seat, knowing she was responsible for her friend's death.

* * * * *

For the rest of the night, Giovanni made calls, trying to find out who was behind the attack. After coming up empty-handed, he decided to take a leave of absence, certain that the hit was more than likely directed at him. "Emilio, you're going to have to step into my shoes sooner than I thought. I'm going to stay out of sight for a while, until I get to the bottom of this."

Emilio agreed with his head, even though his heart harbored doubts. "Okay, Unc."

"I'll brief you daily, and Lurch will be your personal security. You and Lurch will be the only ones who are aware of my whereabouts. Not even the families will know my location," Giovanni explained, still uneasy about the attempt on his life. He planned to set up a meeting with the families as soon as he could to discuss the incident. "I'm beat. I'll see y'all in the morning," Giovanni told them as he headed up to his room, still pondering the day's events.

Emilio and Lurch each went to one of the guestrooms.

Chapter 25

Real was laying in bed thinking about how good it must've felt for Emilio when he walked out of that gate yesterday. He was brought out of his thoughts when he heard his name being called. "Richard Walker, report to the multipurpose room for an attorney visit," the dorm officer yelled across the pod.

He knew the attorney would be visiting him, so he was already prepared and had many questions concerning his case. He grabbed his shirt off of his bed, brushed his hair, and exited his room to see about his freedom. As he made his way around the walk, he heard a group of inmates talking about BodyBag and NoLove being transferred to another institution. He also heard someone mention that B-Low was in the hole, expecting the same fate. He entered the multipurpose room and spotted the attorney, who was already seated in the small office.

"Hi. Richard Walker, I presume?" Bill said as he stood and extended his hand to Real.

"Yes, sir. And you are?" Real asked, gripping the man's hand in a nice firm handshake.

"I'm Bill Leonard, your appeal attorney. Have a seat," Bill said as he pulled up his chair while taking a seat. From his briefcase, he pulled out all the paperwork he had concerning Real's case.

"The case was crazy. I didn't have—" Real started but was abruptly cut off by a wave of the attorney's hand.

"No need," Bill said. "I don't need any explanations. I got your transcripts, and I can say there were many trial misconduct issues. We'll use that to get you some relief," Bill said, aware that the right amount of money to grease the judge's greedy palms, along with the trial misconduct, would be more than enough to free Real.

"Good," Real answered. As he looked over the paperwork, he read between the lines. He knew the lawyer had to have some kind of connections, since he was working with the mob.

"All I need you to do is fill out these papers. Let me handle the rest. Don't speak to anyone about your case or anything else we talk about. I'm going to make a couple of calls and set up some meetings, because what we have here is a blatant case of prosecutorial misconduct. People use the term 'railroading' pretty freely these days, but in this case, even if you were guilty of the crime, they stepped out of line and did a lot of things that weren't proper. Basically, you *were* railroaded. Shit, you weren't even arraigned," Bill said.

Real passed the signed papers back to him. "It was a circus. A lot of people wanted me gone. What kind of timeframe we working with here?" Real asked, trying to hide his anxiousness.

"I can't put a definite date on it, but I'm going to file your paperwork first thing in the morning. It shouldn't be too long, but I can tell you that you have a better position than Emilio had. We are basically dealing with the same people in the same system, though, so just be patient. I'm good at what I do. I'll be in touch," Bill said. He looked at his watch and tucked the papers back into his briefcase.

"All right. I appreciate everything you're doing," Real told him sincerely.

"Don't thank me. Thank Giovanni. He kicked out a nice chunk of change to get you your walking papers."

Real smiled and thought to himself, *More like a nice chunk of change to keep his nephew safe in the lions' den.* "Okay. Take it easy," Real told Bill as he stood and exited.

* * * * *

When Real got back to the dorm, he pulled out his phone and called the number Shonnie had given him.

"Hello?" she answered, knowing the unknown number had to be Real.

"Hey, beautiful. How you doing?" Real asked as he sat behind the towel hanging from the bottom of his bunk.

"Fine. Just thinking about you," Shonnie said as she lay across her bed comfortably for the first time in a long time.

"I just got back from talking to my lawyer. Things gonna be looking up real soon."

"Good! But what's it gonna take to get a city man to settle down with a li'l old country girl?" Shonnie asked playfully, though she was dead serious.

"Loyalty, trust, devotion, love, care…and good sex. Think you can handle that?" Real replied playfully, with a hint of seriousness.

"Oh, I can make all that happen and then some, but I'm going to require the same from you."

"I got that. So from today on, we doing all that, right?" Real asked as he got up off the bunk to check and make sure the officer wasn't making rounds.

"If you with it, I'm with it, but I ain't trying to be caught up in no bull, 'cause I really do need my job," Shonnie said as she peered over at the picture of Moe that was still sitting on the dresser.

"You just play your part, and I'll handle the rest. Since we about to kick this thang off, I guess I need to know everything about you."

"That would help," Shonnie replied, laughing and loving the feeling that was coming over her as she talked to Real.

Real thought back to the black eye Shonnie had tried to hide and recalled how down and out she looked on so many days. Evidently, she was having man problems. He was rather sure she was on the rebound and was looking for someone to take her away from the hurt and pain. He really didn't mind being that person, because deep down, he was feeling her. "So, uh…when is your birthday?" Real asked as he kicked back on the bed to enjoy their conversation.

They talked for hours, until it was time for her to come to work, and they learned a lot about each other. Shonnie was beyond impressed with the man who went by Real. The more they talked, the more she was convinced that he was the perfect man. He was smart, fine, and intellectual, and he had a great sense of humor.

"I'll see you tonight," Shonnie said, and she ended the call, happy to be going to work.

"A'ight, baby," Real replied, laying back on his bunk, thinking about the situation he'd just created.

Chapter 26

Two months later…

"Mr. Walker, I hereby grant you an appeal bond based on the…"

Real couldn't believe his ears; Bill had succeeded in getting him an appeal bond. Even though the case was still pending, Real had Bill's assurance that it would eventually be thrown out. "Bill, thanks, man. I forever owe you," Real said, standing in the same Atlanta courtroom where he was originally convicted.

"Like I told you before, don't thank me…thank Giovanni," Bill said. He made a mental note to call Giovanni, because he hadn't spoken to anyone but Emilio for a while.

"I make it my business to mention that to Emilio every time we speak. I'm just glad he's doing well for himself out there. He the man now in the club," Real said, excited that his old friend was handling business.

"Yes, little Emilio is doing rather well for himself in the business. Do you have clothes? You won't be going back to the prison…Emilio will be waiting for you outside," Bill told Real, who was basically a free man.

"Yeah. I was prepared before I left," Real said, remembering back to when he filled Shonnie in on what could possibly happen and now could wait to give her the good news.

Shonnie prayed all day on the day he left. She kept the faith and believed he would be granted his appeal. Over the short period of time they'd known each other, they'd fallen head-over-heels in love. Shonnie smiled every time she thought about her period being late; she so much wanted it to be the result of Real's seed. They'd made all kinds of plans for his release day. It was the perfect love story, and it was finally about to become a reality.

"See you on the other side," Bill told Real as he gathered his paperwork and exited the courtroom.

"Yeah, okay," Real replied as the jailer came and escorted him back upstairs to await his paperwork being finalized.

Emilio sat outside in a brand-new Rolls Royce Ghost, waiting on his friend. He had big plans for Real to join him in the family business.

As Real exited the jailhouse, he thought about B-Low back at the prison. He'd gotten news from Iron Head, telling him that B-Low had fallen out in the hole and been rushed to the hospital. His HIV had turned to full-blown AIDS. Real had no sympathy for him, and he smiled. He felt good about the outcome of his revenge for Constance's death, and he finally had some closure.

Real walked across the lot, looking for Emilio. He quickly spotted the cream and black Rolls parked in the far corner, glistening in the sunlight. Real couldn't wait to surprise Shonnie with the news, but for the time being, he was eager to get back to his old stomping grounds in the ATL.

Chapter 27

" *D*amn, he fine as fuck! Who is he?" Fire asked Platinum as they watched Emilio give Real a tour of the club.

"Yo, Real! Man, it's good to have you. As soon as we get time, we'll look into upgrading the condo to a more spacious pad for you," Emilio said, happy to have Real working with him.

As soon as Bill called him with the news of Real's possible release, he'd dressed up one of Giovanni's rental properties for his old cellmate. The quarter-million-dollar condo wasn't bad, but it wasn't one of their top properties. Emilio had even turned the keys to his money-green Maserati over to Real just before going on a shopping spree that consisted of Italian shoes and custom-tailored suits, and before long, Real was back in his element with a sleek new car, a custom wardrobe, a luxury condo, and a job in the strip club business.

"Real, man, I'm glad you agreed to join me in the business. Uncle Giovanni wants to meet with you to discuss other opportunities before the week is out."

"Okay, cool. So, uh…" Real was at a loss for words when he eyed a tall, thick Brazilian who was taking the stage, dressed in a skimpy two-piece number that left nothing to the imagination.

"That's Pilar. She's beautiful, ain't she?" Emilio said, grabbing his own eyeful.

"Yeah. So, anyway, what you was explaining to me earlier was that you want me to be some sort of floater, making sure all the clubs are running smoothly and that all revenue is turned in and accounted for by the managers."

"Yes. Basically, you'll be a road manager with an iron fist," Emilio clarified.

Real was really impressed at how Emilio had stepped it up in such a short period. He knew the kid had the mind to run a business, but in the role he was in now, and as well as he'd handled it, it was difficult to imagine the young man had ever been in a prison cell, shaking and scared, being robbed and on the verge of being raped by two young thugs.

"Seems like something I can get used to. So when do I start?" Real asked as he cut his eyes back to the stage.

"Right now. Be ready to fly out tomorrow to our Miami establishment with one of our other managers who keeps track of all of the club books and other financial obligations. I'm sure you'll enjoy her company. She's something else," Emilio said, lust dripping from his tone.

"All right," Real replied as his phone beeped. "Hello?"

"Hey, baby. I'm here. What's the address?" Shonnie asked as she cruised through midday traffic.

Real was as excited to see Shonnie as she was to see him. After he'd called her with the news, she'd wasted no time in putting in for some leave days so she could hit the road. They had become so close that Shonnie had even considered relocating to Atlanta to be with him. She danced in her seat all the way there. She hadn't seen him since he'd gone to fight his case and she couldn't wait to be back in his arms again. This would be their first encounter outside of the prison and she had butterflies just thinking about it. She rarely thought about Moe anymore; he was still sitting in the county jail, awaiting his court appearance on the assault charges. He was furious that Shonnie hadn't been to see him or post the property bond to get him out, but Moe was dead to Shonnie and Real was all that mattered. She typed in the address as he called it out.

"I'll be there in a minute," Real told her as he ended the call.

After he slid his phone back in its case, he looked up and noticed a sexy female walking through the door, dressed in a designer cream-colored power suit, three-inch stilettos, and big designer shades, carrying an expensive Michael Kors bag. As she entered, she stopped and looked around. She had long, flowing hair, and everything about her exuded money and power.

"Hey, beautiful!" Emilio called out as he rushed over to the well-built, beautiful woman.

Real stood back and watched the interaction.

Before long, Emilio was escorting the woman over to where he stood. She did a double-take at the well-dressed, brown-eyed, clean-shaven, smooth-skinned brother who put her in the mind of her ex, Sherm.

"Real, this is Silk. Silk, this is Real, the new addition to the family," Emilio said. He couldn't help staring at Silk, whose only flaw was a scar on her forehead, to the right of her right eye.

"Hi, Real," Silk said, as if she'd known him for years. She extended her freshly manicured hand to him.

"Hey, Silk," Real replied in the same casual tone, still checking out her beauty.

"So, you're gonna be my escort, huh?" Silk said, looking Real up and down. She liked what she saw, but she wondered how he fit into Giovanni's plans.

"Yeah, I guess so. I hear you're the lady in charge of the money, and I'm here to protect the money, so I guess we'll be working hand in hand," Real said, looking at his watch.

"Yep. We're teammates, "Silk said, still looking him up and down.

"Uh, I'm sorry, but I'm gonna have to cut our introduction short, but I have to be getting to the house. Please excuse me. I'll be ready to fly out first thing in the morning," Real said, noticing that Emilio was still looking at Silk in a lustful gaze.

Emilio stood back during their meet-and-greet. He hoped that pairing them up would work out for the best. Ever since he'd taken over the club books, they'd been coming up short, so he took it upon himself to put Silk and Real on the job. "Silk will have your ticket," Emilio called out, breaking his gaze.

"Breakfast first. Here's my number. " She dug a business card out of her bag and handed it to Real. "Call me when you're ready. The flight leaves at 11:15."

"Okay. Got you. Talk to y'all tomorrow," Real said as he tucked the card in his pocket and walked off.

Silk watched him and wondered where the mystery man had come from. She was well into her plans of pulling off her big lick and didn't need any interference. "So you just stick me with someone I don't know shit about? Who is this guy?" Silk spat at Emilio, whom she knew wasn't built for the position Giovanni had put him in. Since Giovanni had fallen back from the scene, she'd been reporting to Emilio. Silk, the gangsta she was, saw straight through Emilio's fake boss persona. She knew he was a coward at heart and she made it her business to keep him in a bitch position every chance she got. She hated weak-ass men and Emilio was just that in her eyes. The only thing that separated him from the rest was that he had the backing of the mob.

"Damn, Silk! Just calm down! Real used to own the G-Spot. He was just released from prison, and I can personally vouch for him. He's a real stand-up guy. He was my roommate for a minute, and the guy's as loyal as they come. Baby, just trust me on this," Emilio explained, as if she was the boss and he had to justify everything to her. He reached over and rubbed her arm.

Silk jerked her arm away from him and slowly removed her shades from her face. "First, Emilio, I ain't your baby. Second, don't ever fuckin' touch me. I ain't one of these li'l hoes who dance for you. I'm a real bitch who's all about the business, and I won't hesitate to body a muthafucker, so please don't get shit confused," Silk snapped, making sure Emilio picked up on the threat as she put him in his place.

"Okay, okay! Just calm down. Real is good people, so just show him the ropes. My word, you in good hands," Emilio said.

Silk beamed down on him like he was her kid. She took in the pitiful excuse of a boss and slid her shades back on, thinking to herself how much she was going to enjoy killing him and his uncle. She also knew it had to be done discreetly, because she didn't want the whole mob out to get her. "Where's Giovanni?" Silk asked, eager to locate her prime target.

"Oh, he's around. He's handling business. When he calls me, I'll let him know you'd like to speak with him," Emilio said, following his uncle's orders of not disclosing his location.

Meanwhile, Giovanni sat behind the walls of his luxurious seven-bedroom mansion up in north Georgia still pondering the attempt on his life. He wanted answers and he wanted a name, but most of all...he wanted revenge.

Chapter 28

"Hey, baby!" Shonnie screamed as she ran over and hugged Real tightly.

"What up, boo?" Real replied, holding Shonnie in his arms. Real was totally feeling Shonnie, a feeling he thought he'd never have again after Constance.

Shonnie had been hiding the news that she was pregnant, but she was about to surprise Real. "Man, I've been missing you like crazy! Damn, my baby clean up real good," Shonnie said as she stepped back and checked out Real, who stood before her looking like a model from a *GQ* magazine.

"Go 'head wit' all that. Come on in," Real said, grabbing her by the waist and leading her into the house.

Before they could even close the door, they were all over each other. Real kissed her hungrily as she wrapped around him like a snake. He carried her to the bedroom, and they both wasted no time in stripping down to nothing.

"Oh yes, baby," Shonnie cooed as Real began planting kisses on her from head to toe while stopping to flick his tongue across her exposed clit.

"Mmmm," Real moaned softly as he buried his head between her legs.

"God, yes! Ohh yeahhh," Shonnie moaned as Real reached under her, grabbing her ass and lifting it up to so he could bury his face deeper into her wetness, as if he was enjoying his favorite dish, face first.

Shonnie's legs were wrapped around his head, and her hips were moving up and down to his rhythm.

Minutes later, Real came up for air and stroked his hard-on getting it ready to replace his tongue.

Shonnie slid her hand down and aided him, lifting up and opening her legs so he could slide in. "Mmm…" she moaned as he filled her up. The feeling with Real in that moment was much more satisfying and intense than any episode she'd ever had with Moe and the occasional quickies they'd had to settle for at the prison.

"Oh ycah, baby," Real called out, long-stroking her until her eyes rolled back in her head.

"Oh, baby, yes! Give me all of you, baby!" Shonnie screamed as she thrust her hips into him faster and faster.

Real followed her lead, turned her over and turned his slow lovemaking into a fast grind, then a hard pounding.

Slap! Slap! Slap!

Shonnie's sweat-covered backside slapped up against his thighs' every stroke while he pounded her in her favorite position, doggy style.

"Fuck this pussy, Real! Get it all!" Shonnie screamed as they both went into a zone of wild, hard, rough sex.

"Throw it to me! Right there, baby!" Real called out as he long-stroked Shonnie hard and fast.

"Oh, I'm…cumming! Ohhhh! Yes!" Shonnie screamed as her body started convulsing violently.

"Fuck!" Real screamed as his body shook and shivered, and he let a hard nut go inside of her.

"Shit!" Shonnie said.

He rolled her over and they both held each other, caught up in the moment, lying there unmoving. Minutes later, they were both asleep in each other's arms—so deeply asleep that they didn't hear someone around back, trying to get into the condo's back door.

* * * * *

The masked man picked the lock on the back door and stepped into the dark kitchen. He crept slowly and quietly through the front room. He had a six-inch blade in his grip as he made his way to the bedroom. He cracked the bedroom door open and looked in and saw someone sleeping in the bed like a baby, even though the room was pitch black. He opened the door just far enough to slide in, holding the blade in an upper-handed grip, ready to tend to the business he'd come for. Just as he reached the bed, a blow to the back of the head caught him totally off guard, causing him to drop the knife. "Umph!" the big masked man cried out as he dropped to his knees and then quickly sprung back up to his feet.

Real was wearing only his boxers as he moved in on the big man. He moved in hard, pummeling the big man with blow after blow, but it was as if he wasn't even hitting him. The huge intruder grabbed Real by the neck and lifted him off his feet.

All the commotion woke Shonnie and she had to make sure she wasn't dreaming when she opened her eyes to Real being choked by a masked man. "Real!" she screamed, jumping up out of the bed, ready to spring into action even though she was butt-ass naked. Shonnie thought back on her tactical prison training and kicked the big man in his groin, causing him to buckle.

Real pried the man's hand away from his neck and noticed he had a missing middle finger. Breaking the man's grip, Real swung and hit him with a solid blow to the side of the head, dazing him.

Shonnie followed up on her attack, trying her best to see in the dark room. The big man pushed Shonnie hard, sending her over the bed, then turned and hit Real in the stomach. He then got his footing and ran out the room, heading out the same way he'd come from. He cursed himself for the botched mission, but he wasn't concerned; he knew he would have plenty more chances.

"You okay?" Real asked Shonnie.

With her adrenaline still running on high, as she sat on the bed, trying to catch her breath. "What in the hell was all that about?" she asked.

"I don't know," Real said. He grabbed his cell phone off the dresser and called Emilio. When he didn't get an answer, he went to the front of the condo to make sure everything was clear and he noticed the back door was wide open.

"So that's how he got in. You must have already been up," Shonnie said, walking up behind Real pulling his robe on.

"Yeah, I'd just gotten up to take a piss and I heard someone creeping."

"You gonna call the police?" Shonnie asked as she walked up behind Real and wrapped her arms around his waist.

"Nah, we good. You know I don't need that heat with me just getting out. Fuck them pigs," Real said, as he closed the door and pulled Shonnie around and took her in his arms.

"Hold up now! I'm one of them pigs!" Shonnie joked.

"You a C.O. flashlight prison cop, baby. But you sho do go hard! I better keep my eye on you with all them moves you got," Real said jokingly. Shonnie had helped him out more than she knew.

"I told you I got your back, ride or die." Shonnie smiled, looking up into his eyes.

"I love you," Real said, hugging her tightly.

"I love you too," she replied, forever wanting to be in his arms.

Chapter 29

" Yeah, nigga you know what it is!" Jalel called out as she and Amber held their cocked and loaded guns on Derwin, one of the city's biggest white-collar scam artists.

Derwin had made millions in real estate and tax scams and other financial fraud. Jalel and Amber had learned from the best when it came to robbing tricks. Silk had taught them all the tricks of the trade, the hook, line and sinker, and now they stood in Derwin's illustrious home, demanding money. Their days of targeting drug dealers were over, being that they were more flash than cash. Their last drug lick had only netted them $12,000, far less than their usual white-collar lick of $80,000 or more. They now only targeted white-collar guys who carried black cards and dressed in designer suits and ties.

"Damn, ladies! I thought we was just gonna have a little fun, but now y'all got guns all up in my face, talking 'bout giving it up. Come on now, y'all. Let's put the guns away and toast to the good life," the sophisticated Derwin said, all calm and cool, hoping the two ladies who'd agreed to a *ménage à trois* hadn't picked up on the fear oozing from his pores.

"Lame-ass nigga! Where the safe at? You got three seconds!" Jalel spat as she stood, with her gun to the side of his head.

Derwin took a sip from the crystal champagne flute he held, set it down, then stood up slowly. "I guess this means y'all ain't feeling me then," Derwin said jokingly, cursing himself for letting his sex drive get him into such a predicament.

"Nah, nigga. We ain't feeling you," Amber said as they led him at gunpoint to the back of his place.

Derwin couldn't believe he was being robbed by two bad bitches in miniskirts and stilettos. He walked into his bedroom and over to the closet that held his top-of-the-line, fireproof, digital safe. "Y'all sure you don't want—"

Clunk!

Amber brought the .9mm down across the back of his faded haircut, instantly drawing blood from the deep gash made by the butt of the gun.

"Umph!" he cried out, grabbing his head.

"Nigga, shut the fuck up and just open the safe!" Jalel screamed.

Derwin shakily punched in the code to the safe and seconds later, it popped open.

The girls were amazed at the piles of new money, neatly stacked from top to bottom.

"A'ight, y'all win," Derwin said as he sat in the closet next to the safe, still holding his head.

"Yeah, we did, didn't we? I still think you're sexy and fine as hell, though, so don't take this personal," Amber said before pulling the trigger on the pistol she held.

Derwin's body hiccupped as the bullets pierced his torso. The last shot tore through his left eye, blowing off the side of his face.

"Let's load this shit up and bounce," Amber called out as they looked around for a bag to carry all the money in.

Chapter 30

arly the next morning, Real sent Shonnie back home while he got ready to join Silk for breakfast before their flight to Miami.

"Baby, make sure you call me," Shonnie told Real as he opened the car door for her.

"I'll hit you when I get settled in. Drive safe, baby," Real said as he leaned in and kissed her softly on the lips.

Real stood in the driveway and watched her drive off before walking back into the house to ponder the night's events. He headed to the kitchen, picked up his cell phone from the table, and called Emilio again.

"Good morning, Real. You good?" Emilio asked as he rode through the city, en route to the club.

"Nah, li'l bro, I got an issue," Real said, taking a seat at the kitchen table.

"What's up? This got something to do with Silk?" Emilio asked.

"No, not at all. It's got something to do with a muthafucker breaking in to the condo last night. I just so happened to be up at the time. He made his way to my bedroom, but I fought him off before he decided to get the hell on. Who was living here before me?" Real asked, thinking maybe the attack was meant for the last tenants.

"Real, being honest, I don't even know, but I will get in touch with my uncle to find out. I can't believe this," Emilio said with a hint of nervousness in his tone.

"Yeah, for real. I'm sitting here with the muthafucker's knife in my hand. If he'd had the chance to use it, I wouldn't be talking to you now. He dropped the shit when I hit him," Real said, admiring the craftsmanship of the sharp hunting knife.

"We'll look into moving you up out of there when you get back in town. Man, Real, I don't understand this shit. First, it was my uncle, then you, and it don't take a rocket scientists to know I'm somewhere on the horizon. After you get back, we'll get in touch with my uncle and see what's going on. Talk to you later," Emilio said, ending the call and quickly dialing Giovanni.

After he hung up, Real got ready to meet Silk, who'd confirmed their breakfast. Real pulled up at the IHOP at 9:00 to meet her for breakfast and picked a corner table next to the window so he could see when she arrived.

"Sir, may I help you?" asked the perky, young, freckle-faced white waitress.

"Just get me a cup of coffee, light sugar and cream. As soon as my company arrives, I'll be ready to order," Real said, scanning the parking lot for Silk.

While he waited, he sat back and pondered what he needed to do to get back on top. He knew he'd have to play his position until he was ready to fend for himself. Real had only ever held one status, boss status, so playing the employee was something he had to get accustomed to. He knew he would have to play the part and play it well to get where he needed to be. The money he was being paid would give him a good start, but he knew he'd also need another source of income to take him over the top. Real's only hang-up was that he'd walked into a mob war or some kind of mess he hadn't signed up for. Real refused to be a casualty of a war when he wasn't even the king on the throne, so he planned to get in, get paid, and get out.

Real was jarred out of his thoughts when an ice-blue, customized Range Rover turned into the lot. Real's thoughts went straight to Constance, since the Range had always been her favorite mode of transportation. A minute later, he set eyes on the sexy dime-piece who stepped out. Silk had grace, looks, a body, class and just the right amount of around-the-way girl underneath. Real worked hard to conceal his attraction to the alluring Silk. He watched her every step as she made her way across the lot in her skin-tight, black designer jeans with gold buckles, a pair of $1,100 Gucci stilettos, a black blouse, a black and gold Gucci bag and an oversized pair of Gucci shades to complement the ensemble. Real eyed her and had to catch himself when he imagined her calling his name in an intimate moment. He had never been the type to be soft or weak for a woman, so he had to check himself; Silk had him feeling vulnerable. He shook off those lustful thoughts as she entered the restaurant and headed in his direction.

"Good morning," Silk said as she sashayed to the table and slid in beside him instead of taking the seat across from him.

"Good morning to you too," Real replied, taking in Silk's good looks and arousing fragrance. "I would have ordered, but I didn't know what you like."

"Good, because we would have had a problem. I would have sworn you were trying to think for me if you'd have ordered and I always think for myself," Silk said, smiling but dead serious.

"I feel you," Real replied, catching another nose full of her sweet perfume.

"So, um, tell me a little about yourself, considering that we're gonna be working together now," Silk said as she turned slightly in her seat, intentionally touching his leg with hers. Silk was a true player and she knew every trick in the book. She was testing Real to see which head he was thinking with. First, she'd squeezed in next to him and now she was making subtle, seemingly innocent contact with her leg. Since Real didn't budge or show any signs of interest, Silk knew he wasn't weak in that category.

"Let me give you a quick rundown on who I am. I'm Real, just released on an appeal bond, and I'm on a mission to get back to the top."

"Interesting. So how did you meet Giovanni?" Silk asked.

"I haven't actually met the man face to face yet. We've only spoken on the phone. I met Emilio while doing my bid. We were cool and his uncle asked me to keep him safe. This is their way of returning the favor."

"Oh okay. So are you fit for your position?"

"What kind of question is that? I used to run this city, but a couple of bids and a few disloyal friends cost me everything. I'm more focused now than ever and losing ain't part of the equation," Real said with much sincerity in his tone.

Silk looked at him attentively. "So you're not associated?" she asked, glad to know his place in the family was just a temporary one.

"Yeah, I like li'l Emilio, and Giovanni really saved my life by getting me out of there, so yeah, my loyalty goes a li'l way with those two," Real replied, reading between the lines. It hadn't taken Real long to figure out that Silk was up to something, even if he wasn't sure what just yet.

"I admire a loyal man," Silk said, moving her leg.

"Right. But enough about me. Tell me a li'l something about the lady behind those shades," Real said, turning in his seat to face her.

"All right. I'm one of the most treacherous, dangerous, cut-throat bitches to walk the Earth. I set niggas up to be robbed. I rob, kill and steal. Matter fact, there ain't no low-down shit I don't do," Silk said as she removed her shades to look him in his eyes.

Real let out a light chuckle, sure the beautiful Silk was just joking. "Whoa, bad girl! So that's what happened to you then, huh?" Real asked, looking at the deep scar that was only partially covered by her hair.

"Yeah, that's just a reminder of just how bad shit can get. It was to the point that I didn't even like myself. A couple years ago, I was sitting in a hotel room, defeated and mad at the world. I put a gun to my head and pulled the trigger, but I guess God wasn't ready for me. The recoil from the gun redirected the barrel, and I was deeply grazed right here," Silk said, moving her hair to let Real see how serious the scar and her life at that time was.

"Musta been hard," Real said softly, feeling a bit of sorrow for the pretty lady.

The waitress came back, and they placed their order. As they enjoyed their breakfast, they got to know each other, and by the time they were finished with their pancakes and eggs, they felt like old friends.

"Shit, we gotta go!" Silk called out, looking down at her diamond-studded Cartier watch and realizing it was close to their flight time.

They trailed each other to the airport, parked their cars, and rushed in to catch their flight to Miami.

Chapter 31

iovanni called the families in for a meeting that would include Emilio and Lurch. After hearing about the attack on Real, Giovanni made it mandatory that the head of each and every family was there. They all sat in Pickett Hall, one of the family's many commercial real estate properties. The hall boasted custom crystal chandeliers, an expensive marble and oak conference table, and other expensive amenities for meetings and conferences. All the heads of the families flew in to assist their mob brother, the one responsible for handling all their finances. They were all ready to help Giovanni deal with his current threat, and they wanted to be briefed on the money being funneled through their respective clubs.

"I'm glad you could all make it today. We've no time for small talk, so I'm going to get right down to the business at hand. Someone is attacking us, and I have no earthly idea who is doing it or why. We have no other outside business going on or any other problems with other families, so I'm rather perplexed right now. The first attack was months ago, and then one of my properties was broken into. My club manager was attacked, barely escaping with his life," Giovanni explained as Emilio and Lurch looked around at the other mob bosses.

"Are you telling us you're being attacked and that you have no other outside interests going on? Something's not right. Let's think about this for a minute. If you're in good standings with every man in this room, which I think you are, and you have no outside business, why would someone be targeting you and your people? It seems to me like someone is indulging in outside business that's caught up with them," Tonelli, the Cali mob boss said. He was one of the most outspoken and least liked of the heads around the table.

Giovanni looked at him in disgust. "What are you saying Tonelli? Are you calling me a liar?" Giovanni asked with venom in his tone.

"No! I'm not calling you a liar, Giovanni. I'm just saying that some of your people might have some things going on that you don't know about. When did these attacks start? Just think about it and add it up. It's all in your face," Tonelli said, looking at Emilio.

Giovanni's nephew knew exactly what Tonelli was getting at. "With all due respect, I have not betrayed my uncle in any kind of way, nor do I have any outside business going. As far as I know, I have no enemies. These attacks are foreign to us all. Also, while I have the floor, I want to thank all the respectable men around this table for trusting me to stand in for my uncle while he's trying to sort these issues out. Uncle Giovanni and I have also brought on another club manager. As we speak, he is headed to our establishment in Miami to make sure all ledgers and accounts are up to par. He will hit all of the establishments and conduct a thorough audit, making sure every penny is accounted for. I know—"

"Wait a minute! You hired a new man, who none of us know, to look through our books? Is he also going to know about our outside, non-club ventures that we're running through the clubs?" Carasco asked. He was, by far, the most respected and dangerous man at the table.

Giovanni cringed in his seat; his nephew was talking too much. He'd planned to bring Real up to the family in the meeting, but Emilio had put it out there as if it wasn't an issue that was up for everyone's agreement. All the men at the table began to whisper amongst themselves and Giovanni could tell by their faces that none of them took the new revelations well. It was okay for him to put Emilio in his place with his direction, but to bring an outsider in without the heads' approval was like a slap in the face to the families.

"Um—" Emilio started up again, but Giovanni broke in.

"I take total blame for this, gentlemen. I gave Emilio the okay to bring on the other manager when the books were not adding up. I felt it was urgent that we bring in someone to assess the situation and make our presence felt in all our spots. A few of our old people are getting lazy, so I felt we needed to send someone to wake them up," Giovanni explained. It sounded like a crock of bullshit to his own ears, so he was sure the men around the table would take it even worse.

"This is totally not acceptable and way out of line. Giovanni, what's gotten into you? Is it possible that such a decision is why you're being targeted now? Who is this new manager? Maybe he is the source of your problems," Carasco asked, glaring at Giovanni, who was now sweating, with a scowl on his face.

Emilio was slumped down in his chair. He'd embarrassed his uncle and put him in an awkward position with the families.

The other heads looked on, waiting for the answer.

"His name is Richard Walker, but he goes by Real. He used to own the G-Spot nightclub, so he's very familiar with the club industry. On top of that, he saved Emilio's life when he was locked up. Our own personal attorney secured him an appeal bond, and we put him in position after witnessing his loyalty firsthand. Besides that, I felt like we owed him," Giovanni explained.

The men didn't go for Real's hero status one bit.

While Giovanni was speaking, he failed to notice that Carasco was digging for his cell phone from his inside jacket pocket. Carasco dialed a number and placed the phone to his ear. "I thought I'd heard it before," Carasco told the person on the other line.

Giovanni was confused at what was going on.

Carasco closed his phone, took off his designer frames, and looked Giovanni directly in the eyes, with hate written all over his face. "You say his name is Richard Walker, better known as Real?"

"Yes."

"And he used to own the G-Spot?" Carasco asked, thinking back on the months of Moretti's and Rossi's deaths.

"Yes. He's a very loyal man from what I've seen so far," Giovanni said, confused at the line of questioning.

"Would you trust him with your life?"

"I would, and I did," Emilio called out, drawing stares from the other men at the table; it was the ultimate disrespect to butt in on a boss conversation.

Carasco cut his eyes over at Emilio, silently warning him to stay out of it.

"I would as well. I apologize to all the men who—" Giovanni began, but his apology was cut short.

"No need, but this is what you're going to do. You're going to bring this man Real before us all and kill him," Carasco demanded, surprising all of the heads.

"What!? I-I don't understand," Giovanni said.

Emilio and Lurch looked at Carasco like he was crazy.

"Giovanni, you just freed the man who killed many of our own—Rossi, Moretti, and Angelo, just to name a few. It's the same man we've been hunting for years. When we heard he'd be dying in prison, we wrote him off. You set one of our worst enemies loose, and now you're letting him go through our books!" Carasco spat, slamming his fist on the table.

"You mean the guy…" Giovanni's words trailed off as the truth hit him. "Fuck!" Giovanni screamed, nervously running his hand through his hair.

"Bring him here, same time, same day next week, and you'll have the pleasure of…no, wait! *You* will kill him," Carasco said, pointing at Emilio.

Naturally, Emilio was totally against Real's death, being that he'd saved his life. He just looked up without saying a word.

"He'll be here," Giovanni said.

All the men around the table started whispering again.

Giovanni felt stupid and was totally humiliated. He'd freed a man the family wanted dead. He looked over at Emilio, who was defeated in every way, knowing it was all his fault.

Chapter 32

Shonnie bopped her head to the Isley Brothers' greatest hits on her two-hour drive home. She smiled as she thought about her new life with Real. As she drove down the street that led to her house, she looked around and decided right then that she wanted a change. *That's it. I'm moving to Atlanta,* she vowed. She pulled up in front of her house, grabbed her overnight bag, and headed in.

As soon as she hit the door, she stripped down and ran some bath water. She couldn't wait to sit back in a nice, warm bath and relive the moments of the night before. Before getting in the tub, she went to the kitchen to retrieve her scented candles and a lighter.

"What the hell!?" she called out when she noticed the back door wide open and hanging off its hinges.

Just as she was turning around, a hard slap across the back of her head sent her sideways.

"Ahh!" she screamed as she hit the floor.

"Yeah, bitch! You think you can just leave me locked up and not bail me out? Then you pressed charges against me!" Moe screamed, reaching back to slap her again. This time, he hit her so hard that bloody spit flew from her mouth.

Earlier in the day, his cousin Mabel had contacted a bail bondsman she knew to get him out on a property bond. After they drank a gallon of vodka and had sloppy, incestuous sex, she dropped Moe off at the house, where he kicked the back door in and waited in the utility room for Shonnie to come home.

"Moe, stop hitting me! Get out, or I'm gonna call the police again!" Shonnie screamed as she quickly got to her feet. She swung wildly at him, then kicked at his groin, but his fat, sloppy thighs kept her foot from connecting.

Moe laughed a sinister laugh as he reached over, grabbed her, and slammed her hard to the floor.

"Oh!" Shonnie cried out as her naked body smacked the hard tile floor.

Moe pinned her down and sat on top of her. "Bitch, I held you down when you ain't have shit! I busted my ass day in and day out to provide for your fuck ass back then, and this is how you fuckin' do me? You call the police and press charges on me?" Moe yelled drunkenly, drool leaking from his mouth.

"Get off me, Moe!" Shonnie said with tears running down her cheeks. She struggled with all her might but couldn't budge.

"Where the fuck you been, huh?" Moe screamed. He could tell she hadn't been home because there was an overnight bag sitting by the door.

"Please, Moe, get off me! I can't breathe!" Shonnie cried out.

Moe moved a little to the side and lifted some of his weight off of her.

When Shonnie realized her pleading was having some effect, she laid it on thick. "Moe, please, baby! Let's not fight. I've been at Tina's all night because her mother passed away, and she didn't wanna be alone. Life is too short for this crazy stuff, Moe. Baby, please let's get back to where we used to be. I-I love you," Shonnie lied, hoping he'd fall for it. The truth was, she no longer cared if he lived or died.

Moe sat there for a minute then rose up off of her. Just as he was getting up, her cell phone beeped, and then the ringtone chimed in. Beyoncé's "Love on Top" played loudly out of the Android phone speaker. Shonnie tried to act as if she didn't hear it, but Moe was curious who she'd given such a ringtone to. As soon as he got to the phone, his temperature rose. There, on the screen, was a shirtless Real, smiling up at him with those perfect teeth.

Shonnie knew what was next, so she made a quick detour to the back to find something to slip on. After she dressed in whatever she could find, she grabbed her keys from the dresser and hurried back out to the front. Just as she was on her way out, she heard Moe on the phone with her new man.

"Fuck, boy, don't call this phone no mo' or else!" Moe spat as he looked up and noticed Shonnie coming his way trying to leave.

"Say, bro, where Shonnie at? I ain't trying to start no trouble. I'm just trying to get in touch with Shonnie," Real told him, remembering what Shonnie had told him about her ex.

"Nigga, fuck you!" Moe screamed. He dropped the phone and grabbed Shonnie before she could get out the door.

"Go on now, Moe!" Shonnie said calmly, hoping her soft tone would keep Moe cool.

"Ho, who is that on the phone? Has your ass been with him?" Moe screamed as he held her like a ragdoll by the arm.

"Moe, let me—"

Before she could get her words out, he hit her with all his might, right in the nose, drawing blood instantly.

"Ow! No!" Shonnie screamed, holding her nose as blood filled her hand.

Real sat on the line, furious that he couldn't be there to protect her from her ex.

"Don't scream now, bitch!" Moe said as he snatched her up by her hair and slung her around.

"Ahhh! Help! Nooo! Please!" Shonnie screamed, trying to pry his hands from her hair.

Moe pulled her up by her hair and kicked her in the stomach. "Yeah, bitch, this is what you want, ain't it?" he screamed as she doubled over, holding her stomach.

Real cringed, listening helplessly to Shonnie being beaten. Flashes of Constance's demise flashed in his mind, and he remembered that horrible message on his voicemail as she took her last breaths.

"Hey, man! Hey!" Real screamed into the receiver, bringing stares from Silk and the baggage handler who was carrying their luggage.

"Please, Moe! Stop!" Shonnie cried out, short of breath.

Moe pulled her face up by her chin and hit her in the mouth, knocking her two front teeth out. Shonnie's head snapped back, and she tumbled over. Next, he stood over her and grabbed a handful of her hair and held it tight while he beat her about the face and head. Real could hear the solid blows on the other end of the line, and a minute later Shonnie blacked out from all the licks to the head. Blood seeped from the many lacerations his fist had made.

"Fuck-ass bitch!" Moe spat drunkenly, landing one last swift kick to her side, breaking her ribs.

The last kick woke Shonnie up, and she instantly spat up blood. She lay in the middle of the floor in a puddle of her own blood, moaning. Moe walked over and picked up the phone.

"Nigga, come get yo' bitch!" Moe spat, then he ended the call and tucked the phone in his pocket. After surveying the damage, Moe went to the back and grabbed a change of clothes, then picked up Shonnie's car keys.

"You a bitch-ass nigga! I swear I'm gonna see you, and when I do, you're a dead man!" Real said through clenched teeth to a dead line.

Silk had now stopped and was staring at him, admiring his deadly side. "You okay?" she asked as he fumbled with his phone.

"Yeah, I'm good. Excuse me for a sec'," Real said as he walked over to an empty corner.

Real dialed 911 and gave the operator Shonnie's name, state, and city. It didn't take them long to match the name with the address.

"We'll dispatch a cruiser immediately, sir. Can you be reached at this number?" she asked.

"Yeah," Real said sadly as he ended the call with a heavy heart.

The first officer to arrive on the scene noticed the front door ajar. He pulled his weapon, called for backup, and approached the front door. Through the cracked door, he could see Shonnie lying facedown in the middle of the floor in a puddle of her own blood. "Send emergency vehicles ASAP!" the officer yelled into his radio as he pushed the front door all the way open and announced his presence. After seeing that no one else was present, he administered first aid on Shonnie. He noticed her heartbeat was faint, and he cursed the person responsible as he checked the house one more time.

Chapter 33

While Real was off to the side taking care of the situation with Shonnie, Silk was calling Amber and Jalel. "He's at this address. Make sure y'all don't fuck it up this time," Silk told Amber.

Amber was sitting across from Jalel, watching her split up their last take. "We got you, Silk," Amber said, rolling her eyes and looking at the address she'd written down.

"Just hit me when it's done," Silk told her, ending the call.

"What's the plan?" Jalel asked as she stacked the remaining crisp bills on the table.

"I got the address for that Giovanni. Let's get this shit over with early so we can go celebrate tonight. We ain't turned it up in the club in a minute," Amber said. She leaned over, grabbed her share of the money from the table, and stuffed it in the plastic bag that sat in the chair.

"I'm wit' that," Jalel said as she took her share and put it in a brown paper sack.

Amber followed Jalel back to the closet, where they both stashed their money. After securing their money, Jalel pulled out the large canvas bag that rested in the corner, filled with high-powered weapons.

"These are a must since we're going so early," Amber called out as she pulled a pair of silencers from the bag.

"For real. I guess that means we're rolling with these," Jalel said, pulling two matching .9mm guns from the bag.

"Yep," Amber said as they exited the closet.

They spent close to an hour getting dressed, and when they walked out of the loft, it looked as if they were headed to an upscale night spot in the middle of the day. They were dressed in designer wear from head to toe, complete with hip-hugging jeans, stilettos, open cleavage, and expensive jewelry. They'd tucked the guns, silencers attached, neatly in their purses. They climbed into their white BMW M3 and headed to north Georgia to pay Giovanni a visit.

* * * * *

"Emilio, do not ever speak up in a meeting again unless you are spoken to. You created a lot of bad blood within our family by blurting all that out back there. I had no idea this Real was a wanted man, and this is a major embarrassment. His fate is sealed. You understand that, don't you?" Giovanni asked as Lurch steered the Benz through the morning traffic.

"Yeah," Emilio answered, hating that he'd been ordered to kill Real.

"When is he scheduled to be back in town?" Giovanni asked, staring out the back passenger window at the passing cars.

"Not sure, but I'll contact him," Emilio said reluctantly. He had no desire to kill the man who'd saved his life in prison.

"Find out and let me know. Emilio, we must always remember that family comes first," Giovanni said, still looking out the window.

A young, thick black female in high heels was at the corner, crossing the street. Giovanni had to do a double-take to make sure it wasn't Black Stallion, because he was still on the hunt for the bitch who'd played him for a fool.

Making a left on Cainwood Drive and a right on Peach Orchard, they came upon Giovanni's secluded mansion.

"All right, I'll get with y'all later," he told Lurch and Emilio. He looked left to right before getting out the car, always on guard.

"Okay," Emilio said.

They watched as Giovanni entered the house, but they didn't notice the two jazzy females riding by in the white BMW, scoping out the estate.

Chapter 34

"You okay?" Silk asked Real as they stood in the elevator, heading to their respective rooms in the Miami Suites five-star hotel.

"Yeah, I'm cool. Shit's just crazy," Real replied. All he wanted to do was hop back on the plane and head home, but he had a job to do and business had to be handled. He just hoped the police and EMTs got to Shonnie in time.

"Is there anything I can help you with?" Silk asked as the elevator doors opened to their floor.

"You can help me by expediting this trip. I need to be in and out and back on the plane tonight," Real said seriously as they stepped off the elevator.

Silk knew after breakfast that Real would be a nice addition to her plans. She was going to need a male counterpart to access Giovanni's accounts, and Real was just the man to pull it off. On top of that, she was growing fond of the handsome gangster. The only problem was that she needed more time to convince him to join her on her mission. "It's that serious? You really need to fly back tonight?" Silk asked, trying her best to think of a way to make him stay.

"Yeah. My ticket was roundtrip, right?" Real asked as they reached her door, two doors up from his.

"All right. If we plan on leaving tonight, we best get freshened up and handle our business in a hurry," Silk said as if she didn't object to his early departure.

"You don't have to leave."

"Nah, it's cool. I'm your escort," Silk said, opening her room door and step-ping in.

"A'ight. Give me twenty minutes," Real said as he picked his bag up and headed to his room. When he reached the room, his phone was beeping. "Hello?" Real answered in an awkward tone, not recognizing the phone number.

"Hello. This is Detective Mundy with the Glennville PD. Who am I speaking with?" the detective asked in an official tone.

"This is James Parker. May I help you?" Real answered, not about to give them his real name.

"You are the gentleman who called 911 about the assault. Am I correct?"

"Yes. Is my friend okay?" Real asked, holding his breath as he stepped into his room, hoping Shonnie was okay.

"Well, she was beaten up pretty bad, but the doctors say she will survive. Do you have any idea who could have done this?"

"I have no idea. She just called me screaming," Real lied, not wanting them to catch up with Moe before he did.

"Can you come down to the station?"

"I'm sorry, sir, but I'm out of town. I will come in as soon as I get back," Real said hurriedly and clicked off the line.

Seconds later, his phone rang again. He looked at the screen and saw that it was the detective again. He ignored the call and sent it to voicemail. In that moment, he wondered whose name Emilio had put the phone under. Considering the business they were in, he was sure it was an alias. Real ignored the phone when it rang yet again. He stripped out of his clothes, took a quick shower, and headed back down to Silk's room. Just as he was about to knock on her door, she was coming out.

"Right on time," she said as they got on the elevator headed back down.

An hour later, they were pulling up into the Pearlz parking lot in the gray Lincoln rental.

"Nice li'l crowd for lunch hour," Silk said, climbing out of the car. She was looking forward to pushing around Cleo, the club manager who was a Danny DeVito lookalike.

As they made their way through the front lobby doors, a pudgy, fat-faced white girl who looked totally out of place amongst the other beautiful women turned her nose up at Silk. She knew her well from past visits.

Silk didn't speak or acknowledge the girl. She simply walked by and rolled here eyes. She couldn't care less that the girl was Cleo's daughter.

Real was highly impressed with the expensive furnishings and décor. The stage was pearl marble, and he was sure it had cost a fortune.

"Follow me," Silk said, heading to the back, where Cleo's office was located. She led Real into a narrow, dimly lit hallway, until they came to an office door. Instead of knocking, Silk just opened his door.

"Oh!" the very tan Pocahontas called out as Silk and Real stepped through the door.

Cleo still wasn't aware they had company, so he kept his head buried between Pocahontas's legs until Silk spoke.

"Damn! You full yet?" Silk called out.

Real couldn't help but crack a smile.

"Who...who in the hell in my office?" Cleo screamed. He lifted up and turned around with a wet mouth. He was surprised to see Silk, with some strange man in tow.

"Let me see the books," Silk said firmly, crossing her arms across her ample chest.

"Get out!" Cleo told Pocahontas, wiping his mouth and straightening his tie.

"Damn, Silk! You were just here, and may I ask who your companion is?" Cleo asked, looking at Real.

"I'm Real. Where are the books?" Real asked in a serious tone, ready to take care of business.

Cleo didn't say a thing. He simply turned and headed over to his desk, with

Silk on his heels.

"We're doing things different now, so get used to Real. He'll be in here a lot," Silk said, standing behind him, looking over his shoulder as he sat at his desk.

"Could y'all please give me about ten minutes to get everything up to date? I'll also give you a safe count and a deposit count. Things have been real busy around here, and I've fallen a little behind. I just need a few minutes to get things straight," Cleo said, pulling his glasses from his pocket and the account papers from his desk.

"Fine. Ten minutes. We'll be right out front," Silk replied, walking back over to the door as Real opened it for them to exit.

"His ass knows he been stealing, and now he needs time to doctor the accounts. It's all good, as long as it adds up. This is my last trip dealing with this bullshit. I've got bigger and better things to do," Silk said, wondering how Real would react.

Real gave her just the look she was looking for.

Silk had made many trips to clubs for Giovanni, but it wasn't so he could be informed. She'd always had an ulterior motive and her own agenda. She now knew exactly how much she was going to pick up when she put her plan in motion. "You want to make some extra money?" Silk asked as they walked to the bar.

"You know I'm always for making a dollar. What you got in mind?" Real asked as he climbed up on the leather barstool.

"I'm going to kill Giovanni and empty out all his accounts that I have access to," Silk said calmly and coolly, waving the bartender over.

Real was totally caught off guard by her plans, but he looked at her without breaking his stare, just to see if she was serious. "You for real?" Real asked as the bartender walked up.

"Dead serious," she said, grinning at him. "Can I have a double-shot of Hennessy, light ice with a splash of Sprite?" she said to the bartender. "What are you having Real?"

"It's a little too early for me. I'm—"

"Give him the same," Silk said, cutting him off.

"You calling shots now?" Real asked with raised brows.

"Yeah, I'm that bitch—real gangsta," Silk said in a joking tone, though she really meant it.

"Well, let me enlighten you. I'm a real nigga, one of the realest you'll ever meet. If I don't like things, I change it. If I can't change it, I get rid of it. You'll come off better working with me than you would trying to work against me. I'm a stone-cold killer, and a bitch—even a gangsta bitch—don't stand a chance. They don't call me Real for nothing. That name was earned, not given," Real said, leaning over to look her right in the eyes and having no idea how much he was turning Silk on.

"Excuse me then." Silk laughed out loud. She reached in her pocket and pulled out the money for their drinks while making sure her stash was intact.

"Your plan seems kind of tempting. Let me think about it on the way home tonight."

"Okay, but can I trust you with my intentions?" Silk asked as the bartender set their drinks on the counter.

"You know it, or you wouldn't have told me," Real said. He chose his words carefully, as he thought it might all be a test from Giovanni, and he wanted to pass that test.

"All right," Silk said.

Just then, a drop-dead gorgeous stripper hit the stage.

"Now that's a bad bitch," Silk called out.

Real turned around and checked out the girl onstage, who was working the pole like a pro.

Silk took the few minutes while he was turned around to dig in her pocket and retrieve the crushed up ecstasy, mixed with cocaine. She quickly unwrapped the plastic that held the powder and dumped it in his drink.

"Yeah, she is a bad bitch," Real said when Silk handed him his drink.

A minute into their drinks, Cleo stepped out the office and waved them over. They went back to the office and went over the books and saw that everything added up.

Silk anxiously waited on the call from the girls while they checked the books. She was eager to make her move, but she had to wait until Giovanni was out of the way. "A'ight, Cleo, you good. We'll be in touch," Silk said as they exited his office and headed to the car.

"Damn! That one drink got me feeling…feeling…damn!" Real said as they walked out of the club and to the car.

Silk climbed behind the wheel, and Real got in on the passenger side. She looked over at him and knew the drugs had taken their toll. She planned to join him in his hotel room and have some fun before convincing him to join her in her mission. There was no way he was flying back liked he planned.

Chapter 35

$\mathscr{A}$mber and Jalel rode by the house a second time before pulling the BMW over on the curb right outside Giovanni's palatial home. They adjusted their clothes and popped the hood. Amber sat on the curb, acting like she was on her cell phone, while Jalel was under the hood, acting like something was wrong with the brand-new ride.

"Give 'em ten minutes," Amber said, continuing to act like she was mad at her car.

"Okay," Jalel said, not looking up from under the hood.

The two women played their parts well, but when the ten-minute timeframe passed, they agreed to move on to Plan B.

"I'll go up to the door, and you stay here. When you see me go in, you need to…" Jalel stopped mid-sentence when the front door of the mansion opened. "Hey! He just opened the door," Jalel whispered to Amber, who was sitting with her back to the house.

"What's he doing? Does he see us?" Amber asked, still holding her cell phone to her ear.

"He's coming down the driveway now," Jalel replied.

Giovanni had been lounging around, hoping to find some peace of mind after the stressful meeting. He got up for a minute to grab a snack and noticed two attractive women having car trouble out front. He didn't suspect any foul play. All he saw were long, firm legs, pretty faces, and plump asses. The last thing on his mind was being gunned down by the damsels in apparent distress. As he made his way down the driveway, he played eenie-meenie-miney-moe to decide which female he should focus on, because they were both beautiful. Before he reached them, he decided there was nothing wrong with taking a shot at both of them. Giovanni hadn't had any female company in a minute and he missed the clandestine sexual affairs he'd often had in his club office. He had his heart set on bedding both of the distressed women, and he was excited for the threesome. "Hello, ladies. Car trouble?" Giovanni asked as he stood with his hands in the pockets of his designer slacks that perfectly brushed the tops of his Italian loafers.

"Yeah. The damn thing won't start!" Jalel said with an attitude.

Amber turned, still pretending someone was on the line. "Sir, could you help us out here? I've got AAA on the way, but my bladder is about to bust," Amber said as she told the empty line she would call back.

"Anything for you beauties. By the way, I'm Giovanni, and you are?" he asked as motioned for them to follow him.

"I'm Valencia, and this is Shalan," they lied as they followed him up the driveway, holding their purses tight.

"What are y'all doing out in these parts?" Giovanni asked curiously.

"House-hunting. My realtor told me this is the perfect spot for me," Jalel said.

"What do you do? What's your profession?" Giovanni asked curiously, since the houses in the area started off in the seven-figure price range.

"I own a line of spas, thanks to my cheating husband. We divorced a year ago, and I took half of all his hard-earned surgeon's pay. I think I did quite well for myself. What do you do?" Jalel asked smiling.

"I'm in the nightclub business. I think I've done pretty well for myself as well, if I do say so myself," Giovanni said as he opened the door to his illustrious million-dollar home.

"Well, you've sure got a nice place here," Amber said as she stepped in behind Jalel.

"Thanks. Um, could you ladies wait here for a second?" Giovanni said with a smile before he retreated to the back room.

Amber stepped to the left and looked around the corner to make sure they were alone before she spoke. "Let's get this shit over with as quick as possible."

"We need to make sure there ain't nobody else in here," Jalel said, looking around the foyer of the beautiful home.

Just as they were deciding on the best time to make their move, Giovanni stepped back in the room with a Colt .45 in his grip. "Both of y'all sit down," he said, leveling the gun in their direction.

Chapter 36

"Damn, killer, you let one li'l Hen and Sprite knock you off your feet?" Silk said as she pulled the rental in front of the hotel.

The valet rushed over to the car and opened the doors for them to exit.

"Man, that shit got me tingling all over," Real slightly slurred, feeling good.

Silk made it her business to invade his personal space as she walked over to him and grabbed his hand. "Come on, handsome," she said, squeezing his hand lightly. She knew after she finished with him that night, he'd be down with her program. She also knew dealing with a headstrong man like Real, who was already in a relationship, she'd need a little help breaking his shell. The drugs would loosen him up, and that would make it all the easier for her to have her way with him. Over time, she could have pulled off the feat without the spiked drink, because she was pretty desirable, but she was pressed for time. Besides that, the sex would be all that much better if he was high.

"I gotta get to Atlanta to check on Shonnie," Real mumbled as Silk led him by the hand to the elevator.

"You'll get there," she replied as the elevators doors closed. When they stepped off the elevator, she was still holding his big, firm hand.

Real's head was spinning, and he was having hot flashes by the time they stepped into his room. He stood in the middle of the floor and stripped out of his shirt. "Damn, I'm hot! Something ain't right."

Silk stepped back and admired his six-pack and well-defined chest, now wet with perspiration. His sweaty physique turned her on. "Damn, he;s fine," Silk mumbled to herself as she walked over and gently pushed him back to the bed. "Here, baby," Silk said, handing him a glass of water and knowing full well it would only boost the ecstasy high.

Real gulped the water down like a thirsty refugee. "I gotta get to Atlanta," Real repeated, but he didn't move.

"How about you spend some time with me before you go?" she said in a seductive voice. She reached over and lightly brushed her long nails across his chest, sending chills all over his body. When he tensed up, she did the same thing to his back.

"Maybe I've got a few minutes," Real said, looking at Silk like he wanted to eat her up. It was as if he had no control and the feeling he was having was very familiar. He remembered it from long ago, when he used to do cocaine. He'd kicked that habit a while back and hadn't done any since, so he blamed the crazy high on the liquor, since he hadn't had any of that in a while either.

Silk stood up and pulled her shirt over her head, exposing a perfect set of perky C-cups that stood erect without the help of a bra. "You like what you see?"

Silk asked, stripping out of her remaining clothes.

"Fuck yeah!" Real called out as he reached out and started caressing and kissing her breast and stomach, lost in the high.

"Lie back," she coaxed softly as she reached over and unbuckled his belt.

Real helped her out and pulled off his pants and boxers.

Silk didn't waste any time climbing on top of the perfectly sculptured man, bringing her mouth down on his.

Real took her kiss invitingly, and his erection became rock hard. In the midst of the kiss, his mind flashed back to Shonnie, but the drugs and a naked Silk on top of him made him quickly dismiss the thought.

"Mmm…" Silk moaned as she kissed him deeply.

Real's high, scattered thoughts went back and forth from Silk to Shonnie to Constance. The drugs had him zoning out and he couldn't get control of his mind. After fighting with himself, he gave up and reached up under Silk. He cupped her hairless wet spot and massaged it, getting her all worked up.

"Put it in, Real," Silk moaned as her juices flowed over his fingers. She hadn't been involved with anyone for a minute, and she applauded herself for working the extra perk in her plan. She was long overdue, and Real was right on time. "Come here," she said softly as she reached down, grabbed his erection, and guided it in her waiting wetness. She knew the cocaine and ecstasy would have her in for a long ride, and she'd longed for that since she'd first set eyes on him. She felt his manhood throbbing as he buried it deep inside of her. "Ohhh, baby!" Silk cooed as she perched herself on top of him and rotated her hips to his rhythm.

"Yeah! Ride that dick, baby," Real called out as his body tingled all over. The drugs had him feeling like every stroke was an orgasm. He loved the feeling and never wanted it to end. Twenty minutes later, Silk was on her third orgasm and worn out, but Real showed no signs of slowing down or wanting to stop. He'd sexed her in every position, until she was hurting and sore.

"Cum with me, baby!" she called out, hoping he'd end it. It had started as pure pleasure, but now she was in pain.

"Oh yeah, baby!" Real called out as he increased his pace while she fondled his balls.

Silk could tell by his facial expression that he was about to cum. She squeezed her vaginal muscles tight and threw her hips into him. "I'm cumming, baby!" Silk screamed, hoping her cries would make him follow her lead.

"Oh fuck yess! Ahhhh!" Real screamed as he let himself go inside of her tight, wet center. He was still shaking minutes later from the hard, long, intense climax.

Silk knew after their session, he would be all hers—or at least down with her plans.

They lay in each others arms until they dozed off.

Chapter 37

"What's going on?" Amber asked as Giovanni stood holding the gun on them.

"Who y'all work for?" Giovanni spat as his bent his face up in a frown.

"Work for? I told you I own spas. Please don't hurt us. We don't know what you're talking about, mister! Our car broke down, and we were just looking for some help and a place to use the restroom! Please, sir, don't hurt us," Jalel cried out, angry at herself for slipping.

"We have no clue what's going on here! I-I don't want to die," Amber sobbed, trying to squeeze her eyes to bring real tears.

"I'll give y'all three seconds. If you don't tell me who you work for, I'll kill both of you right here, right now. One…two…thr—"

"Wait! Please! I swear we don't work for nobody!" Amber screamed, bracing herself for a gunshot that never came.

"Okay. Y'all are clean. The bathroom is through that door and around the corner," Giovanni said as he laid the gun on the counter and started talking to Jalel, who was still trying to regain her composure. "Would you like something to drink or a snack?" Giovanni asked, as if nothing out of the ordinary had happened.

As Amber hastily walked off to the bathroom with her purse tucked under her arm, Jalel wiped the sweat from her brow. "Why did you just do that? Should we just go wait outside for AAA?" she asked, pissed. She'd almost given in, but the look in his eyes told her to ride it out. The girls had always been on the safe side of the high-powered weapons, but this time, they'd gotten a taste of their own medicine. As they saying goes, ain't no fun when the rabbit got the gun, and neither of them liked it. Jalel took a seat on the couch with her purse in her lap and waited for Amber to return.

"Just trying to be sure. I apologize."

"I really don't know what to say right now. You scared the shit out of me," Jalel said shakily.

"I'm truly sorry, but there's been some crazy things happenings in my life, and I just wanted to make sure you weren't one of them," he said as he took the seat on the adjoining couch.

"Well, we're not crazy, and I appreciate you letting us chill while we wait for help," Jalel said. She eyed Amber coming from the back and made sure to keep Giovanni's attention.

Amber stepped back in the room quietly with the .9mm in her grip as Giovanni entertained Jalel. "Let's get this shit over with!" she yelled, causing Giovanni to turn around.

"Damn," Giovanni said softly as he looked back at Amber, aiming a gun right at him.

"Yeah, we've been here way too long," Jalel said, standing and pulling her own weapon out.

"I knew it!" Giovanni screamed. He dropped his head and ran both his hands through his hair.

"Where's your safe? Give us what we came for, and you'll live another day," Amber demanded.

Giovanni was confused. He knew he was a marked man, even though he wasn't sure who his enemy was, but the two intruders made it sound like a simple robbery and not a hit. "I understand. I'll give you what you want. Please just stay calm," he said as he eyed his Colt on the counter.

"Not today, sir," Amber said, following his line of sight. She walked over and picked up his gun.

"Take us to the safe," Jalel said. Since they already had the drop on him, they figured they might as well take off with some of his loot.

Giovanni turned and led them to the back office, where his safe was. "Ladies, this is not necessary. I can put you both in positions that will have you set for life," he said as he entered his office. Before he got to his desk, he stopped and turned to face the women. "Look, this is your last chance to take me up on my offer, or I'm going to kill both of you," he said out of nowhere in a menacing tone, as if he could really make it happen. He hoped the ladies would give in to his crazy scheme.

His threat had Amber looking around the office, all jittery and confused.

Jalel, on the other hand, relied on her common sense. "Just open the safe and shut the fuck up!" she bellowed, sticking the gun in his face.

"I'm gonna give you three seconds," Giovanni repeated. "One…two…thr—"

Before he could finish his countdown, a loud blast went off in the room, and blood splattered on the side wall.

Jalel looked over at Amber, her mouth wide open. "Amber! Why the fuck you shoot him before we got in the safe? Rule fuckin' number one is don't shoot until the damn safe is open!" she screamed, rushing around the office and looking for anything of value.

"He was going to—" Amber started.

"He wasn't gonna do shit! How was he gonna kill us, huh? You really ain't cut out for this shit no more," Jalel said as Amber stepped over Giovanni's body and helped with the search.

Ring! Ring! Ring!

"Hello. I'm not available right now. Please leave a message…*BEEP!*"

"Hey, Unc, when you get this message, please give me a call," Emilio said on the answering machine as he and Lurch sat in the back office at the club.

"Let's go! Ain't shit in here," Jalel called out, listening to Emilio on the answering machine while they thoroughly searched and trashed the office.

They exited the office, tucked their guns, and grabbed their purses on the way out the door. They smiled and laughed like giggly school girls as they exited the house, just in case someone was looking out at them. Jalel walked around and closed the hood, while Amber climbed behind the wheel of the BMW.

As they pulled off, Jalel pulled out her phone and called Silk.

Chapter 38

" Ah, man, my head," Real said, realizing it was the next day.

"You good?" Silk asked, standing over the bed in a pair of light blue Gucci slacks, black Gucci heels with gold accents, and a black and blue signature Gucci blouse.

Real looked up at her and thought about their intense lovemaking. "Yeah. What time is it?" Real asked, rubbing his eyes.

"It's 10:30, almost time to check out," Silk said. She needed him to be on the phone with the bank, since she'd gotten the message from Jalel to confirm that Giovanni was dead.

"I got to get up out of here. That shit last night had me gone," Real said, sitting up in the bed.

"You sayin' it wasn't me who had you gone?" Silk asked seductively, trying to keep her feelings intact just in case she had to kill Real.

"I ain't saying that. You played a big part," Real said. He felt guilty that he'd sexed Silk up while Shonnie was more than likely laid up in the hospital.

"Before you leave, we need to call the bank and get access to these accounts. I have all the information we need," she said, digging in her pocket and pulling out a piece of paper with the bank and account information on it.

"Hold up. What's the plan here?" Real asked groggily as he climbed out of bed and headed to the bathroom. After using the bathroom, Real sat on the corner of the bed and listened to Silk's plan.

"We're gonna empty out all of the accounts, and then I'm going to make rounds to each club and clean out the safes. It won't be a problem since I'm the accountant. Emptying the safes will be the easy part. The hard part will be getting access to these accounts. That will be our only hassle. You're gonna have to put on your best act," she said, tossing two fake driver's licenses and a Social Security card on the bed.

Real picked up the IDs and checked their authenticity. They were close as they were going to get to the real deal. "Looks like you were pretty sure I'd be down with all this. How did you get my old license picture?" Real asked, looking closely at the IDs.

"I know all the right people," Silk said, recalling the $5,000 she'd handed over earlier while he was in bed asleep. Maxine, her DMV contact, had no problem whipping up the fake IDs.

"While we're emptying all of these accounts, you think Giovanni's gonna be sitting there twiddling his thumbs?" Real asked as he slipped into his pants and shirt.

"He ain't going to be saying or doing shit. He's dead," Silk said, then smiled a sinister smile.

"Dead? But…how?" Real asked in disbelief.

"Dead, and don't worry about how," Silk replied.

Real shrugged and tucked the ID in his pocket, then headed to his room to freshen up. "Let's do this then."

Thirty minutes later, they were headed to the bank. As they traveled down the narrow Miami streets, he tried to question her further about Giovanni's death, but the look in her eyes reaffirmed her earlier statement. He also thought about the loyalty and love Emilio had shown in getting him out and setting him up with a job and a place to stay. Then he thought about the money he stood to make with Silk when he gained access to those accounts. It was hard for Real to betray the people who had freed him, but he knew pulling the heist off with Silk would be his quickest way back to the top.

Two hours later, Real was exiting The Federal Bank of Miami with two small bags that contained a combined total of $1.3 million.

"I knew I had the right man for the job!" Silk said excitedly. "Let's go back down to the club and empty the safe," Silk said, holding the trunk open so Real could drop the money in.

"What's next for you after this?" Real asked as they drove. "Obviously, you won't be sticking around."

"To tell you the truth, I haven't really thought about it, but I'll be leaving Atlanta. I've got to hit the other clubs before word get out within the family," she said as they pulled up in front of the club that wasn't open for business yet. Silk picked up her phone and dialed Cleo's number. "We're out front. Open the door," she ordered.

"Fuck! Baby, go to the dressing room until I handle this business," Cleo told Sweetie, the half-black, half-Mexican new hire. Once she was gone, he pulled up his pants and headed to the front door. "What's going on?" he asked, holding the front door open for them to enter.

"Everything's cool. I just need to do a safe count," Silk said as she and Real walked by him to the back.

Real stood to the side while Silk and Cleo headed over to the safe.

"It's the same as it was yesterday, $123,937 to the penny. Do we really have to count all of this again?" Cleo asked, hoping they'd give him a pass. He was ready to get back to Sweetie.

"Nah, you're right. Real, bag all this up for me please," Silk said, pulling a black trash bag from her purse and handing it to Real as he made his way across the room.

"Wait! Hold up. You know I have to make a call before I let you just empty the safe," Cleo said firmly as he walked around the desk and picked up his phone.

"No need. I already spoke with him, and we need to get on the road," Silk said.

Real looked over at Cleo, who kept on dialing Giovanni's number.

Cleo decided not to leave a message on Giovanni's voicemail when he didn't answer. "No answer. Let me see if I can reach Emilio."

Silk knew if he got Emilio on the line, her plans would be ruined, and he would surely alert the other clubs. "Put the phone down, Cleo," she said with aggression in her voice.

Real grabbed the bag and knelt in front of the safe.

Cleo turned and stared down the barrel of a chrome .44 Magnum. "Oh shit! No problem, Silk. Just take whatever you need. I know you guys need to be getting on the road," he said, nervously stumbling over his words.

Silk kept the gun trained on him as Real emptied the safe.

"All clear. Take that watch off. I need it," Real told Cleo, knowing the platinum Westinheimer was worth all of $50,000, or more.

"You're right. This will look far better on you than it ever has on me," Cleo stuttered. He shakily unbuckled the watch and handed it over to Real.

Real grabbed the watch, then tied up the bag and handed it to Silk. "Let's go," he said, pulling his Glock .40 from his waist.

"What? Hold on! Please, y'all! Don't—" Cleo stuttered as Real put two bullets in his face, sending him crashing to the floor. Cleo didn't have time to feel a thing before the bullet entered his right eye and punctured his brain. He tumbled back over the chair and landed face first on the floor with a huge hole in his head.

"Damn! Could you let me know before you decide to shoot next time? What if I had a personal issue with him and wanted to kill him myself?" Silk joked as she opened the office door and stepped out.

"My bad," Real replied sarcastically, following Silk out the office.

They were stopped in their tracks when Sweetie came running from the back, half-naked. "Cleo? Where's Cleo? I heard gunshots and—"

Pop! Pop! Pop!

Silk didn't even give Sweetie a chance to finish her sentence before she pulled the trigger and watched the hollow points lift the young girl off her feet. She walked around and inspected the dancer to make sure she wouldn't be able to serve as a witness later. "Poor thing. Wrong place, wrong time," she said with a callous shrug before putting a single shot in the girl's head to stop her from whimpering and breathing.

"All right, let's go!" Real shouted.

They pushed the doors open and rushed out to the car. Ten minutes later, they were headed to the airport, just in time to catch their flight to Atlanta. Real gave Silk the .40. She threw it and her .44 Magnum out the window after wiping them clean.

When they got to the terminal, she popped the trunk of the car so she could divide up the money and pack it in two separate leather carryon bags, while Real went to turn in the keys to the rental. When he came back, she handed over his half of the money, text her TSA connection who would assure their bags make it through the scanner and they headed in to board their flight back to Atlanta.

Chapter 39

"*I* wonder why Unc ain't called me to let me know the plans for the club in Texas," Emilio said to Lurch while drying his hands on a paper towel after using the club's restroom.

Lurch just shrugged his shoulders and went back to reading the newspaper while waiting for the time to open the club doors for the night.

Emilio pulled out his phone and called Giovanni again and still got no answer. He tried the house phone and got no answer there either, which wasn't like Giovanni. He waited twenty minutes and called back but still got no answer. "What the hell is going on with him?" Emilio asked as he dialed frantically.

When he still didn't get an answer, he grabbed his keys off of the coffee table and headed out the door with Lurch in tow. They weaved in and out of traffic, exceeding the speed limit as they made their way to Giovanni's house. Deep down, Emilio felt something wasn't right, and he told Lurch so.

Lurch never moved his gaze from the front window.

They pulled up in front of Giovanni's mansion, and Emilio hurriedly jumped out and ran up to the door. The first thing he noticed was that the front door was slightly ajar. "Uncle!" Emilio screamed, pushing the door all the way open. He ran straight to his office, hoping to see his uncle sitting at his desk. There, lying in a pool of blood, was Giovanni.

Lurch walked in and stood over the body, then slowly looked around the room, frowning.

"Damn! Fuck!" Emilio cried out, burying his hands in his face as his eyes watered. He then walked around the room checking things out. Seeing nothing that could lead him to the murderer, he pulled out his cell phone and called Carasco.

"Hello?" Carasco answered, knowing it had to be an urgent call because nobody normally calls him after his dinner hour.

"Hi, Mr. Carasco. This is Emilio! My uncle's dead! What should I do?" Emilio cried out as he looked down at the lifeless mob boss on the floor. "Should I call 911?"

"No! Do not call the police. Are you at his place?" Carasco asked.

"Yeah," Emilio answered, still in shock.

"I'll send some men over. Did you see anyone?"

"No. There's no one here but me and Lurch."

"Okay. Just go out front and wait for my men to arrive. Tell me the address."

After telling Carasco where they were, Emilio and Lurched went out to wait by their car.

"This cant be happening! Who knew he was here? No one knew about this place but me and you. Somebody must have followed us. God, no!" Emilio cried like a baby as Lurch sat silently, waiting on Carasco's men to arrive.

Thirty minutes later, a black Expedition turned into the driveway.

"Carasco's men," Emilio said, moving to greet them. While he was talking to the men, his phone beeped. He pulled it out and saw that it was Carasco calling back.

Yeah?"

"Emilio, did you withdraw money from the club bank accounts today?" Carasco asked uneasily.

"No, sir. No one has access to those accounts but Uncle and you. Why?" Emilio asked in a concerned tone.

"I just read an an email from the bank asking me if we have been dissatisfied with their service, because the accounts were closed out today," Carasco said flatly as he pinched the bridge of his nose.

"Closed? Mr. Carasco, I have no idea what's going on here."

"Don't worry. I'll call my FBI connect to see if I can get surveillance footage from the bank where the withdrawal was made," Carasco said, pissed. He ended the call with Emilio and dialed up his old friend Felton.

"Hi, Felton. Can you get me a picture or some video footage of The Federal Bank of Miami? I need to see who closed my account. I'll make sure to thank you generously," Carasco blurted out as soon as Felton was on the line.

"Let me make a couple calls. Give me half an hour," Felton said, thumbing through his Rolodex.

A half-hour later, Carasco's phone beeped, and a message flashed across the screen telling him to check his email. Carasco pulled up his email and clicked on the attachment, a video footage of the bank. There stood Real, plain as day, acting as the account holder. The footage clearly showed the money being handed over to him and him leaving the bank. What disturbed Carasco the most was the woman standing outside of the car holding the trunk up. He couldn't believe who it was. He'd met her on several occasions, and she worked for Giovanni, and he couldn't believe she was behind it all. He knew exactly who she was and recognized her gold-streaked hair that cascaded down her back. Carasco made a call, then sent the footage to the other family members, who confirmed the identity of the man in the video. They'd wanted Real before, but since the Georgia prison system had failed to steal his life away, they were all eager to do it now—at all costs.

Chapter 40

mber and Jalel arrived at the airport twenty minutes late. They'd stopped by their place to change clothes, then got caught up in the downtown traffic.

Silk was pissed that she had to stand out front with all the cash in the bag. "What's up with you? Are you staying here?" Silk asked Real, who was pondering what his next move would be after going to see Shonnie.

"I'm thinking about it. I've got a lot of unfinished business around here, but I'll be in touch," he said as Jalel and Amber rounded the curve in the BMW.

Silk spotted the girls from afar and waved her hands in the air to get their attention.

Jalel saw Silk and brought the car to a stop in front of them.

"Where y'all been? I should've been outta here thirty minutes ago," Silk barked, angry that she was falling further and further behind schedule.

"Shit got seriously crazy," Amber said, looking Real up and down as he opened the back door and climbed in the back seat.

"Hey, ladies. I'm Real. I appreciate the ride," he said with humor, trying to ease the tension Silk was creating. It didn't take long to pick up on the fact that Silk was indeed the shot caller.

"Hey. I'm Jalel, and this is Amber." The girls didn't pick up on Silk's sideways look from the back seat from her displeasure with them giving him their real names.

They arrived at Silk's townhouse thirty minutes later.

"Let me put this up, Real, and then we'll drop you off at your place so you can handle your business. Matter fact, y'all go ahead and drop Real off, and I'll meet y'all at your place in twenty," Silk said as she dropped her bags and headed straight to the back to grab her .45 automatic, which she felt naked without.

"Okay, but, uh—" Amber started, but Silk cut her short.

"We'll handle all of that then," she said, knowing the girls were looking for their cut for the work they'd put in getting rid of Giovanni.

The three of them got back in the car and rode in silence, weaving in and out of traffic as they headed to Real's condo.

"I appreciate it, y'all. Take it easy," Real said as he exited the car with the leather bag. He climbed the stairs to his condo and mentally made plans to relocate as soon as possible.

Opening the door and stepping in, he looked up and saw Emilio and Lurch standing in the middle of the front room with uneasy looks on their faces.

"Hey, Real, we need you to come with us. The family needs to speak with you," Emilio said with caution and fear in his voice, knowing Real was not to be taken lightly.

"Right now I gotta see about my lady, but after that, I'll meet with the family," Real said. He picked up on the scent of trouble in the air, so he didn't close the door behind him.

"I don't think the family will be in town much longer. We need to meet with them now," Emilio said while Lurch stood off to the side, ready to move on his order.

Real couldn't believe the same little punk he'd saved from getting raped was now trying to order him around. "Didn't you hear me? I'll say it again. I'm gonna check on my lady, and then I'll meet with the family. What's so urgent anyway? What's got y'all creepin' up on me like this?" Real asked, knowing they had to be on to him.

"I really don't know, but my uncle just called and told me the family wants to see you," Emilio lied, trying to get a reaction out of Real.

No stranger to games, Real never flinched. "All right, but I ain't got long. I need to be hitting the road," he said, eyeing Lurch, who had his hand in his pocket, probably resting on a weapon. Real turned and walked out the door with the two men on his heels. He walked over to the Maserati and forgot he didn't have his keys. "Damn! Forgot my keys," he said, patting his pocket and turning around.

"No need. You'll ride with us," Emilio said.

Lurch opened the door to the Yukon Denali.

Real had been around long enough to know that if he climbed in the Yukon, he'd never be seen again. "I'll drive myself. I…" Real stopped mid-sentence as Emilio pulled a gun and pointed it at him.

"Real, man, don't make it come to this. Just get in so we can get this over with," Emilio said, motioning with the gun for him to get in.

Real looked over at both men and took a deep breath as he walked in their direction. Just as he got close to the truck, the condo security patrol rounded the corner, making rounds in the lot. Real took the small window to make a run for it. Just as the car reached the bumper of the truck, Emilio tucked the gun, and Lurch watched the security pass. As soon as Real saw Emilio tuck the gun, he struck out running with the leather bag swinging wildly in his grip.

"Shit!" Emilio screamed. He was about to give chase but saw that it was no use. Real had a tremendous lead on him and was way too fast, and Emilio knew it would draw too much unwanted attention if he gave chase.

Lurch just shook his head as Real disappeared over the parking lot gate with the leather bag tight in his grip.

"Fuck! Let's go!" Emilio grumbled as he climbed up in the truck and told Lurch to head out to Pickett Hall where the family meeting was about to start.

Chapter 41

"We should be all the way situated when we get this cut from Silk. There she goes now," Amber said as they sat in the front room of their two-bedroom, plush apartment, counting their recent come-up.

They watched Silk through the front window as she got out of the car with a Gucci duffle bag and admired her style. She was their mentor and idol, the type of woman they strived to be. Silk was classy, pretty, nicely figured, smart, and deadly. Amber and Jalel admired every single quality about her. They watched as she took the stairs slowly, and seconds later she was stepping in the door.

"Hey, y'all," Silk said as she stepped through the door with the bag in hand.

"Hey!" Amber replied as Silk walked over and set her bag on the table.

"What y'all got going on? Where that come from?" Silk asked, looking at the stacks of money they were dividing up.

"A li'l somethin'-somethin'," Jalel said, dividing the money up.

"A li'l bonus, I see," Silk called out as she reached around and pulled her gun from the small of her back. "Both of y'all get over there," Silk ordered, using the barrel of the gun to direct them over to the couch.

"Silk, what's this all about? What's up?" Jalel asked in disbelief, looking at the woman she admired, totally confused.

"What do you mean, what's this all about? It's about the game of life. Like I've always told you, keep your enemies close but your friends closer," Silk said as she lifted the gun and pulled the trigger. The loud blast echoed through the front room. Boom! Boom!

Amber couldn't move fast enough as the two shots tore through her stomach and chest.

"No!" Jalel screamed. She jumped up and flipped the coffee table, throwing Silk's aim off as she pulled the trigger.

Silk ran behind her letting off shots but saw that it was no use; she was gone. "Bitch," Silk spat as she walked over to the table and packed the money in the plastic bag they'd taken it out of. After packing the bag, she rushed out of the apartment. By the time she reached her car, there were sirens blaring in the distance. She jumped in and sped away.

Jalel had run into the woods next to the apartment and hidden behind a big oak tree. She watched Silk pull off, then rushed back up to the apartment. She tried her best not to look at Amber, who was sitting straight up on the couch, lifeless. Jalel didn't have to go far before she saw that Silk had taken all the money off the table. "Fuck! Bitch, if it takes me years, I'm gonna get that ass!" Jalel muttered to herself as she turned and exited the apartment, knowing that the police would be there soon.

" Emilio, where is Real?" Carasco asked as the other heads of the families stood around in Pickett Hall, discussing business and the death of Giovanni.

"Um, he ran away," Emilio said.

Lurch looked over at Toko, Carasco's personal enforcer, who was just as big and strong as he was.

All the men in attendance stopped talking and looked at Emilio with disgust, angry that he'd allowed the man to get away when they'd been chasing him for years.

"Are you telling me, telling us that you let Real get away? Sit down," he ordered.

The other heads took a seat, leaving only Toko and Lurch standing.

"First, you free the man responsible for killing some of our own, and then you bring him on and he empties all of our accounts, over a million dollars. To top it off, Silk, the manager you brought on, served as his accomplice. We just got a call telling us that our Miami club manager Cleo and one of the dancers is dead, and the safe in the club was found open and empty. Emilio, the fault for all of this falls on you and your dead uncle," Carasco said firmly, interlacing his fingers and staring hard at the boss's nephew.

Emilio was terrified and had cut his eyes in Lurch's direction. "Mr. Carasco, I swear we had no idea what was going on. We didn't know about any of this. They had to have something to do with my uncle's death," Emilio said nervously as the men around the table all focused on him.

"I'm with you 100 percent on that, Emilio. Just so we're clear, you're a made man now, aren't you?" Carasco asked, leaning back in his chair.

"Yes," Emilio answered proudly.

"And you are filling in for your uncle, his predecessor?" Carasco asked, looking around at the men at the table.

"Yes," Emilio answered proudly, with bass in his voice this time.

"Good. I just wanted to make sure we were clear on that. Toko!" Carasco called out, making a finger-across-the-throat gesture.

Toko rose off the wall and started over to the table.

Lurch started behind him, until he realized the other men at the table reaching into their jackets.

Emilio turned just as the big man reached his chair. "Mr. Carasco, wait!" Emilio called out as he started to stand.

"Since you're standing in for your uncle and he is dead, you must bear full responsibility for this," Carasco said as Toko wrapped his big arms around his neck and squeezed.

"Uggggghh," Emilio squealed, trying his best to wiggle free from the big man's grip, but the man was way too strong.

"We have no room for these kinds of mistakes," Carasco said as a loud, cracking sound silenced the room.

After breaking the young man's neck, Toko dragged him like a old ragdoll out the chair and into the hallway, where Carasco's clean-up men would pick him up and dispose of him.

"Lurch, you are free to stay on. Alfretti is taking over the clubs," Carasco said as all the men turned their gaze to Lurch, who hadn't spoken a word.

Lurch just nodded and looked over at his new boss.

"Alfretti, make us all proud. We'll be in touch," Carasco said, concluding the meeting.

Alfretti and Lurch rode in silence out to the club in Emilio's truck. Lurch used Emilio's keys to enter the club and held the door for Alfretti.

Alfretti smiled as he entered the expensively furnished club, ecstatic that he had finally been promoted within the family. "Where's the office?" he asked in a bossy tone, taking on the boss role instantly.

Lurch pointed to the back, and as soon as Alfretti turned around, he imitated Toko's move. He wrapped his massive arm around Alfretti's neck.

"Ugh!" he coughed out as Lurch squeezed the life out of him. After making sure he was dead, he let him drop to the floor. Stepping over him, he rushed to the back and emptied the safe, then hurried back out of the club.

$\mathcal{R}$ eal flagged down a taxi and instructed the driver to drop him off at a buy-here/pay-here car lot. Pick and Drive was one of many shabby car lots that lined the street. Real paid the cabbie and got out.

"Hey there! Looks like you could use a little help," the old white hillbilly car salesman said as he walked over, chewing on a mouthful of tobacco.

"Yeah. I need something dependable. I'm looking to spend about $3,000," Real said as he gripped the bag he'd been carrying all day.

"Well, you're in luck. I just got a van in with your name written all over it. Follow me," he told Real as he led him through the line of cars and stopped in front of a Chrysler minivan.

"This one?" Real asked, looking at the green van.

"Yep, this is the one. This baby's got everything you need in a dependable ride. Just overlook the chipping paint, hanging bumper, and cracked windshield, and you've practically got yourself a brand-new ride here," the man said, spitting a wad of tobacco juice from his mouth.

"Okay, I'll take it," Real said, ready to get on the road to see Shonnie.

"Good choice. Come on in so we can write this thang up," the man told Real, leading him up into a trailer that doubled as his office.

"Where's you bathroom?" Real asked, not wanting the man to see the money that filled the bag.

"Over there," he said, pointing.

While the salesman completed the paperwork, Real went in the bathroom and opened the bag. He moved the plastic around, and his heart dropped when he realized he wasn't carrying anything but some folded-up newspapers. "Fuck-ass, trifling bitch!" he said through clenched teeth as he dumped the contents of the bag out on the floor.

"Got you all ready. Only thang I need is your ID and money, and she's all yours," the salesman said, smiling an ugly smile at Real as he exited the bathroom.

Real was fuming on the inside, thinking about how Silk had played him. "Okay. Where do I need to sign?" Real asked as he walked over to the desk.

"Right here and here," the man said, pointing to the lines and a box.

Real looked out the front window and made sure the coast was clear before he grabbed the back of the man's head and slammed it into the desk with all his might, knocking the man out cold.

Clunk!

Real snatched the keys to the van off the desk and exited the trailer. He jumped in the van, turned the key, and was relieved when the engine roared to life. The van wasn't much to look at, but the motor ran smoother than a sewing machine.

Real pulled out the lot and made a left, heading to Glennville in search of Shonnie.

On the ride down the long, winding highway, Real thought about Silk and began to make plans for revenge. On top of that, he was now back on the mob's radar, and he hadn't even capitalized on the dirty deeds that had landed him in such a spot.

The ride down south seemed to take forever. As soon as he got to the Glennville city limits, he pulled out his cell phone and called the local hospital to see if Shonnie was there. "Has a Shonnie Turner been admitted, ma'am?" Real asked the perky operator.

"Um, let me see. Yes, Shonnie Turner is in Room 213. She came in yesterday," the receptionist said, then went back to posting on her Facebook page.

"Could you give me directions please? I'm coming from Atlanta," Real asked as he grabbed a pen and a piece of scrap paper from the console. A few minutes later, Real had the directions and Shonnie's room number. "Thanks," he said and hung up.

Ten minutes later, he was rushing through the hospital doors and up to Room 213. His heartbeat quickened when he stepped inside and saw a man sitting next to the bed, holding Shonnie's hand, crying. He stepped backwards out the room and stood by the door listening as the man was trying to apologize. He knew then who the man was…it was Moe. He remembered hearing that voice on the cell phone. Although he was begging and pleading, Shonnie wasn't responding.

Real stepped over to the nurse's station and asked about Shonnie's condition. After convincing the nurse he was her supervisor and a very dear friend of Shonnie's, she gave him the information. The blows she'd sustained had caused her to slip into a coma. She had a broken jaw and swelling of the brain. Real thanked the nurse and headed to the room.

"What up, bro?" Real said, taking in the strong smell of liquor that Moe emitted.

"Who you?" Moe said, jumping up out of the hospital chair and facing Real.

"I'm a friend from the prison, just stopping by to see how she's coming along. Who did this to her?" Real said, looking at the big man and wanting to beat him to a pulp. Nevertheless, he kept his cool and tried to keep his facade under wraps.

"I don't know, but when I find out, it's gonna be trouble," Moe lied, looking at Real with bloodshot eyes.

"Damn, it looks like the coward beat her bad," Real said. He wanted to go over to the bed and pour his heart out to her, but he couldn't.

"Yeah, real bad," Moe said, regretting his actions and not recognizing Real from the picture on Shonnie's cell phone.

"Damn," Real said. He walked over and looked at his baby girl, all bandaged and bruised. The more he looked at her, the angrier he got. He kept a straight face as he looked over at Moe, whom he knew was responsible. It took everything in Real not to beat Moe to death right there in the hospital room. He looked up at the ceiling counted to ten and calmed himself down.

"Excuse me, gentlemen, but it's time for me to change the patient's bandages and clothes. I'm gonna have to ask y'all to leave the room," the old gray-haired nurse said as she pulled on some latex gloves.

Neither Real nor Moe said anything, they just turned and exited the room.

Real followed Moe out to the pickup truck he was driving. "You going back in?" Real asked as he rounded the back of the truck, looking in at all the tools sprawled out in the bed.

"No. I'll stop back by tomorrow," Moe said as he struggled to get the key in the door.

"Man, I know it's hard," Real said, discreetly reaching in the bed of the truck and grabbing the crowbar lying next to the toolbox.

Moe didn't pay Real any mind as he jiggled the key in the door and finally clicked it open. "Yeah, it's hard," Moe said as he grabbed the door handle to open the door.

"Man, you're a real bitch-ass nigga!" Real blurted out as he brought the crowbar down. He missed Moe's head by inches but connected with his shoulder.

"Nigga!" Moe screamed out, grabbing his shoulder while trying to run.

Real chased him down, and as soon as he was within striking distance, he raised the crowbar again and brought it down on the back of the man's head.

Blood spewed out like a faucet as Moe fell forward.

Real looked around the parking lot to make sure no one was around, then continued his assault. "Bitch nigga, beat me like you beat Shonnie!" Real screamed as he stood over Moe, who was balled up on the ground, holding his head and moaning. Real raised the crow bar again and brought it down on Moe's head, breaking his finger and cracking his skull. The last lick was fatal and killed the man instantly.

Real wiped the crowbar off, dropped it in the grass, and ran back to the van. He planned on checking with the hospital daily for updates on Shonnie's condition, and after he finished his business with Silk, he would relocate to Glennville to lay low for a while.

Chapter 44

*L*ater in the evening, Silk packed her bags and headed to the private runway where her chartered flight was scheduled to fly her out to LA.

Unbeknownst to her, Real had arrived back in town and didn't waste any time heading out to her townhouse. When he arrived at her place, he saw that she wasn't home. He rounded the place and broke the back door window out to give himself entry. He opened the door and started through the house. He knew it was a long shot, but he searched the house for a stash anyway. After thirty minutes of searching, he gave up. "Bitch! Bitch! Bitch!" Real bellowed. He began to trash the place, but the ringing of the phone paused him.

The phone rang three time before the answering machine picked up. "Hi, Miss Crisp. Your flight on Lux Way is set to depart at 4:00. This is just a courtesy call to make sure that..."

Real hurriedly grabbed a pen and a piece of paper and jotted down all the info from the message. It was already 3:00, and Silk's plane was scheduled to leave at 4:00, so Real skipped some of the stairs as he ran out the door, determined to make it to the airport before her plane took off. Real pushed the van way past the posted speed limit as he raced to the private air strip. Being familiar with the area, it didn't take him long to get to where he needed to be. He whipped the van into the air strip parking lot and jumped out.

* * * * *

Dominic arrived back from Florida rejuvenated and feeling like a new man. As soon as he walked in the house his housekeeper rushed up to him with a slip of paper with all his urgent calls scribbled on it.

"Thanks Carmen," Dominic said as he walked his well fit seventy-one year old body over to his hand crafted bar and sat down.

He looked at all of the messages and saw that all of them were from Ponelli, his young protégé who he mentored up until he took a seat at the table with the rest of the heads of the family. Dominic had fallen back from the rank a couple of years ago so his son Giovanni could get acquainted with representing the family within the Mob. After looking at the paper, he picked the phone up off of the bar and dialed Ponelli's number.

"Hello?" Ponelli answered on the second ring while sitting at his dining room table looking over his recent stock purchases.

"Ponelli, how are you? I see you've been trying to reach me," Dominic said, wheezing after every word.

"Yeah Dominic things have turned for the worst. I hate to be the bearer of bad news especially when you're just returning from a long relaxing vacation.

"Oh man don't tell me that Giovanni has overplayed his hand in some kind of way with the family," Dominic said knowing how Giovanni could get at times.

"Worse than that…Giovanni is dead presumably killed by the man named Real from years—" he was cut off in mid sentence.

"I know that name well I thought he was still in prison. Doesn't matter I want his body delivered to me personally…to my doorstep by next week!" Dominic snapped, showing his Godfather persona.

"That's not all," Ponelli continued.

"What else is there Ponelli?" Dominic huffed.

"Your grandson was released from prison and—"

"Great, he can now head the family we—"

Dominic, Carasco had him killed," Ponelli blurted out causing Dominic's heart to skip a beat.

"Carasco? He had my grandson killed? He never even reached out to me on the matter! Call a meeting and I want every head in attendance and make sure Carasco is up front and center!" Dominic screamed, then slammed the phone down.

* * * * *

"Buckle up, y'all!" the pilot said as he closed the door to the Cessna 347.

Silk saw the green van enter the parking lot from afar but thought nothing of it until she saw a man jump out and begin running across the lot. She watched out the window as the man ran full speed, headed directly toward the plane.

"Stop! Stop!" Real screamed at the pilot, who didn't see him.

As Real ran beside the plane, he could clearly see Silk looking at him. Then he noticed a man in the next window behind her. The man lifted his hand and waved. The sight of the hand caught Real by surprise because the man's middle finger was gone.

Then it all hit him. Real stopped mid stride.

"Lurch…Fuck!" he screamed.

Just as he turned and headed back to his van, a car full of heavily strapped Italians jumped out of their car and rushed through the airport. They had also gotten word of Silk's departure and had been ordered to stop her at all costs.

"Where is she?" the man asked the attendant, Carasco's direct contact.

"That way!" the attendant yelled, pointing toward the direction of the last plane to take off.

As they rushed the runway, they looked right past Real, who was most definitely going to be their next target.

Real dropped his head and walked quickly back to the van.

The Italians were in an uproar, seeking revenge, Real was back in a mob war, Shonnie was still fighting for her life, and Lurch was headed to LA with his boss lady. Silk was over a million dollars strong and was looking for a new life, and Jalel was contemplating her next move, guaranteed to make Silk wish she'd never crossed her. When their paths cross, it will certainly be a BLACK OUT like no other!

We'd like to thank you for supporting G Street Chronicles and invite you to join our social networks. Please be sure to post a review when you're finished reading.

Facebook
G Street Chronicles Fan Page
G Street Chronicles CEO Exclusive Readers Group

Twitter
@GStreetChronicl

Email us and we'll add you to our mailing list
fans@gstreetchronicles.com

George Sherman Hudson, CEO
Shawna A., COO